P9-BYH-927

The Penguin Book of Italian Short Stories

THE
PENGUIN BOOK
of
ITALIAN
SHORT
STORIES

———

Introduced, edited and with selected translations by
JHUMPA LAHIRI

PENGUIN BOOKS

PENGUIN BOOKS

UK | USA | Canada | Ireland | Australia
India | New Zealand | South Africa

Penguin Books is part of the Penguin Random House group of companies
whose addresses can be found at global.penguinrandomhouse.com.

This translation first published in Penguin Books 2019

002

Set in 11.25/14.75 pt Adobe Caslon Pro
Typeset by Jouve (UK), Milton Keynes
Printed and bound in Great Britain by Clays Ltd, Elcograf S.p.A.

A CIP catalogue record for this book is available from the British Library

ISBN: 978–0–241–29983–8

www.greenpenguin.co.uk

Contents

Contents

Contents

Contents

Introduction

Poiché dispongo di input ibridi, ho accettato volentieri e con curiosità la proposta di comporre anch'io un' 'antologia personale', non nel senso borgesiano di auto-antologia, ma in quello di una raccolta, retrospettiva e in buona fede . . .

Always inclined to a hybrid input, I accepted willingly and with curiosity the proposal to compile a 'personal anthology', not in the Borgesian sense of an auto-anthology but in that of a harvesting, retrospectively and in good faith . . .

Primo Levi, *La ricerca delle radici*[1]

One evening in Rome, in the kitchen of the Italian writer Caterina Bonvicini, I expressed a desire to assemble a collection of Italian short stories translated into English. It was March of 2016, during a brief trip back to Italy. Six months before, my family and I had returned to the United States after living for three years in Rome.

My life as a reader had, by that time, taken an unexpected turn; since 2012, shortly before moving to Rome, I had chosen to read only Italian literature, mostly from the twentieth century, and to read those works exclusively in Italian, a language I had diligently studied for many years but had yet to master. I was forty-five years old, and I believed, even before this new phase began, that I was already fully formed as a reader and writer. And yet I surrendered to an inexplicable urge to distance myself, to immerse myself and to acquire a second literary formation.

It was one thing to read only Italian when living in Italy, where the winds were favourable, where my state of voluntary literary exile made sense. I read with an adolescent's zeal, transported to another dimension, standing before a new group of gods. I had an Italian teacher who came to my home twice a week and, at the start, brought me chapters and excerpts equipped with footnotes for elementary readers. I befriended Italians who mentioned authors I had never heard of before. I began frequenting bookstores, especially those that sold secondhand volumes, combing the shelves for their works. I purchased them and read them, and copied down sentences by hand, taping them over my desk for inspiration. I realized that, for the first time in decades, I was reading to satisfy only myself. I was no longer influenced by the expectations and broader cultural consensus that dictate what one should be reading – such frames of references had fallen away. The more people remarked on my new inclination – But don't you miss English? – the more I clung to my newfound freedom, not wanting it to end.

But it did end; while in Italy, I was offered a job at Princeton University to teach Creative Writing, and so my family and I returned to the United States. Crossing the Atlantic, I read Primo Levi's *Se questo è un uomo* (*If This Is a Man*), a first book which recounts the eleven months that Levi, a young chemist from Turin who became one of the twentieth century's greatest writers, spent imprisoned in a German concentration camp before it was liberated in 1945. It was my first time reading that work in Italian, and the pure truth and beauty of those pages that transform one man's experience of hell into a masterpiece of literature transformed not only the hours on the plane but also me personally, instilling in me an abiding awe – there is no other word for it – that even today governs my own newfound liberty as both a reader and a writer.

Teaching at Princeton, I wanted to transmit this awe, to share my admiration for Levi and the other Italian authors who had spoken to me deeply, who had taught me so much and who were now a part of me. And given that my classes were held in English, the only way to do so was to teach them in translated form. And so I searched for English versions of the works I wanted to talk about. I was struck by how many translations were either out of print or outdated, difficult to track down, and I was even more struck by the many great Italian authors who had scarcely been translated at all.

After dinner that evening at Caterina's, she and I wandered from the kitchen into her study and began pulling books off her shelves. I already had a dozen authors in mind, and Caterina suggested a dozen others. I took out my diary and wrote all the names down, twenty-four in total. Of that group, twenty-three are represented in the current volume. The authors jotted down that evening comprised a wish list. Back in Princeton,

I made do with photocopies of translations that I hoped my students would enjoy. Then, not long after my second semester had come to an end, Penguin Classics asked me to assemble this anthology.

I was impressed by the passion with which my Italian friends and acquaintances reacted to the project. This passion was by no means exclusive to writers. I was struck by the degree to which Italians from different walks of life knew and cared about specific short stories. People would email me the names of authors and titles of works they felt were worthy of anthologizing, or thrust books from their personal libraries into my hands. My list began to grow, as did my reading, and back in Princeton that fall, I had accumulated well over fifty names.

At a certain point, I realized I had to set down some basic parameters. The first was to eliminate all living authors from my list. The second was to arrive at a number. Fifty felt celebratory and auspicious, but I worried that it would amount to an unwieldy physical object, and so, with some anguish, I whittled the list down to the forty featured here. The fruit of my research was the discovery of a potent, robust tradition of the short form in Italy, a harvest far more vast and varied than I'd anticipated.

What were my criteria? To gather together as many of the authors who have inspired and nourished my love for Italian literature, and for the Italian short story in particular. I wanted a volume I and others would be excited to teach from, and that students, ideally, would be eager to read. I wanted to include a wealth of styles, and a range of voices. The resulting collection, by no means comprehensive, reflects my judgement and sensibility, and also encapsulates a specific moment of my reading trajectory. I cast a wide net and, as is inevitably the case, a somewhat arbitrary one. Some authors – including several particularly dear to me – were consciously excluded due to one rationale or the other; others simply escaped unseen.

Once the list was final, it struck me that these forty Italian authors would not necessarily be familiar to any one Italian reader. Many of them have fallen out of favour, or have been sporadically published, and are therefore hard to come across in Italian bookstores. Ironically, I could only get my hands on them thanks to Firestone Library in Princeton or, if I was lucky, at the Porta Portese flea market, which brings hundreds of secondhand books, every Sunday, to Rome. Even after I had made my choices, people kept mentioning other writers I ought to have included, and suggestions will surely only proliferate now that the book exists.

I have focused predominantly on the twentieth century, though a few of the authors were born and began writing in the nineteenth, and others remained active into the twenty-first. It was my priority to feature women authors, lesser-known and neglected authors, and authors who practised the short form with particular vehemence and virtuosity. My aim is to present a portrait of Italy that reflects its reality. I prefer to work against a reassuring but ridiculous perception encapsulated by an American who once said to me, 'Nothing bad can possibly happen in Italy.' Of course, it is one thing to experience Italy as a tourist, another thing to live there. Then again, one has only to read the literature of any given place to recognize that bad things happen to everyone, everywhere.

Several members of this group knew one another during their lifetimes. They sustained, influenced, promoted, edited, reviewed and were at odds with one another. They formed part of a community, a network, bound together by vital personal and professional friendships and, in one case, even by marriage. And as I stood back to absorb the details of their lives and the nature of their creativity, I realized that they were all, by and large, hybrid individuals, with multiple proclivities, identities, signatures and shadows. They were writers of fiction and at the same time they were almost always other things: poets, journalists, visual artists, musicians. Many had demanding editorial responsibilities, were critics, were school teachers. Some were professional scientists and politicians. They served in the military, held bureaucratic positions, had diplomatic careers. And the vast majority were translators, living, reading and writing astride two languages or more.

The act of translation, central to their artistic formation, was a linguistic representation of their innate hybridity. The majority of these writers shuttled between dialect and standard Italian; though they all wrote in Italian, it was not necessarily the language they grew up speaking, or the first they learned to read and write in or were originally published in. Four were born outside of present-day Italy, and most of them spent significant amounts of time either studying, travelling or residing abroad. A few turned to other languages, writing novels in French or Portuguese, experimenting with German and English, teaching themselves different dialects, complicating their texts and their identities further still. Whether linguistic or stylistic, their creative paths were marked by experimentation, by wilful mutation. They were artists who questioned and redefined themselves over time, some defiantly distancing themselves from earlier phases of their work.

A central underpinning of their hybridity is manifested in the striking number of invented or altered names. Elena Ferrante is a pseudonym that has taken the literary world by storm, but long before her, Italian writers created alter-egos for political or personal reasons, either to protect themselves from the law or to disassociate themselves from their origins. Eight of the authors on this list were born with different names, and others published specific works under pseudonyms. To rename oneself is to edit one's destiny, to insist upon an autonomous identity, and for a writer it is a means, quite literally, of rewriting the self. Not surprisingly, many of these stories address the theme of identity, of fluctuating selfhood, and accentuate the issue of naming in particular. Characters have complicated relationships to their names, and a few lack names altogether – perhaps a nod to one of the most intriguing characters in Alessandro Manzoni's novel *The Betrothed* (*I promessi sposi*), who is called is 'l'innominato', literally, 'the unnamed'.

Always pertinent to the discussion of identity is the question of women in Italy: how they were defined, how they were seen. Many of these stories are portraits of women, some confronting and challenging patriarchal ideology, others revealing attitudes in which women are objectified, belittled, maligned. One option, on my part, would have been to exclude such stories in order to protest against these objectionable depictions. But this would misrepresent a society and its history as reflected in its literature. As a woman, and a woman writer, these stories help me to better understand the cultural context of Italian feminism, and to admire the great strides that Italian women have made. The fact of the matter is that many of the most moving depictions of women in this collection were written by men. Marriage is a recurrent theme – to be precise, how a woman's identity can be altered, compromised and negated by a man, and also by maternity. But the whole of the twentieth century, which witnessed the collapse of a series of powerful social institutions, including marriage, was a laboratory in which individual identities were being lost and found, regained and shed.

Hybridity is also manifested in the number of animal characters that abound in these pages, a recurrent metaphor that calls into question the porous barrier between the animal and human worlds. In this sense, some of these works can trace their lineage to the fables of Aesop, to the *Metamorphoses* of Ovid and to folkloric tradition, in which the animal kingdom has always played a delightful and prominent role. The significance of animals in literary satire was appreciated by the poet Giacomo Leopardi (1798–1837), whose *Paralipomeni della Batracomiomachia* (translated into English as *The War of the Mice and the Crabs*) is a mock epic, inspired by an ancient Greek poem, adapted by Leopardi to criticize imperial politics and false patriotism in Italy.[2] A great number of these stories feature animals that talk, behave, think and feel just as people do. They substitute as friends, lovers, philosophical interlocutors, a spouse. They serve as mirrors and filters that reflect and reveal myriad emotional and psychological states. The reader will note various characters who feel more animal than human, or are themselves both animal and human. The paradoxical valence of animals merits close attention in that they represent both a state of freedom as well as subservience, both innocence and savagery. As these stories make clear, they are creatures both cherished and consumed, both worshipped and sacrificed, beings that both define and question what 'human' even means.

In the course of pondering the diverse and intriguing encounters between man and beast in this anthology, I was struck by the following words by Benito Mussolini: 'Fascism denies the validity of the equation, well-being-happiness, which would reduce men to the level of animals, caring for one thing only – to be fat and well-fed – and would thus degrade humanity to a purely physical existence'.[3] This observation, antithetical to the in-between, transversal, protean essence of so many of these writers and their work, also allows us to make room for another, more troubling organizing principle: the reality of Fascism. Giovanni Verga was the first of the authors gathered in these pages to die, in 1922, the year Mussolini marched to power in Rome. All the rest lived under Fascism at some point or another, and were affected directly by its legacy. The ugliest manifestation of Fascism was to dehumanize, to treat people as animals, or worse. The irony of course was that in order to achieve their aims, it was those in power who behaved like beasts.

Fascism, in Italy, was declined linguistically, to the extent of enforcing a 'pure Italian' free from foreign words and expressions. Under Fascism a croissant became a *cornetto*, a bar became a *quisibeve* ('here one drinks') and football, invented by the English, became *calcio*. Even the pronoun *lei* (as opposed to *voi*) was prohibited as a second-person pronoun because it was claimed to be a Spanish grammatical import, and also because it sounded 'feminine'. In any overview of Italian literature in the twentieth century, the history of the language must come into consideration. The regime sought to standardize and flatten the language, to weed out dialect and other anomalies, above all, to turn it inward. And it was in that very moment that Italy's writers, at least a considerable number of them, turned defiantly outward. The entire twentieth century can be read as a battle of wills between the wall Fascism sought to erect around Italy and Italian culture, and those – many of the writers represented here very much among them – determined, despite running grave risks, to break it down.

The forty authors on my list hailed from all parts of Italy, though I acknowledge that my base in Rome and my love for southern Italy contributes a slant. They came from rich families and poor ones. They had all sorts of political leanings and varying degrees of political commitment. Stylistically, they covered the spectrum: Realist, neoRealist, avant-garde, fantastic, Modernist, postmodernist. Some cultivated literary fame; others actively shunned it. Many were celebrated, powerful, influential figures. A few never saw their work published in their lifetime.

If there is a dominant point of reference, it is the Second World War. The writer Cristina Campo called it 'the abyss that had split apart the century';[4] indeed, this cataclysmic caesura is what links the vast majority of these authors. Two were in Nazi concentration camps, and another escaped en route to one. At least a dozen were forced to live, for a time, in hiding, either because they were members of the anti-Fascist Resistance, or because they were Jews. The Second World War and its aftermath drastically and irrevocably altered Italian society, penetrating the collective consciousness, traumatizing it, but eventually reinvigorating it culturally and economically. The proliferation of literary magazines after the war, the redoubled and innovative publishing initiatives and the spirit of community and collaboration among writers, means that this time is now regarded as something of a golden age in Italian literary culture. Having said this, and in spite of the myriad personal connections among many of these authors, the anthology contains powerful meditations on alienation, estrangement, states of solitude. The only true common ground for each of these authors is the Italian language, an invention in and of itself, described by Leopardi as *'piuttosto un complesso di lingue che una sola'* ('a complex of languages as opposed to a single one').[5] It was imposed upon a linguistically and culturally diverse population, late in the nineteenth century, when the separate regions of Italy were unified in the name of national identity.

The roots of the modern Italian short story are themselves hybrid: at once deep and shallow, at once foreign and domestic. In assembling this anthology, one indispensible font of information was the anthology dedicated to the Italian short story in the twentieth century edited by Enzo Siciliano (1934–2006), for Mondadori's *i Meridiani* series. Siciliano was a writer, critic and journalist from Rome, and he became the editor of the influential literary journal *Nuovi Argomenti* after the death of its founder, Alberto Moravia. There are in fact two versions of Siciliano's anthology: a single volume running to nearly fifteen hundred pages without notes (featuring seventy-one authors, published in 1983) and then across three volumes (with a revised introduction and a grand total of two hundred and ninety-eight authors, including himself, published in 2001).

In his introduction, Siciliano traces the Italian short story back to the Middle Ages, to the anonymously written, thirteenth-century *Novellino*, containing episodes and characters drawn from the Bible and classical and medieval mythology, to Giovanni Boccaccio's *Decameron* (likely composed between 1349 and 1351) and to Matteo Bandello, whose sixteenth-century *Novelle* (he wrote over two hundred of them) may have inspired the plots of Shakespeare's *Twelfth Night* and *Much Ado about Nothing* via French translation. Between Bandello and Boccaccio one must also acknowledge Masuccio Salernitano, whose own *Novellino*, a collection of fifty posthumously published tales, included one noted for being among the sources for *Romeo and Juliet*.

What, the reader may ask, is a *novellino*? It is a book that gathers together various *novelle* (the plural of *novella*), which, in Italian, is not a slim novel, but rather, a word used to describe a short story or a tale. Though Boccaccio titled his great work *The Decameron*, he explicitly refers to the tales themselves as *novelle*. Siciliano investigates the difference between the term *novella* and *racconto* in Italian, seemingly interchangeable terms, both to be differentiated from *romanzo*, the word for novel. The word *racconto*, with its Latin root, is etymologically connected to the English 'recount': a telling again. A *racconto* aims to communicate a story, personally and purposefully, to a listener. Thus *raconteur*, a French word that has also become English, refers specifically to a human figure, a storyteller, especially a captivating one. The spirit of the *racconto* implies a dynamic relation, with at least two people involved; though distinct from dialogue, it indicates a form, immediate and typically brief, of exchange. In modern Italian, the verb *raccontare* is commonly used, in conversation, when people want to narrate something casually but colourfully, imbuing this literary term with ongoing quotidian currency. That Siciliano's anthology promotes the word *racconti* in the title (*Racconti Italiani del Novecento*) is in and of itself making a statement, positing the form along a decidedly modern axis where Guy de Maupassant, Gustave Flaubert and Anton Chekhov serve as coordinates, thereby distinguishing the *racconto* from the more classically rooted *novella*.

Fleeting by nature, short stories, in spite of their concision and concentration, are infinitely elastic, expansive, probing, elusive – suggesting that the genre itself is essentially unstable, hybrid, even subversive in nature. In discussing Moravia's *Roman Tales*, called *Racconti romani*, and a cornerstone of the twentieth-century Italian short-story tradition, Siciliano cites Moravia's illuminating observation that a *racconto* is something born from *intuizione*, intuition. I agree. In some sense it is the novel, in Italy, which is the interloper, the imported genre. Alessandro Manzoni and Giovanni Verga looked to France and to England for models, Grazia Deledda to the Russians, Italo Svevo to the central European tradition. The novel, according to Moravia, derives from reason, and is imbued with structure, elements that short stories routinely undermine and resist. Indigenous to Italy, *racconti* have thrived for centuries, and they constitute a continuum, cross-pollinating with the world's literature in ways that the longer Italian form has not.

Siciliano's volumes were indispensable to me, travelling back and forth across the Atlantic, those navy-blue bricks with their sewn-in ribbons to mark one's place lined up on my desk, and I recommend them to those who read Italian and wish to broaden their perception of the short form in Italy. Even for those who don't read Italian, the index alone, listing all the authors' names, is the first place I would direct those in search of suggested further reading. To leaf through them is to glimpse the thrilling sweep of the ocean from above, as opposed to navigating the more manageable but partially uncharted bay I have demarcated.

Every language is a walled entity. English is a particularly fortified one. To step outside the Anglophone world is to grow aware of the near-total domination of the English language when it comes to what is being read and celebrated as literature today. It is a domination that few, at least on the English-speaking side of the border, stop to question. I am aware that my orientation at the moment – to look outside English, and to put forth for consideration what is now overlooked even in Italy – separates me from the literary mainstream both in the Italian- and English-language context. In Italy, I note the overwhelming number of English-language authors prominently displayed in bookshops, and reviewed, each week, in newspapers and magazines; the number of prizes and residencies and festivals designed to host and honour English-language authors in Italy. I myself have been the grateful recipient of such invitations, prizes and residencies. And yet the discrepancy is clear. The fact remains that Italian writers, for good and for ill, for well over a century now, have looked outside their own literature for inspiration, and the tradition of translation out of English, at least on behalf of Italian publishers, is critical, not peripheral, to the literary landscape.

Of these forty stories, sixteen have not been translated into English until now, and nine have been retranslated intentionally for this anthology. The vast majority, I imagine, will be fresh discoveries for English readers. And of these forty authors, a great many have been ignored and thus practically forgotten in Italy as well. Most of the magazines in which they originally appeared no longer exist. There was a period, particularly after the Second World War, when small literary journals, many of them founded by the authors in this anthology, flourished in Italy. Some were short-lived but editorially clamorous. Each represented a hope, a different direction, a new cultural climate or point of view. They put short stories at the forefront. Their presence corresponded to a period of extraordinary literary ferment, and their editors prided themselves on promoting new, innovative, heterodox voices. They were proof of how individually published short stories, free from the economic machinery of book publishing, are by definition autonomous texts: a source of resistance, a means for creative risk and experimentation. Fortunately, there are still talented young writers in Italy who embrace the short form, and once in a while, in Italy as in other places, a short-story collection creeps on to the shortlist for a major literary prize. Another promising sign is Racconti Edizioni, a Roman publishing house founded in 2016, dedicated exclusively to publishing short-story collections.

Until recently, schools of creative writing were unheard of in Italy. They are beginning to grow in numbers, though they remain independent from academic institutions. The term *scrittura creativa* (creative writing) and the borrowed term 'storytelling' have entered the vocabulary, but their meanings are still largely shrouded in mystery, regarded, rightly, as foreign phenomena. What has happened in the United States and, to a lesser degree, also in Great Britain – the reign of the Master of Fine Arts and the calculated marriage between art and academy – has not yet been sanctioned in Italy, and as a result, most Italian writers still have, by and large, a different centre of gravity, either as journalists or scholars or editors, or, in some cases, all of the above. The separation between writers and publishers is less rigid in Italy, and the editorial milieu, more intimate, less corporate than its American counterpart, is an engrossing story in and of itself. Tracing its evolution and dynamics is fundamental to understanding how and why so many short stories were written in Italy in the course of the previous century, and in such a rich array of styles. The Chronology at the end of this volume operates on two tracks: providing background on the historical and political events that accompanied these authors' lives, while paying attention to the country's publishing history as well.

As I was nearing the completion of this project, Italy was in the process of electing a new government, with xenophobic parties gaining electoral sway. NeoFascist violence towards immigrants has been on the rise, and the government still denies birthright citizenship to Italians with foreign-born parents. In spite of this distressing reality, Italy has become a second home to me, and Italians have, on the whole, welcomed my efforts to explore their literature and experiment with their language with an outsider's sensibility. In spite of those who aim to control borders, deny passage and to restrict Italy to 'Italians first' (*'Prima gli italiani'*), Italy's identity – including the very definition of 'Italian' as it applies to the current population – is radically changing, and its literature, always an open system, further enriched by these changes, continues to diversify.

Language is the substance of literature, but language also locks it up again, confining it to silence and obscurity. Translation, in the end, is the key. This volume, which honours so many writer-translators, is as much a tribute to the Italian short story as it is validation of the need – aesthetic, political, ethical – for translation itself. I am enormously grateful to the team that has worked to bring the works of these writers into English for the first time, or to retranslate stories with greater accuracy and intuition. In the process of editing their contributions I have deepened my own awareness and respect for what it means to transport literature from one language to another, and I have redoubled my commitment to doing so. Only works in translation can broaden the literary horizon, open doors, break down the wall.

I have ordered these stories in reverse alphabetical order, by author's last name. It is an arbitrary sequence, but it is also serendipitous that Elio Vittorini appears first. In 1942, Vittorini published *Americana*, an anthology of thirty-three largely unknown American authors – among them, Nathaniel Hawthorne, Henry James and Willa Cather. But this was no mere gathering of authors; it was a massive, collective translation enterprise, featuring contributions by some of the most important Italian writers of the time, including Alberto Moravia, Cesare Pavese and the Nobel Laureate poet Eugenio Montale. The objective of *Americana* was to introduce iconic American voices to Italian readers. For America, too, was a fabulous projection in the minds of many Italians of that generation: a legendary place that stood for youth, rebellion, freedom and the future. But this projection, at least Vittorini's version of it, was no escapist disconnect from reality, but rather, a form of both creative and political dissidence, a heroic, courageous connection, by means of literature, to a new world.

Introduction

The first edition of *Americana*, to be published by Bompiani, was banned by Mussolini's regime. It passed the censors only after Vittorini removed his critical commentaries on the individual authors, and Emilio Cecchi, a critic in good graces with the Fascist government, wrote an introduction. To leaf through the book today – it runs to over one thousand pages long – is to traverse a bridge that feels nothing short of revolutionary. Vittorini was my guiding light as I assembled this book. I followed his example in writing the brief author biographies – intended as partial sketches and not definitive renderings – that preface each story, and it is in homage to him and to that landmark work – to the spirit of saluting distant literary comrades, of looking beyond borders and of transforming the unknown into the familiar – that I offer the present contribution.

Rome, 2018

NOTES

1. From the preface to *La ricerca delle radici*, in Primo Levi, *Opere complete*, vol. I, ed. Marco Belpoliti (Torino: Einaudi, 2017). Published in English as *The Search For Roots: A Personal Anthology*, ed. and trans. Peter Forbes (Chicago: Ivan R. Dee, 2002). Originally commissioned and published by Einaudi in 1981, the anthology – a miscellany of formative readings particularly dear to Levi – consisted of thirty texts chosen, excerpted, introduced and, in five cases, translated by the author. Among the selections were works by Charles Darwin, Marco Polo and Paul Celan. (The reference within the citation itself is to Jorge Luis Borges' *A Personal Anthology*, a compilation of Borges' works edited by himself, first published in Spanish in 1961 and translated and published in Italian in 1962.)

2. Leopardi's poem is based on the *Batrachomyomachia*, a parody of Homer's *Iliad* which has been translated from Ancient Greek into English as *The Battle of Frogs and Mice*. Leopardi translated the *Batrachomyomachia* and conceived of the *Paralipomeni* as a continuation of that work. Leopardi's title for the latter work literally means 'omissions' (to the *Batrachomyomachia*).

3. *The Political and Social Doctrine of Fascism*, trans. Jane Soamers (London: The Hogarth Press, 1933), p. 14.
4. The citation comes from '*La noce d'oro*' ('The Golden Nut'), the story by Cristina Campo which is included in this anthology. In Italian it reads, '*l'abisso che avrebbe spezzato un secolo*'.
5. Giacomo Leopardi, *Zibaldone: The Notebooks of Leopardi*, ed. Michael Caesar and Franco Ditino, trans. Kathleen Baldwin et al. (London: Penguin, 2013), p. 202 [321], 13 Nov. 1820.

A Note on the Citation of Titles and Their Translations

Careful effort has been made to ascertain whether or not there are published English translations of Italian works included or cited in this volume.

When an Italian work has been published in English, its title appears in italics, as is common practice. When such a work has not been published in English, a literal translation of the title is given, and appears without italicization. When an Italian novel published in English has a very differently worded title to that of the original, a literal translation has also been provided. Titles of individual short stories are placed within quotation marks and unitalicized.

ELIO VITTORINI

1908–66

The tiny Sicilian island of Ortigia, where Vittorini was born, is connected by an isthmus to Siracusa, home of an Ancient Greek theatre. A railway worker's son, Vittorini left Sicily when he was nineteen years old to work on a construction site in the region of Venezia-Giulia. He was a proofreader for a newspaper in Florence, and it was there, thanks to a co-worker, that he learned English during his breaks, by translating, word for word, Daniel Defoe's *Robinson Crusoe*. At the foreign books division of Mondadori, he was commissioned to translate a book by D. H. Lawrence, and he also translated Edgar Allan Poe, William Faulkner, William Saroyan and John Steinbeck. His passion for translation would culminate in assembling the epic anthology *Americana* (see Introduction). But as one of the prime movers at Einaudi, Vittorini was also part of the ingenious editorial collective that galvanized Italian literature after the Second World War. His first book, *Piccola borghesia* (Petty Bourgeoisie), published in 1931, contained stories that had appeared in the anti-Fascist journal *Solaria*, criticized at the time for featuring the works of Jewish writers. His first major novel, *Conversazione in Sicilia* (*Conversations in Sicily*), reflects the cadences of the English language which he'd read, translated, absorbed and reconstituted into Italian. The American edition contains a glowing preface by Ernest Hemingway. This story, elusive, unadorned and understated, is a parable combining quotidian and supernatural elements. It showcases Vittorini's penchant for dialogue, and places the acts of writing and naming at its very centre.

Name and Tears

Translated by Erica Segre and Simon Carnell

I was writing in the gravel in the garden and it was dark already; lit for a while now by the lights from all the windows.

The guard passed by.

'What are you writing?' he asked.

'A word,' I replied.

He bent down to have a look, but couldn't make it out.

'What word is it?' he asked again.

'Well,' I said. 'It's a name.'

He jangled his keys.

'With no 'Long live . . .'? No 'Down with . . .'?'

'Oh no!' I exclaimed.

And I laughed as well.

'It's the name of a person,' I said.

'A person you're waiting for?' he asked.

'Yes,' I replied. 'I'm waiting for her.'

Then the guard walked away, and I resumed my writing. I wrote and reached the earth beneath the gravel: I dug and wrote, and the night turned blacker still.

The guard returned.

'Still writing?' he asked.

'Yes,' I said. 'I've written a bit more.'

'What else have you written?' he asked.

'Nothing else,' I replied. 'Nothing except that word.'

'What?' the guard shouted. 'Nothing except that name?'

And he rattled his keys again, and lit his lantern to have a look.

3

'So I see,' he said. 'There's nothing there but that name.'

He raised the lantern and looked into my face.

'I've written it deeper,' I explained.

'Is that right?' he replied. 'If you want to continue, I'll give you a hoe.'

'Give it to me,' I said.

The guard gave me the hoe, then went off again, and with the hoe I dug and wrote the name deep into the ground. In truth I would have inscribed it as far down as seams of coal or iron are found, down to the most secret metals, which bear ancient names. But the guard came back again and said: 'You have to leave now. It's closing time.'

I climbed out of the name ditch.

'All right,' I replied.

I put down the hoe, wiped my brow and looked at the city around me, through the dark trees.

'All right,' I said. 'All right.'

The guard grinned.

'She hasn't come, right?'

'She hasn't come,' I said.

But immediately afterwards I asked: 'Who hasn't come?'

The guard lifted his lantern and looked into my face like before.

'The person you were waiting for.'

'Yes,' I said, 'she hasn't come.'

But then once again, straight away I asked: 'What person?'

'Damn it!' the guard said. 'The person with the name.'

He shook his lantern, rattled his keys and added: 'If you'd like to wait a little longer, don't mind me.'

'That isn't what matters,' I said. 'But thanks.'

But I didn't leave, I stayed and the guard stayed with me, as if to keep me company.

'Lovely night!' he said.

'Lovely,' I said.

Then, carrying his lantern, he took a few steps towards the trees.

'I wonder,' he said. 'Are you sure she's not there?'

I knew that she could not have come, yet I was startled.

'Where?' I whispered.

'Over there,' said the guard. 'Sitting on the bench.'

The leaves rustled as he said these words; a woman stood up in the dark and started to walk on the gravel. On hearing her footsteps, I closed my eyes.

'So she had come after all, had she?' said the guard.

Without answering, I followed after the woman.

'We're closing!' the guard shouted. 'We're closing!'

Shouting 'We're closing', he disappeared amongst the trees.

I followed the woman out of the garden and through the streets of the city.

I followed after what had been the sound of her steps on gravel. Or you might say, rather, that I was guided by the memory of her footsteps. And it turned out to be a long walk, a long pursuit, now amidst the crowd, now along deserted pavements until, raising my eyes, I saw her for the first time, a passer-by, by the light of the last shop.

What I saw, actually, was her hair. Nothing else. And fearing that I would lose her, I started to run.

The city in these parts alternated between meadows and tall houses, dimly lit parks and lit-up funfairs, with the red eye of the gasworks in the background. Many times I asked: 'Did she come this way?'

Everyone told me that they didn't know.

But a mocking child came up, quickly, on roller-skates, and laughed.

'Haah!' she laughed. 'I bet you're looking for my sister.'

'Your sister?' I exclaimed. 'What's her name?'

'I'm not telling you,' the girl replied.

And again she laughed, doing a dance of death around me on her roller-skates.

'Haah!' she laughed.

'Then tell me where she is,' I said.

'Haah!' laughed the girl. 'She's in a doorway.'

She skated her dance of death around me again for a moment, then sped off up the endless avenue, laughing.

'She's in a doorway,' she called back from afar, still laughing.

The doorways were all occupied by abject couples, but I arrived at one that was abandoned and empty. The door opened when I pushed it. I went up the stairs and began to hear someone crying.

'Is it her crying?' I asked the concierge.

This old woman was sitting asleep, halfway up the stairs with her rags in her hand – and she woke up and looked at me.

'I don't know,' she replied. 'Do you want the lift?'

I did not want it, I wanted to go to where the crying was, and I continued to climb the stairs between the black, wide-open windows. I finally came to where the crying was, behind a white door. I went in, felt her close to me and turned on the light.

But I saw no one in the room, and heard nothing more. And yet there, on the sofa, was the handkerchief, damp with her tears.

'*Nome e lagrime*'

First published in the magazine *Corrente* (31 October 1939). It then became the title of Vittorini's first novel, published by Parenti in 1941, and then, the same year, by Bompiani as *Conversazione in Sicilia*.

GIOVANNI VERGA

1840–1922

Catania, on the eastern coast of Sicily, was destroyed more than once by earthquakes and eruptions of Mount Aetna. The effect of its late baroque reconstruction begun in 1693, from lava stone, is at once grim and spectacular. Still charged with the weight of disaster, the city personifies drama, destruction and rebirth. Verga, astride the nineteenth and twentieth centuries and the eldest author of this collection, was raised there, but to produce his art he had to get away, first to Florence, immersing himself in its literary culture, and then to Milan, where he lived for twenty years (although he made frequent journeys back to Sicily). He was born three months after Thomas Hardy, an author with whom he bears comparison. Both wrote about hardship, family and fatal passions with lyricism and pessimism. Both had complex relationships with their places of origin, which both inspired and alienated them. Verga's realistic approach – called the school of *Verismo* in Italian – was a reaction to a movement in the same period called *Scapigliatura* (devoted, broadly speaking, to interiority, individualism and ideals). Realism, in Verga's time, was considered an anti-conformist approach to literature: alert to social tensions, refusing to elevate or evade. In reproducing elements of dialect, he allowed characters to sound as they actually would have in real life, and described the poor without sentimentality. In doing so, he broke definitively with the literary aesthetic in Italy that had come before him. Verga wrote seven collections of short stories in his lifetime. 'Fantasticheria' ('Picturesque Lives'), a description of a fishing village, is considered an antecedent to his later masterpiece, a novel called *I Malavoglia* (The Malavoglia, translated as *The House by the Medlar Tree*). It was adapted, in 1948, into the neoRealist cinematic classic *La terra trema* (The Earth Trembles) by Luchino Visconti. But it is more than preparatory work, striking for its epistolary structure, its imagery, its precise yet panoramic vision.

Picturesque Lives

Translated by G. H. McWilliam

Once, when the train was passing by Aci Trezza, you looked out of the carriage window and exclaimed, 'I'd like to spend a month down there!'

We went back there and spent, not a month, but forty-eight hours. The villagers who stared in disbelief at your enormous trunks must have thought you would be staying for a couple of years. On the morning of the third day, tired of seeing nothing but green fields and blue sea, and of counting the carts as they trundled up and down the street, you were at the station, fiddling impatiently with the chain of your scent bottle, and craning your neck to catch sight of a train that couldn't arrive too soon. In those forty-eight hours we did all it was possible to do in Aci Trezza. We walked down the dusty street and we scrambled over the rocks. Under the pretext of learning to row you got blisters beneath your gloves that had to be kissed better. We spent a marvellously romantic night at sea, casting nets so as to do something to convince the boatmen it was worth their while to be catching rheumatism. Dawn came upon us at the top of the beacon rock. I can still see that dawn – pale and unassuming, with broad, mauve-coloured shafts of light playing across a dark-green sea, caressing the tiny group of cottages that lay huddled up asleep on the shore, while above the rock, silhouetted against the dark and cloudless sky, your tiny figure stood out clearly in the expert lines designed for it by your dressmaker, and the fine, elegant profile of your own making. You were wearing a grey dress that seemed to have been specially made to blend with the colours of the dawn. A truly pretty picture! And you certainly knew it, to judge from the way you modelled yourself in your shawl and smiled with those enormous, tired, wide-open eyes at that strange spectacle, and at the strangeness, too, of being there

9

yourself to witness it. What was going on at that moment in your little head, as you faced the rising sun? Were you asking it to tell you where in the world you would be, a month into the future? All you said, in that ingenuous way of yours, was, 'I don't understand how people can spend the whole of their lives in a place like this.'

But you see, the answer is easier than it looks. For a start, all you need is not to have an income of a hundred thousand lire, and to take comfort in suffering a few of the many hardships that go with those giant rocks, set in the deep blue sea, that caused you to clap your hands in wonder. Those poor devils, who were nodding off in the boat as they waited for us, need no more than that to find, in among their ramshackle, picturesque cottages, that seemed to you from a distance to be trembling as if they too were seasick, everything you search for, high and low, in Paris, Nice and Naples.

It's a curious business, but perhaps it's better that way for you, and for all the others like you. That cluster of cottages is inhabited by fishermen, who call themselves 'men of the sea' as opposed to your 'men about town', people whose skins are harder than the bread that they eat, when they eat any bread at all, for the sea is not always as calm as it was when it was planting kisses on your gloves. On its black days, when it roars and it thunders, you have to rest content with standing and gazing out at it from the shore, or lying in your bed, which is the best place to be on an empty stomach. On days like that, a crowd gathers outside the tavern, but you don't hear many coins rattling on the tin counter, and the kids, who throng the village as if poverty was a good way to multiply their numbers, go shrieking and tearing around as though possessed by the devil.

Every so often typhus, or cholera, or a bad harvest, or a storm at sea come along and make a good clean sweep through that swarm of people. You would imagine they could wish for nothing better than to be swept away and disappear altogether, but they always come swarming back again to the very same place. I can't tell you how or why they do it.

Did you ever, after an autumn shower, find yourself scattering an army of ants as you carelessly traced the name of your latest boyfriend in the sand along the boulevard? Some of those poor little creatures would have remained stuck on the ferrule of your umbrella, writhing in agony, but all the others, after five minutes of rushing about in panic, would have returned to cling on desperately to their dark little ant-heap. You wouldn't go back there, certainly, and neither would I. But in order to understand that kind of stubbornness, which in some respects is heroic, we have to reduce ourselves to the same level, restrict our whole horizon to what lies between a couple of mounds of earth, and place their tiny hearts under a microscope to discover what makes them beat. Would you, too, like to take a look through this lens here, you who contemplate life through the other end of a telescope? You'll think it a curious spectacle, and it might amuse you, perhaps.

We were very close friends (do you remember?), and you asked me to dedicate a few pages to you. Why? *à quoi bon*, as you would put it. What value does anything I write possess for anyone who knows you? And to those who don't, what are you anyway? But never mind all that, I remembered your little whim, on the day I set eyes once again on that beggarwoman you gave alms to, with the pretext of buying the oranges she'd laid out in a row on the bench outside the front door. The bench is no longer there, they've cut down the medlar tree in the yard and the house has a new window. It was only the woman that hadn't changed. She was a little further on, holding out her hand to the cart-drivers, crouching there on the pile of stones blocking the entrance to the old outpost of the National Guard. As I was doing the rounds, puffing away at a cigar, it struck me that she too, poor as she is, had seen you passing by, fair of skin and proud of bearing.

Don't be angry if I've remembered you in such a way, and in such a context. Apart from the happy memories you left me, I have a hundred others, indistinct, confused, all different, gathered here, there and everywhere – some of them mere daydreams, perhaps – and in my confused state of mind, as I walked along that street that has witnessed so many happy and painful events, the frail-looking woman crouching there in her mantilla made me somehow feel very sad, and made me think of you, glutted with everything, even with the adulation heaped at your feet by the fashion magazines, that often splash your name in the headlines of their elegant feature articles – glutted to such a degree as to think up the notion of seeing your name in the pages of a book.

Perhaps, when I have written the book, you won't give it a second thought. But meanwhile, the memories I send you now, so far away from you in every sense, inebriated as you are with feasting and flowers, will bring a refreshing breeze to play upon the feverish round of your endless revelry. On the day you go back there, if you ever do go back, and we sit together again, kicking up stones with our feet and visions in our thoughts, perhaps we shall talk about those other breezes that life elsewhere has to offer. Imagine, if you like, that my mind is fixed on that unknown little corner of the world because you once stepped into it, or in order to avert my gaze from the dazzling glare of precious stones and fevered expectation that accompanies your every movement, or because I have sought you out in vain in all the places smiled upon by fashion. So you see, you always take the lead in my thoughts, as you do in the theatre!

Do you also recall that old man at the tiller of our boat? You owe it to him to remember, because he saved you a dozen times from soaking your fine blue stockings. He died down there, poor devil, in the town hospital, in a huge white ward, between white sheets, chewing white bread, assisted by the white hands of the Sisters of Charity, whose only weakness was their failure to comprehend the string of woes that the wretched fellow mumbled forth in his semi-barbaric dialect.

But if there was one thing he would have wanted above all else, it was to die in that shaded little corner beside his own hearth, where he had slept for so many years 'below his own roof', which is why, when they carried him away, he was in tears, whining as only the old are able to.

He had spent his whole life between those four walls, looking out on that lovely but treacherous sea with which he had had to wrestle every day of his life to extract what he needed to survive without coming to a watery end. And yet for that brief moment in time when he was silently relishing his place in the sun, huddled on the thwart of the boat with his arms round his knees, he wouldn't have turned his head to admire you, and you would have looked in vain into those spellbound eyes for the proud reflection of your beauty, as when so many of the high and mighty bow their heads as they make way for you in the fashionable salons, and you see your reflection in the envious eyes of your best women friends.

Life is rich, as you see, in its inexhaustible variety, and you can enjoy that part of its richness that has come your way just as you please.

Take that young woman, for instance, who peeped out from behind the pots of basilico when the rustling of your dress set off a clamour in the street. When she espied your famous face in the window opposite she beamed as though she too were dressed in silk. Who knows what simple joys filled her thoughts as she stood at that window behind the fragrant basilico, her eyes fixed intently on the house opposite, bedecked with branches of vine. And the laughter in her eyes would not have turned later into bitter tears in the big city, far away from the four walls that had witnessed her birth and watched her grow up, if her grandfather hadn't died in the hospital, and her father hadn't drowned, and her family hadn't been scattered by a puff of wind that had blown right through it – a puff of ruinous wind, which had carried one of her brothers off to prison on the island of Pantelleria, or 'into trouble', as they say in those parts.

A kinder fate lay in store for those who died, one in the naval battle of Lissa. He was the eldest son, the one you thought resembled a David sculpted in bronze, as he stood there clutching his harpoon with the light from the flame of the lanterns playing about his features. Big and tall as he was, he too glowed with pleasure whenever you darted your brazen eyes in his direction. But he died a good sailor, standing firm at the rigging of the yardarm, raising his cap in the air and saluting the flag for the last time with the primitive shout of the islander bred and born. The other man, the one who was too timid to touch your foot on the island to free it from the rabbit trap where you got it caught in that heedless way of yours, was lost on a dark winter's night, alone at sea amid the raging foam, when between his boat and the shore – where his loved ones awaited his return, rushing here and there as though possessed – there lay sixty miles of storm and darkness. You would never have guessed the amount of sheer dauntless courage that man was capable of, who allowed himself to be overawed by the handiwork of your shoemaker.

The ones who are dead are better off. They are not eating 'the king's bread', like the poor devil locked up on Pantelleria, or the kind of bread his sister is eating, nor do they go around like the woman with the oranges, living on the charity of God, which doesn't flow too freely in Aci Trezza. At least the dead need nothing any more! That's what the son of the woman who keeps the tavern said, the last time he went to the hospital to enquire about the old man and smuggle in some of those stuffed snails that are so good to suck for anyone who has no teeth, and he found the bed empty, with the blankets neatly folded upon it. He crept out into the hospital yard and planted himself at a door with a lot of wastepaper piled up against it, and through the keyhole he spied a large empty room, hollow-sounding and icy even in summer, and the end of a long marble table, with a thick, starched sheet draped over it. And thinking to himself that the ones inside no longer needed anything, and the snails were of no use to them any more, he began to suck them one after the other to pass away the time. It will comfort you to think, as you hug your blue fox muff to your bosom, that you gave a hundred lire to the poor old fellow.

Those village kids who followed you like stray dogs and raided the oranges are still there. They are still buzzing round the beggarwoman, pawing at her clothes as though she's hiding a crust of bread, picking up cabbage stalks, orange peel and cigar stubs, all the things thrown away in the street but obviously still having some value because the poor live on them. They live so well on them, in fact, that those starving, blown-out ragamuffins will grow up in the mud and the dust of the street, and turn out big and strong like their fathers and grandfathers. Then they in turn will populate Aci Trezza with more ragamuffins, who will cling on to life as long as they can by the skin of their teeth, like that old grandfather, wanting nothing else but simply praying to God they will close their eyes in the place where they opened them, attended by the village doctor who goes round every day on his donkey, like Jesus, to succour the departing ones.

'The ambition of the oyster!' you may say. Exactly, and the only reason we find it absurd is that we were not born oysters ourselves.

But in any case, the tenacious clinging of those poor souls to the rock on to which fortune decreed they should fall, as it scattered princes here and duchesses there, their brave resignation to a life full of hardships, their religion of the family, reflected in their work, their homes and the walls that surround them, seem to me, for the time being at any rate, deeply serious and worthy of respect. It seems to me that the anxieties of our wandering thoughts would find sweet solace in the tranquil calm of those simple, uncomplicated feelings that are handed down, serene and unchanging, from one generation to the next. It seems to me that I could watch you passing by, to the sound of your horses' trotting hooves and the merry jingling of their brasses, and greet you without a care in the world.

Perhaps because I have tried too hard to penetrate the whirlwind that surrounds and pursues you, I have now learned to understand the inevitable need for that solid, mutual affection among the weak, for the instinct of the underprivileged to cling to one another to survive the storms of their existence, and I have tried to unravel the humble, undiscovered drama that has dispersed to the four winds its plebeian actors whom we once got to know together. The drama of which I speak, which perhaps one day I shall unfold to you in its entirety, would seem to me to depend essentially on this: that whenever one of the underprivileged, being either weaker, or less cautious, or more selfish than the others, decided to break with his family out of a desire for the unknown, or an urge for a better life, or curiosity to know the world, then the world, like the voracious fish that it is, swallowed him up along with his nearest and dearest. From this point of view you will see that the drama is not without interest. The main concern of oysters must be to protect themselves from the snares of the lobster, or the knife of the diver that prises them from the rock.

'Fantasticheria'
First published in the weekly magazine *Il fanfulla della Domenica* (14 March 1880), and, in the same year, in the collection *Vita dei campi* (Treves).

GIUSEPPE TOMASI DI LAMPEDUSA
1896–1957

Tomasi di Lampedusa, born in Palermo, was a learned prince, and his literary legacy remains a cause-célèbre. His most celebrated published work was composed within the two years leading up to his death, including the novel, *Il gattopardo* (*The Leopard*), feverishly written between 1955 and 1956, only to be rejected by various publishers, including Vittorini, who didn't think it was the right fit for his *Gettoni* series. It was another writer, Giorgio Bassani – having received a partial manuscript from the writer Elena Croce, daughter of the famous philosopher – who travelled to Palermo the year after Tomasi di Lampedusa's death, obtained his papers from his Latvian widow and quickly published *Il gattopardo*. An engrossing historical and psychological novel about the decline of the Sicilian aristocracy as Italy moved towards unification, it sold over three million copies, was translated into twenty-seven languages, and was turned, in 1963, into a film by Luchino Visconti. In addition to *Il gattopardo*, Tomasi di Lampedusa had also left behind critical essays and a few short stories, including this one, unquestionably his most powerful. A story within a story, everything about it is doubled: it contains two narrative planes, two central protagonists, two settings, two tonal registers, two points of view. There are even two titles; though published as '*La Sirena*' ('The Siren'), it was originally called '*Lighea*', (the title provided by the author's wife), which refers to the name of the siren at the heart of this mysterious tale. Fusing elements at once carnal and intellectual, both pagan and modern, it is a story about the revitalizing and transformative things that can happen while learning another language – in this case, Ancient Greek. Tomasi di Lampedusa wrote it in the final months of his life, with certain knowledge of his imminent death from lung cancer.

The Siren

Translated by Stephen Twilley

Late in the autumn of 1938 I came down with a severe case of misanthropy. I was living in Turin at the time, and my local girl no. 1, rifling my pockets in search of a spare fifty-lire note as I slept, had also discovered a short letter from girl no. 2. Spelling mistakes notwithstanding, it left no room for doubt concerning the nature of our relations.

My waking was both immediate and violent. Outbursts of angry dialect echoed through my modest lodgings on Via Peyron, and an attempt to scratch my eyes out was averted only by the slight twist I administered to the dear girl's left wrist. This entirely justified act of self-defence put an end to the row, but also to the romance. The girl dressed hurriedly, stuffing powder puff, lipstick, and a little handkerchief into her bag along with the fifty-lire note, 'cause of so great a calamity,' thrice flung a colourful local alternative to 'Swine!' in my face, and left. Never had she been so adorable as in those fifteen minutes of fury. I watched from the window as she emerged and moved away into the morning mist: tall, slender, adorned with regained elegance.

I never saw her again, just as I never saw a black cashmere sweater that had cost me a small fortune and possessed the woeful merit of being cut to suit a woman just as well as a man. All she left were two of those so-called invisible hairpins on the bed.

That same afternoon I had an appointment with no. 2 in a patisserie in Piazza Carlo Felice. At the little round table in the western corner of the second room – 'our' table – I saw not the chestnut tresses of the girl whom I now desired more than ever but the sly face of Tonino, her twelve-year-old brother. He'd just gulped down some hot chocolate with a double

19

portion of whipped cream. With typical Turinese urbanity, he stood as I approached.

'Sir,' he said, 'Pinotta will not be coming; she asked me to give you this note. Good day, sir.'

He went out, taking with him the two brioches left on his plate. The ivory-coloured card announced that I was summarily dismissed on account of my infamy and 'southern dishonesty.' Clearly, no. 1 had tracked down and provoked no. 2, and I had fallen between two stools.

In twelve hours I had lost two usefully complementary girls plus a sweater to which I was rather attached; I also had to pick up the bill for that infernal Tonino. I'd been made a fool of, humiliated in my very Sicilian self-regard; and I decided to abandon for a time the world and its pomps.

There was no better place for this period of retreat than the café on Via Po where, lonely as a dog, I now went at every free moment, and always in the evening after my work at the newspaper. It was a sort of Hades filled with the wan shades of lieutenant colonels, magistrates and retired professors. These vain apparitions played draughts or dominoes, submerged in a light that was dimmed during the day by the clouds and the arcade outside, during the evenings by the enormous green shades on the chandeliers. They never raised their voices, afraid that any immoderate sound might upset the fragile fabric of their presence. It was, in short, a most satisfactory Limbo.

Being a creature of habit, I always sat at the same little corner table, one carefully designed to provide maximum discomfort to the customer. On my left two spectral senior officers played trictrac with two phantoms from the appeals court; their military and judicial dice slipped tonelessly from a leather cup. On my right sat an elderly man wrapped in an old overcoat with a worn astrakhan collar. He read foreign magazines one after another, smoked Tuscan cigars, and frequently spat. Every so often he would close his magazine and appear to be pursuing some memory in the spirals of smoke; then he would go back to reading and spitting. His hands were as ugly as could be, gnarled and ruddy, with fingernails that were cut straight across and not always clean. Once, however, when he came across a photograph in a magazine of an archaic Greek statue, the kind with widespread eyes and an ambiguous smile, I was surprised to see his disfigured fingertips caress the image with positively regal delicacy. When he realized that I'd seen him, he grunted with displeasure and ordered a second espresso.

Our relations would have remained on this plane of latent hostility if not for a happy accident. Usually I left the office with five or six daily papers, including, on one occasion, the *Giornale di Sicilia*. Those were the years when the Fascist Ministry of Popular Culture, or MinCulPop, was at its most virulent, and every newspaper was just like all the others; that edition of the Palermo daily was as banal as ever, indistinguishable from a paper published in Milan or Rome, if not by its greater share of typographical errors. My reading of it was accordingly brief, and I soon set it aside on the table. I had already begun to contemplate another product of MinCulPop's vigilance when my neighbour addressed me: 'Pardon me, sir, would you mind if I glanced at this *Giornale di Sicilia* of yours? I'm Sicilian, and it's been twenty years since I came across a newspaper from my part of the world.' His voice was as cultivated as any I'd ever heard, the accent impeccable; his grey eyes regarded me with profound indifference.

'Be my guest. I'm Sicilian myself, you know. If you like, I can easily bring the paper every evening.'

'Thank you, but that won't be necessary; my curiosity is a purely physical one. If Sicily remains as it was in my time, I imagine nothing good ever happens there. Nothing has for the past three thousand years.'

He glanced through the paper, folded it, and gave it back to me, then plunged into reading a pamphlet. When he stood to go, it was clear that he hoped to slip out unnoticed, but I rose to introduce myself; he quietly muttered his name, which I failed to catch, yet neglected to extend his hand. At the threshold of the café, however, he turned, doffed his hat, and loudly shouted, 'Farewell, fellow countryman.' He disappeared down the arcade, leaving me speechless while the shades at their games grumbled disapprovingly.

I performed the magical rites necessary to conjure a waiter; pointing at the empty table, I asked him, 'Who was that gentleman?'

'That,' he replied, 'is Senator Rosario La Ciura.'

The name said a great deal even to an ignorant journalist. It belonged to one of the five or six Italians with an indisputable international reputation – to the most illustrious Hellenist of our time, in fact. I understood the thick magazines and the caressing of the illustration, the unsociability and hidden refinement, too.

In the newspaper offices the following day I searched through that peculiar drawer of the obituary file containing the 'advancers.' The 'La Ciura' card was there, for once tolerably well drafted. I read how the great man had been born into an impoverished petit bourgeois family in Aci Castello (Catania), and that thanks to an astonishing aptitude for Ancient Greek, and by dint of scholarships and scholarly publications, he had at the age of twenty-seven attained the chair of Greek literature at the University of Pavia. Subsequently he had moved to the University of Turin, where he remained until retirement. He had taught at Oxford and Tübingen and travelled extensively, for not only had he been a senator since before the Fascists came to power and a member of the Lincean Academy; he had also received honorary degrees from Yale, Harvard, New Delhi and Tokyo, as well as, of course, from the most prestigious European universities from Uppsala to Salamanca. His lengthy list of publications included many that were considered fundamental, especially those on Ionic dialects; suffice to say that he had been commissioned to edit the Hesiod volume in the Bibliotheca Teubneriana, the first foreigner so honoured, to which he had added an introduction in Latin of unsurpassed scientific rigour and profundity. Finally, the greatest honour of all, he was *not* a member of the Fascist Royal Academy of Italy. What had always set him apart from other exceedingly erudite colleagues was a vital, almost carnal sense of classical antiquity, a quality on display in a collection of essays written in Italian, *Men and Gods*, which had been recognized as a work not only of great erudition but of authentic poetry. He was, in short, 'an honour to a nation and a beacon to the world,' as the card concluded. He was seventy-five years old and lived decorously but far from lavishly on his pension and senator's benefits. He was a bachelor.

There's no use denying that we Italians – original sons (or fathers) of the Renaissance – look on the Great Humanist as superior to all other human beings. The possibility of finding myself in daily proximity to the highest representative of such subtle, almost magical, and poorly remunerated wisdom was both flattering and disturbing. I experienced the same sensations that a young American would on meeting Mr Gillette: fear, respect, a certain not ignoble envy.

That evening I descended into Limbo in quite a different spirit than that of the previous days. The senator was already at his spot and responded to my reverential greeting with a faint grumble. When, however, he'd finished reading an article and jotted down a few things in a small notebook, he turned toward me and, in a strangely musical voice, said, 'Fellow country-man, from the manner in which you greeted me I gather that one of these phantoms has told you who I am. Forget it, and, if you haven't already done so, forget the aorist tense you studied in secondary school. Instead tell me your name, because your introduction yesterday evening was the usual mumbled mess and I, unlike you, do not have the option of learning who you are from others. Because it's clear that no one here knows you.'

He spoke with insolent detachment. To him I was apparently some-thing less than a cockroach, more like a dust mote whirling aimlessly in a sunbeam. And yet the calm voice, precise speech and use of the familiar *tu* radiated the serenity of a Platonic dialogue.

'My name is Paolo Corbera. I was born in Palermo, where I also took my law degree. Now I work here for *La Stampa*. To reassure you, Senator, let me add that on my exit exams I earned a "5 plus" out of 10 in Greek, and I suspect that the "plus" was only added to make sure I received my diploma.'

He gave a half smile. 'Thank you for telling me this. So much the bet-ter. I detest speaking with people who think they know what they in fact do not, like my colleagues at the university. In the end they are familiar only with the external forms of Greek, its eccentricities and deformities. The living spirit of this language, foolishly called "dead," has not been revealed to them. *Nothing* has been revealed to them, for that matter. They are poor wretches, after all: How could they perceive this spirit without ever having had the opportunity to hear Greek?'

Pride is fine, sure, it's better than false modesty, but it seemed to me the senator was going too far. I even wondered whether the years might have succeeded in softening somewhat his exceptional mind. Those poor things, his colleagues, had had just as much opportunity to hear Ancient Greek as he had – that is, none.

He went on: 'Paolo, you're lucky to bear the name of the one apostle who had a bit of culture and a smattering of reading under his belt. Though Jerome would have been better. The other names you Christians carry around are truly contemptible. The names of slaves.'

I was disappointed again. He really seemed like nothing more than a typical anticlerical academic with a pinch of Fascist Nietzscheism thrown in. Could it be?

He voice rose and fell appealingly as he continued to speak, with the ardour, perhaps, of someone who had passed a great deal of time in silence. 'Corbera . . . Is that not one of the great names of Sicily, or am I mistaken? I remember that my father paid the annual rent for our house in Aci Castello to the administrator of a House of Corbera di Palina, or Salina, I can't recall which. He'd always joke and say that if there was one thing that was certain in this world, it was that those few lire weren't going to end up in the pockets of the "demesne," as he called it. But are you one of those Corberas, or just a descendant of some peasant who took his master's name?'

I confessed that I really was a Corbera di Salina, the sole surviving specimen, in fact. All the opulence, all the sins, all the uncollected rents, all the unpaid debts, all the political opportunism of the Leopard were concentrated in me alone. Paradoxically, the senator seemed pleased.

'That's fine, just fine. I have a great deal of respect for the old families. Their memory is . . . miniscule, of course, but still it's greater than the others'. It's as much of physical immortality as your sort can hope for. Think about getting married soon, Corbera, seeing as how your sort haven't found any better way to survive than scattering your seed in the strangest places.'

He was definitely trying my patience. 'Your sort.' Who was that? The whole contemptible herd that was not fortunate enough to be Senator La Ciura? Who'd attained physical immortality? You'd never know it from looking at his wrinkled face, his sagging flesh . . .

'Corbera di Salina,' he continued, undeterred, 'You don't mind if I call you *tu*, as I do with my students in their fleeting youth?'

I professed to be not only honoured but delighted, and I was. Moving beyond questions of names and protocol, we now spoke of Sicily. It had been twenty years since he'd set foot on the island, and the last time he'd been 'down there,' as he called it in the Piedmontese manner, he'd stayed a mere five days, in Syracuse, to talk to Paolo Orsi about the alternating choruses in classical theatre.

'I remember they wanted to take me in a car from Catania to Syracuse; I accepted only when I learned that at Augusta the road passes far from the sea, whereas the train follows the coastline. Tell me about our island. It's a beautiful places, even if it is inhabited by donkeys. The gods once sojourned there – and perhaps in some endless Augusts they return. But don't on any account speak to me about those four modern temples of yours, not that that's anything you'd understand, I'm sure.'

So we spoke about eternal Sicily, the Sicily of the natural world; about the scent of rosemary on the Nebrodi Mountains and the taste of Melilli honey; about the swaying cornfields seen from Etna on a windy day in May, some secluded spots near Syracuse, and the fragrant gusts from the citrus plantations known to sweep down on Palermo during sunset in June. We spoke of those magic summer nights, looking out over the gulf of Castellammare, when the stars are mirrored in the sleeping sea, and how, lying on your back among the mastic trees, your spirit is lost in the whirling heavens, while the body braces itself, fearing the approach of demons.

The senator had scarcely visited the island for fifty years, and yet his memory of certain minute details was remarkably precise. 'Sicily's sea is the most vividly coloured, the most romantic of any I have ever seen; it's the only thing you won't manage to ruin, at least away from the cities. Do the trattorias by the sea still serve spiny urchins, split in half?'

I assured him that they did, though adding that few people ate them now, for fear of typhus.

'And yet they are the most beautiful thing you have down there, bloody and cartilaginous, the very image of the female sex, fragrant with salt and seaweed. Typhus, typhus! They're dangerous as all gifts from the sea are; the sea offers death as well as immortality. In Syracuse I demanded that Orsi order them immediately. What flavour! How divine in appearance! My most beautiful memory of the last fifty years!'

I was confused and fascinated: a man of such stature indulging in almost obscene metaphors, displaying an infantile appetite for the altogether mediocre pleasure of eating sea urchins!

Our conversation stretched out, and on leaving he insisted on paying for my espresso, not without a display of his peculiar coarseness ('Everyone knows kids from good families are always broke'). We parted friends, if you disregard the fifty-year difference between our ages and the thousands of light years separating our cultures.

We proceeded to see each other every evening; even as my rage against humanity began to wane, I made it my duty never to fail to meet the senator in the underworld of Via Po. Not that we chatted much; he continued to read and take notes and only addressed me occasionally, but when he spoke it was always a melodious flow of pride and insolence, sprinkled with disparate allusions and strands of impenetrable poetry. He continued to spit as well, and eventually I observed that he did so only while he read. I believe that he also developed a certain affection for me, but I didn't delude myself. If there was affection it wasn't anything like what one of 'our sort' (to adopt the senator's term) might feel for a human being; instead it was similar to what an elderly spinster might feel for her pet goldfinch, whose vacuousness and lack of understanding she is well aware of, but whose existence allows her to express aloud regrets in which the creature plays no part; and yet, if the pet were not there, she would suffer a distinct malaise. In fact, I began to notice that when I arrived late the old man's eyes, haughty as ever, were fixed on the entrance.

It took roughly a month for us to pass from topical observations – always highly original but impersonal on his part – to more indelicate subjects, which are after all the only ones that distinguish conversations between friends from those between mere acquaintances. I was the one who took the initiative. His spitting bothered me – it had also bothered the guardians of Hades, who finally brought a very shiny brass spittoon to his spot – such that one evening I dared to inquire why he didn't seek a cure for his chronic catarrh. I asked the question without thinking and immediately regretted risking it, expecting the senatorial ire to bring the stucco work on the ceiling raining down on my head. Instead his richly toned voice replied calmly, 'But my dear Corbera, I have no catarrh. You who observe so carefully should have noticed that I never cough before spitting. My spitting is not a sign of sickness but of mental health: I spit out of disgust for the rubbish I happen to be reading. If you took the trouble to examine that contrivance' – (and he gestured at the spittoon) – 'you would realize that it contains hardly any saliva and no trace of mucus. My spitting is symbolic and highly cultural; if you don't like it, go back to your native drawing rooms, where people don't spit only because they can't be bothered to be nauseated by anything.'

His extraordinary insolence was mitigated solely by his distant gaze; I nevertheless felt the desire to stand up and walk out on him then and there. Fortunately I had the time to reflect that the fault lay in my rashness. I stayed, and the impassive senator immediately passed to counterattack. 'And you then, why patronize this Erebus full of shades and, as you say, catarrh sufferers, this locus of failed lives? In Turin there's no shortage of those creatures your sort finds so desirable. A trip to the Castello hotel in Rivoli, or to the baths in Moncalieri and your squalid aspiration would soon be fulfilled.'

I began to laugh at hearing such a cultured mouth offer such precise information about the Turinese demimonde. 'But how do you come to know about such places, Senator?'

'I know them, Corbera, I know them. Anyone spending time with politicians or members of the Academic Senate learns this, and nothing more. You will, however, do me the favour of being convinced that the sordid pleasures of your sort have never been stuff for Rosario La Ciura.' One could sense that it was true: In the senator's bearing and in his words there was the unmistakable sign of a sexual reserve (as one said in 1938) that had nothing to do with age.

'The truth is, Senator, it was precisely my search for some temporary refuge from the world that first brought me here. I'd had trouble with two of just the sort of women you've so rightfully condemned.'

His response was immediate and pitiless. 'Betrayed, eh, Corbera? Or was it disease?'

'No, nothing like that. Worse: desertion.' And I told him about the ridiculous events of two months earlier. I spoke of them in a light, facetious manner; the ulcer on my self-regard had closed, and anyone but that damned Hellenist would have teased me or possibly even sympathized. But the fearful old man did neither; instead he was indignant.

'This is what happens, Corbera, when wretched and diseased beings couple. What's more, I'd say the same to those two little trollops with respect to you, if I had the revolting misfortune to meet them.'

'Diseased, Senator? Both of them were in wonderful shape; you should have seen how they ate when we dined at Gli Specchi. And as for wretched, no, not at all: Each was a magnificent figure of a young woman, and elegant as well.'

The senator hissingly spat his scorn. 'Diseased, I said, and made no mistake. In fifty, sixty years, perhaps much sooner, they will die; so they are already now diseased. And wretched as well. Some elegance they've got, composed of trinkets, stolen sweaters and sweet talk picked up at the movies. Some generosity too, fishing for greasy banknotes in their lover's pockets rather than presenting him, as others do, with pink pearls and branches of coral. This is what happens when one goes in for those little monstrosities with painted faces. And were you all not disgusted – they as much as you, you as much as they – to kiss and cuddle your future carcasses between evil-smelling sheets?'

I replied stupidly, 'But Senator, the sheets were always perfectly clean!'

He fumed. 'What do the sheets have to do with it? The inevitable cadaver stink came from you. I repeat, how can you consent to carouse with people of their kind, of your kind?'

I, who already had my eyes on an enchanting sometime seamstress, took offense. 'It's not as if one can sleep with nothing but Most Serene Highnesses!'

'Who said anything about Most Serene Highnessess? They're bound for the charnel house like the rest. But this isn't something you'd understand, young man, and I was wrong to mention it. It is fated that you and your girlfriends will wade ever further into the noxious swamps of your foul pleasures. There are very few who know better.' Gazing up at the ceiling, he began to smile; a ravished expression spread over his face; then he shook my hand and left.

We didn't see each other for three days; on the fourth I received a telephone call in the editorial office. 'Is this Signor Corbera? My name is Bettina Carmagnola, I'm Senator La Ciura's housekeeper. He asks me to tell you that he has had a bad cold, and that now he is better and wishes to see you tonight after dinner. Come to 18 Via Bertola at nine, second floor.' The call, abruptly interrupted, became unappealable.

The building at 18 Via Bertola was a dilapidated old structure, but the senator's apartment was large and – thanks, I suppose, to the diligence of Bettina – well maintained. In the entrance hall began the parade of books, of those modest-looking, economically bound volumes found in all living libraries; there were thousands of them in the three rooms I crossed. In the fourth sat the senator, wrapped in a very ample camel-hair dressing gown that was smoother and softer than any I'd ever seen. I learned later that the fabric wasn't camel at all but was made from the precious wool of a Peruvian animal, and that the gown was a gift from the Academic Senate of Lima. The senator refrained from rising when I entered but welcomed me with considerable warmth. He was better, completely fine, in fact, and planned to be back in circulation as soon as the bitter cold spell that had descended on Turin in those days had passed. He offered me some resinous Cypriot wine, a gift from the Italian Institute of Athens; some atrocious pink *lokums* from the Archaeological Mission of Ankara; and some more sensible Turinese sweets purchased by the provident Bettina. He was in such good humour that he gave two full-mouth smiles and even went so far as to apologize for his outbursts in Hades.

'I know, Corbera, I know. I was excessive in my words, however restrained – believe me – in my concepts. Don't give it another thought.'

I really didn't think about it; indeed I was full of respect for the old man, whom I suspected of being tremendously unhappy notwithstanding his triumphant career. He devoured the revolting *lokums*.

'Sweets, Corbera, ought to be sweet and nothing but. If they have another flavour they are like perverted kisses.' He gave large crumbs to Aeacus, a stocky boxer that had entered the room at some point. 'This creature, Corbera, for those capable of appreciating him, more closely resembles the Immortals, despite his ugliness, than your little temptresses.' He refused to show me his library. 'It's all classics, stuff that wouldn't interest someone like you, a moral failure in Greek.' But he did lead me around the room we were in, which was his study. There were few books, among which I noted the theatre of Tirso de Molina, Fouqué's *Undine*, Giraudoux's play of the same name, and, to my surprise, the works of H.G. Wells; but in compensation, on the walls, were enormous life-size photographs of archaic Greek statues, and not the typical photographs that any of us could procure for ourselves but stupendous reproductions, clearly requested with authority and sent with devotion by museums around the world. They were all there, the magnificent creatures: the Louvre's

Horseman, the *Seated Goddess* from Taranto that is in Berlin, the *Warrior* from Delphi, one of the *Korai of the Acropolis*, the *Apollo of Piombino*, the *Lapith Woman* and the *Phoebus* from Olympia, the famous *Charioteer* . . . The room shone with their ecstatic and at the same time ironic smiles, gloried in the calm arrogance of their bearing. 'You see, Corbera, perhaps these, if one is so fortunate; the local "maidens," no.' Above the fireplace, ancient amphorae and craters: Odysseus tied to the mast of his boat, the Sirens casting themselves down onto the rocks in expiation for having let their prey escape. 'Lies, Corbera, the lies of petit bourgeois poets. No one escapes, and even if someone did, the Sirens would never destroy themselves for so little. In any case, how could they die?'

On an end table stood a faded old photograph, simply framed, of a young man around twenty, almost nude, his curly hair disheveled, with a bold expression and features of rare beauty. Perplexed, I stopped myself for a moment. I thought I understood. Not at all. 'And this, countryman, this was and is, and *will be*,' he stressed, 'Rosario La Ciura.'

The broken-down senator in a dressing gown had been a young god.

Our conversation then turned to other matters. Before I left he showed me a letter in French from the rector of the University of Coimbra inviting him to be a guest of honour at a Greek studies conference in Portugal in May. 'I'm very pleased. I'll go aboard the *Rex* in Genoa along with the French, Swiss and German participants. Like Odysseus I'll plug my ears in order not to hear the drivel of those moral cripples, and there'll be beautiful days of sailing: the sun, the blue sky, the smell of the sea.'

On my way out we again passed the shelf containing the works of Wells, and I ventured to show my surprise at seeing them there. 'You're right, Corbera, they're ghastly. There's one novella there that, were I to reread it, would make me spit nonstop for a month; and even you, salon lapdog that you are, you would be appalled.'

Following my visit our relations became decidedly cordial – on my part at least. I went to great lengths to have some exceptionally fresh sea urchins brought in from Genoa. When I learned that they would arrive the following day I procured some Etna wine and farmer's bread and nervously invited the senator to visit me in my tiny apartment. To my great relief he very happily accepted. I picked him up in my Fiat 508 and dragged him all the way to Via Peyron, which is something of a backwater. In the car he displayed some fear and no confidence whatsoever in my driving skills. 'I know you now, Corbera; if we're unlucky enough to encounter one of your abortions in a frock, you're liable to turn your head and send us both smashing into the corner of a building.' We met no skirted monstrosity worthy of note and arrived safely.

For the first time since I met him I saw the senator laugh – when we entered my bedroom. 'So then, Corbera, this is the theatre of your vile exploits.' He examined my few books. 'Fine, fine. Perhaps you're less ignorant than you seem. This one here,' he added as he picked up a volume of Shakespeare, 'this one here understood something. "A sea-change into something rich and strange."[1] "What potions have I drunk of Siren tears?"[2]

When the good Signora Carmagnola entered the drawing room carrying the tray of sea urchins, lemons, and the rest, the senator was ecstatic. 'This was your idea? How did you know they are the thing I long for more than any other?'

'You can safely enjoy them, Senator; this morning they were still in the Ligurian Sea.'

'Yes, of course, your sort are always the same, slaves to your decadence, to your putrescence; your long, asinine ears always straining to make out the shuffling steps of Death. Poor devils! Thank you, Corbera, you've been a good famulus. It's a shame they're not from the sea down there, these urchins, that they haven't been steeped in our algae; their spines have surely never drawn a drop of divine blood. You've done what was possible, certainly, but these urchins, having dozed on the cold reefs of Nervi or Arenzano, they're almost *boreal*.' It was clear that he was one of those Sicilians for whom the Ligurian Riviera – considered a tropical region by the Milanese – may as well be Iceland. The urchins, split in half, revealed their wounded, blood-red, strangely compartmentalized flesh. I'd never paid attention before now, but after the senator's bizarre comparisons they really did seem like cross sections of who knows what delicate female organs. He consumed them avidly but without cheer, with a meditative, almost sorrowful air. He didn't want to squeeze any lemon over them.

'Your sort, always combining flavours! Sea urchins have to taste also like lemon, sugar also like chocolate, love also like paradise!' When he finished he took a sip of wine and closed his eyes. After a bit I noticed, slipping from beneath his shriveled eyelids, two tears. He stood up and walked to the window, where he furtively dried his eyes. Then he turned. 'Have you ever been to Augusta yourself, Corbera?' I'd spent three months there as a recruit; during off-duty hours two or three of us would take a boat out on the transparent waters and explore the gulfs. After my answer he was silent; then, in an irritated voice: 'And did you grunts ever arrive as far as the inland gulf past Punta Izzo, behind the hill overlooking the saltworks?'

'We certainly did, it's the most beautiful spot in Sicily, yet to be discovered, thankfully, by the Dopolavoro crowds.[3] The coast is wild there, right, Senator? It's completely deserted, and you can't see a single house; the sea is the colour of peacocks; and behind it all, beyond the shifting waves, rises Mount Etna. From no other spot is it so beautiful – calm, powerful, truly divine. It's a place where you can see the island in one of its eternal aspects, as it was before it so foolishly turned its back on its vocation, which was to serve as pasture for the Cattle of the Sun.'

The senator was silent. Then: 'You're a good kid, Corbera; if you weren't so ignorant, something might have been made of you.' He came toward me and kissed my forehead. 'Now bring round your jalopy. I want to go home.'

In the weeks that followed we continued to see each other regularly. Now we also took late-night walks, generally down Via Po and across the martial expanse of Piazza Vittorio; we went to gaze at the rushing river and the Turin hills, elements that introduced a drop of fantasy into the geometrical rigour of the city. Then began the spring, that affecting season of threatened youth; the first lilacs sprouted on the banks, and the most impetuous of the young couples without a place to retreat to braved the dampness of the grass. 'Down there the sun already blazes, the algae blooms, the fish appear at the surface of the water on moonlit nights and flashes of bodies can be made out between the lines of luminous foam. We stand here before this insipid, lifeless current of water, before these big ugly buildings that look like soldiers or monks all in a line, and we hear the sobs of these dying creatures coupling.' It cheered him, however, to think about the impending voyage to Lisbon, not far off now. 'It will be pleasant. You ought to come along as well. A shame that it's not open to those deficient in Greek; with me at least you can speak Italian, but if Zuckmayer or Van der Voos found out you didn't know the optative of every irregular verb, you'd be done for. This even though you may be more in touch with Greek reality than they are; not through cultivation, clearly, but through animal instinct.'

Two days prior to his departure for Genoa he told me that he would not be returning to the café the following day, but that he would expect me at his house at nine that evening.

The protocol was identical to the last time: The images of the gods of three thousand years ago radiated youth as a stove radiates heat; the faded photograph of the young god of fifty years ago seemed dismayed at watching his own metamorphosis into a white-haired old man sunk in an armchair.

When the Cypriot wine had been drunk the senator called Bettina and told her she could go to bed. 'I will see Signor Corbera out myself when he goes.' Then: 'Believe me, Corbera, if I've asked you here this evening at the risk of upsetting any Rivoli fornication plans you might have had, it's because I need you. I leave tomorrow, and when you go away at my age you never know if it won't be necessary to stay away forever, especially when you go by sea. Please know that I genuinely care for you: Your ingenuousness touches me, your unconcealed carnal intrigues amuse me, and it seems to me that, as is sometimes the case with the best kind of Sicilians, you have managed to achieve a synthesis of the senses and reason. Therefore you deserve not to be left empty-handed, without hearing me explain the reason behind some of my eccentricities, of some sentences I've spoken in your presence that will certainly have appeared to you worthy of a madman.'

I protested weakly: 'I haven't understood many of the things you've said, but I've always attributed my incomprehension to the inadequacy of my own mind, never to an aberration of yours.'

'Don't worry, Corbera, it doesn't matter. All of us old people seem crazy to you young people, and often in fact the opposite is true. To explain myself, however, I'll have to tell you about my adventure, an uncommon one. It happened when I was "that young gentleman there," and he pointed at his photograph. 'I have to go back to 1887, a time that will seem pre-historic to you but is not for me.'

He moved from his place behind the desk and came to sit down beside me on the same couch. 'Pardon me, but from now on I'll have to speak in a low voice. Important words cannot be bellowed; the "cry of love" or hate is to be found only in melodrama or among the most uncultivated people, which comes to the same thing in the end. In 1887, then, I was twenty-four years old; I looked like the person in that photograph. I already had my degree in ancient literature and had published two articles on Ionic dialects that had caused a certain stir in my university; and for the previous year I'd been preparing for a competition for a post at the University of Pavia. Also, I had never known a woman. As a matter of fact, I have never known women either before or after that year.' I was sure that my face had remained stonily impassive, but I was deceived. 'Your eyelash fluttering is very ill-mannered, Corbera. What I say is the truth – the truth and a boast. I know that we Catanesi are held to be capable of impregnating our own nannies, and that may even be true. Not in my case, however. When one passes one's days and nights with goddesses and demigoddesses, as I did during that period, there remains little desire to climb the stairs of the brothels of San Berillo. At the time I was also held back by religious scruples. Corbera, you really should learn to control your eyelashes; they betray you constantly. Yes, I said religious scruples. I also said "at the time." Now I no longer have them; but they were worthless in any case.

'You, young Corbera, who probably obtained your position at the newspaper thanks to a note from some Party official, you don't know what it is to prepare for a competition for a university chair of Greek literature. For two years you slog away, to the limits of sanity. I already knew the language fairly well, fortunately, as well as I know it now; and I don't say so just for the sake of it, you know . . . But the rest: the Alexandrine and Byzantine variants of the texts; the passages cited, always poorly, from Latin authors; the countless connections between literature and mythology, history, philosophy, science! I repeat, it's enough to drive you mad. So I studied like a dog, and also gave lessons to students who'd flunked the subject, to pay the rent on my place in the city. You could say I subsisted on nothing but black olives and coffee. On top of all this came the disastrous summer of 1887, one of those truly infernal summers that we have every so often down there. At night Etna vomited back the fire of the sun that it stored up fifteen hours a day; if you touched the railing of a balcony at noon you'd have to run to the emergency room; volcanic paving stones seemed on the point of returning to their liquid state; and almost every day the sirocco swatted you in the face with sticky bats' wings. I was on the verge of collapse when a friend came to my aid. He found me wandering the streets, exhausted, muttering Greek verses I no longer understood. My appearance troubled him. "Look, Rosario, if you stay here you'll go mad, and then so much for the competition. Myself, I'm off to Switzerland" – the fellow had money – "but in Augusta I've got a three-room cabin twenty yards from the sea, far from the village. Pack a bag, take your books and go stay there for the rest of the summer. Come by my place in an hour and I'll give you the key. Just wait till you see, it's something else. Ask for the Carobene place at the station, everyone knows it. But you're really got to leave – tonight."

'I followed his advice and left that same evening. On awaking the next morning, rather than the toilet pipes across the courtyard that used to greet me at dawn, I found before me a pure expanse of sea, and beyond it a no longer pitiless Etna, wrapped in the morning mist. The spot was completely deserted, as you said it still is now, and of a singular beauty. The little house's dilapidated rooms contained just the sofa on which I'd slept, a table, and three chairs; the kitchen, a few earthenware pots and an old lamp. Behind the house were a fig tree and a well. Paradise. I went into the village and tracked down the farmer of the small Carobene estate, and worked out that every few days he would bring me some bread, pasta, vegetables and kerosene. Olive oil I had, from the supply my poor mother had sent me in Catania. I rented a dinghy that the fisherman brought round that afternoon along with a wicker fish basket and a few hooks. I'd decided to stay there for at least two months.

'Carobene was right: It really was something else. The heat was violent in Augusta too, but, no longer reflected back by walls, it produced not dreadful prostration but a sort of submissive euphoria; the sun, shedding its executioner's grimace, was content to be a smiling if brutal giver of energy, and also a sorcerer setting mobile diamonds in the sea's slightest ripple. Study ceased to be toil: Gently rocked by the boat in which I spent hours on end, each book seemed no longer an obstacle to be overcome but rather a key offering me passage into a world, a world I already had before my eyes in one of its most enchanting aspects. I often happened to recite the verses of poets aloud, and thus the names of those gods, which most people have forgotten or never knew, again skimmed the surface of the sea that would have once, at their mere mention, risen up in turmoil or subsided into dead calm.

'My isolation was absolute, interrupted only by visits from the farmer who brought me my few provisions every three or four days. He would only stay for five minutes; seeing me so exhilarated and dishevelled, he must have thought me dangerously close to madness. And in truth, the sun, the seclusion, the nights passed beneath the wheeling stars, the silence, the scant nourishment, the study of remote subjects wove around me a spell that predisposed me to marvels.

'This came to pass on the morning of 5 August, at six o'clock. I hadn't been up for long before I was in the boat; a few strokes of the oars took me away from the pebbled shore. I'd stopped at the base of a large rock whose shadow might protect me from a sun that was already climbing, swollen with dazzling fury and turning the whiteness of the auroral sea gold and blue. As I declaimed I sensed that the side of the boat, to my right and behind me, had abruptly been lowered, as if someone had grabbed on to climb up. I turned and saw her: The smooth face of a sixteen-year-old emerged from the sea; two small hands gripped the gunwale. The adolescent smiled, a slight displacement of her pale lips that revealed small, sharp white teeth, like dogs'. This, however, was not a smile like those to be seen among your sort, always debased with an accessory expression of benevolence or irony, of compassion, cruelty or whatever the case may be; it expressed nothing but itself: an almost bestial delight in existing, a joy almost divine. This smile was the first of her charms that would affect me, revealing paradises of forgotten serenity. From her disordered hair, which was the colour of the sun, seawater dripped into her exceedingly open green eyes, over features of infantile purity.

'Our suspicious reason, howsoever predisposed, loses its bearings in the face of the marvellous, and when it perceives it, tries to rely on the memory of banal phenomena. Like anyone else would have, I supposed that I'd met a swimmer. Moving cautiously, I pulled myself up to her level, leaned toward her and held out my hands to help her aboard. Instead she rose with astonishing strength straight out of the water to her waist, encircled my neck with her arms, wrapping me in a never before experienced perfume and allowed herself to be pulled into the boat. Her body below the groin, below the buttocks, was that of a fish, covered with tiny pearly blue scales and ending in a forked tail that slapped gently against the bottom of the boat. She was a Siren.

'She lay back, resting her head on interlaced fingers, displaying with serene immodesty the delicate little hairs of her armpits, her splayed breasts, her perfect stomach. She exuded what I have clumsily referred to as a perfume, a magical smell of the sea, of decidedly youthful sensuality. We were in the shade but twenty yards from us the seashore reveled in the sun and quivered with pleasure. My near-complete nudity ill concealed my own emotion.

'She spoke and thus was I overwhelmed, after her smile and smell, by the third and greatest of her charms: her voice. It was a bit guttural, husky, resounding with countless harmonics; behind the words could be discerned the sluggish undertow of summer seas, the whisper of receding beach foam, the wind passing over lunar tides. The song of the Sirens, Corbera, does not exist; the music that cannot be escaped is their voice alone.

'She spoke Greek and I struggled to understand her. 'I heard you speaking to yourself in a language similar to my own. I like you: take me. I am Lighea, daughter of Calliope. Don't believe the stories about us. We don't kill anyone, we only love.'

'I bent over her as I rowed, staring into her smiling eyes. When we reached the shore I took her aromatic body into my arms and we passed from the blazing sun into the deep shade; there she poured into my mouth such sensual pleasure that it is to your terrestrial kisses as wine is to insipid water.'

The senator narrated his adventure in a low voice. I who in my heart had always set my own varied experiences with women against those he regarded as mediocre, and had derived from this a foolish sense of reduced distance, was humiliated: in matters of love as well, I saw myself sunk to unfathomable depths. Never for a moment did I suspect he was lying to me, and had anyone else been there, even the most sceptical of witnesses, he too would have perceived the certainty of truth in the old man's tone.

'So began those three weeks. I have no right, nor would it be merciful to you, to go into details. Suffice to say that in those embraces I enjoyed the highest form of spiritual pleasure along with the greatest physical gratification, devoid of any social resonance, the same that our solitary mountain shepherds experience when they couple with their goats. If the comparison repels you, it's because you're not capable of performing the necessary transposition from the bestial to the superhuman plane – planes that were, in this case, superimposed.

'Think about how much Balzac dared not express in "Une Passion dans le désert." From her immortal limbs flowed such life force that any loss of energy was immediately compensated, increased, in fact. In those days, Corbera, I loved as much as a hundred of your Don Juans put together, over their entire lives. And what love! Sheltered from conventions and crimes, the rancor of commendatori and the triviality of Leporellos, far from the claims of the heart, the lying sighs, the phony melting weakness that inevitably mark your sort's wretched kisses. To be honest, a Leporello did disturb us the first day, and it was the only time: Around ten I heard the sound of the farmer's boots on the path that leads down to the sea; just in time, with the farmer at the door, I managed to throw a sheet over the uncommon body of Lighea. Her uncovered head, throat, and arms led our Leporello to believe this was some commonplace affair and hence commanded his sudden respect. His stay was shorter than usual. As he went he winked his left eye, and with his right thumb and index finger at the corner of his mouth made the motion of curling an imaginary mustache; and he returned up the path.

'I spoke of our having spent twenty days together. However, I wouldn't want you to imagine that during those three weeks she and I lived, as they say, "conjugally," sharing our bed, meals and occupations. Lighea's absences were quite frequent. Without any advance notice she would dive into the sea and disappear, sometimes for many hours. When she returned, almost always first thing in the morning, either she found me in the boat or, if I was still in the cabin, wriggled up the pebbled shore till she was half out of the water, on her back and pushing with her arms, calling to be helped up the slope. "Sasà," she would call, because I'd told her this was the diminutive form of my name. In this manoeuvre made awkward by the same part of her body that granted her agility in the sea, she gave the pitiable impression of a wounded animal, an impression immediately obliterated by the smile in her eyes.

'She ate nothing that was not alive. I often saw her rise out of the sea, delicate torso sparkling in the sun, teeth tearing into a still-quivering silver fish, blood running down her chin; after a few bites the mangled hake or bream would be tossed over her shoulder and sink into the water, staining it red, while she shouted in childish delight and ran her tongue over her teeth. Once I gave her some wine. Drinking from a glass was impossible for her, so I was obliged to pour some into her small and slightly greenish hand; she lapped up the liquid as dogs do, her eyes registering surprise at the unfamiliar flavour. She said it was good but afterward always refused it. From time to time she came to shore with hands full of oysters or mussels, and while I struggled to open the shells with a knife, she crushed them with a stone and sucked down the throbbing mollusk along with bits of shell that did not trouble her in the least.

'I told you before, Corbera: She was a beast and at the same time an Immortal, and it's a shame that we cannot continuously express this synthesis in speaking, the way she does, with absolute simplicity, in her own body. Not only did she display in the carnal act a cheerfulness and a delicacy altogether contrary to wretched animal lust, but her speech was of a powerful immediacy, the likes of which I have only ever found in a few great poets. Not for nothing was she the daughter of Calliope: Oblivious to all cultures, ignorant of all wisdom, disdainful of any moral constraint whatsoever, she was nevertheless part of the source of all culture, of all knowledge, of all ethics, and she knew how to express this primitive superiority of hers in terms of rugged beauty. "I am everything because I am only the stream of life, free of accident. I am immortal because all deaths converge in me, from that of the hake just now to that of Zeus; gathered in me they once again become life, not individual and particular but belonging to nature and thus free." Then she said, "You are young and handsome. You should follow me into the sea now and escape sorrows and old age. You would come to my home beneath enormous mountains of motionless dark water, where all is silent calm so innate that those who possess it no longer even perceive it. I have loved you, and so remember: When you are tired, when you can truly bear it no longer, all you have to do is lean out over the sea and call me. I will always be there, because I am everywhere, and your dream of sleep will be fulfilled."

'She told me about her life below the sea, about bearded Tritons and glaucous caverns, but she said that these too were vain appearances and that the truth lay much deeper indeed, in the blind, mute palace of formless, eternal waters, without sparkle, without murmurs.

'Once she told me she would be away for some time, until the evening of the following day. "I must travel far, to where I know I will find a gift for you."

'In fact she returned with a stupendous branch of deep red coral encrusted with shells and algae. For a long while I kept it in a drawer and every night I would kiss the spots where I recalled the Indifferent, that is the Beneficent, one had placed her fingers. Then one day my housekeeper, Maria – Bettina's predecessor – stole it to give to one of her pimps. I later found it in a Ponte Vecchio jeweller's shop, deconsecrated, cleaned up and smoothed to the point of being virtually unrecognizable. I bought it back and that same night threw it into the Arno: It had passed through too many profane hands.

'She also spoke to me of the many human lovers she'd had during her thousand-year adolescence: fishermen and sailors – Greeks, Sicilians, Arabs, Capresi – including survivors of shipwrecks clinging to sodden debris, to whom she'd appeared in a flash of lightning during a storm to transform their last gasp into pleasure. "They all accepted my invitation and came to see me, some immediately, others after having lived what to them seemed a long time. Only one failed to show. He was a big beautiful young man with red hair and exceptionally white skin; I joined myself to him on a beach far away, where our sea flows into the great Ocean. He smelled of something stronger than the wine you gave me the other day. I believe that he failed to show not, surely, because he was happy, but because when we met he was so drunk as not to understand anything anymore. I must have seemed like one of his usual fisherwomen."

'Those weeks of high summer flew by as rapidly as a single morning; when they'd passed I realized that in fact I had lived centuries. That lascivious girl, that cruel little beast, had also been the wisest of Mothers;

with her mere presence she'd uprooted faiths, dispelled metaphysics; with her fragile, often bloodstained fingers she'd shown me the path toward true eternal peace, and also toward an asceticism based not on sacrifice but on the impossibility of accepting other, inferior pleasures. I will certainly not be the second man to fail to heed her call, will not refuse this sort of pagan Grace that has been granted me.

'In accordance with its own violence, that summer was short. Not long after August 20 the first clouds timidly gathered; a few isolated blood-warm drops of rain fell. The nights brought to the distant horizon slow mute flashes of lightning, deduced one from the other like the cogitations of a god. Mornings the dove-gray sea suffered for its hidden restlessness; evenings it rippled without any perceptible breeze, in gradations from smoke grey to steel grey to pearl grey, all extremely soft colours and more affectionate than the splendour before. Faraway shreds of fog skimmed the water; on the coasts of Greece, perhaps, it was already raining. The colour of Lighea's mood also changed, from radiance to grey affection. She was silent more often; spent hours stretched out on a rock, staring at the no longer motionless horizon; spent less time away. "I want to stay here longer with you; if I were to take to the open sea now my marine companions would keep me there. Do you hear them? They're calling me." At times I truly did seem to hear a different, lower note among the seagull calls, to make out flashes of movement from rock to rock. "They're blowing their conches, calling Lighea to the festival of the storm."

'This set upon us at dawn on the twenty-sixth day. From our rock we saw the approaching wind as it battered distant waters; closer by, sluggish leaden waves swelled ever larger. Soon the gusts arrived, whistling in our ears, bending the withered rosemary bushes. The sea churned below us and the first white-capped surge advanced. "Farewell, Sasà. You won't forget." The billow broke upon the rock; the Siren dove into the iridescent spray. I never saw her come down; she seemed to dissolve into the foam.'

The senator left the next morning; I went to the station to see him off. He was surly and cutting as usual, but, when the train began to move, his fingers reached through the window to graze my head.

The next day at dawn a telephone call came into the newspaper from Genoa: During the night Senator La Ciura had fallen into the sea from the deck of the *Rex* as it sailed toward Napoli; though lifeboats had been deployed immediately, the body was not found.

A week later came the reading of his will: To Bettina went the bank account and furniture; the library was donated to the University of Catania; in a recently added codicil I was named legatee of both the Greek crater with the Siren figures and the large photograph of the Acropolis kore.

I had the two objects sent to my house in Palermo. Then came the war and while I was stuck in Marmarica with a pint of water a day, the 'Liberators' destroyed my house. When I returned I found the photograph had been cut into strips and used by the looters for torches. The crater had been smashed to bits; the largest piece showed the feet of Odysseus tied to the mast of his ship. I still have it today. The books had been stored underground by the university, but, for lack of money for shelves, there they slowly rot.

'*The Siren*'

Written in the winter 1956–1957 and published posthumously (with the title '*Lighea*') in *Racconti* (Feltrinelli, 1961).

ANTONIO TABUCCHI

1943–2012

Writing, for Tabucchi, was often an act of crossing borders, of switching from one set of coordinates to the next. Implicit to his creative journey was an enduring and transformative dedication to another language, its literature and its people. In his case, the language was Portuguese, first encountered in the work of the writer Fernando Pessoa, famous for creating separate literary identities known as heteronyms. In translating and introducing Pessoa's work to Italy, Tabucchi fabricated a unique postmodern identity for himself. He travelled to Portugal, met and married a Portuguese woman, and founded, with his wife, a magazine dedicated to Portuguese literature. In Italy he taught Portuguese for decades, in Bologna, Genoa and Siena, and then became the director of the Institute for Italian Culture in Lisbon in the late 1980s. He wrote long novels and short ones, his style also crossing the borders of conventional narrative technique over the course of his creative career. He composed his novel, *Requiem*, directly in Portuguese, a book he did not himself translate into Italian. An outspoken public intellectual, Tabucchi collaborated with Italy's major newspapers until his articles, fiercely critical of the Berlusconi government, marginalized him to the realm of overtly leftist publications. He wrote four books of short stories. This selection appears at the end of his final collection, *Il tempo invecchia in fretta* (*Time Ages in a Hurry*): nine cyclical, deeply elegiac tales in which time, place and memory form a thematic triad. Each is set in a series of different international cities. The book was published three years before the author's death in Portugal. By then Tabucchi had been made a Portuguese national, and so his ashes rest in a tomb dedicated to Portuguese writers in Lisbon's Prazeres Cemetery. His funeral was conducted in Italian, French and Portuguese.

Against Time

Translated by Martha Cooley and Antonio Romano

It'd gone like this:

The man had boarded at an Italian airport, because everything began in Italy, and whether it was Milan or Rome was secondary, what matters is that it was an Italian airport where you could take a direct flight to Athens, and from there, after a brief stopover, a connecting flight to Crete on Aegean Airlines, because this he was sure of, that the man had travelled on Aegean Airlines, so in Italy he'd taken a flight that let him connect in Athens for Crete at around two in the afternoon, he'd seen it on the Greek company's schedule, which meant this man had arrived in Crete at around three, three-thirty in the afternoon. The airport of departure is not so important, though, in the story of the person who'd lived that story, it's the morning of any day at the end of April of 2008, a splendid day, almost like summer. Which is not an insignificant detail, because the man taking the flight, meticulous as he was, gave considerable importance to the weather and would watch a satellite channel dedicated to meteorology around the world, and the weather in Crete, he'd seen, was really splendid: 29 degrees Celsius during the day, clear sky, humidity within normal limits, good seaside weather, ideal for lying on one of those white beaches described in his guide, for bathing in the blue sea and enjoying a well-deserved vacation. Because this was also the reason for the journey of that man who was going to live that story: a vacation. And in fact that's what he thought, sitting in the waiting lounge for international flights at Rome-Fiumicino, waiting for the boarding call for Athens.

And here he is finally on the plane, comfortably installed in business class – it's a paid trip, as will be seen later – reassured by the courtesies of the flight attendants. His age is difficult to determine, even for the person

45

who knew the story that the man was living: let's say he was between fifty and sixty years old, lean, robust, healthy-looking, salt-and-pepper hair, fine blond moustache, plastic glasses for far-sightedness hung from his neck. His work. On this point too the person who knew his story was somewhat uncertain. He could be a manager of a multinational, one of those anonymous businessmen who spend their lives in an office and whose merit is one day acknowledged by headquarters. But he could also be a marine biologist, one of those researchers who observe seaweed and micro-organisms under a microscope, without leaving their laboratory, and so can assert that the Mediterranean will become a tropical sea, as perhaps it was millions of years ago. Yet this hypothesis also struck him as not very satisfying, biologists who study the sea don't always remain shut up in their laboratory, they wander beaches and rocks, perhaps they dive, they perform their own surveys, and that passenger dozing in his business-class seat on a flight to Athens didn't actually look like a marine biologist; maybe on weekends he went to the gym to keep fit, nothing else. But if he really did go to the gym, then why did he go? To what end did he maintain his body, stay so young-looking? There really was no reason: it'd been over for quite a while with the woman he'd considered his life companion, he didn't have another companion or lover, he lived alone, stayed away from serious commitments, apart from some rare adventures that can happen to everybody. Perhaps the most credible hypothesis was that he was a naturalist, a modern follower of Linnaeus, and he was going to a convention in Crete along with other experts on medicinal herbs and plants, abundant in Crete. Because one thing was certain, he was going to a convention of fellow researchers, his was a journey that rewarded a lifetime of work and commitment, the convention was taking place in the city of Retimno, he'd be in a hotel made of bungalows a few kilometres from Retimno, and a car service would shuttle him in the afternoons, but he'd have mornings to himself.

The man woke up, pulled out the guide from his carry-on and looked for his hotel. What he found was reassurring: two restaurants, a pool, room service, the hotel had closed for the winter and had only reopened in mid-April, and this meant very few tourists would be there, the usual clients, the northern Europeans thirsty for sunlight, as the guide described them, were still in their little boreal houses. The pleasant voice from the loud-speaker asked everyone to buckle their seat-belts, they'd begun the descent to Athens and would land in about twenty minutes. The man closed the folding tray table and put his seat upright, replaced the guide in his carry-on and from the pocket of the seat in front of him pulled out the newspaper that the flight attendant had distributed, to which he'd paid no attention. It was a newspaper with many full-colour supplements, the usual weekend ones, the economics-financial supplement, the sports supplement, the interior-design supplement and the weekend magazine. He skipped all the supplements and opened the magazine. On the cover, in black and white, was the picture of the atomic bomb's mushroom cloud, with the title: THE GREAT IMAGES OF OUR TIME. He began leafing through, somewhat reluctantly. First came an ad by two fashion designers showing a young man naked to the waist, which at first he thought was a great image of our time, but then there was the first true image of our time: the stone facade of a house in Hiroshima where the heat from the atomic bomb had liquefied a man, leaving only the imprint of his shadow. He'd never seen this image and was astonished by it, feeling a kind of remorse: that thing had happened more than sixty years before, how was it possible he'd never seen it? The shadow on the stone was a silhouette, and in this profile he thought he could see his friend Ferruccio, who for no apparent reason, on New Year's Eve of 1999, shortly before midnight, had thrown himself from the tenth floor of a building on to Via Cavour. Was it possible that the profile of Ferruccio, squashed into the soil on the thirty-first of December in 1999, looked like the profile absorbed by stone in a Japanese city in 1945? The idea was absurd, yet that's what passed through his mind in all its absurdity. He kept riffling the magazine, and meanwhile his heart began beating erratically, one-two-pause, three-one-pause, two-three-one, pause-pause-two-three, the so-called extrasystole, nothing pathological, the cardiologist had reassured him after an entire day of testing, only a matter of anxiety. But why now? It couldn't be those images provoking his emotions, they were faraway things. That naked girl, arms raised, who was running towards the camera in an apocalyptic land-scape: he'd seen this image more than once and it hadn't made such a violent impression, and yet now it produced in him an intense turmoil. He turned the page. There was a man on his knees, palms together, at the edge of a pit, a kid sadistically pointing a gun at his temple. Khmer Rouge, said the caption. To reassure himself he made himself think that these things were also from faraway places and distant times. But the thought wasn't enough: a strange form of emotion, almost a thought, was telling him the opposite, that the atrocity had happened yesterday, it'd happened just that morning, while he was on this flight, and by sorcery had been imprinted on the page he was looking at. The voice over the loudspeaker stated that the landing would be delayed by fifteen minutes due to air traffic, and meanwhile the passengers should enjoy the view. The plane traced a wide curve, banking to the right, from the little window opposite he could glimpse the blue of the sea, while in his own, the white city of Athens was framed, with a green spot in the middle, no doubt a park, and then the Acropolis, he could see the Acropolis perfectly, and the Parthenon, his palms were damp with sweat, he asked himself if it weren't a sort of panic provoked by the plane going round in circles, and meanwhile he looked at the photo of a stadium where policemen in riot gear pointed submachine guns at a bunch of barefooted men, under it was written: Santiago de Chile, 1973. And on the opposite page was a photo that seemed a montage, surely retouched, it couldn't be real, he'd never seen it: on the balcony of a nineteenth-century palazzo was Pope John Paul II next to a general in uniform. The Pope was without doubt the Pope, and the general was without doubt Pinochet, with that hair full of brilliantine, that chubby face, that little moustache and the Ray-Ban sunglasses. The caption said: His Holiness the Pope on his official visit to Chile, April 1987. He began quickly leafing through the magazine, as though anxious to get to the end, barely looking at the photographs, but he had to stop at one of them, it showed a kid with his back turned to a police van, his arms raised as though his beloved soccer team had scored a goal, but looking closer you could see he was falling backward, something stronger than he was had struck him. On it was written: Genoa, July 2001: Meeting of the eight richest countries in the world. The eight richest countries in the world: the phrase provoked in him a strange sensation, like something that is at once understandable and absurd, because it was understandable and yet absurd. Every photo was on a silvery page as though it were Christmas, with the date in big letters. He'd arrived at 2004, but he hesitated, he wasn't sure he wanted to see the next picture, was it possible the plane was still going around in circles? He turned the page, it showed a naked body collapsed on the ground, a man apparently, though in the photo they'd blurred the pubic area, a soldier in camouflage extended a leg towards the body as though he were kicking a garbage can, the dog he held on a leash was trying to bite a leg, the muscles of the animal were as taut as the cord that held it, in the other hand the soldier held a cigarette. The caption read: Abu Ghraib Prison, Iraq, 2004. After that, he arrived at the year he found himself in now, the year of our Lord 2008, that is, he found himself in sync, that's what he thought even if he didn't know with what, but in sync. He couldn't tell what image he was in sync with, but he didn't turn the page, and meanwhile the plane was finally landing, the landing strip was running beneath him with the intermittent white bands blurring to a single band. He'd arrived.

Venizelos Airport looked brand new, surely they'd built it for the Olympic Games. He was happy with himself for being able to reach the boarding gate for Crete without reading the signs in English, the Greek he'd learned at school was still useful, curiously. When he landed at the Hania airport at first he didn't realize he'd reached his destination: during the brief flight from Athens to Crete, a little less than an hour, he'd fallen fast asleep, forgetting everything, it seemed, even himself. To such a degree that when he came down the airplane's staircase into that African light, he asked himself where he was, and why he was there and even who he was, and in that amazement at nothing he even felt happy. His suitcase wasn't long in arriving on the conveyor belt, just beyond the boarding gates were the car-rental offices, he couldn't remember the instructions, Hertz or Avis? It was one or the other, fortunately he guessed right, along with the car keys, they gave him a road map of Crete, a copy of the programme of the convention, his hotel reservation and the route to the tourist village where the convention-goers were lodged. Which by now he knew by heart, because he'd studied and restudied it in his guide, nicely furnished with road maps: from the airport you went straight down to the coast, you had to go that way unless you wanted to reach the Marathi beaches, then you turned left, otherwise you wound up west and he was going east, towards Iraklion, you passed in front of the Hotel Doma, went along Venizelos, and followed the green signs that meant highway, though it was actually a coastal freeway, you exited shortly after Georgopolis, a tourist spot to avoid, and followed the directions for the hotel, Beach Resort, it was easy.

The car, a black Volkswagen parked in the sun, was boiling, but he let it cool down a little by leaving the doors open, entered it as though he were late for an appointment, but he wasn't late and he didn't have any appointments, it was four o'clock in the afternoon, he'd get to the hotel in a little more than an hour, the convention wouldn't start till the evening of the following day, with an official banquet, he had more than twenty-four hours of freedom, what was the hurry? No hurry. After a few kilometres a tourist sign indicated the grave of Venizelos, a few hundred metres from the main road. He decided to take a short break to freshen up before the drive. Next to the entrance to the monument was an ice-cream shop with a large open terrace overlooking the little town. He settled himself at a table, ordered a Turkish coffee and a lemon sorbet. The town he saw had been Venetian and then Turkish, it was nice, and of an almost blinding white. Now he was feeling really good, with an unusual energy, the disquiet he'd felt on the plane had completely vanished. He checked the road map: to get to the freeway to Iraklion he could pass through the town or go around the gulf of Souda, a few kilometres more. He chose the second route, the gulf from up above was beautiful and the sea intensely azure. The descent from the hill to Souda was pleasant, beyond the low vegetation and the rooftops of some houses he could see little coves of white sand, a strong urge to swim came over him, he turned off the air-conditioning and lowered the window to feel the warm air smelling of the sea on his face. He passed the little industrial port and the residential zone and arrived at the intersection where, turning to the left, the road merged with the coastal highway to Iraklion. He put on his left blinker and stopped. A car behind him beeped for him to go: there was no oncoming traffic. He didn't move, just let the car pass him, then signalled right and went in the opposite direction, where a sign said Mourniès.

And now we're following him, the unknown character who arrived in Crete to reach a pleasant seaside locale and who at a certain moment, abruptly, for a reason also unknown, took a road towards the mountains. The man proceeded till Mourniès, drove through the village without knowing where he was going, though as if he did. Actually he wasn't thinking, just driving, he knew he was headed south: the sun, still high, was already behind him. Since he'd changed direction, that sensation of lightness had returned, which he'd briefly felt at the table in the ice-cream shop, looking down on the broad horizon: an unusual lightness, and with it an energy he no longer recalled, as though he were young again, a sort of light euphoria, almost a happiness. He arrived at a village called Fournès, drove through the town confidently as though he already knew the way, stopped at a crossroads, the main road went to the right, he took the secondary road with a sign that said: Lefka Ori, the white mountains. He drove on calmly, the sensation of wellbeing was turning into a sort of cheerfulness, a Mozart aria came to mind and he felt he could reproduce its notes, he began whistling them with amazing ease, but then went hopelessly out of tune in a couple of passages, which made him laugh. The road slipped into the rugged canyons of a mountain. They were beautiful and wild places, the car went along a narrow asphalt road bordering the bed of a dry creek, at a certain point the creek bed disappeared among the rocks and the asphalt ended in a dirt road, in a barren plain among inhospitable mountains, meanwhile the light was fading, but he kept going as though he already knew the way, like someone obeying an old memory or an order received in a dream, and at a certain point he saw a crooked tin sign riddled with holes as if from gunshots or from time, and the sign said: Monastiri.

He followed it as though he'd been expecting it all along, until he came to a tiny monastery, its roof in ruins. He realized he'd arrived. Went down. The dilapidated door of those ruins sagged inward. He figured no one was there any longer; a beehive under the little portico seemed the only housekeeper. He went down and waited as if he had an appointment. It was almost dark. Then at the door a monk appeared, he was very old and moved with difficulty, he had the look of an anchorite, with his hair down to his shoulders and yellowish beard, what do you want? he asked in Greek. Do you know Italian? answered the traveller. The old man nodded. A little, he murmured. I've come to change places with you, said the man.

So it'd been like this, and no other conclusion was possible, because that story didn't call for any other possible conclusions, but the person who knew this story was aware that he couldn't let it conclude in this way, and at this point he made a leap in time. And thanks to one of those leaps in time that are possible only in the imagination, things landed in the future with regard to that month of April of 2008. How many years ahead no one knows, and the person who knew the story remained vague, twenty years, for instance, which in the lifetime of a man is a lot, because if in 2008 a man of sixty still has all his energy, in 2028 he'll be an old man, his body worn out by time.

And so the person who knew this story imagined it continued like this, and so let's accept that we're in 2028, as the person who knew the story had wanted and had imagined it would continue.

And at this point, the person who imagined how the story would continue saw two young people, a guy and a girl wearing leather shorts and trekking boots, who were hiking in the mountains of Crete. The girl said to her companion: I think that old guide you found in your father's library doesn't make any sense, by now the monastery will be a pile of stones full of lizards, why don't we head towards the sea? And the guy responded: I think you're right. But just as he said this she replied: no, let's keep on for a bit, you never know. And in fact it was enough to walk around the rugged red-stone hill that cut through the countryside and there it was, the monastery, or rather ruins of the monastery, and the two of them approached, a wind blew in from the canyons raising the dust, the monastery's door had collapsed, wasps' nests defended that empty cave, the two of them had already turned their backs on that gloom when they heard a voice. In the empty space of the door stood a man. He was very old, looked dreadful, with a long white beard to his chest and hair down to his shoulders. Oooh, called the voice. Nothing else. The couple stood still. The man asked: do you understand Italian? They didn't respond. What happened in 2008? asked the old man. The two young people looked at each other, they didn't have the courage to exchange a word. Do you have photographs? asked the old man, what happened in 2008? Then he gestured for them to go away, though perhaps he was brushing away the wasps that whirled under the portico, and he returned to the dark of his cave.

The man who knew this story was aware that it couldn't finish in any other way. Before writing his stories, he loved telling them to himself. And he'd tell them to himself so perfectly, in such detail, word by word, that one might say they were written in his memory. He'd tell them to himself, preferably, late in the evening, in the solitude of that big empty house, or on those nights when he couldn't sleep, those nights in which insomnia yielded nothing but imagination, not much, yet imagination gave him a reality so alive that it seemed more real than the reality he was living. But the most difficult thing wasn't telling to himself his stories, that was the easy part, it was as though he'd see the words of the stories he told himself written on the dark screen of his room, when fantasy would keep his eyes wide open. And that one story, which he'd told himself in this way so many times, seemed to him an already printed book, one that was very easy to express mentally but very difficult to write with the letters of the alphabet necessary for thought to be made concrete and visible. It was as if he were lacking the principle of reality to write his story, and in order to live the effective reality of what was real within him, yet unable to become truly real, he'd chosen this place.

The trip was planned in fine detail. He landed at the Hania airport, got his luggage, went into the Hertz office, picked up the car keys. Three days? the clerk asked, astonished. What's so strange about it? he said. No one comes to Crete on vacation for three days, the clerk replied, smiling. I have a long weekend, he responded, it's enough for what I have to do.

The light in Crete was beautiful. It wasn't Mediterranean but African; he'd reach the Beach Resort in an hour and a half, at most two, even going slowly, he'd arrive there around six, a shower and he'd start writing immediately, the hotel restaurant was open till eleven, it was Thursday evening, he counted: all of Friday, Saturday and Sunday, three full days. They'd be enough: in his head everything was all already written.

Why he turned left at that light, he couldn't say. The pylons of the freeway were clearly visible, another four or five hundred metres and he'd be at the coastal freeway to Iraklion. But instead he turned left, where a little blue sign indicated an unknown place. He thought he'd already been there, for in a moment he saw everything: a tree-lined street with a few houses, a plain square with an ugly monument, a ledge of rocks, a mountain. It was a flash of lighting. That strange thing which medical science can't explain, he told himself, they call it déjà vu, already-seen, it'd never happened to him before. But the explanation he gave himself didn't reassure him, because the already-seen endured, it was stronger than what he was seeing, like a membrane enveloping the surrounding reality, the trees, the mountains, the evening shadows, even the air he was breathing. He felt overcome by vertigo and was afraid of being sucked into it, but only for a moment, because as it expanded that sensation went through a strange metamorphosis, like a glove turning inside out and bringing forth the hand it covered. Everything changed perspective, in a flash he felt the euphoria of discovery, a subtle nausea, a mortal melancholy. But also a sense of infinite liberation, as when we finally understand something we'd known all along and didn't want to know: it wasn't the already-seen that was swallowing him in a never-lived past, he instead was capturing it in a future yet to be lived. As he drove among the olive trees on that little road taking him towards the mountains, he knew that at a certain point he'd find an old rusty sign full of holes on which was written: Monastiri. And that he'd follow it. Now everything was clear.

'Controtempo'
Published as part of the collection *Il tempo invecchia in fretta* (Einaudi, 2009).

ITALO SVEVO

1861–1928

Trieste, in Italy's extreme north-east, belonged to the Hapsburg Empire until 1918, when it was incorporated into the kingdom of Italy. Svevo, a profound hybrid with deeply doubled roots, was born there with the name Aron Ettore Schmitz. Today he is hailed as one of the first great Italian Modernists, but Svevo is in fact a literary Janus figure, his artistic orientation as Italian as it is central European (the pseudonym represents, quite literally, the cultural and geographical amalgam that constituted his essence; '*Italo*' represents Italy, and '*Svevo*' describes a person from Swabia – '*Svevia*' in Italian – which is in south-western Germany). The son of an Austrian Jewish father and an Italian Jewish mother, he was educated in German, spoke dialect at home and was an Austrian citizen. He converted from Judaism to Catholicism in order to marry, but had a Jewish funeral. He worked in a bank and, after marriage, for his father-in-law's company, which produced underwater paints. But his passion, since adolescence, was literature; he nurtured himself on the philosophy of Arthur Schopenhauer and the psychoanalytic works of Sigmund Freud, and he mixed the Triestine dialect and German to create his signature, unconventional Italian. His English teacher in Trieste was James Joyce, whom he befriended. Perpetually conflicted between his artistic calling and familial responsibilities, Svevo's most important novel, *La coscienza di Zeno* (translated into English not as The Conscience of Zeno, but as *The Confessions of Zeno*), was published in 1923. Until then his work went largely unnoticed; the silence that followed *Senilità* (Senility, given the English title *As a Man Grows Older*), a novel published over two decades before, almost caused him to stop writing. But Joyce adored *Senilità*, to the point of committing pages of it to memory and providing its English title. Physical decline, ineptitude and idleness were ongoing themes, and almost all of Svevo's stories, published towards the end of his career, describe the battlefield of old age. The protagonist of this selection is typical of Svevo's warrior-heroes, in part both neurotic and noble, infantile and enlightened.

Generous Wine

Translated by John Penuel

A niece of my wife's was getting married at that age at which girls stop being girls and start becoming old maids. Until shortly before, the poor thing had rejected life, but pressures from the entire family had then persuaded her to return to it and, renouncing her desire for purity and religion, she had agreed to speak to a young man the family considered a good match. Immediately thereafter, it was Goodbye, religion, Goodbye, dreams of virtuous solitude, and the date of the wedding was set for sooner even than the families would have preferred. And now we were sitting down to dinner on the eve of the wedding.

As an old satyr, I had to laugh. What had the young fellow done to get her to change her mind so quickly? He had probably taken her in his arms to make her feel the joy of living and seduced her rather than convinced her. So they really had to be wished all the best. All people, when they marry, need good wishes, but that girl needed them more than anybody. What a disaster if one day she were to regret having let herself be led back into a life that, by instinct, she had abhorred. And I, too, accompanied a drink or two of mine with good wishes, which I managed even to tailor to that particular case: 'May you be happy for a year or two, since it will be easier then for you to put up with the other long years, out of gratitude for having enjoyed yourselves. Joy gives way to longing, and it, too, is a sorrow, but a sorrow that masks the fundamental one, the sorrow of life.'

It seemed that the bride didn't feel the need for a lot of good wishes. In fact, it seemed to me that her face was practically fossilized into an expression of trusting abandon. But it was the same expression she had worn when she was announcing her intention to withdraw into a cloister.

This time, too, she was making a vow, a vow to be happy her entire life. Some people in this world are always making vows. Would she fulfil this vow any better than she had the earlier one?

Everyone else at that table was cheerful, with great naturalness, as spectators always are. I was missing naturalness altogether. It was a momentous evening for me, too. My wife had gotten permission from Dr Paoli for me to eat and drink like everybody else. The freedom was made more precious by the warning that it would be taken from me immediately afterward. And I acted exactly the way those young fellows who are given the keys to the house for the first time act. I ate and drank, not out of hunger or thirst but out of eagerness for freedom. Each bite, each sip, had to be a declaration of independence. I opened my mouth more than what was necessary for me to put the individual bites in it, and the wine went from the bottle to overflowing in my glass, and I left it there for but an instant. I felt an urge to move, and, riveted to that chair there, I somehow had the feeling I was running and jumping like a dog freed of its chain.

My wife made my state worse by telling a woman next to her about the diet I was usually on, while my daughter Emma, fifteen years old, was listening to her and giving herself airs by adding to her mother's remarks. So they wanted to remind me of the chain even at that moment at which it had been lifted from me? And the entirety of my torture was described: how they weighed the little bit of meat I was allowed at midday, depriving it of all taste, and how there was nothing to weigh in the evening because dinner was a roll with a sliver of ham and a glass of warm milk without sugar, which nauseated me. And as they spoke, I offered up a critique of the doctor's knowledge and their affection. If my body were really in such bad shape, after all, how was it possible that that evening – seeing as we had managed to get someone who wouldn't have married had she been left to her own devices to get married – it could suddenly take so much indigestible and harmful food? And as I drank I readied myself for the rebellion of the next day. They were going to be in for a tough one.

The others were on the champagne, but after having had a glass or two of it in response to the several toasts, I'd gone back to the ordinary dinner wine, a dry and sincere Istrian wine a friend had sent for the occasion. I loved that wine the way one loves memories and wasn't wary of it; nor was I surprised that, instead of procuring me joy and heedlessness, it was making me angrier.

How could I not get angry? I had been forced to endure a wretched period of life. Frightened and impoverished, I had let any generous instinct of mine die out to make room for pills, drops and powders. No more Socialism. What could it matter to me if the world, contrary to all of the most scientific conclusions, remained under private ownership? If many people, for that reason, were not allowed their daily bread or the portion of freedom that should adorn man's every day? Did I perhaps have either?

I tried to become my essential self that blessed evening. When, in his stentorian voice, my nephew Giovanni, a gigantic man who weighs more than two hundred pounds, started telling a few stories about his own cunning and other people's credulity in business, I found the old altruism in my heart again.

'What will you do,' I shouted at him, 'when the struggle is no longer a struggle over money?'

For a second, Giovanni was stunned by my dense phrase, which happened to shake his world. He stared at me with his eyes made bigger by his glasses. He was examining my face for explanations by which to get oriented. Then, while everybody was looking at him, hoping to be able to laugh at one of the retorts of that ignorant and intelligent oaf, at his ingenuous and malicious wit, which is always surprising despite having been used even before Sancho Panza, he stalled for time by saying that for everyone else wine altered the view of the present, whereas for me it muddled the future. That wasn't bad, but then he thought he had come up with something better and shouted:

'When no one fights over money any more, I'll have it all to myself, without a fight, all of it, all of it.'

He laughed a lot, in particular at a repeated movement of his big arms, which at first he held out all the way and then drew towards him with his fists closed to suggest that he had grabbed the money that was supposed to flow towards him from all sides.

The discussion went on, and no one noticed that when I wasn't talking I was drinking. And I drank a lot and said little, intent as I was on studying my core, to see if it was finally going to fill with benevolence and altruism. That core was burning slightly. But it was a burning that would later turn into a pleasant, diffuse warmth, into the feeling of youthfulness provided – but briefly, alas – by wine.

And, expecting this, I shouted at Giovanni:

'If you take the money others refuse, they'll throw you in the clink.'

But Giovanni quickly shouted:

'And I will bribe the jailers and have those who don't have the money to bribe them locked up.'

'But money will no longer corrupt anyone.'

'Then why not let me keep it?'

I got immoderately angry:

'We'll hang you,' I yelled. 'It's what you deserve. A noose around your neck and weights on your legs.'

I stopped in astonishment. I had the impression I hadn't said exactly what I was thinking. Was that really how I was? No, of course not. I reflected: how to recover my fondness for all living creatures, of which Giovanni was surely one? I immediately gave him a smile, making a huge effort to mend my ways and to excuse him and love him. But he kept me from doing so, as he paid my benevolent smile no heed whatsoever and, as if resigning himself to the observation of a monstrosity, said:

'Well, in practice, all Socialists end up resorting to the hangman.'

He had defeated me, but I hated him. He perverted my entire life, even the part of it preceding the doctor's intervention, a part I looked back on as highly luminous. He had defeated me because he had revealed the very doubt that had assailed me terribly even before his words.

Another punishment awaited me immediately thereafter.

'He looks well,' my sister had said, looking at me with satisfaction, and it was an infelicitous phrase, because my wife, as soon as she heard it, foresaw the possibility that the excessive wellbeing that was colouring my face would degenerate into a proportionally great illness. She was as frightened as if she had been warned of imminent danger just then and turned fiercely on me:

'Enough, enough!' she shouted. 'Put that glass away.'

She appealed for help from the man next to me, one Alberi, who, slender, dry and healthy but, like Giovanni, bespectacled, was one of the tallest men in the city.

'Be so kind as to take that glass from his hand.'

And since Alberi hesitated, she got emotional, agitated:

'Signor Alberi, please. Take that glass from him.'

I wanted to laugh; that is, I sensed that a well mannered person would do well to laugh then, but it was impossible for me. I had readied my rebellion for the next day and it wasn't my fault if it broke out right away. Those public rebukes were really insulting. Alberi, who didn't give a fig for me, my wife and all those people who were giving him food and drink, aggravated my situation, making it ridiculous. He looked over his glasses at the glass I had in my grip, moved his hands over as if he were going to take it from me, and ended up pulling them back with a quick jerk, as if he were afraid of me for looking at him. Everybody was laughing at me behind my back, Giovanni with a shouted laugh of his that caused him to get out of breath.

My daughter Emma thought her mother needed her help. With a tone that struck me as excessively imploring, she said:

'Papà, stop drinking.'

And it was on that innocent creature that I poured my wrath. I said to her a harsh and threatening word dictated by an old man's and a father's resentment. Her eyes immediately filled with tears, and her mother stopped concerning herself with me to concentrate entirely on comforting her.

My son Ottavio, thirteen years old then, came running to his mother just then. He hadn't noticed anything, either his sister's distress or the dispute that had caused it. He wanted permission to go to the movies the following evening with a few friends of his who had suggested it to him just then. But my wife, completely given over to her position as Emma's consoler, wasn't listening to him.

'Yes,' I shouted, trying to assert myself with an act of authority, 'of course you can go to the movies.'

Ottavio, not hearing anything else, went back to his friends after having told me:

'Thank you, Papà.'

A pity, that haste of his. If he had stayed with us, his happiness, the product of my act of authority, would have raised my spirits.

The good mood at the table was wrecked for a minute or two, and I sensed that I had wronged the bride, for whom that good mood was meant to be a good omen and a sign of things to come. And yet it was she alone, or so it seemed to me, who understood my distress. She was looking at me downright maternally, willing to excuse me and flatter me. That girl had always had that look of certainty in her judgements.

As when she was aspiring to a cloistered life, she thought now she was better than everyone else for having renounced it. Now she was prevailing upon me, upon my wife and upon my daughter. She felt sorry for us, and her lovely grey eyes fell on us, serenely, to look for the flaw that, in her view, had to be present wherever there was distress.

That heightened my resentment of my wife, whose behaviour was humiliating us. It made us inferior to everybody else at the table, even the most wretched figures. Down at the far end, even my sister-in-law's children had stopped chatting and had brought their little heads together to talk about what had just happened. I clutched my glass, unsure whether to drain it or to hurl it at the wall or even at the facing windowpanes. I ended up draining it in one go. That, a declaration of independence, was my most energetic act: it seemed to me the best wine I had had that evening. I lengthened the act by pouring myself more wine, which I also sipped a bit of, into the glass. But joy wasn't forthcoming, and all the overly intense energy that was enlivening my body was rancour. An odd idea came to me. Not everything was clarified by my rebellion. Could I not also ask the bride to rebel with me? Fortunately, she smiled gently just then at the trusting man by her side. And I thought: 'She doesn't know yet, and she is convinced she does.'

I remember, too, that Giovanni said:

'But let him drink. Wine is old men's milk.'

I gave him a look, wrinkling my face up to feign a smile, but I couldn't find it in me to wish him well. I knew that he was concerned only about the good-mood atmosphere and that he wanted to content me, the way one does an excited child who is disturbing a gathering of adults.

Then I drank little and only if people were looking at me, and not a word more did I say. All around me was cheerful shouting, and it bothered me. I wasn't listening, but it was hard not to hear. An argument between Alberi and Giovanni had broken out, and everybody was having fun watching the fat man contend with the thin man. What the argument was about I don't know, but I heard fairly aggressive words coming from both of them. I saw Alberi, who, standing up, stretched out toward Giovanni, was putting his glasses almost in the middle of the table, very near his adversary, who had comfortably laid his 260 pounds in a deckchair offered him as a joke at the end of the dinner, and was studying him intently, like the good fencer he was, as if he were weighing where to aim his own thrust. But Alberi was fine too, so very lean, though still healthy, mobile and serene.

And I remember, too, the good wishes and the endless farewells as we took leave of each other. The bride gave me a kiss with a smile that seemed maternal to me again. I took that kiss absent-mindedly. I was thinking about when I would be given leave to explain to her a thing or two about this life.

Just then a name was mentioned by someone, that of a friend of my wife and old friend of mine: Anna. By whom or for what reason I don't know, but it was the last name I heard before being left in peace by the dinner guests. For years I had been seeing her with my wife and greeting her with the friendliness and indifference of people who have no reason to complain about having been born in the same city and at the same time. But now I was remembering that, years earlier, she had been my sole offence. I had wooed her almost up to the moment I had married my wife. But no one had ever spoken of my act of betrayal, which had been so sudden I hadn't even tried to cushion it with a single word, because shortly thereafter she, too, had gotten married and been very happy. She hadn't taken part in our dinner because she was in bed with a light bout of the flu. Nothing serious. What was odd and serious was that I should remember my offence, which came now to weigh on my already troubled conscience. I had the feeling I was being punished for my old offence just then. From her bed, in which she was probably convalescing, I could hear my victim protest: 'It wouldn't be fair if you were to be happy.' I went off to my bedroom in very low spirits. I was a bit confused, because the fact is it didn't seem right to me that my wife should have been entrusted with avenging the person whose place she herself had taken.

Emma came to wish me goodnight. She was smiling, rosy, fresh. Her brief fit of tears had given way to a reaction of joy, as happens in all young and healthy bodies. I had been reading other people's states of mind well for a little while, and, besides, my daughter was clear water. My outburst of anger had conferred importance on her in front of everybody, and she was savouring it with complete naivety. I gave her a kiss and am sure I thought it was lucky for me that she was so happy and pleased. To bring her up, to be sure, it would have been my duty to warn her that she had not shown me sufficient respect. She left, and nothing remained of my attempt to come up with those words but a worry, a vagueness, an effort that stayed with me for some time. To calm down, I thought: 'I'll talk to her tomorrow. I'll tell her my reasons.' But it did no good. I had offended her, and she had offended me. And I was offended again that she should no longer be thinking about it, whereas I still was.

Ottavio came to say goodnight to me as well. An odd kid. He said goodnight to me and to his mother almost without seeing us. He had already left when I reached him with my shout:

'Glad to be going to the movies?'

He stopped, made an effort to remember, and, before resuming his flight, said drily:

'Yes.'

He was very sleepy.

My wife handed me the pillbox.

'These are the ones?' I asked, a chilly mask on my face.

'Yes, of course,' she said nicely.

She examined me and, not knowing how to read me otherwise, asked me hesitantly:

'Are you feeling all right?'

'Perfectly fine,' I said resolutely, taking off a boot.

And at that very instant my stomach started burning frightfully. This was what she wanted, I thought, with a logic I doubt only now.

I took the pill with a sip of water and got a bit of relief from it. I kissed my wife on the cheek mechanically. It was a kiss such as could accompany the pills. I couldn't avoid it if I wanted to spare myself arguments and explanations. But I was unable to retire for the night without spelling out my position in the fight that, for me, had still not ended, and as I settled into bed I said: 'I think the pills would work better taken with wine.'

She turned off the light, and very soon the regularity of her breathing told me her conscience was clear; that is, I immediately thought, the uttermost indifference to anything that had to do with me. I had been awaiting that instant eagerly, and immediately I told myself I was finally free to breathe noisily, as it seemed to me the state of my body required, or even to sob, as I would have liked to in my despondency. But the anxiety, as soon as it was free, became an even more real anxiety. This was certainly not liberty. How to give vent to the anger raging in me? I could do nothing other than turn over in my mind what I would say to my wife and daughter the next day. 'Are you really so concerned about my health, when you annoy me in front of everybody?' It was absolutely true. And here I was, alone, racking my brains in bed, and they were sleeping peacefully. What a burning sensation! A large expanse that was flowing into my throat had overrun my body. The bottle of water had to be on the night table by the bed, and I put my hand out for it. But I hit the empty glass, and it took only the light clink to wake up my wife. As it is, she always sleeps with one eye open.

'Are you feeling bad?' she asked me in a whisper.

She wasn't sure she had heard and didn't want to wake me up. I speculated a bit, but I attributed to her the odd intention of rejoicing in that suffering of mine, which was none other than proof that she had been right. I did without the water and lay back down very quietly. She immediately fell back into that light slumber of hers that enabled her to keep an eye on me.

In short, if I didn't want to put up with that fight with my wife, I was going to have to sleep. I closed my eyes and curled up on one side. Right away, I had to change position. But I was determined and didn't open my eyes. But every position sacrificed a part of my body. With a body made this way, I thought, there won't be any sleeping. I was all movement, all wakefulness. A person who is running cannot imagine sleep. I was out of breath, as if from running, and in my ears was the pounding of my feet: of heavy boots. I thought I was perhaps moving too gently in bed to be able to get into the right position and with all of my limbs all at once. Better not to seek it. Better to let everything find the spot that suited its form. I turned over with complete violence. 'Are you OK?' my wife immediately muttered. But I didn't want to respond to those words that alluded offensively to our argument.

Keeping still had to be really easy. What could be so hard about lying, really lying, in bed? I reviewed all of the great difficulties we bump into in this world and found that, by comparison, lying without moving was a trifle. Every swine is able to keep still. My determination came up with a complicated but unbelievably tenacious position. I put my teeth in the upper part of the pillow and twisted around in such a way that my chest was resting on the pillow too, while my right leg hung off the bed and was nearly touching the floor and my left leg went stiff in the bed, chaining me to it. Yes. I had discovered a new system. I wasn't clinging to the bed; it was the bed that was clinging to me. And this firm belief in my inertia meant that even when my feeling of oppression increased I didn't give in. When, later, I did have to yield, I consoled myself with the thought that a part of that horrendous night had gone by, and I also had the recompense that, freed from the bed, I felt relieved like a wrestler who has freed himself from his rival's hold.

I don't know how long I stayed still for then. I was tired. Surprised, I noticed a strange glow in my closed eyes, a whirling of flames I imagined caused by the fire I felt in me. They weren't real flames, but colours that simulated them. And then they died out, little by little, and became roundish forms, which soon went all blue, soft, but ringed by a bright red band. They were falling from a high spot, lengthening, and, once they dropped off, disappearing below. It was I who first thought those drops could see me. At once, to see me better, they turned into a lot of little eyes. As they lengthened, falling, a small circle formed in their centre, a circle that, doing without the blue layer, revealed a real eye, malicious and malevolent. I was being chased by a throng that wished me ill. I rebelled in bed, moaning and crying out: 'My God!'

'Are you feeling bad?' my wife immediately asked.

Some time must have gone by before the response. But then I happened to notice that I was now clinging to the bed, not lying in it, and that it had become a steep slope I was sliding down.

'I feel bad,' I shouted, 'very bad.'

My wife had lit a candle and was by my side in her pinkish nightgown. The light reassured me and in fact I had the clear feeling of having slept and of having awoken only then. The bed had straightened back out, and

I was lying effortlessly in it. I looked at my wife in surprise, because now, since I had realized I had slept, I was no longer sure of having called for her help.

'What do you want?' I asked.

Sleepy, fatigued, she looked at me. My cry had been enough to have her leap out of bed, not to take from her desire for rest, next to which not even being right mattered to her any longer.

'Do you want some of those drops the doctor prescribed for sleeping?' she asked to hurry up and be done.

I hesitated, even though the desire to feel better was nearly overpowering.

'If you like,' I said, trying to appear only resigned. Taking drops is hardly tantamount to a confession of feeling bad.

Then there was an instant in which I enjoyed great peace. It lasted as long as my wife, in her pinkish nightgown, in the dim light of that candle, was by my side counting the drops. The bed was a real horizontal bed, and my eyelids, if I closed them, were enough to shut any light whatsoever out of my eyes. But I opened them now and then, and that light and the pink of that nightgown gave me as much relief as total darkness. But she didn't want her help to last an instant longer, and I was dropped back into the night to struggle for peace on my own. I remembered that, as a youth, to bring on sleep more quickly, I would force myself to think of a dreadfully ugly old woman who would make me forget the beautiful visions that were obsessing me. Here it was then that now, by contrast, it was granted me to call without danger upon beauty, which would of course help me. It was the advantage – the only one – of old age. And I imagined, calling them by name, several beautiful women, desires of my youth, of a time in which beautiful women had abounded in an unbelievable way. But they didn't come. They didn't yield then, either. And I went on evoking, evoking, until a single beautiful figure emerged from the night: Anna, she of all people, as she was so many years earlier, but with her face, her lovely rosy face, wearing an expression of distress and reproach. Because she wanted to bring me not peace, but remorse. That was clear. And seeing as she was present, I spoke with her. I had left her, but she had immediately married another man, which was altogether fair. But then she had brought into the world a girl who was now fifteen years old and who looked like her mother in her soft colours, the gold of her head and the blue in her eyes, but her face was affected by the intervention of the father who had been chosen for her: the gentle waves of the hair turned into a mass of frizzy curls, big cheeks, a wide mouth and overly thick lips. But her mother's colouring in her father's features ended up being a shameless kiss, a kiss in public. What did she want from me now, after she had so often shown herself to me fascinated by her husband?

And it was the first time that night I was able to believe that I had triumphed. Anna got meeker, as if changing her mind. And then her company no longer displeased me. She could stay. And I fell asleep admiring her, beautiful and kind, persuaded. I soon fell asleep.

An awful dream. I found myself in a complicated structure, but which I understood right away as if I had been part of it. A huge, primitive cave, without those decorations nature has fun creating in caves, and thus certainly the work of man; I was sitting in the dark on a three-legged wooden stool next to a glass chest feebly lit by a light I took to be one of its qualities, the only light in the vast space, and which lit me, a wall made of large uncut stones, and, beneath it, a cement wall. How expressive dream structures are! You might say they are so the person who designed them can understand them easily, and that would be correct. But the surprising thing is that the architect doesn't know he has built them, and he doesn't remember it even when he is awake, and thinking about the world it emerged from and where structures pop up with such ease he might be surprised to find that everything there is understood with no need for a single word.

I knew right away that that cave had been built by men who were using it for a cure they had come up with, a cure that would be lethal for one of those put away there (a lot of them must have been down there in the shadows), but beneficial to all of the others. Exactly! A kind of religion, which needed a sacrifice, and by that I was naturally not surprised.

It was quite a bit easier to guess that, since I had been placed so close to the glass chest in which the victim was supposed to be asphyxiated, I had been chosen to die, to everyone else's advantage. And I was already anticipating the pains of the horrible death that was awaiting me. I was having trouble breathing, and my head was hurting and feeling heavy, as a result of which I held it in my hands, my elbows propped on my knees.

All at once everything that I already knew was spoken by a lot of people concealed in the darkness. My wife spoke first: 'Hurry up, the doctor said you're the one who has to go into that chest.' It seemed distressing to me, but very logical. So I didn't protest, but I pretended not to hear. And I thought: 'My wife's love has always struck me as stupid.' A lot of other voices were shouting imperiously: 'Have you decided to obey?' Among them I made out, very clearly, Dr Paoli's. I couldn't protest, but thought: 'He is doing it to be paid.'

I lifted my gaze for another look at the glass chest that was awaiting me. I then saw, sitting on the lid, the bride. There, too, she maintained her constant air of easy assurance. Frankly, I despised that silly woman, but I was immediately informed that she was very important for me. I would have found this out in real life too, seeing her seated on that device that was supposed to kill me. And so, eagerly, I looked at her. I felt like one of those tiny little dogs that win favour by wagging their tails. What degradation!

But the bride spoke. Without any ferocity, as if it were the most natural thing in the world, she said: 'Uncle, the chest is for you.'

I had to fight for my life on my own. This, too, I divined. I had the feeling of being able to make a huge effort without anyone's noticing it. Just as I had earlier sensed in myself an organ that enabled me to win over my judge without speaking, so I discovered within me another organ – what it was I don't know – with which to fight without moving and thus to attack my unthreatened adversaries. And the effort paid off right away. Here was Giovanni, fat Giovanni, sitting in the bright glass chest on a wooden stool similar to mine and in the same position as me. He was hunched over, the chest being too low, and had his glasses in his hands so they wouldn't fall off his nose. But that way he sort of looked as if he were working on a deal and had taken off his glasses to think better without seeing anything. And, in fact, although he was sweaty and out of breath, instead of thinking about his coming death, he was full of malice, as you could tell from his eyes, in which I caught sight of the same effort I had made shortly before. So, because I feared him, I was unable to take pity on him.

Giovanni's effort paid off as well. Shortly thereafter, Alberi, the tall, slender and healthy Alberi, was in his spot in the chest, in the same

69

position as Giovanni had been in but made worse by the size of his body. He was altogether bent double and would really have aroused compassion in me had there not also been in him, in addition to agitation, great malice. He was looking me up and down, with an evil smile, knowing that not dying in that chest depended on him alone.

From on top of the chest, the bride spoke again: 'Now it's your turn, of course, Uncle.' She stressed each syllable with great pedantry. And her words were accompanied by another sound, very distant, very much from on high. From that long-lasting sound, let out by a person moving quickly away, I could tell that the cave ended in a steep corridor that led to the surface of the earth. It was a single hiss, but a hiss of approval, and it was coming from Anna, who was once again showing her hatred for me. She didn't have the courage to put it in words, because I had in fact convinced her she had wronged me more than I had wronged her. But when it comes to hatred conviction counts for nothing.

I was condemned by everybody. A long way from me, somewhere in the cave, waiting, my wife and the doctor were pacing back and forth, and I sensed that my wife had a resentful appearance. She was moving her hands energetically, reciting my wrongs. Wine, food and my brusque manners with her and with my daughter.

I felt myself drawn to the chest by Alberi's gaze, turned triumphantly on me. I went slowly over to it with the stool, less than an inch at a time, but I knew that when I got within a yard of it (such was the law) I would find myself, in a single bound, made captive and gasping for breath.

But there was still hope for salvation. Giovanni, perfectly recovered from the fatigue of his tough struggle, had shown up by the chest, which he no longer had to fear, as he had already been in it (this, too, was law down there). He was standing up straight, right in the light, looking at times at Alberi, who was gasping and making threats, and at times at me, as I was slowly approaching the chest.

'Giovanni!' I shouted. 'Help me keep him in there . . . I'll pay you.'

The entire cave resounded with my shout, and it seemed like a scornful laugh. I understood. It was no use begging. Neither the first person nor the second person who had gotten into the chest was meant to die in it, but the third person was. This, too, was a law of the cave, which, like all the other laws, was the ruin of me. And it was hard to have to acknowledge it hadn't been made just then to harm me in particular. It, too, stemmed from that darkness and that light. Giovanni didn't even answer, and he shrugged to convey to me his distress at being unable to save me or sell me salvation.

And then I screamed again: 'If there's no other way, take my daughter. She's sleeping right here. It will be easy.' These shouts, too, were brought back by a tremendous echo. I was befuddled by them, but I shouted for my daughter again: 'Emma! Emma! Emma!'

And in fact Emma's answer came to me from the depths of the cave, the sound of her still childish voice: 'Here I am, Daddy, here I am.'

It seemed to me I hadn't answered right away. Just then there was a violent start caused, so I thought, by my leap into the chest. 'This daughter,' I thought, 'always slow when it comes to obeying.' This time her slowness was going to be the ruin of me, and I was full of rancour.

I woke up. That was the start. The leap from one world to the other. My head and my trunk were off the bed, and I would have fallen had my wife not come to hold me up.

'Were you dreaming?' she asked me.

And then, moved: 'You were calling your daughter. You see how you love her?'

At first, I was dazzled by that reality in which it seemed to me that everything was twisted and perverted. And I said to my wife, who certainly had to know everything as well:

'How will we ever win our children's forgiveness for having given them this life?'

But she, in her simplicity, said: 'Our children are delighted to be alive.'

The life I then felt to be the real one, the dream life, was still enveloping me, and I wanted to declare it: 'Because they don't know anything yet.'

But then I went quiet and withdrew into silence. The window by my bed was getting light, and by that light I immediately sensed I shouldn't recount that dream, as the shame of it had to be concealed. But soon, as the sunlight, so light blue and soft, but pressing, went on flooding the room, I no longer even felt that shame. Dream life wasn't my life, and I wasn't the man who had grovelled and been ready to sacrifice his own daughter to save himself.

But the return to that horrendous cave had to be avoided. And it is thus that I became submissive and conformed eagerly to the doctor's diet. If, through no fault of mine – that is, as a result not of excessive libation but of the final fever – I should have to return to that cave, I would immediately jump into that glass chest, if it's there, to keep from grovelling and to keep from being a traitor.

'Vino generoso'

First published in the journal *La fiera letteraria* (28 August 1927). It was then included in the collection *La novella del buon vecchio e della bella fanciulla e altri scritti* (Morreale, 1929).

LEONARDO SCIASCIA

1921–89

Sciascia assembled a volume of thirteen short stories in the final decades of his life and called it *Il mare colore del vino* (*The Wine-dark Sea*), invoking the Homeric epithet. One of Sicily's most celebrated public intellectuals, he was born in the province of Agrigento, where magnificent Greek temples still stand, and the island was his subject from beginning to end. He wrote about its people, its politics, its beauty and its corruption, its Mafia violence, its rich cultural history, its incantatory effect. He explored the island's relationship, always fraught, to the rest of Italy, and he tackled, with a combination of compassion and steely documentation, the great theme of justice. Sciascia confronted the major controversies and cataclysmic events of his day, including Italian terrorism, writing cogently about the abduction and assassination of Aldo Moro, a former prime minister of Italy, during the 1970s. In addition to writing essays and political and investigative journalism, he composed a series of tough, terse novels that elevated crime fiction to a high literary form. *Il giorno della civetta* (*The Day of the Owl*) and *A ciascuno il suo* (*To Each His Own*), among his most famous novels, are two exemplary works of concision. Before he became a full-time writer he taught in elementary school. He was elected to the Palermo city council in 1976 with Communist Party support, and was also a member of the European Parliament. The stories in *Il mare colore del vino* were published between 1959 and 1972 in various newspapers and magazines. In the author's note to the collection, which he arranged in order of publication, he speaks of the satisfaction of assembling the book in spite of his 'general and continuous dissatisfaction'. Sciascia's sentences are rich and dark like the sea he invokes, his figurative language precise and unnerving. This story has a mythic grace to it, and takes us where we least expect.

The Long Voyage

Translated by Erica Segre and Simon Carnell

It was a night that seemed made for it, shrouded in a darkness you could almost feel the weight of as you moved. And it was frightening, the breathing of that beast of a world, the sound of the sea: a breathing that came right up and expired at their feet.

They stood, with their cardboard suitcases and their bundles, on a stony stretch of beach, protected by the hills, between Gela and Licata: they had reached there at nightfall, they had left their villages at daybreak; villages of the interior far removed from the sea, clustered in the arid plague of feudal lands. For some, it was the first time they had seen the sea: the thought of having to cross the whole of it from that deserted beach in Sicily, at night, to get to another deserted beach in America, also at night, was deeply disconcerting. Because the deal was this: 'I take you on board at night,' the man had said, a kind of travelling salesman, judging by the style of his patter, though with a serious and honest face, 'and I land you at night: you'll land on the beach in Nugiorsi. I'll put you ashore a short walk from Nuovaiorche . . . Those who have relatives in America can write and tell them to go wait for you at Trenton Station, twelve days after we set sail . . . You do the calculation . . . Of course, I can't guarantee the exact date you'll get there: let's suppose that the sea might be rough, let's suppose that the coastguards might be on the lookout . . . One day here or there will make no difference to you. The important thing is to land in America.'

To land in America really was the important thing: how or when hardly mattered, in the end. If their letters had succeeded in reaching their relatives, with those confused and scrawled addresses that they'd managed to inscribe on the envelopes, then they would make it too. Whoever has a tongue shall cross the sea, as the proverb rightly had it. And they would

75

have crossed the sea, that great dark ocean; and they would have reached the *stori* and the *farme* – the stores and farms – of America, the welcoming circle of brothers uncles nephews cousins, the warm luxurious spacious houses, the automobiles that were as big as houses.

Two hundred and fifty thousand lire: half on departure, half on arrival. They kept the money, in the style of scapularies, between their skin and shirts. They had sold everything they had in order to scrape it together: the house, the land the mule the donkey that year's provisions the chest of drawers the blankets. The craftier ones had resorted to moneylenders, with the secret intention of cheating them at least this once, after years of harassment. They relished the thought of how the faces of those money-lenders would look when they received the news that they'd gone. 'Come and find me in America, bloodsucker, and maybe you'll get your money back. But without interest, even if you do manage to track me down.' The dream of America was awash with dollars, with cash no longer clutched in a shabby wallet or hidden beneath their shirts, but stuffed casually into trouser pockets and pulled out by the handful the way they'd seen their relatives do it – relatives who had left half starved, thin as rakes and scorched by the sun, then returned after twenty or thirty years, though only for a short vacation, with their round rosy-cheeked faces handsomely contrasting with their white hair.

It was eleven o'clock already. One of them lit the lantern: the signal that they were ready to be collected and taken aboard the steamer. When he extinguished it again, the darkness seemed even thicker and more menacing. But just a few minutes later, from the relentless breathing of the sea a more human, domestic sound emerged from the water, like that of buckets being rhythmically filled and emptied. And then came the sound of voices, a muffled chatter. They found themselves in the presence of Signor Melfa, which was the name they knew the organizer of their great adventure by, even before realizing that the boat had touched land.

'Is everyone here?' he asked. Signor Melfa turned on a torch and counted heads. Two people were missing. 'Maybe they've had second thoughts, maybe they'll turn up later . . . Either way, so much the worse for them. What's the point of waiting for them, with the risks that we're running already?'

Everyone agreed that it was not worth waiting.

'If any of you doesn't have the cash ready,' warned Signor Melfa, 'they might as well start walking home again right now – because if anyone thinks that they're going to spring that little surprise when we're already on board they're making a big mistake. If that happened I swear I'd drop the whole lot of you back off again. Then everyone would suffer, thanks to one person, which isn't fair – and that person would be made to pay with a beating from me, and from his mates too, that he'll remember for as long as he lives. If he's lucky, that is . . .'

Everybody swore that they had the necessary cash, down to the last lira.

'Get aboard then,' said Signor Melfa. And suddenly each of the travellers became a formless mass, a confused bundle of luggage.

'Christ! – and have you brought the kitchen sink with you as well?' Signor Melfa began to blurt out curses, only stopping when the whole cargo – men, bags and baggage – had been bundled into the boat, at the risk of persons or luggage ending up overboard. For Signor Melfa, the difference between a person and an item of luggage was that the person had two hundred and fifty thousand lire on him, stitched into his coat or held between his shirt and skin. He knew them; he knew them only too well: these peasant bastards, these louts.

The journey did not last as long as expected: eleven nights, including the one on which they'd left. And the nights were counted rather than the days, because they were nights of suffocating, atrocious overcrowding. They felt submerged in the combined reek of fish, diesel and vomit – as if in a hot, black, bituminous liquid. They were oozing it at daybreak, exhausted as they climbed on deck seeking light and air. If for them the idea of the sea was associated with a verdant, undulating plain stirred by the wind, the real sea terrified them: their insides clenched and knotted, their eyes were painfully blinded if they so much as attempted a glance towards the horizon. But on the eleventh night Signor Melfa ordered them on deck. At first they thought they could see dense constellations that had descended on to the sea, like flocks – but these turned out to be towns; the towns of wealthy America glittering like jewels in the night. And the night itself was enchanting: calm and gentle, a half-moon sailing amidst a transparent fauna of clouds, with a lung-clearing breeze.

'This is America,' said Signor Melfa.

'Is there any danger it might be some other place?' someone asked, since he had spent the entire journey thinking about the fact that there are no roads or tracks on the sea, and that it was a godlike feat to find the right route, without mistakes, steering a boat between sky and water.

Signor Melfa gave him a pitying look, and asked everyone else: 'Have you ever seen a skyline like this one, in your neck of the woods? Can't you feel that even the air is different? Can't you see how brilliantly the towns here sparkle?'

Everyone agreed, looking with pity and resentment at that companion of theirs who had dared to ask such a stupid question.

'Let's settle the bill,' said Signor Melfa.

They fumbled beneath their shirts and extracted the money.

'Get your things ready,' said Signor Melfa, after stashing it away.

They only needed a few minutes: having almost exhausted the provisions they'd supplied themselves with for the journey, all they were left with was the odd item of linen and the presents for their relatives in America: a chunk of *pecorino*, a well-aged bottle of wine, something embroidered to put at the centre of a table or on the back of a sofa. They disembarked walking on air, weightless, laughing and humming tunes – and one burst into full-throated song just as soon as the boat began to move off.

'So you've understood nothing,' hissed Signor Melfa angrily. 'You're determined to land me in it? . . . As soon as I've put you ashore you can rush up to the first cop you see and get yourselves deported on the next available boat: I don't give a shit, you're free to kill yourselves in any way you like . . . I've kept to my side of the bargain: this is America and I've dumped you here . . . Now, for Christ's sake, give me the chance to get back on board!'

They gave him more than enough time to get back on board: they remained sitting on the fresh sand, undecided, not sure of what to do next, blessing and cursing the night which gave them protection as long as they stayed still on the beach, but that would turn into a terrible ambush if they dared to leave it.

Signor Melfa had advised them to 'scatter', but no one felt inclined to separate from the others. Who knew how far away Trenton was, and how long it would take to get there?

Then they heard in the distance, sounding unreal, a song. 'It sounds like one of our own carters,' they thought – and that the world must be the same everywhere: that everywhere man expresses in song the same melancholy, the same sorrow. But they were in America now: the cities that blazed beyond the horizon of sand and trees were the cities of America.

Two of them decided to head off as scouts. They went in the direction of the lights that the nearest town cast into the sky. Almost immediately they found a road: 'Tarmaced, well maintained – how different roads are here compared to back home!' But really they had expected it to be wider and straighter. They kept away from it to avoid meeting anyone: they walked alongside it, through the trees.

A car passed. 'It looks like a *seicento*.' Then another, looking like a *millecento*, and then another. 'They keep cars like ours for amusement; they buy them for their kids like people back home buy bicycles for theirs.' Two deafening motorbikes passed, one chasing the other. It was the police, they couldn't afford to make any mistakes – thank goodness that they'd stayed off the road.

And there, finally, were the signs. They looked along the road in both directions, stepped on to it and went near enough to them to read: Santa Croce Camarina/Scoglitti.

'Santa Croce Camarina: I've heard of the place before.'

'It sounds familiar to me too; and even Scoglitti rings a bell.'

'Maybe one of our relatives lived there – perhaps it was my uncle, before he moved to Philadelphia. If I remember rightly he was living in a different city before Philadelphia.'

'My brother also lived some place before heading for Brucchilin . . . But I really can't remember what it was called. And anyway, we're saying 'Santa Croce', we're saying 'Scoglitti', but we've no idea how they pronounce these words here: American isn't pronounced like it's written.'

'That's true, and the great thing about Italian is just that: it sounds exactly like it's written . . . But we can't spend the night out here, we've got to take a risk. The next car that passes, I'm stopping. I'll just say 'Trenton?' . . . People are more polite here . . . Even if we don't understand what they're saying they're bound to point, to give a sign, and that way we'll work out where to find this blasted Trenton.'

Around the curve, twenty metres away, a *cinquecento* emerged: the driver saw them dart out with their arms raised, waving for him to stop. He slammed on the brakes, cursing: he didn't think it could be a hold-up in an area as quiet as this, and opened the door thinking that they wanted a lift.

'Trenton?' one of them asked.

'*Che?*' asked the driver.

'Trenton?'

'What effing Trenton are you on about!' the driver exclaimed, cursing.

'He speaks Italian,' they both said, looking at each other to see what to do next: if perhaps the time had come to reveal their situation to a fellow countryman.

The driver shut the door and switched the engine back on. The car jerked forwards: and only then did he shout out to the two men standing in the road like statues, 'Drunkards, drunken cuckolds, cuckolds and sons of—' The rest was drowned out as he accelerated away.

There was a protracted silence.

'Now I remember,' said the one, a moment later, who'd thought the name Santa Croce sounded familiar, 'my father went to Santa Croce Camarina one year when things had gone badly in our region. He went there for the harvesting.'

Then they flung themselves down as if they had been knocked into the ditch at the side of the road. There was no hurry, after all, to deliver the news to the others that they had disembarked in Sicily.

'*Il lungo viaggio*'
First published in the newspaper *l'Unità* (21 October 1962), then included in *Racconti siciliani*, a non-commercial edition of Sciascia's short stories published in Urbino in 1966. It was subsequently published in *Il mare colore del vino* (Einuadi, 1973).

ALBERTO SAVINIO
1891–1952

A man who refused to stick to any one identity, Savinio titled his first book *Hermaphrodito*: a diary that oscillates between genres (poetry and prose), languages (French and Italian, in addition to a little Greek) and tones (high and low). An accomplished musician, painter and writer – though he claimed to be a dilettante in all three – he was born Andrea Francesco Alberto de Chirico, in Athens. He studied classical piano and composition in Greece and Germany, then moved to Paris when he was nineteen, along with his older brother, who would become the world-renowned painter Giorgio de Chirico. As André Breton later admitted, the brothers' artistic activity in Paris at the time sowed the seeds for the Surrealist movement which would explode in the 1920s. Savinio initially wrote in French, and Guillaume Apollinaire sponsored his first avant-garde recital in 1914. He became Alberto Savinio for the occasion. The new name was fundamental not only to inaugurate his creative self, but to distinguish himself from Giorgio. The following year the brothers left Paris for Ferrara to serve in the First World War – it was the easiest way to gain Italian citizenship – and it was there that Savinio abandoned music for writing. But in 1926, back in Paris, he started painting seriously, and his first exhibit was presented by Jean Cocteau. His paintings are oniric, with allusions to travel, classical antiquity, animals, childhood toys. They are also whimsical (he depicted his parents fused into their favourite armchairs, partially transformed into birds). In 1931, upon his return to Italy, he shifted gears again, and began writing seriously. He became a luminary of the avant-garde, but remained in the shadow of Giorgio's greater fame. The selected story below, from a 1945 collection called *Tutta la vita* (The Rest of Life) exemplifies the Surrealists' love of confounding the animate and inanimate worlds.

Bago

Translated by Michael F. Moore

'Good morning, Bago.'

This is what Ismene says every day the moment she wakes up, and every night before going to bed she says, 'Goodnight, Bago.' Otherwise she'd feel as if she had started or ended the day wrong, indeed as if she had not started or ended it at all. The same way she would have felt in the past if she hadn't said 'Good morning' and 'Goodnight' to Daddy and Mummy. And then only to Mummy after Daddy died. Then only to Bug after Mummy died too. Then only to Bago, after the death of Bug, with all that hair over his eyes and oh so human look. Sometimes Ismene forgets to say 'Good morning' or 'Goodnight' to her husband, but that doesn't make her feel as if she has begun or ended the day wrong. Besides, Rutiliano is so rarely at home, so often on a trip . . . One morning when Rutiliano opened the door and asked, 'Who were you speaking to?' Ismene answered, 'Maybe in my sleep', an answer she had no trouble inventing. She didn't even have the impression she was lying. The best part of her life is like a dream she dreams when she's awake and when she's asleep, and her secret conversations with Bago belong to the dream world, too. When she said that by saying 'Good morning, Bago' she was talking in her sleep, Ismene wasn't lying.

'Good morning, Bago.'

Ismene is sitting on the bed, her head leaning to one side, her hands clasped together and still warm from the night, smiling in the direction of Bago, as if he were a strong, protective father. She sits there listening. The bedroom smells of dreamt dreams, like wilted flowers. The only trace the dreams leave behind is this smell, and if the bedroom stinks in the morning it's because we've had bad dreams. The morning light peeks through the blinds in stripes, shining like the rungs of a golden ladder through the drawn curtains. The furniture is a heavy shadow emerging from the pallor of the wall. Ismene's undergarments glow white on a chair. A crown of light of unknown origin trembles on the ceiling, a halo within which the head of an angel might appear. But Billi is no angel.

What is Ismene waiting to hear? What does she hear? What did she hear?

(Ismene alights from the bed and races barefoot to open the window.)

Nothing echoed in the room, yet Ismene has still heard and is content. This morning she is more impatient than usual for the awaited voice, more happy that she has heard it. Today Billi is coming back from his long trip. Today more than other days Ismene needs to feel the presence and protection of Bago.

Now the room is bright, the smell of withered dreams has dissipated. Ismene lingers at the window; down in the valley some vapours are still floating. She is content. Beneath her nightgown her body turns pink, and darkens at the fold of her thighs and hips in a triangular shadow like the eye of a mysterious god. But who apart from Bago can see the skinny body of Ismene beneath the veil of her nightgown, like a big pink fish beneath a sliver of water? Ismene isn't embarrassed by Bago ... Yet she is. But it's another kind of embarrassment. It's the fear of doing something to Bago that shouldn't be done to Bago. Before opening Bago's doors Ismene stands there, unsure of herself, like when she was a little girl and was about to unbutton her daddy's jacket and fish his pocket-watch out of his vest to hear it chime the hours and quarter hours.

Daddy, Mummy, Bug, Bago, Billi. Rutiliano was a name so different from those names, which seem to have been shaped deliberately by the mouth of a child, a stutterer, a weak little baby. What a strange name, Rutiliano!

The moments of embarrassment are another matter. When Rutiliano comes to Ismene at night, Ismene gets out of bed, pulls out the big folding screen, and opens it up between the bed and Bago, in order to hide the bed. Rutiliano is always dismayed by this gesture, and he asks for an explanation. Ismene says she is afraid of the air. The air? Yes, the air that passes under the door. And to reinforce the shelter, Ismene drapes a coverlet over the screen, which she folds back up and places on a chair at night. Rutiliano watches these actions with an uncomprehending eye. Well, what does Rutiliano understand anyway? What does he understand about her? Rutiliano is serious and distant. He never laughs and he busies himself with mysterious jobs that require frequent trips. Despite the mystery that envelops them, Ismene has no interest in finding out about Rutiliano's jobs. For as far back as her childhood memories can reach, Ismene remembers Rutiliano. He was as much a part of the household as a sofa is part of the living room, as a sideboard is part of a dining room. For Christmas and the Epiphany, Rutiliano used to arrive with an armload of packages, from which he would meticulously extract presents. Ismene would then kiss him on the forehead and say, 'Thank you, Uncle Rutiliano.' Uncle was an honorary title and, for Ismene, a synonym for 'old'. Ismene didn't like kissing the forehead of Uncle Rutiliano and especially didn't like being kissed by him. Yet when Mummy died, too, the only thing she could do was marry Uncle Rutiliano. Whom did this marriage benefit? Certainly not Uncle. At least that's what he said. He no longer expected anything from life. To Ismene, instead, the marriage assured her of a comfortable life and protection. 'People like us don't get married just for pleasure.' This is what Uncle Rutiliano said. He spoke so rarely, but the very few times that he did he uttered indisputable truths. 'Lucky he speaks so rarely!' said Billi to Ismene, and he bowed his head. The silk dress, the white veil, the presents, the guests, the dinner could have made their wedding day a happy day, but on that very day Billi left to enlist in the navy. 'How happy your poor mummy would be, how happy your poor daddy would be!' said Uncle Rutiliano, who on that day was even quieter than usual.

At the table, in front of the thirty guests who were stuffing their faces, Ismene called her husband 'Uncle Rutiliano', and immediately the ice cream went down the wrong way. A few days later, to keep Ismene from making the same mistake, Rutiliano changed his name and had everyone call him Ruti. But it wasn't true that Ruti was always right. Ismene did not find in her husband the security, the confidence that she had felt with her parents, things she'd hoped to regain in marrying him. She found them instead in Bug, with all that hair over his eyes and oh so human look, and after Bug's death she found it in Bago. And it was impossible for Bago to die. One day Ruti talked about getting new bedroom furniture, putting in furniture that was lighter, fresher, more suitable for the bedroom of a young bride. Ismene defended 'her' furniture with an obstinacy that shocked Ruti. He was dismayed by such a strong attachment to furniture that was worth so little, but deep down he was pleased that he did not have any new expenditures. Ismene, especially when her husband was home, would spend the day in her room, near Bago. The 'old' armoire had witnessed her birth, safeguarded her clothes as a little girl and then as a young lady, and now it safeguarded her clothes as a woman. She sits next to the partially closed doors, as if to hear the beating of that dark but profoundly good heart. She confides in him. She tells him things she would never tell others and especially Ruti. She tells him about the return of Billi.

Ruti appeared at the door and announced with a gloomy air that he was leaving in the car and would not be back until the next day. Ismene kissed him on the forehead, just like when Ruti was still 'Uncle Rutiliano' and brought her Christmas presents.

Now Ismene and Billi are sitting quietly across from each other, as if they have nothing to say. Was Billi perhaps embarrassed to find himself in Ismene's bedroom? She wanted to feel close to Bago, especially now that Billi was in her bedroom.

The loud rumble of an automobile arriving. The crunching of the gravel beneath the wheels. The yanking of the hand-brake in front of the main door.

The alarmed voice of Ancilla in the hall. 'The signor has come back! The signor has come back!'

Billi jumps to his feet. He's pale as a sheet. He looks around. Why is Ancilla's voice so alarmed? What is so dangerous about the return of the 'signor'?

A howl. A deep howl. More powerful than the most powerful human voice, but completely 'inside'. A howl that is 'embodied' and circumscribed within a tight radius. A howl for local consumption. A 'domestic' howl. A 'cubicular' howl. A howl 'for close friends only'.

In that howl, the doors of the armoire burst open. Billi takes a leap and dives inside the armoire, which suddenly closes its doors. Did Billi jump voluntarily inside the armoire or was he sucked into the armoire?

The moment the doors of the armoire opened, all of Ismene's clothes flew out in swarms, and now they were lying scattered all around the room, like laundry day in the countryside.

Ruti appears at the door, gloomier than ever.

'Impossible people,' said Ruti. 'They make me drive one-hundred-and-fifty kilometres and then don't . . . What's this mess? Why are your clothes spread out on the furniture, on the floor? With what a dress costs today!'

Ismene looks at her clothes spread around the room. But are they really her clothes? Now all her clothes are white. Ismene looks at her evening dress draped over the back of the armchair, like a castaway flattened against a cliff. The shape is the same, but the colour is no longer red but white. While Ismene, astonished, looks at her dress and struggles to recognize it, the dress starts to turn red and little by little regains the colour that fear had drained away.

Ismene instead doesn't regain her colour: fear is still blanching her when Ruti opens the armoire to put back, in his very meticulous way, the scattered clothes.

Ruti says, 'Neatness is the first quality of a good lady of the house. Remember that.' And he leaves.

Now Ismene starts to turn pink in the midst of the scattered clothes, which little by little regain their colour: red, light blue, green, orange, violet.

When Ismene has regained her colour, too, she goes to open the armoire. The armoire is empty.

From that day Ismene stayed right next to the armoire. She refused food and the few hours that she did sleep she slept on the armchair next to Bago's half-closed doors.

She lived for fifteen days in all. When they removed the blanket that had covered her legs, they found a card with childish handwriting resting on her knees. 'I want to be locked inside the dark and good body of Bago too. The clothes mustn't be removed: they are my friends.' At the bottom of the card was a reminder. 'Bago is the name of the armoire in my bedroom.'

Rutiliano hated absurdity in all its forms, but since custom demanded respect for the wishes of the deceased, no matter how absurd, Rutiliano ordered that the arrangements be followed as written on the card.

Ismene was placed inside the armoire and the armoire was lowered into the grave: a tomb with double doors that was too big for such a small body. Like a father folding a daughter against his chest.

'Bago'

First published in the newspaper *La Stampa* (3 July 1943) and then in the magazine *Il risveglio* (6–13 February 1946). It was included in the collection *Tutta la vita* (Bompiani, 1945).

UMBERTO SABA

1883–1957

The heart of Trieste contains one of the most magnificent piazzas in Italy, with one side that looks out onto the sea. Around the corner is a beautiful secondhand bookshop that Saba purchased in 1919 and worked in for most of his life. Grouped with Eugenio Montale and Giuseppe Ungaretti as one of the three most influential Italian poets of his time, Saba was born with the surname 'Poli' (he adopted 'Saba', which means 'Grandfather' in Hebrew, in his late twenties). His best-known work in verse, *Il canzoniere* (*Songbook*), is a vast container of successive collections of poems that he structured as an ongoing autobiography. But he had an equally sophisticated control of prose. *Scorciatoie e raccontini* (Short-cuts and Very Short Stories) is a dense, aphoristic text of micro-narratives, at once intellectually rigorous and immensely readable. His posthumous autobiographical novel, *Ernesto*, about an adolescent boy's sexual awakening with an older male worker and a female prostitute, is a distressing masterpiece. Bisexual, Jewish on his mother's side, and raised without a father, he wrote moving poems both to his wife and in memory of his young male muse, Federico Almansi. In 1938, when the Racial Laws targeting Jews took effect, he and his wife changed various domiciles, including Ungaretti's apartment in Rome. Saba's mental health plagued him; he suffered his first crisis at twenty-one and underwent psychiatric treatment throughout his adulthood. He spent the last two years of his life institutionalized, and died in a clinic outside Trieste, of a heart attack, while writing *Ernesto*. This story below, about an adolescent boy's love for an animal, is a powerful account of the loss of innocence. Saba is one of the few authors in this volume who was deeply sceptical of translation.

The Hen

Translated by Howard Curtis

Odone Guasti, who was later, under another name, to acquire a degree of fame in the republic of letters, was, at the age of not yet fifteen, an office and warehouse apprentice in a small firm in Trieste dealing in citrus fruits. Thinking himself perhaps a born merchant, he had been overjoyed to abandon his classical studies, to which he believed himself unsuited, in favour of a commercial career. But he had not spent even a month in his new life when, faced with crates of oranges to be marked and letters to be copied into the book, the restlessness fundamental to his nature had caught up with him just as it had over the Ministry-approved Greek and Latin texts which he had defaced with caricatures in the margins. He hated his boss, the 'exploiter' of his clear handwriting and his long adolescent legs, with a hatred very similar to that which he had borne the class monitor; and he felt as much contempt for his only workmate, an elderly clerk, as he had felt at school for his classmates, who always got good marks at the end of the year and were always well treated by the masters. This hatred was, of course, unjust, but many years were to pass, and many sorrows overcome, before Odone, thinking over the past and comparing it with the present, realized that the blame was entirely his, that he had done too much and too little to succeed either as a good pupil or, later, as a good employee. It is an inestimable privilege of maturity to find the roots of our ills only in ourselves, whereas the young man cannot help but blame the outside world, and with all the more ferocity the greater his own defects. And besides, who was there to explain Odone to himself and provide him with constructive criticism when his own father had gone, God alone knew where, even before he was born and had never returned, and he lived alone with his mother, a poor, deeply unhappy woman who understood little of life beyond the need for her only son to be physically well and to soon earn enough to relieve the two of them of a humiliating dependence on their relatives? Signora Rachele (that was Odone's mother's name) loved the boy with an almost sinful intensity, with that exaggerated maternal love peculiar to women who have married in vain; and the loved one had until then returned a similar affection, although tinged with selfishness; because parents love for what they give, and children for what they receive. There comes a moment in the life of a young man when filial love, before burning itself out in reaction to the family, to be replaced by love in the strictest sense of the word, flares up one last time in the most resplendent fashion: so it was that, on the afternoons of feast days, the few loving couples in the half-deserted Passeggio Sant'Andrea would see Odone, already in long trousers and with the beginnings of a moustache on his lips, walking arm in arm with his mother, who was much shorter than he and wore a black veil and such a strange, tiny hat as to make the observer feel sorry for her. In the same way, after dinner, mother and son would indulge in the tenderest of conversations, in which their differences of opinion, already beginning to become marked in the young man, were not yet such, compared with the certainty of a common future, as to cause his filial submission to degenerate into open revolt, and their romance into quarrels. As far as his mother was concerned, Odone was still a child who every evening, before going to bed, never forgot to thank God in his prayers for having granted him the most beautiful, the best, the wisest of all the many mothers who have inhabited, for the happiness of their sons, the splendid and never sufficiently praised work of creation.

It was, therefore, thinking of how pleased his mother would be that the young man replied to his employer with a touched and grateful 'Thank you' when the latter, one evening at the end of the month, threw a banknote down on his desk and informed him: 'From today, you're on the payroll. You'll get ten crowns a month.' These were his first wages: how would the dear, hitherto unrewarded creature react when he put the money in her hand and said: 'Take this, Mother, it's for you!' with the implication: Though all this is nothing compared to what I'll be able to give you one day. Those ten crowns dispelled the doubts that, in his several months of apprenticeship, he had begun to have about his commercial vocation; they also dispelled that touch of remorse that he could not help but feel when, being out on an errand, he met a former classmate on the street and tried – alas, in vain! – to convince him of the immense good that had befallen him in leaving school for work, and the other either replied rudely or kept silent, as if to say: We'll see about that in a few years, you poor drudge! His day over, he ran home, walked upstairs with the beating heart of a man in love taking a first gift to his beloved and, stammering and kissing his mother, gave her the great news. Signora Rachele seemed touched (less so, though, than Odone had hoped) and even forgave him for having made her angry at lunchtime by refusing to eat his soup, the memory of which had made the thought of the satisfaction he would give her when he came home all the dearer to him. She suggested that Odone put aside half the amount for himself, for whatever he pleased, although not without advising him to spend it as well as he had earned it and warning him of certain dangers about which young men are more typically taught by their fathers than their mothers; but to her, who never uttered certain words or never indicated them with a periphrasis without first spitting on the ground (such was the disgust she felt towards them), fell the burden of having to speak of such things to her son; and she did her best, even in such a sad task; so that she might, when it so pleased the Lord, sleep in peace and without any regrets on her conscience.

Her advice was unnecessary: Odone did not yet turn to look at women, and never passed down certain alleyways crowded in the evenings with sailors and raucous-voiced women without hurrying on; and besides, he had already decided how to spend his five crowns: he would use them to buy his mother a gift: only, he was torn between a round tobacco tin with silver decorations and a black fan with sequins. But as long as man proposes and God disposes, nobody has the right to believe himself safe from temptation, however strong he feels in broad terms. For Odone, the temptation did not come in the form of a human female, but came instead in that of a beautiful hen; and I will now recount how and why he was unable to resist this temptation, and how cruelly he was subsequently punished.

Passing at about two in the afternoon of the following day through the Piazza del Ponterosso, where there was, and still is, a market for birds and live poultry, Odone, who had left home to return to work and loiter a little on the way, quite determined not to go back to his prison a moment too soon, stopped to observe the merchandise displayed in the cages. First, he was struck by certain exotic little birds with bright shiny colours, which reminded him of the stamps from the English colonies and the barbaric states which he often admired in his modest collection; then his desire came to rest on a blackbird, a totally mysterious-looking animal, from whose golden beak half a dozen little worms were struggling to escape, while the bird swallowed them no more than one at a time, at regular intervals, half closing with pleasure its round little eyes encircled with the same fine gold as the beak; he looked with scant sympathy at the parrots, and with revulsion at a monkey; finally, his attention was drawn to the chickens, packed closely together in their cramped wooden cages, from which their necks stuck out alternately, and where they complained bitterly or took it out on one another for the thirst and lack of space. It was not the glutton in him that was moved by this spectacle: Odone liked live hens very much, but they were a matter of more than indifference to him when served at table. When on a solitary walk in the country, one of those adolescent walks that have the length of a forced march and the solemnity of a conquest, he would spot crests and wattles in front of a farmhouse or amid the green of the meadows, he would cheer up at the sight, as if they were brushstrokes in which the feeling of the landscape was concentrated; and he would gladly stroke the hen who was sufficiently tame or rendered so awkward by fear as not to escape in time from his lovingly held-out hand. Where others hear only monotonous, unpleasant sounds, Odone listened to the voices of the henhouse as if they were constantly varied music, especially as evening fell and the drowsy hens would complain in a very gentle manner. He did not like roosters as much. The pride and magnanimity of these sultans of the farmyard, shown when faced with a caterpillar or some other exquisite morsel which is lusted after and then, not without a visible inner struggle, left to the females, can only be appreciated by a man already expert in life, capable of understanding the nobility of that renunciation and the masculine lordliness that lies behind every true sacrifice. If at that time anyone had asked him why he was so fond of those stupid birds, which others only associate with thoughts of gastronomy, the young man might not have known what to reply. To the many who did in fact ask him, he only replied twenty years later, in a poem; only, that, too, was little understood. He felt that those feathered bodies were genuinely imbued with air and countryside and the different hours of the day: add to this aesthetic reason a sentimental one: for a long time, in his childhood devoid of siblings and friends, Odone had played with a hen. His mother had bought it to kill and eat; but Odone had cried and begged so much that Signora Rachele had finally agreed to keep it alive and let it roam freely about the house, like a dog. From that day on, as well as sucking its warm eggs, the boy had company; and even his mother ended up enjoying watching the way the bird leapt against the glass door of the kitchen, where it was shut in on the rare occasions that she had visitors; and when, sweaty and panting, she came back from the market carrying her shopping basket, Cò-Cò (as mother and son had agreed to call the hen) would run to meet her, beak open, wings outspread and fluttering. 'And they say hens are stupid,' Signora Rachele would say admiringly. But often she would become irritated, seeing her son talking to a fowl as if it were a person: that struck her as almost a sign of idiocy. For Odone, on the other hand, the hours he spent with the hen were truly his, he would make the bird 'sit' (perch) next to him on the steps leading from the kitchen to the dining room, brick steps that turned strangely red in the sunset and reminded him of those of ante-purgatory, as he had seen them depicted in a sacred image; he would clasp the hen to his heart so tightly that it shrieked, thinking with joy that he had so much time ahead of him to live and enjoy in this world (and then he would still have eternity); he would talk to Cò-Cò of journeys and adventures, of joys to come, of everything, in short, that went through his head. But after two years of domestic seclusion and excessively tasty and warming food, the heart of this strange companion of a sacrificed, ecstatic childhood burst (according to a female neighbour who knew about such things) – burst from being too fat (it looked like an odalisque); in short, it died, and was buried by its friend. Odone would have liked another immediately; a wish his mother absolutely refused to grant: he was already too old for that kind of diversion: his stamp album and an occasional stroll with her were – had to be – sufficient recreation. But a wish ungranted is a wish protracted; and Odone recalled it now as he stood looking at these cages of poultry with his first wages in his pocket. There was one animal in particular that he liked: a really beautiful specimen, with a tiny expressive head, shiny black plumage and a long arched tail, which reminded Odone of the feathers on the caps of the

Italian Bersaglieri. He asked the price, at first more out of curiosity than with the firm intention of acquiring it (God knows how much he thought it cost); and the poultry merchant, surprised because this customer was not the usual sex and age, answered rudely, and as if certain of taking his breath away: 'Three *Kronen* and fifty *heller.*'

'So little?' Odone exclaimed. The other man looked at him more offended than astonished, and more than ever convinced that he was being made fun of by a brat. Then, realizing that the latter was serious, he opened the cage, took out the bird and breathed into its feathers to show off how fat it was, how appetizing the colour of the meat.

'Enough, enough!' Odone exclaimed, pained by the shrill cries the victim was emitting and the efforts it was making to hold its head up and not die of suffocation. 'I'll buy her,' he said, 'if you can send her to my house right away.'

'Right away,' the awful man replied; he called the boy who worked for him and handed him the fowl, holding it by the legs. Odone paid, gave his address, plus twenty *heller* as a tip for the boy, and instructed the latter to give his name to whoever opened the door. Then he looked at his watch. It was almost a quarter past two, and he hurried back to the office, trying to persuade himself that he had spent his own money well. With that aim in mind, he exaggerated to himself the joy he would feel when he got home and found Cò-Cò reborn. But the more he tried to dismiss the thought, the more afflicted he was by the suspicion that he had done something pointless, if not actually ridiculous. Cò-Cò had died once and for all, he felt, and could not be replaced by all the hens in the world; his childhood had also died, and it was a foolish thing to want to bring its sweet aspects back to life other than in memory; his mother's hair had already turned completely white, she grew tired ever more quickly, and she might die before she could enjoy the affluence that he, Odone, had promised her; he had done the wrong thing in leaving school for work; an error had been committed in his life, he could not say what or when, a mistake, a sin that distressed his heart more every day, one that he believed was his alone, not yet knowing (as he was to know only too well later) that such pain was the pain of man, of any creature living as an individual; it was the pain that religion calls original sin.

Outside the warehouse, Odone found the day labourers waiting for him with a consignment of oranges in crates, and he forgot himself easily in the task of labelling and supervision; then he wrote out some invoices; he transcribed into fine commercial handwriting a long letter of which the boss had given him a rough draft; he went to run an errand on the other side of the city; returned with the reply, and had to go out again to the Adria shipping company to pay a bill for shipment; he washed the canvas sheets and put the letters in the press; finally, he helped the caretaker to close up. He ought also to have hurried to the central post office to make sure the correspondence should leave within the day, but that evening, as soon as he was out of sight of the boss, he threw it into an ordinary letterbox (the first he found); and he arrived home almost at a run. His mother, who had been waiting for him at the window, opened the door without asking: 'Who is it?' She took his hat from his hand, handed him his spare jacket and then said with a smile:

'Thank you for the nice gift you gave me. How much did it cost you?'

'Three *Kronen* fifty,' Odone replied cheerfully, 'plus a twenty-*heller* tip. Not much, is it?' He was happy and surprised that his mother had welcomed with pleasure, and as a gift for her, that forbidden animal, in truth more adapted to a farmyard than a dwelling, which soiled everything in its path.

'Where is she?' he said. 'Let me see her.'

She opened a door. Behind it, the hen hung on a nail, already plucked, in the rigidity of death. The sight froze Odone's heart.

'I don't know,' his mother said, 'how you managed to find such a nice fat one. It looks more like a capon than a hen. It really was a lucky find. Tomorrow, I'll add a bit of beef and make you an excellent broth. For this evening, you'll have to be content with an omelette. The poor beast was so full of eggs, it was almost a sin to kill it.'

Odone did not want to hear any more and ran to take shelter in his room. His heart was pounding and tears of grief stung his eyes, not only for the miserable end of the fowl – which had served a purpose so different from the one for which he had bought it – but at the thought that his mother – his own mother! – had not understood. Was it possible that a mother did not understand her son? That a son, to make himself understood by his mother, had to explain himself as if to a stranger? Was that how mothers (ten years later he would say 'women') were, or only his? He felt no great desire to talk; nevertheless, when the guilty party entered his room, with the oil lamp already lit in her hand, Odone tried to explain the misunderstanding: the immense pain she had caused him, however involuntarily.

Signora Rachele shrugged her shoulders, surprised and annoyed, and said that a boy who was going to be fifteen in two months' time does not play with hens. Then she advised him to go out for a while, because dinner was not ready yet and a little walk would do him good.

'Who killed her?' Odone asked.

'I did. Why do you ask me that?'

'Because I didn't think you had the courage to kill poultry.'

'When I was a girl,' Signora Rachele said, 'I wouldn't have killed a bird even for a hundred francs. But since I became a mother, it's stopped having any effect on me. When you were recovering from typhoid, I really relished wringing a fowl's neck, thinking of the fine nourishing broth it would make for my son.'

Odone fell silent, feeling that what he had to say on the matter was more for himself than for others. But from that evening on, he loved his mother less and less.

'La gallina'
Written in 1912–13. First published in the journal *La tribuna* (15 November 1913), then included (with significant changes) in *Ricordi-Racconti*, the fifteenth volume of Saba's complete works (Mondadori, 1956).

LALLA ROMANO

1906–2001

Romano's first book of prose shares the title of the Roman poet Ovid's magnum opus, which celebrates the act of transformation: *Le metamorfosi* (*The Metamorphoses*). She began her creative life as a painter before becoming a writer (soon after her Turin home and studio were bombed in the Second World War). Her canvases are moody, murky, full of greys. Towards the end of her life, this intensely visual writer had gone nearly blind. She continued writing, on enormous sheets of paper, sometimes just a word. These tenacious efforts are collected in the *Diario ultimo* (Last Diary), posthumously published. In it she writes, 'La mia cecità = un punto di vista' ('My blindness = a point of view'), an aphoristic equation as paradoxical as it is profound. All of Romano's prose is startling for its spareness, its incisiveness. She was contradictory in that she maintained a boundary between her public and private selves – she was not called Lalla but Graziella, her given name, by friends and family – and yet she wrote in a deeply autobiographical, even confessional vein. *Nei mari estremi* (In Extreme Seas), written after her husband's death, is a plangent work about the physical loss and decline of a companion, while in *Le parole tra noi leggere* (The Light Words between Us), for which she won the Strega in 1969, she wrote frankly about her troubled relationship with her son. Though Romano settled in Milan after the war, this story is set in the mountains of Cuneo, her place of origin. Its carefully gauged point of view reveals the attitude of an artist alert to gestures and nuance. Discreetly erotic, it is a celebration, albeit ironic, of the female gaze, and also a study of political and class distinctions. In addition to being a writer and painter, Romano worked as a librarian and translated Flaubert's *Three Tales*, an experience, according to Romano, which inspired her to turn to writing prose.

The Lady

Translated by Jhumpa Lahiri

In the hotel dining room, the lady started to observe the gentleman seated at the table across from her, and upon preliminary inspection, surmised that he was interesting.

The essential thing – that is to say, the hands – were perfect. The lady never gave a second thought to men who had rough, neglected hands. The man at the opposite table took excellent care of his hands. They were slender, anxious hands, and the noble curve of the nails was free of impurities. His hair was smooth, grey at the temples, and moulded to his round, rather small head. As the lady factored each new element into her analysis, approval mounted in her heart, and her whole being was poised for happiness.

The gentleman had finished lunch without raising his head, so the lady hadn't been able to catch his eye. He got up and left the room, not only without glancing at the lady, but without even a nod. For a moment the morsel of food that the lady had just swallowed stuck in her throat, but she hastened to think that maybe she'd been mistaken, and then she abandoned herself to pleasant daydreams, looking out the window at the slope of the mountain where small fields of rye seemed to be fleeing below steady gusts of wind.

Someone brought the lady a note. The lady had been waiting for it, because she hadn't seen Nicola Rossi when she'd arrived on the morning coach. Nicola Rossi apologized for not being there, and invited the lady to come up to his hotel. Nicola Rossi was a music critic and a friend of the lady's husband. The whole afternoon, Nicola Rossi talked about the stomach ailment that had kept him from coming to meet her. It was the altitude that gave him this trouble, and unfortunately the pharmacy in town didn't carry effective remedies. Nicola Rossi talked about nothing else all afternoon, and in the evening the lady was grateful to the man at the opposite table for being there.

After three days, the lady had only managed to make eye contact with the man two or three times, though she hadn't been able to hold his gaze for even an instant. Later, questioning herself about that look, which had made a distinct impression on her, the lady tried to discern some warmth in it, a flash of kindness or sensuality, but she doubted this had been the case.

A certain restlessness began to take root in the lady's spirit. But it was still linked to a subtle joy, owed in part to the sheer difficulty of the undertaking. And yet the lady realized that this particular joy or, rather, pleasant excitement, was growing much less spontaneous, so that she had to seek it out, provoke it; and so the joy was turning less vivid, maybe even a little insincere and false.

On previous occasions, a unique quality of this joy was that the lady felt it precisely when she exchanged more or less neutral glances or words with the new individual in question. This time, though, the strangest thing was that she couldn't feel joy in the gentleman's presence. Meanwhile she fell prey to an inexplicable embarrassment that could only be called shyness. That was the strangest thing. The lady was certain, however, that she would regain full control once she could speak.

At this point the lady burned with curiosity to know who the man was, and what his profession might be. His anxious hands suggested a pianist, or a surgeon.

Inventing an excuse, the lady asked to see the hotel register, but all she learned was that the gentleman was forty years old. The box for profession was left blank. The lady was irked that she'd written, on her part, 'set-designer' – she gave advice to her architect husband – so she now replaced it with 'painter', which struck her as less odd. She also regretted having put down her exact age, but she didn't dare correct it. Besides, compared to the gentleman, the lady was still quite young.

The lady had just stood up from the table and was looking, leaning against the window, at the small fields of rye rippling in the wind. The gentleman was finishing his lunch, and the window was behind his back. Now and then the lady looked away from the landscape and stared at the gentleman's neck, which wasn't rigid or straight, but pliant, like a boy's. It was impossible to detect cruelty in it.

The gentleman stood up and, rather than head for the door as he usually did, turned towards the lady and, without saying a word, offered her a cigarette. The lady was both delighted and disturbed, as if she were a shy teenager, and the way the gentleman brought the lit match up to her cigarette felt like a small gesture of intimacy.

It wasn't a real conversation; just a few words about the hotel, the location. Mulling over it later, the lady noted that a cue hadn't been lacking, in fact, the gentleman had provided one, and she regretted not having picked up on it. That evening in bed, for the twentieth time, the lady repeated the morning's exchange, and with no trouble at all, she found infinite ways of starting up an interesting conversation. The gentleman had mentioned that the hotel manager had got married that very year, but it was only because his mother had died and he needed a woman in the hotel; otherwise he would have remained a bachelor, because he and the gentleman had similar thoughts about marriage. She could have asked him to elaborate on this topic, thus getting to know what he thought about women.

On the other hand, the lady knew that it wasn't just the brevity of the gentleman's conversation that had disappointed her. She knew he had a lovely voice, but that his pronunciation was marred, betraying the fact that he spoke dialect. Above all, she knew it was too late. The moment of realizing that she'd been deceived, a moment she'd been through on other occasions – during which she'd always made a quick decision – was somehow already behind her, without ever having been reached.

The lady began envisioning favourable scenarios, ranging from the adventurous to the catastrophic. For example, a fire at night in the little hotel: mayhem, people scrambling to escape. She remembered that similar fantasies had consoled her in childhood, when she wanted to be noticed by an older classmate who paid her no attention. Back then those imaginary disasters served as pretexts for rescues, heroic actions, feats of self-sacrifice. Whereas now they served as occasions for escaping in one's pyjamas, or wearing even less. The lady ended up falling asleep to these fantasies, and her dreams almost always picked up the cue, granting it unexpected developments.

On her solitary walks – she avoided going to see Nicola Rossi, who was still stuck in his hotel with stomach troubles – the lady reflected at length on the fragmented escapades of her dreams. The dreams ended up creating some sort of complicity between herself and the gentleman. But they only managed to intrigue her further, without ever instilling confidence in her, not only because she was aware of their one-sided nature, but because they weren't enough to convince her, even in an illusory way, of a change in the gentleman's attitude, since he'd always behaved, even in her dreams, implacably like himself.

These dreams weren't lacking a more playful side – though what it meant escaped the lady – that may have represented a sort of unconscious revenge.

One took place in the museum. When she was a little girl, the lady had visited a sculpture museum and had been quite taken by a statue of a male nude that didn't have the customary fig leaf over its sex. But the reason for her astonishment, and the mild discomfort she felt, wasn't because she'd seen what was usually hidden, but rather because it looked so small and slender compared to figure's stature. At the time, her knowledge of the subject was rather vague, and she wasn't precocious by nature. The matter had upset her unconsciously, and she had ended up forgetting the whole episode.

In the dream, the statue appeared to her at night, in a garden that was very dense and dark. It was extremely tall, and the head was lost in the shadows. The lady recognized the statue, and once again felt that same discomfort, though it was much stronger and more distressing. Her gaze hastened to the place that had upset her, but there was no trace of what she'd glimpsed back then. There was only the customary fig leaf. The lady knew it was the man in the hotel.

In another dream, the man turned up in an even more obvious manner. The whole town was on fire, and a terrified crowd was fleeing to the mountains. The lady tarried because she was looking for someone. At this point the gentleman entered the scene. He moved with long, slow strides, even though he was running. He ran fluidly, like someone filmed in slow-motion. The lady immediately recognized the gentleman's legs, and their strange movements didn't surprise her because she was used to observing the gentleman when he got up from the table. She'd noticed that he had long, agile legs, like a boy, but that his stride was slow and pliant, almost springing at the knees. The embarrassing thing was that the gentleman was wearing a flowing white nightshirt, the kind the lady had never seen, other than perhaps in some silent comedy from her childhood. All of a sudden, the lady knew she was dreaming, and she took advantage of this to satisfy her curiosity. She approached the gentleman and extended her hand, with the intention of lifting up the flowing gown, but just as she did this she woke up; or at least, that was the part of the dream she remembered.

There was a second conversation. The gentleman said he was waiting for a friend to arrive, to go up the glacier. This conversation was also very brief, but it didn't end like the earlier one, because the gentleman didn't leave. Instead something else happened.

The lady and the gentleman were seated across from each other, close to their usual window. All of a sudden, even before finishing his cigarette, the gentleman leaned his head against the window jamb and closed his eyes. The lady wasn't offended, but she felt her heart clench in a brief burst of anguish. She looked at the gentleman's face, nobly agitated even in sleep, and felt like crying. Then she turned towards the mountain, where the familiar fields of rye rippled in the wind like small lakes in a storm.

The gentleman really was sleeping, but he soon roused himself, and said that in order to sleep well, one needed to go and lie out on a meadow, under the sun. The lady went to change and get a dressing gown. She put on her shorts and didn't forget to bring a book; because she assumed, though she was rushing, that nothing would happen.

The lady climbed up a path behind the hotel, until she reached a small meadow hemmed by the shadow of a beech forest. She opened her dressing gown on the grass, and she had just lain back when the gentleman reached her, then went on ahead, working his way through the bushes, perhaps in search of another meadow higher up. The lady was grateful that the sun was hot.

A good deal of time passed. The shade of the beech trees reached the lady, and she started to shiver. The sun already looked sad above the snowcaps. She heard the sound of shifting stones: the man was slowly coming down the path. The lady looked at his naked torso, on the thin side, graceful. Without thinking, she impulsively said hello. The gentleman stopped, and the lady thought he was looking at her legs, as she saw him blushing discreetly below his tan. She felt no pleasure, just a sharp sense of shame. She stood, and picked up her dressing gown.

In the evening the seat across from the gentleman was occupied. A large man dressed in brown corduroy, with his back to the lady, prevented her from gazing at her idol and intercepting his distracted glances. Through the window, above the man's massive shoulders, the lady no longer saw the neighbouring mountain, only a pink blade of sunlight about to be extinguished on the patches of snow on the facing valley.

After lunch, the new man introduced himself. He was friendly and had big, stubby, good-natured hands. With him was his eighteen-year-old son. The lady went up to her room and chose, from among her dresses, a white evening gown she'd set aside the first day, deeming it inappropriate for that sort of hotel. It was a dress that exposed her shoulders, to be worn with a short red velvet cape. The lady put it on and changed her hairstyle, gathering it at the top of her head with little combs. She applied her make-up carefully, then went back down to the room. No one paid attention to her.

The small group was gathered around the radio, dominated by a giant man, the chief technician of the power plant, who was in charge of making the device work. The friend's son started staring persistently at the lady, and then, encouraged by a nod, asked if she liked the music and invited her to dance. The large friend winked over at them now and then, and the gentleman was deep in conversation with him. Between dances, the lady could hear the man's voice, and the unpleasant inflection of his dialect. She realized at a certain point that she could hear what they were saying, and she started listening.

The lady's husband was a leftist intellectual, as were Nicola Rossi and all the lady's friends. The conversation the gentleman and his friend were having was unbelievably reactionary, especially on the part of the gentleman, while the friend seemed less convinced and, above all, less rabid. The chief technician also joined the conversation and, to the lady's astonishment, loudly proclaimed his opinions, which were even more backward. Since she was obviously following their conversation, the lady was questioned. She tried to respond in kind, and felt strange pleasure at the thought that none of her friends was there to witness her degradation.

During a pause, the gentleman started to study the lady's sandals, then praised them soberly. The lady felt acute pleasure, but was also embarrassed, as always, and she then observed, in turn, the gentleman's shoes. The gentleman's shoes were marvellous. They were made of white suede, with raised spirals in brown. The lady expressed her amazement and her admiration, and thus, for the first time, she saw the gentleman smile unabashedly. At that point, the friend said that if the gentleman didn't have beautiful shoes, who would? Given that he made them.

The gentleman clarified that he worked in leather, cutting uppers, and gave the lady some advice about buying shoes.

Though she suffered, the lady didn't feel anything close to spite or rancour towards the gentleman. And she didn't despise herself either: in truth she was so consumed by passion that she didn't have time to dwell on peripheral feelings. She knew nothing would happen, and yet she experienced the anguished sensation – though not entirely disheartening – of risk, as if she were walking on the edge of an abyss. She had the great clairvoyance to sense that, for the first time in her life, something terrible had been born inside of her, no less strong for that, but destined inevitably to defeat her. So great was her revelation that it would forever alter and undermine her certainty, her every illusion. The lady even felt a vague self-respect, or rather, respect for what she recognized was happening inside her. She knew it wasn't a matter of a stubbornness, but something that went beyond vanity and pride. All her faculties were thus taut, in a state of useless expectation.

The friend's presence was of no use to the lady. The son brought her flowers when he returned from his walks and, looking deep into her eyes, confided his disappointment in the immaturity of his classmates. The lady thought he was boring, but in those moments preferred him to Nicola Rossi and to anyone else.

Nicola Rossi, meanwhile, still felled by his stomach troubles, decided to go back to the city, and the lady told him to tell her husband that she was bored.

The gentleman and his friend had organized their trip to the glacier. The hotel manager, also a guide, was accompanying them. The boy pleaded with the lady to join them. The lady harboured no illusions of lending the least bit of substance to their adventure, but she couldn't help but daydream about this trip to the glacier and imagine endless scenarios. But she didn't make up her mind.

The night before, in the hotel lobby, she saw ice axes, ropes, crampons. They needed to leave before dawn. Around four o'clock in the morning, the lady thought she heard a car. After an hour, since she couldn't get back to sleep, she got out of bed, thinking she'd go up the mountain on her own. But she found everyone in the lobby, with the ropes and crampons. No one said hello. The car that was supposed to take them up to the cable car hadn't come, and now they were waiting for the milk truck.

The hotel manager surveyed the street and called them after half an hour. The milk truck was enormous, without side rails, and was already crammed with people sitting on milk canisters. The lady nodded yes when the guide called her, and this was how she let herself be hoisted on to the truck.

Keeping balance on the truck was extremely difficult: the road snaked uphill, and as the truck rounded each turn, it would veer to one side. The villagers, with their baskets, were anchored to the vehicle, but the gentlemen, including the guide, were an endangered bunch, and they clutched the shoulders of older women who seemed to be made of stone. The lady, seated on a basket between two canisters, was the most stable, and she was already starting to forget about herself and about her affliction. She was intent on drinking in, at every turn, apparitions of the tall white mountain, continually swallowed up by the dark pine forests. But she was aware that the gentleman was close to her, looking uncomfortable, because he was searching with one hand for something to hold on to. She was quick to grab the hand. She glanced at him and saw, through the wind, that he, a bit embarrassed, was thanking her.

As soon as she made contact with his hand, the lady experienced intense pleasure. The hand was smooth, dry and warm, and it clasped her own only as a means of support, that was all. The lady knew he could give her nothing more. But rather than feeling the usual humiliation, she felt a calm sense of possession.

That clasp, untethered from the ground, in the middle of the whirlwind of jolts, sharp turns and the ghostly backdrop of the unfurling mountains, was closer to the deceptive intimacy of their encounters in her dreams, as opposed to real contact. But even though, as in those dreams, it contained a precariousness and, above all, a sense of solitude, the warmth it gave off was real and comforting, almost familiar.

When it was time to step down from the truck, she sensed that the gentleman hurried to pull back his hand. She had already dismissed him, in any case. A car accompanied her back to the hotel, where she found a telegram from her husband. She had just enough time to pack her bags, and left on the afternoon coach.

'*La signora*'
Written in 1948, first published in the collection *La villeggiante* (Einaudi, 1975).

FABRIZIA RAMONDINO

1936–2008

Ramondino is the youngest writer in this anthology, and *Althénopis*, a fugue-like autobiographical first novel, inspired by her itinerant childhood, is her masterpiece. A leftist intellectual and community organizer, she was raised largely outside Italy, in Spain, France and Germany. Her father, a diplomat, died when she was young. In her mid-twenties she came to Naples and made it her base. Despite her vagabond nature, or perhaps because of it, she was fascinated by spaces that contained and confined, writing a meditative book called *L'isola riflessa* (The Reflected Island), about the time she spent, in a period of acute crisis, on Ventotene, a tiny island off the coast between Rome and Naples where the Emperor Augustus banished one of his daughters for adultery, where Mussolini interned enemies nearby and where, in 1941, the confined writer Altiero Spinelli, in collaboration with others, wrote a pioneering manifesto that paved the way for European unification (and the European Union). Ramondino dedicated another work to the experiences of women in a mental institution in Trieste. Spatial constriction is central to this story, which focuses tightly on a handful of characters simultaneously bound together and splintered. Despite being a chamber piece, it comments broadly and caustically on the effects of the economic boom that followed the Second World War, the consequences of the great migration of southern Italians to the north, and the dissolution of the traditional family structure. Ramondino writes with exceptional lucidity about states of emotional and physical distress. She also writes candidly about her struggle with alcoholism. In 1996 she joined a film crew that shot a documentary, partly commissioned by Unicef, about the exiled Sahrawi community in

West Africa. Ramondino loved the sea, such that it was an element in nearly everything she wrote. She died suddenly after feeling ill while swimming close to the shore of southern Italy. Her last novel, *La via* (The Way), was published the following day.

The Tower

Translated by Jhumpa Lahiri

The bus dropped them off on Saturday: the father, the mother, the cat in its basket, the daughter. The house, the father's, was like his others. On the kitchen table, the woman set out a few of the provisions she'd brought with her, along with some other things she'd found in the house, including lots of wine. They ate cheerfully. The father said: 'It's like an Easter anti-pasto.' Indeed, there were hard-boiled eggs, cheese and olives. The woman was tired – her menstrual period had just started – and she went to bed with a novel and the radio, that alternated between opera arias and pro-grammes on RAI3.[1] Daughter and father, armed with flashlights, went to explore the tower. 'Careful not to fall, there's a step missing!' the father said, or: 'A thousand years ago, soldiers kept watch through these embra-sures,' just as children were told thirty years ago. At the top of the tower: wind, stars, the cat between their feet, disoriented by strange smells.

Sunday morning, the woman woke up to find the daughter next to her in bed. She left the bedroom. She went to the kitchen. Light filtered in through the embrasures, constricted but intense. She moved around the room. From every slit, on each wall, that dazzling sun, and segments of the town, immersed in a din that merged with the light. The woman took a tranquillizer, because the left side of her chest was hurting, and she made herself some coffee, which she drank from a bowl, without sugar, with a little milk. Then she started to smoke.

They'd already used up the water in the bathroom. It shut off at seven, they would turn it on again in the evening. She washed up with what was left in the tank and glanced, with remote satisfaction, at the voluminous hairstyle, Geisha-like, that the hairdresser had given her the day before, which still looked good.

The house was familiar to her, like his previous ones.

While she smoked and drank coffee in the narrow kitchen, waiting for the tranquillizer to get rid of the tightness in her chest – enveloped by the din of voices that came from down below – the others woke up. There wasn't much in the house for breakfast. And so they decided to go to the sea, and to have breakfast at a bar. But before heading out, the daughter wanted her mother to explore the tower the way she had, excited, in the dark, the night before. The woman didn't want to; she felt crabby, and didn't want to pretend to be charmed. But she went.

The light, which had been broken up, in the rooms, by the slender contours of the embrasures, reassembled in a circle at the top of the tower: the red roof-tiles of the town, the ilex-lined avenue, the piazza in front of the castle with a horrid white statue of San Francesco from the 1930s[2] (replacing the usual unknown soldier), the orange and yellow fields, the lakes formed by the distant lagoon, the narrow strip of beach, the sea, the islands; all of it bathed in the clear, fresh, strong September light.

They went into town. A few small shops, built up around the castle, replacing the old stables and oil mills. The bar, the dairy, the barber. They entered the bar thronged with men: the woman ordered a brandy, the daughter had a *buondì* snack and a fruit juice, the father a coffee. While waiting for the bus they walked around the little streets: houses painted white, with peppers and tomatoes hung out to dry, and chairs, those too hung up high, on hooks; there were large plates of figs exposed to the sun, and conserves kept safe from children and animals. They felt a bit uncomfortable walking there, because every tiny alley was like a house, and people in those nestled towns weren't used to tourists. They proceeded to walk along the walls, which had small dwellings built into them. The daughter was tired of walking and seeing stones, fields, houses.

The bus wasn't due for another hour, and while they waited in the piazza, they bought the newspaper. The festival for L'Unità[3] was taking place, and on page one of the newspaper they read that some thousand copies had been sold, and that the Metalworkers' Union had declared that civil disobedience was a legitimate way to protest against the rise in transportation fares, and maybe also electricity rates.

The bus finally arrived. They skirted orange and yellow fields, vineyards and olive groves, the red-tiled roofs of a town that ran along the single road that passed through it, up to the rail-yard, where the sea was. The bus left immediately. The daughter wanted to wait, to watch a train go by, but none arrived – the train and bus schedules almost never coincided. Beyond the platforms, a few buildings, deserted by now: restaurants, bars, hotels open in August, destined for the boisterous tourism of southern labourers who had migrated north, and who, in dance halls, bars and cheap hotels, had twenty days at best to revel, love, relax and spend all their money in an ongoing clamour of car horns and transistor radios. Apart from these migrants, tourism didn't flourish here. This was also the case along other parts of the Adriatic coast, because of the state forest situated along the shoreline.

That Sunday in late September there was hardly a soul: four young people, who clambered out of a Fiat 500, rapidly undressing and diving into the water; a prudent mother and child holding hands, both impeccably dressed, strolling along the water's edge.

Father and daughter went into the sea and started up endless shenanigans, splashing each other, diving in, racing, swimming.

The woman lay out in the sun, at first with her clothes on; then she took them off, since the black bra and underpants weren't that unlike a real bathing suit. Her body was thin, youthful, adorned by her puffy Geisha hairstyle. Reassured by her appearance, she wanted to abandon herself to the sun. But the feverish warmth of her period, which held her in a state of levitation and discomfort, didn't mix well with the sun, brazen and direct but not powerful enough to vanquish her inner heat. That sun, broken up by the wind, called for races and swims, not distraught levitations. She was stretched out, her arms spread, before the sea. Her body formed a cross. Many kilometres in the distance, she thought, to the left and right of her, on both sides, were two other places on the Adriatic she knew well.

Ten years ago, in Rimini, in September, before they had a daughter, when they'd hitchhiked carefree on three hundred lire a day, they'd stayed with some friends in an abandoned cabin, breaking in through a window. The next morning she'd woken up on a vast desert of sand and cabins. A drunken lifeguard, taking advantage of a moment in which she'd hung back from the others, had grabbed her breast: that cold September, deprived of women, his eyes had popped from the orbits of his ruddy face, while a little boy dragged a wooden spool at his feet by a string.

And just fifteen days ago, further south, beyond the lagoon lakes, she'd carved out the time for a youthful weekend getaway. She'd left without her daughter, going with three friends who fished underwater, they, too, without girlfriends or wives. They'd tooled around in a small car through camping grounds, bays, Saracen towers, fields of prickly pear, white towns, abandoned plains; sun gave way to stormy weather, wind and sea took turns riling one another up, discouraging her companions from fishing, either by skin diving or scuba diving. And so in the end, in addition to being on their own, they were also rudderless. In the deserted camping ground, two of the friends had engaged for hours in a fight, like warriors in the *Iliad*, making shields out of the plastic lids of garbage cans, jousting with leafy torn-off branches, or even iron bars pried off the roof of the diving shop, among battle cries confused by the wind. At night, inside her small tent, she'd heard one of the men complaining; he wanted a woman. And he only calmed down on the third day, as they rode back, when each of them was immersed in thoughts of everyday hassles, and the loved ones they'd left behind.

The woman thought back to those two adolescent moments – each so far apart in years, both so turbulent and raw. She thought back to that friendly camaraderie with men – at first it had drawn out a spell of eternal, unscathed expectation, but then it had led to disenchantment.

Sun, sea, wind and the daughter's frenzied playing, which the father continued to indulge, were poorly suited that day – she saw this more and more clearly – to that sense of mild levitation and illness. So she got dressed and headed over to the small establishment managed by the person who had once administered the assets since squandered by her ex-boyfriend's parents.

She had to chat with the wife, a thin blonde woman, mother of two children: chat about the car, her husband, the new stove she wanted, having seen it in the pages of *Grazia*, and about hairdressers, holidays, the dishwasher, her kids' school, *Emmanuelle*,[4] the pill, her family. She also exchanged a word or two with the woman's mother-in-law, an elderly peasant nostalgic for conversations that would take place on the little street she'd long since left behind, who showed her bobbin lace, pulling them out from a box, lace destined for the countless children and grandchildren who got rich in the north during the boom; lace that was previously scorned but, now that the family had grown sophisticated, was highly coveted. Just like the oils and preserves that the other old women who still lived in the village sent to their children and grandchildren, factory workers in Milan who, back in '55, used to be ravenous for them. But then, in later years – years, precisely, of economic growth – hand-made goods would only be barely tolerated, out of sentimentality – Sasso oil was better, it didn't ruin your liver, so were jellies from Massalombarda, and Pavesini biscuits, and *zampone* wrapped in aluminum foil and hermetically sealed – only to be fancied again, when it became fashionable, in motels along the highways, to have fake rustic genuine preserves, sealed in old glass jars, with hand-written labels glued to them.

This was the chit-chat; and the woman was gripped by an aristocratic yearning to be sitting in a café in Istanbul or Vienna, where nobody knew her, where no one would say a word to her or divert her from her state of weary concentration.

Then a huge racket arose, from the clearing between the pier and the sea: children, not joyful but petulant, asking for gelato, a cookie, gum, and: 'When, when can we watch TV?'

After that there was the trip back in the car; the daughter, still full of energy, who wanted to go down to the gate-keeper's house and watch TV, who wanted gelato, a cookie, gum. Dinner at home because, as everyone knew, kids had to eat. But there wasn't much in the kitchen. The father went out to buy some milk and a fancy tin of cookies – also a bottle of grappa for the two of them. The girl had dinner, she frolicked a bit on the tower steps and with the cat; she fell asleep, exhausted, reading the same comic books she'd been reading all week.

The father and mother were also tired, but not from air, motion, sea and sun; they were tired of themselves, and they were even more tired of being together again, because of the daughter.

Grappa had always kept them company in those final years: at first for the difficulty of being together, then for the boredom of being together again. Grappa when they had money, otherwise wine. And that night they still had some money.

He'd taught her how to drink grappa and wine, and inebriation. He taught all this as if it were a form of bliss, as if it were a pledge. He'd accompany the initiation with a smile, now gentle and radiant, now winking with intelligence, now muffled with secret suffering, now airy and engrossing, now sorrowful, as if offended by the hardships of the world;

it was the smile of perennial adolescence, though sometimes it turned mean, belonging to someone who couldn't bear the weight of being unmasked. Then, more and more with the passing of years, the smile was darkened by the offences of misunderstanding and those, yet more serious, of understanding. A smile that had seduced her in the beginning because she'd warped it, that is to say, made it out to be more than it was, the way children do when they see beauty in ordinary faces, or enormity in the village piazza, or think that animals can talk. Or maybe it really had been beautiful back then, and life was what had distorted it.

Now, occasionally, the smile seemed petty or afraid: not gentle but pusillanimous, not radiant but kitschy; the winking intelligence was still there, but it was ensnared by petty daily grievances – and if it rose to a higher plane, it seemed like a delirium or a trap set for others who were more naive; the sorrowful irony had become a tic, a sign of offences suffered and dealt. Then, more recently, nothing moderately appealing about that smile remained; instead it seemed to turn people away; and often it turned into a grimace, like someone who puts his hands over his ears because of a screeching sound, or covers his eyes from a blinding light. Tolerance had turned to cynicism, compassion to self-pity and acrimony.

They wouldn't be seeing each other this way, recalling, over a bottle of grappa, a world they'd shared, had it not been for the daughter. But this conviction – the woman thought – was also a salvation. She objected to the evasions of the past; deep down, in fact, she was severe. But how it weighed on her! He would have wanted her to be unhappy, in fact, like some men want their mothers to be. Mater Dolorosa. No, not her.

At the start of their scheduled encounters she had always ended up drunk, because the effort of deciphering the enigma still flummoxed her: there it was in front of her, unfathomable, some meaning looming, dreadful, neither able nor willing to reveal itself. On either side a Yes and a No, leaning in, at loggerheads, among the falsely obliging fumes of alcohol; and this eventually left them exhausted, muddled by an ambiguous complicity.

But now, for quite some time, everything had changed. On either side of the table there was only the obligation of staying together for the sake of their daughter; but at times the age-old habit of seeking an impossible, mutual understanding took hold of them, like a bad habit. Then they were bogged down in a perilous swamp of memories.

Like all people who are profoundly alone, the woman was naive and violent. They hadn't spoken to each other in a long time. So she fell back, again, into the bad habit of complicity, mistaking it for sharing. Their conversations seemed like ancient sophisms, harmful to the world and to themselves. Paltry ruins of ancient wisdom. She surrendered to the alcohol until she threw up, liberated. An acute discomfort followed.

When the ritual had been carried out, she went to bed, next to her daughter. But the discomfort intensified. Waves rose up as if from a swamp, not from memory but from nothing; deep waves, and rapid fog. She wanted someone beside her to quell them, to shoo them away; the way her mother did.

She got up, went to his bed, and hugged him tight, but kept to the edge of the mattress so she wouldn't bother him, so she wouldn't be pushed away; just like she would with her mother who, when she didn't push her away, would indulgently call her 'my little ivy-leaf'. That was how tightly she'd squeeze into her mother in bed.

He tried to chase her away, he'd misunderstood. But she insisted, deaf, until the discomfort gave way to sleep.

In the morning, father and daughter decided to go to back to the sea. The woman had a massive headache, as well as the morbid heat of her period, so she stayed in bed. But after a while she felt the urgent need to escape the distressing odour of her blood. She got up; the sun was coming in again through the embrasures, along with the din of the piazza. She read all day. She finished *The Confessions of Zeno*. She started *One Hundred Years of Solitude*.

In the afternoon she went down to the piazza to buy food; people stared at the 'foreigner'. Who knows what they take me for, she said to herself. Maybe they think I'm the wife of a new office worker, or a whore.

She thought of him in the town, more of a foreigner than an office worker. Sheltered in that dilapidated abandoned tower none of his relatives would claim. Limited to spending time with only a few people: the gate-keeper – a woman who'd known him since he was little, when his parents had money, who now, seeing him poor, treated him with a calculated informality – and a boyhood friend, a decent man, a shopkeeper entirely devoted to work and family. She imagined him living for weeks on rice, olive oil from Puglia, and packs of Nazionali, as if he were in solitary confinement, in voluntary exile, after the suicide (or accidental death) of a friend.

He spoke to the daughter, at length, about the mouse who lived in his drawer, his faithful companion fattened up on cheese rinds; the unusual light at certain hours or on certain days that unveiled or lit up the islands; old stories about the tower: traps, assassins, labyrinths. He spoke of a happy, hard-working future, when, who knew, he might plant basil, tomatoes, aubergines and lettuces in the tower's dried-up moat – maybe even roses and geraniums.

The daughter, one day, had asked her: 'Why doesn't he live with us?' And she, lying, had replied: because he wants to be like a bird, free. Instead he seemed to her, in that tower, an ensnared bird who had lost its bearings and could no longer get out.

It was late to shop for food. The market was empty. She found a little shop and chose something from the leftover fruits and vegetables. They threw in some wilting basil, bereft of its proud scent. She bought bread and cheese. Everything was complicated in that mistrustful town, where no one seemed to know anything, not even where the little shop was. Where eyes stared at her, half closed or still, like thick wax seals.

She had to make dinner, set the table. The family triangle, there at the table. She was overtaken by frenzy. She had a wicked impulse. There was no one watching her. She undid the triangle: she stacked the three plates in the middle and put the silverware on top, next to the glasses, one inside the other. A kind of buffet. Father and daughter paid it no heed, they didn't even notice. He merely recreated the triangle. And since the child didn't like certain foods, he started to amuse her, to instruct her, to convince her that she had to try every new thing out of curiosity, not obligation.

After dinner everyone was sleepy, for different reasons: the little girl because it had been an active day at the beach; the woman because she was hungover from the day before, and because of her period; as for him, who knew – in those days he fell asleep easily, maybe to thin his delirium down to a fog.

The following Tuesday, after breakfast, that sunny din still came through the embrasures; but the sky was no longer as clear. The wind had picked up and clouds approached from the sea. The daughter went down to play at the gate-keeper's. And while the woman settled down to read in the only armchair, by the only window adorned with lush reddish ivy, he called her into a room, an old chicken coop, where he'd set up a small desk. I've consulted the *I Ching*, he said. He'd looked up the word 'wife' and what came up was 'damage and devastation'. Then the woman, reacting to his ambiguous smile, remembered how he'd interpreted her nocturnal act of lying down beside him a few nights ago, reading it as nothing other than the behaviour of a woman who wants to sidle up to a man. Of course this hadn't been the truth, nor could it ever be again. She turned sullen at their lack of understanding of each other. But she didn't want to stoop to petty explanations. She left without a word.

And she observed this silence, not as if it were a pact, or an order, but instinctively.

Four more days went by. The air had turned chilly, and there were storms at night. In the morning, the sun-lit din no longer arrived through the embrasures: the sky was gloomy, the piazza deserted. The woman sat next to the window wrapped in blankets and shawls; the rain streamed down the wall of the house across the street; or it let up, and the drops glistened on the pigeons. The daughter kept playing her exciting games: up and down the tower stairs, with the cat; in the piazza, with the other children; she spent the evenings in front of the gate-keeper's television. At times the father indulged her in her games – it was only with children that he resembled his former self. More frequently he sat at his desk in the chicken coop among crates of books, clothes and records he hadn't bothered to open, though he'd been living there for several months.

The woman read. Or, inevitably, she remembered. She abstained from alcohol; she drank the cold water of recollection.

The tumult of the years spent in Milan, their cheerful ex-pat brigade: from one little job to another, one furnished room to the next, bar-hopping in the evenings. They'd left behind Posillipo, their neighbourhood in Naples. Ahead of them lay a future rich with promise. No one wanted to make money. Then those years ended for everyone. But he was still ensnared in his youth.

Now and then, lifting her eyes from the book, she observed the little room where she was holed up for those days; it felt like a bow window, or a boudoir.

Everything looked as if it had been salvaged from a shipwreck: the revolving bookcase saved from the ruin of his family, the mirror saved from the failure of their living together; the photograph of the young man she'd once loved; the photo of the daughter, about whom he'd once said: 'It's such a drag to raise a kid'; paintings by an old friend from their Brera days. But all this wreckage had been reorganized by a common aura she struggled to define: faded fabrics laid over the armchairs and beds; subdued light; rounded angles and nooks; a suffused pastel shade. A baroque disorder that evoked rosy children among the bushes; white skirts with thin sky-blue stripes that got snagged on the grass; playful, rotund priests; English prof-iteers and southern Italian *viveurs*; last rites, solemn and grotesque, because the dying had lived too long. Hence indefinably similar to his mother's rooms, she around whom every place became an alcove or a boudoir, where every colour muted into a pastel hue, every sound sank into the carpets, every misfortune settled into good manners, every belief faded into a tolerance that seemed fatuous, but was actually insidious, lethal.

On Friday night there was some friction. They'd gone through almost all the money, and each blamed the other. The woman had paid the bills before leaving, while he'd been counting on that money. Only some spare change remained for her ticket. He and the daughter would go to his mother and sister's, getting a ride with his cousin. The woman also asked him to lend her a copy of *Don Quixote* to read on the journey; she'd latched on to that book since the previous day. But he didn't want to give it to her. He said it meant a lot to him. She felt unjustly deprived. And the hidden meaning of those petty actions also embittered her: the infantile hatred he harboured towards her, because he felt exposed by her. What he needed was to be surrounded by that aura, drowsy and ambiguous, which belonged to his family: the aura that sowed the seeds of his exile, in a world that called for definitions instead.

The next day it rained. The bus would be leaving at noon. The woman, as usual, got up before the others. In the kitchen, through the embrasures, a malevolent wind brought in the rain. She lit a cigarette, waiting.

'*La torre*'
Part of the collection *Arcangelo e altri racconti* (Einaudi, 2005).

LUIGI PIRANDELLO
1867–1936

Pirandello, who won the Nobel Prize in 1934, is perhaps best known as a playwright who revolutionized theatrical conventions, but his astonishing output of short fiction was also a locus of ongoing experimentation. In 1922, the year after his groundbreaking play *Sei personaggi in cerca d'autore* (*Six Characters in Search of an Author*) earned him international fame, he told his publisher, Mondadori, that he wanted to create a massive work called *Novelle per un anno* (*Short Stories for a Year*), consisting of three hundred and sixty-five tales that had originally appeared in newspapers and magazines. Fifteen volumes were published, a total of two hundred and forty-two stories, but the project was left incomplete. Pirandello was born in Agrigento, Sicily, but moved to Rome when he was twenty, and spent the next twenty-five years there teaching Italian language and literature. His personal life was tormented; economic hardship drove his wife insane, and she was committed to an asylum for four decades. In 1924, he sent Mussolini a telegram and publicly joined the Fascist Party, an allegiance providing Pirandello with financial backing to form a theatre company. And yet his work, obsessed with masks and doubles, interrogating the silence at the heart of existence, was subversive to the core. This story was published in 1912, more than ten years before his masterful novel *Uno, nessuno e centomila* (*One, No one, One Hundred Thousand*), a radical work about identity. Anguished and essential, it is stylistically distant from his earlier folkloric work. According to a dear friend from Palermo, 'the soul of a Sicilian is in it'. Though he was eligible for a state funeral, Pirandello's final wishes were to be carried in a humble wagon and cremated without ceremony. His last published work – a short story – appeared the day before he died.

The Trap

Translated by Giovanni R. Bussino

No, no, how can I resign myself? And why should I? If I had any responsibilities towards others, perhaps I would, but I don't! So, why should I?

Listen to me. You can't say I'm wrong. No one reasoning in the abstract like this can say I'm wrong. What I'm feeling, you and everyone else feels too.

Why are all of you so afraid of waking up at night? Because for you the reasons for living are strengthened by the light of day, by the illusions produced by that light.

Darkness and silence terrify you. You light a candle but the candlelight seems dismal to you because that's not the kind of light you need, right? The sun! The sun! All of you desperately seek the sun because illusions no longer arise spontaneously with the artificial light you yourselves procure with a trembling hand.

Like your hand, all your reality trembles. It reveals itself to you to be fake and flimsy. Artificial like that candlelight. All your senses keep watch, painfully tense in the fear that beneath the reality that you discover to be flimsy and hollow, another reality may be revealed to you: an obscure and horrible one – the real one. A breath of air . . . What's that? What's that creaking sound?

Suspended in the horror of that uncertain wait, amid chills and sweat, you see your daytime illusions in that light. They move about the room with the appearance and gait of ghosts. Look at them carefully. They have the same puffy and watery bags under their eyes that you have, the same jaundiced look brought on by your insomnia, and your arthritic pains too. Yes, the same dull torment caused by the gout in the joints of your fingers.

What a strange appearance, what a strange appearance the pieces of furniture in your room assume! They too seem suspended in a bewildering stillness that troubles you.

You slept with them around you.

But they do not sleep. They remain there both day and night.

For now, it's your hand that opens and closes them. But tomorrow it'll be another hand. Who knows whose other hand! . . . But for them it's all the same. For now they contain your clothes: empty forms that have been hung up and that have taken on the shape and wrinkles of your tired knees and bony elbows. Tomorrow they'll contain someone else's forms hanging there. The mirror on the wardrobe reflects your image now, but it doesn't preserve a trace of it, nor will it preserve a trace of someone else's image tomorrow.

The mirror itself cannot see. The mirror is like truth.

Do you think that I'm delirious, that I'm talking nonsense? Come on, you understand me, and you understand even what I am not saying since I find it very hard to express this obscure feeling that rules me and overwhelms me.

You know how I've lived up till now. You know that I've always felt revulsion and horror about giving myself some sort of form, becoming congealed and fixing myself even momentarily in it.

I've always made my friends laugh because of the great many . . . what do you call them? Alterations? Yes, alterations in my personal characteristics. But you've been able to laugh at them because you've never condescended to consider my urgent need to look at myself in the mirror, with a different appearance; to trick myself into believing that I was not always the same person, to see myself as someone else!

But of course! What could I alter? It's true that I went so far as to shave my head to see myself bald before my time. At times I shaved off my moustache, leaving my beard, or vice versa. At times I shaved off my moustache and beard, or I let my beard grow now one way, now another. A goatee, parted on the chin or running along the line of the jaw . . .

I played around with the bristles.

I couldn't at all alter my eyes, nose, mouth, ears, torso, legs, arms or hands. Did I put on make-up like a theatre actor? I sometimes had that temptation. But then I thought that, under my mask, my body always remained the same . . . and was growing old!

I tried to make up for it with my spirit. Oh yes, with my spirit I was able to play around better!

Above all, you value and never tire of praising the constancy of feelings and the coherence of personality. Why? Always for the same reason! Because you are cowards. Because you're afraid of yourselves. That is, you're afraid that if you change, you'll lose the reality you have given yourselves and you'll recognize, therefore, that it was nothing more than an illusion of yours and, consequently, that no reality exists other than the one we give ourselves.

But, I ask, what does giving oneself a reality mean if not fixing oneself in a feeling, becoming congealed, stiff and encrusted in it? Therefore, arresting in ourselves the perpetual vital movement, making of ourselves so many small miserable pools destined for putrefaction, while life is a continuous flux, incandescent and indistinct.

See, this is the thought that perturbs me and makes me furious!

Life is wind. Life is sea. Life is fire. Not earth, which becomes encrusted and takes on form.

All form is death.

All that is removed from the state of fusion and congeals amid this continuous flux, which is incandescent and indistinct, is death.

We are all beings that have been caught in the trap, separated from the ceaseless flux and fixed to die.

The movement of this flux is in us, in our form, which is separated, detached and fixed, and will last for a brief moment more. But, see, little by little, it slows down. The fire cools down. The form dries up and finally movement ceases completely in the form, which has become rigid.

We have finished dying and we have called this life!

I feel caught in this death trap that has separated me from the flux of life in which I flowed without form, and has fixed me in time, in this *time*!

Why in this time?

I could still have flowed on and become fixed a little later, at least in another form, a little later . . . You think it would have been the same, right? Well, yes, sooner or later . . . But I would have been someone else a little later. Who knows who and who knows how! Trapped in another fate. I would have seen other things or, perhaps, the same things but with different appearances, arranged differently.

You can't imagine what hatred the things I see arouse in me, the things caught with me in the trap of this time that is mine. All the things that end up dying with me, a little at a time! Both hatred and pity! But more hatred, perhaps, than pity.

Yes, it's true, if I had fallen into the trap a little later, I would then have hated that other form as I now hate this one. I would have hated that other time as I do this one now, and all the illusions of life that *we the dead of all time* fabricate for ourselves with that small amount of movement and heat that remains shut up within us and that comes from that continuous flux that is true life and that never stops.

We are so many busy corpses who are deceiving ourselves into believing that we are creating our lives.

We copulate, a dead man with a dead woman, and we think we are giving life but we give death . . . Another being in the trap!

'Here, my dear, here. Begin to die, dear . . . Begin to die . . . You're crying, eh? You're crying and wriggling about . . . You would have liked to flow on some more? Relax, my dear! What can you do about it? Caught, co-ag-u-la-ted, fixed . . . It won't last but a short while! Relax . . .'

Oh, as long as we're very young, as long as our body is fresh and grows and weighs little, we do not clearly realize that we are caught in the trap! But then the body becomes a tangled mass and we begin to feel its weight. We begin to feel that we can no longer move as we did before.

With disgust I see my spirit struggling in this trap to avoid, it too, being fixed in a body already worn out by the years and grown heavy. I immediately drive away every idea that might become stale in me. I immediately interrupt every act that might become a habit in me. I don't want responsibilities, I don't want tender attachments and I don't want my spirit to harden into a crust of concepts either. But I feel that from day to day my body finds it ever more difficult to follow my restless spirit. It continually slumps. It has tired knees and heavy hands . . . It wants rest! I'll give it that.

No, no, I'm unwilling and unable to resign myself to offering, me too, the miserable spectacle given by all those old people who end up dying slowly. No. But first . . . I don't know what, but I'd like to do something enormous, something unheard of, to give vent to this rage that's devouring me.

I'd like at least . . . See these fingernails? I'd like to dig them into the face of every beautiful woman who passes down the street, teasing men provocatively.

What stupid, miserable and thoughtless creatures all women are! They dress up, put on their fineries, turn their laughing eyes here and there and show off their provocative shapes as much as they can. But they don't realize that they too are in the trap and are fixedly formed to die, and have the trap in themselves for those that are to come!

For us men the trap is in them, in women. For a moment they put us once again in a state of incandescence to wrest from us another being who is sentenced to death. They say and do so much until they finally make us fall, blind, passionate and violent, into their trap.

Me too! Me too! They made me fall too! In fact, most recently. That's why I'm so furious.

An abominable trap! If only I had seen it . . . A demure young lady. Timid, humble. As soon as she would see me, she would lower her eyes and blush because she knew that otherwise I would never have fallen.

She used to come here to put into practice one of the seven corporal works of mercy: to visit the sick. She used to come for my father, not for me. She used to come to help my old governess look after and clean my poor father, who's in the other room . . .

She used to live here in the adjoining apartment and had become friends with my governess, to whom she would complain about her idiotic husband, who always reproached her for not being able to give him a son.

But do you understand how it is? When you begin to stiffen and you can no longer move as before, you want to see other small corpses around, very young corpses that still move as you did when you were very young; other small corpses that resemble you and do all those little things that you can no longer do.

There's nothing more amusing than to wash the faces of small corpses that still don't know they are caught in the trap, and to comb their hair and take them out for a little stroll.

As I was saying, she used to come here.

'I can imagine,' she would say, blushing, her eyes downcast, 'I can imagine what a torment it must be, Signor Fabrizio, to see your father in this condition for so many years!'

'Yes, Signora,' I would answer gruffly and I would turn around and go away.

I'm certain now that as soon as I would turn around and go away, she would laugh to herself, biting her lip to hold back her laughter.

I would go away because, in spite of myself, I felt that I admired that woman. Not indeed because of her beauty – she was very beautiful, and the more she showed she had no regard for her beauty, the more seductive she was – but because she didn't give her husband the satisfaction of putting another unfortunate in the trap.

I thought she was the one. Instead, no, it wasn't her problem. It was his. And she knew it or, at least, if she didn't actually have the certainty, she must have entertained the suspicion. That's why she laughed She laughed at me because I admired her for that presumed incapacity of hers. She laughed silently in her evil heart and waited. Until one evening . . .

It happened here, in this room.

I was here in the dark. You know that I like to go to the window and watch the day die and let myself be taken and wrapped gradually by the darkness, and to think, 'I'm no longer here!' To think, 'If there were someone in this room, he would get up and light a lamp. I won't light the lamp because I'm no longer here. I'm like the chairs in this room, like the little table, the drapes, the wardrobe, the couch, that don't need light and don't know and don't see that I'm here. I want to be like them and not see myself and forget I'm here.'

Now then, I was here in the dark. She came tiptoeing in from my father's room, where she had left a small night-lamp lit whose glimmer came through the small opening in the door and faintly spread through the darkness, almost without diminishing it.

I didn't see her. I didn't see that she was about to bump into me. Perhaps she didn't see me either. When we collided, she let out a cry and pretended to faint in my arms, on my chest. I lowered my head. My cheek brushed up against hers. I felt the ardour of her eager mouth, and . . .

After a while, her laugh roused me. A diabolical laugh. I can still hear it! She laughed and laughed as she ran off, that wicked woman! She laughed because she had set a trap for me with her modesty. She laughed because my ferocity was vanquished. And she laughed because of something else that I learned about later.

She went away three months ago with her husband, who was assigned to the position of high-school teacher in Sardinia.

Certain assignments come in the nick of time.

I will never see my remorse. I will not see it. But at certain moments I am tempted to run off and find that wicked woman and choke her before she puts into the trap that unfortunate whom she wrested from me with such treachery.

My friend, I'm happy I never knew my mother. Perhaps if I had known her, this ferocious thought would not have arisen in me. But since it has, I'm happy I never knew my mother.

Come, come, come here with me into this other room. Look! This is my father.

For seven years he has been here. He's nothing any more. Two eyes that cry, a mouth that eats. He can't speak, can't hear and can't move any more. He eats and cries. He is spoonfed. He cries in private without reason or, perhaps, because there's still something in him, a vestige of something that, though it began to die seventy-six years ago, doesn't want to end yet.

Don't you find it atrocious to remain still caught in the trap like that because of a single remaining moment and not to be able to free yourself?

He cannot think of his father who, seventy-six years ago, fixed him for death, which is so frightfully late in coming. But I, I can think about him, and I think about the fact that I am a germ of this man who can no longer move, and that if I am trapped in this time and not in another, I owe it to him!

He's crying, see? He always cries like that . . . and he makes me cry too! Perhaps he wants to be freed. I'll free him some evening together with myself. It's now beginning to get cold. One of these evenings we'll light a little fire . . . If you'd like to join us . . .

No, eh? You're thanking me? Yes, yes, let's go outside, let's go outside, my friend. I can see that you need to see the sun again, on the street.

'La trappola'

First published in the newspaper *Corriere della Sera* in 1912 (23 May). It was later part of the collection *La trappola* (Treves, 1915), in the fourth volume of *Novelle per un anno (L'uomo solo)* (Bemporad, 1922), and in the final edition of *Novelle per un anno* (Mondadori, 1937).

CESARE PAVESE

1908–50

Pavese's version of *Moby Dick*, translated at the age of twenty-three with a rudimentary knowledge of English, has come to be criticized by many for its errors, omissions and liberties. And yet it speaks volumes about Pavese, a tormented genius from Turin who was an obsessive student of the English language and wrote his university thesis on Walt Whitman. His visionary love for American literature, both aesthetically and politically motivated, opened a floodgate, forever altering the course of Italian writing. He spent time interned for anti-Fascist activity in Calabria, a setting for some memorable stories, and upon return to Turin, after the war, became a legendary editor at Einaudi, working alongside Vittorini (they were born in the same year), and mentoring Italo Calvino, whose writing career Pavese essentially launched. He turned to fiction only in the last creative phase of his life; it followed his prodigious activity as translator, poet, critic and editor. Much of his work, occupying sixteen volumes, is autobiographical, and has a primordial underpinning of nature, myth and sacrifice. Like Hemingway, he was a master of the lacuna, the unsaid. And again, like Hemingway, he had an ear for just how people spoke, with a particular penchant for slang. Pavese's stories can be bleak, astringent. The selected story was written in 1936, but not published until after the author's death. The first-person narrator, rueful and self-critical, sheds light on Pavese's perpetually conflicted relationships with women. He set his final novel, *La luna e i falò* (*The Moon and the Bonfires*), published the year he died, partly in America, powerfully evoking the California landscape without having ever gone there. Until 1950, Pavese was a figure both aloof and at the very centre of post-war Italy's literary world. In August of that year, two months after winning the Strega Prize, he killed himself in a hotel room; the note he left asked people to 'not gossip too much'.

Wedding Trip

Translated by A. E. Murch

I.

Now that I, shattered and full of remorse, have learned how foolish it is to reject reality for the sake of idle fancies, how presumptuous to receive when one has nothing to give in return, now – Cilia is dead. Though I am resigned to my present life of drudgery and ignominy, I sometimes think how gladly I would adapt myself to her ways, if only those days could return. But perhaps that is just another of my fancies. I treated Cilia badly when I was young, when nothing should have made me irritable; no doubt I should have gone on ill-treating her, out of bitterness and the disquiet of an unhappy conscience. For instance, I am still not sure after all these years, whether I really loved her. Certainly I mourn for her; I find her in the background of my inmost thoughts; never a day passes in which I do not shrink painfully away from my memories of those two years, and I despise myself because I let her die. I grieve for her youth, even more for my own loneliness, but – and this is what really counts – did I truly love her? Not, at any rate, with the sincere, steady love a man should have for his wife.

The fact is, I owed her too much, and all I gave her in return was a blind suspicion of her motives. As it happens, I am by nature superficial and did not probe more deeply into such dark waters. At the time I was content to treat the matter with my instinctive diffidence and refused to give weight or substance to certain sordid thoughts that, had they taken root in my mind, would have sickened me of the whole affair. However, several times I did ask myself: 'And why did Cilia marry me?' I do not know whether it was due to a sense of my own importance, or to profound ineptitude, but the fact remains that it puzzled me.

There was no doubt that Cilia married me, not I her. Oh! Those depressing evenings I endured in her company – wandering restlessly through the streets, squeezing her arm, pretending to be free and easy, suggesting as a joke that we should jump in the river together. Such ideas didn't bother me – I was used to them – but they upset her, made her anxious to help me; so much so that she offered me, out of her wages as a shop assistant, a little money to live on while I looked for a better job. I did not want money. I told her that to be with her in the evenings was enough for me, as long as she didn't go away and take a job somewhere else. So we drifted along. I began to tell myself, sentimentally, that what I needed was someone nice to live with; I spent too much time roaming the streets; a loving wife would know how to contrive a little home for me, and just by going into it I should be happy again, no matter how weary and miserable the day had made me.

I tried to tell myself that even alone I managed to muddle along quite well, but I knew this was no argument. 'Two people together can help each other,' said Cilia, 'and take care of one another. If they're a little in love, George, that's enough.' I was tired and disheartened, those evenings; Cilia was a dear and very much in earnest, with the fine coat she had made herself and her little broken handbag. Why not give her the joy she wanted? What other girl would suit me better? She knew what it was to work hard and be short of money; she was an orphan, of working-class parents; I was sure that she was more eager and sincere than I.

On impulse I told her that if she would accept me, uncouth and lazy as I was, I would marry her. I felt content, soothed by the warmth of my good deed and proud to discover I had that much courage. I said to Cilia: 'I'll teach you French!' She responded with a smile in her gentle eyes as she clung tightly to my arm.

2.

In those days I thought I was sincere, and once again I explained to Cilia how poor I was. I warned her that I hardly ever had a full day's work and didn't know what it was to get a pay packet. The college where I taught French paid me by the hour. One day I told her that if she wanted to get on in the world she ought to look for some other man. Cilia looked troubled and offered to keep on with her job. 'You know very well that isn't what I want,' I muttered. Having settled things thus, we married.

It made no particular difference to my life. Already, in the past, Cilia had sometimes spent evenings with me in my room. Love-making was no novelty. We took two furnished rooms; the bedroom had a wide, sunny window, and there we placed the little table with my books.

Cilia, though, became a different woman. I, for my part, had been afraid that, once married, she would grow vulgar and slovenly – as I imagined her mother had been – but instead I found her more particular, more considerate towards me. She was always clean and neat, and kept everything in perfect order. Even the simple meals she prepared for me in the kitchen had the cordiality and solace of those hands and that smile. Her smile, especially, was transfigured. It was no longer the half-timid, half-teasing smile of a shop-girl on the spree, but the gentle flowering of an inner joy, utterly content and eager to please, a serene light on her thin young face. I felt a twinge of jealousy at this sign of a happiness I did not always share. 'She's married me and she's enjoying it,' I thought.

Only when I woke up in the morning was my heart at peace. I would turn my head against hers in our warm bed and lie close beside her as she slept (or was pretending to), my breath ruffling her hair. Then Cilia, with a drowsy smile, would put her arms around me. How different from the days when I woke alone, cold and disheartened, to stare at the first gleam of dawn!

Cilia loved me. Once she was out of bed, she found fresh joys in everything she did as she moved around our room, dressing herself, opening the windows, stealing a cautious glance at me. If I settled myself at the little table, she walked quietly so as not to disturb me; if I went out, her eyes followed me to the door; when I came home she sprang up quickly to greet me.

There were days when I did not want to go home at all. It irritated me to think I should inevitably find her there, waiting for me, even though she learned to pretend she took no special interest; I should sit beside her, tell her more or less the same things, or probably nothing at all. We should look at one another with distaste and a smile. It would be the same tomorrow and the next day, and always. Such thoughts entrapped me whenever the day was foggy and the sun looked grey. If, on the other hand, there was a lovely day when the air was clear and the sun blazed down on my head, or a perfume in the wind enfolded and enraptured me, I would linger in the streets, wishing that I still lived alone, free to stroll around till midnight and get a meal of some sort at the pub on the corner of the street. I had always been a lonely man, and it seemed to me to count for a great deal that I was not unfaithful to Cilia.

She, waiting for me at home, began to take in sewing, to earn a little. A neighbour gave her work, a certain Amalia, a woman of thirty or so, who once invited us to dinner. She lived alone in the room below ours, and gradually fell into the habit of bringing the work upstairs to Cilia so that they could pass the afternoon together. Her face was disfigured by a frightful scar – when she was a little girl she had pulled a boiling saucepan down on her head. Her two sorrowful, timid eyes, full of longing, flinched away when anyone looked at her, as if their humility could excuse the distortion of her features. She was a good girl. I remarked to Cilia that Amalia seemed to me like her elder sister. One day, for a joke, I said: 'If I should run away and leave you, one fine day, would you go and live with her?'

'She's had such bad luck all her life. I wouldn't mind if you wanted to make love to her!' Cilia teased me. Amalia called me 'Sir' and was shy in my presence. Cilia thought this was madly funny. I found it rather flattering.

3.

It was a bad thing for me that I regarded my scanty intellectual attainments as a substitute for a regular trade. It lay at the root of so many of my wrong ideas and evil actions. But my education could have proved a good means of communion with Cilia, if only I had been more consistent. Cilia was very quick, anxious to learn everything I knew myself because, loving me so much, she could not bear to feel unworthy of me. She wanted to understand my every thought. And – who knows? – if I could have given her this simple pleasure I might have learned, in the quiet intimacy of our joint occupation, what a fine person she really was, how real and beautiful our life together, and perhaps Cilia would still be alive at my side, with her lovely smile that in two years I froze from her lips.

I started off enthusiastically, as I always do. Cilia's education consisted of a few back numbers of serial novels, the news in the daily papers, and a hard, precocious experience of life itself. What was I to teach her? She very much wanted to learn French and indeed, heaven knows how, she managed to piece together scraps of it by searching through my dictionaries when she was left alone at home. But I aspired to something better than that and wanted to teach her to read properly, to appreciate the finest books. I kept a few of them – my treasures – on the little table. I tried to explain to her the finer points of novels and poems, and Cilia did her best to follow me. No one excels me in recognizing the beauty, the 'rightness' of a thought or a story, and explaining it in glowing terms. I put a great deal of effort into making her feel the freshness of ancient pages, the truth of sentiments expressed long before she and I were born, how varied, how glorious, life had been for so many many men at so many different periods. Cilia would listen with close attention, asking questions that I often found embarrassing. Sometimes as we strolled in the streets or sat eating our supper in silence, she would tell me in her candid voice of certain doubts she had, and once when I replied without conviction or with impatience – I don't remember which – she burst out laughing.

I remember that my first present to her, as her husband, was a book, *The Daughter of the Sea*. I gave it to her a month after our wedding, when we started reading lessons. Until then I had not bought her anything – nothing for the house, no new clothes – because we were too poor. Cilia was delighted and made a new cover for the book, but she never read it.

Now and then, when we had managed to save enough, we went to a cinema, and there Cilia really enjoyed herself. An additional attraction, for her, was that she could snuggle up close to me, and now and then ask me for explanations that she could understand. She never let Amalia come to the cinema with us, though one day the poor girl asked if she could. She explained to me that we got to know each other best of all in a cinema, and in that blessed darkness we had to be alone together.

Amalia came to our place more and more often. This, and my well-deserved disappointments, soon made me first neglect our reading lessons, and finally stop them altogether. Then, if I was in a good mood, I amused myself by joking with the two girls, and Amalia lost a little of her shyness. One evening, as I came home very late from the college with my nerves on edge, she came and stared me full in the face, with a gleam of reproof and suspicion in her timid glance. I felt more disgusted than ever by the frightful scar on her face, and spitefully I tried to make out what her features had been before they were destroyed. I remarked to Cilia, when we were alone, that Amalia, as a child, must have been very like her.

'Poor thing,' said Cilia. 'She spends every penny she earns trying to get cured. She hopes that then she'll find a husband.'

'But don't all women know how to get a husband?'

'I've already found mine,' Cilia smiled.

'Suppose what happened to Amalia had happened to you?' I sneered.

Cilia came close to me. 'Wouldn't you want me any more?'

'No.'

'But what's upset you this evening? Don't you like Amalia to come up here? She gives me work and helps me . . .'

What had got into me – and I couldn't get rid of it – was the thought that Cilia was just another Amalia. I felt disgusted and furious with both of them. My eyes were hard as I stared at Cilia, and the tender look she gave me only made me pity her, irritating me still more. On my way home I had met a husband with two dirty brats clinging round his neck, and behind him a thin worn-out little woman, his wife. I imagined what Cilia would look like when she was old and ugly, and the thought clutched me by the throat.

Outside, the stars were shining. Cilia looked at me in silence. 'I'm going for a walk,' I told her with a bitter smile, and I went out.

4.

I had no friends and I realized, now and then, that Cilia was my whole life. As I walked the streets I thought about us and felt troubled that I did not earn enough to repay her by keeping her in comfort, so that I needn't feel ashamed when I went home. I never wasted a penny – I did not even smoke – and, proud of that, I considered my thoughts were at least my own. But what could I make of those thoughts? On my way home I looked at people and wondered how so many of them had managed to succeed in life. Desperately I longed for changes, for something fresh and exciting.

I used to hang around the railway station, thrilled by the smoke and the bustle. For me, good fortune has always meant adventure in faraway places – a liner crossing the ocean, arrival at some exotic port, the clang of metal, shrill, foreign voices – I dreamt of it all the time. One evening I stopped short, terrified by the sudden realization that if I didn't hurry up and travel somewhere with Cilia while she was still young and in love with me, I should never go at all. A fading wife and a squalling child would, for ever, prevent me. If only we really had money, I thought again. You can do anything with money.

Good fortune must be deserved, I told myself. Shoulder every load that life may bring. I am married but I do not want a child. Is that why I'm so wretched? Should I be luckier if I had a son?

To live always wrapped up in oneself is a depressing thing, because a brain that is habitually secretive does not hesitate to follow incredibly stupid trains of thought that mortify the man who thinks them. This was the only origin of the doubts that plagued me.

Sometimes my longing for faraway places filled my mind even in bed. If, on a still and windless night, I suddenly caught the wild sound of a train whistle in the distance, I would start up from Cilia's side with all my dreams reawakened.

One afternoon, when I was passing the station without even stopping, a face I knew suddenly appeared in front of me and gave a cry of greeting. Malagigi: I hadn't seen him for ten years. We shook hands and stood there exchanging courtesies. He was no longer the ugly, spiteful ink-spotted little devil I knew at school, always playing jokes in the lavatory, but I recognized that grin of his at once. 'Malagigi! Still alive, then?'

'Alive, and a qualified accountant.' His voice had changed. It was a man speaking to me now.

'Are you off somewhere, too?' he asked. 'Guess where I'm going!' As he spoke he picked up a fine leather suitcase that toned perfectly with his smart new raincoat and the elegance of his tie. Gripping my wrist he went on: 'Come to the train with me. I'm going to Genoa.'

'I'm in a hurry.'

'Then I leave for China!'

'No!'

'It's true. Can't a man go to China? What have you got against China? Instead of talking like that, wish me luck! Perhaps I may stay out there.'

'But what's your job?'

'I'm going to China. Come and see me off.'

'No, I really can't spare the time.'

'Then come and have coffee with me, to say goodbye. You're the last man I shall talk to, here.'

We had coffee there in the station, at the counter, while Malagigi, full of excitement, told me in fits and starts all about himself and his prospects. He was not married. He'd fathered a baby, but luckily it died. He had left school after I did, without finishing. He thought of me once, when he had to take an exam a second time. He'd gained his education in the battle of life. Now all the big firms had offered him a job. And he spoke four languages. And they were sending him to China.

I said again that I was in a hurry (though it was not true), and managed to get away from him, feeling crushed and overwhelmed. I reached home still upset by the chance meeting, my thoughts in a turmoil. How could he rise from such a drab boyhood to the audacious height of a future like that? Not that I envied Malagigi, or even liked him; but to see, unexpectedly superimposed on his grey background, which had been mine, too, his present colourful and assured existence, such as I could glimpse only in dreams, was torment to me.

Our room was empty, because now Cilia often went downstairs to work in our neighbour's room. I stayed there a while, brooding in the soft darkness lit only by the little blue glow of the gas jet under the saucepan bubbling gently on the stove.

5.

I passed many evenings thus, alone in the room, waiting for Cilia, pacing up and down or lying on the bed, absorbed in that silent emptiness as the dusk slowly deepened into dark. Subdued or distant noises – the shouts of children, the bustle of the street, the cries of birds – reached me only faintly. Cilia soon realized that I didn't want to be bothered with her when I came home, and she would put her head out of Amalia's room, still sewing, to hear me pass and call to me. I didn't care whether she heard me or not, but if she did I would say something or other. Once I asked

Amalia, quite seriously, why she didn't come up to our room any more, where there was plenty of light. Amalia said nothing; Cilia looked away and her face grew red.

One night, for something to say, I told her about Malagigi and made her laugh gaily at that funny little man. Then I added: 'Fancy him making a fortune and going to China! I wish it had been me!'

'I should like it, too,' Cilia sighed, 'if we went to China.'

I gave a wry grin. 'In a photograph, perhaps, if we sent one to Malagigi.'

'Why not one for ourselves?' she said. 'Oh, George, we haven't ever had a photograph of us together.'

'No money.'

'Do let's have a photograph.'

'But we oughtn't to afford it. We're together day and night, and anyway I don't like photographs.'

'We are married and we have no record of it. Let's have just one!'

I did not reply.

'It wouldn't cost much. I'll pay for it.'

'Get it done with Amalia.'

Next morning Cilia lay with her face to the wall, her hair over her eyes. She would not take any notice of me, or even look at me. I caressed her a little, then realized she was resisting me, so I jumped out of bed in a rage. Cilia got up, too, washed her face and gave me some coffee, her manner quiet and cautious, her eyes downcast. I went away without speaking to her.

An hour later I came back again. 'How much is there in the savings book?' I shouted. Cilia looked at me in surprise. She was sitting on the stool, unhappy and bewildered.

'I don't know. You've got it. About three hundred lire, I think.'

'Nearly three hundred and sixteen. Here it is,' I flung the roll of notes on the table. 'Spend it as you like. Let's have a high old time! It's all yours.'

Cilia stood up and came over to face me. 'Why have you done this, George?'

'Because I'm a fool. Listen! I'd rather not talk about it. When money is in your pocket it doesn't count any more. D'you still want that photograph?'

'But, George, I want you to be happy.'

'I am happy.'

'I do love you so much.'

'I love you, too.' I took her by the arm, sat down, and pulled her on my knee. 'Put your head here, on my shoulder.' My voice was indulgent and intimate. Cilia said nothing and leaned her cheek against mine. 'When shall we go?' I asked.

'It doesn't matter,' she whispered.

'Then listen!' I held the back of her neck and smiled at her. Cilia, still trembling, threw her arms around my shoulders and tried to kiss me.

'Darling!' I said. 'Let's make plans. We have three hundred lire. Let's drop everything and go on a little trip. Quickly! Now! If we think it over we'll change our minds. Don't tell anyone about it, not even Amalia. We'll only be away a day. It will be the honeymoon we didn't have.'

'George, why wouldn't you take me away then? You said it was a silly idea, then.'

'Yes, but this isn't a honeymoon. You see, now we know each other. We're good friends. Nobody knows we're going. And, besides, we need a holiday. Don't you?'

'Of course, George. I'm so happy. Where shall we go?'

'I don't know, but we'll go at once. Would you like us to go to the sea? To Genoa?'

6.

Once we were on the train, I showed a certain preoccupation. As we started, Cilia was almost beside herself with delight, held my hand and tried to make me talk. Then, finding me moody and unresponsive, she quickly understood and settled down quietly, looking out of the window with a happy smile. I remained silent, staring into nothingness, listening to the rhythmic throb of the wheels on the rails as it vibrated through my whole body. There were other people in the carriage, but I scarcely noticed them. Fields and hills were flashing past. Cilia, sitting opposite and leaning on the windowpane, seemed to be listening to something, too, but now and then she glanced swiftly in my direction and tried to smile. So she spied on me, at a distance.

When we arrived it was dark, and at last we found somewhere to stay, in a large, silent hotel, hidden among the trees of a deserted avenue, after going up and down an eternity of tortuous streets, making enquiries. It was a grey, cold night that made me want to stride along with my nose in the air. Instead, Cilia, tired to death, was dragging on my arm and I was only too glad to find somewhere to sit down. We had wandered through so many brightly lit streets, so many dark alleys that brought our hearts into our mouths, but we had never reached the sea. No one took any notice of us. We looked like any couple out for a stroll, except for our tendency to step off the pavements, and Cilia's anxious glances at the houses and passers-by.

That hotel would do for us: nothing elegant about it. A bony young fellow with his sleeves rolled up was eating at a white table. We were received by a tall, fierce-looking woman wearing a coral necklace. I was glad to sit down. Walking with Cilia never left me free to absorb myself in what I saw, or in myself. Preoccupied and ill-at-ease, I nevertheless had to keep her beside me and answer her, at least with gestures. Now, all I wanted – and how I wanted it – was to look around and get to know in my heart of hearts this unknown city. That was precisely why I had come.

We waited downstairs to order supper, without even going upstairs to see our room or discussing terms. I was attracted by that young fellow with his auburn whiskers and his vague, lonely manner. On his forearm was a faded tattoo mark, and as he went away he picked up a patched blue jacket.

It was midnight when we had our supper. At our little table, Cilia laughed a great deal at the disdainful air of the landlady. 'She thinks we're only just married,' she faltered. Then, her weary eyes full of tenderness, she asked me: 'And are we really?' as she stroked my hand.

We enquired about places in the neighbourhood. The harbour was only a hundred yards away, at the end of the avenue. 'Let's go and see it for a minute,' said Cilia. She was fit to drop, but she wanted to take that little walk with me.

We came to the railings of a terrace and caught our breath. The night was calm but dark, and the streetlamps floundered in the cold black abyss that lay before us. I said nothing, and my heart leapt as I breathed the smell of it, wild and free. Cilia looked around her and pointed out to me a line of lights, their reflection quivering in the water. Was it a ship? A breakwater? We could hear waves splashing gently in the darkness. 'Tomorrow,' she breathed ecstatically, 'tomorrow we'll see it all.'

As we made our way back to our hotel, Cilia clung tightly to my side. 'How tired I am! George, it's lovely! Tomorrow! I'm so happy! Are you happy, too?' and she rubbed her cheek against my shoulder.

I did not feel like that. I was walking with clenched jaws, taking deep breaths and letting the wind caress me. I felt restless, remote from Cilia, alone in the world. Halfway up the stairs I said to her: 'I don't want to go to bed yet. You go on up. I'll go for another little stroll and come back.'

7.

That time, too, it was the same. How I hurt Cilia! Even now, when I think of her in bed as dawn is breaking, I am filled with a desolate remorse for the way I treated her.

Yet I couldn't help it! I always did everything like a fool, a man in a dream, and I did not realize the sort of man I was until the end, when even remorse was useless. Now I can glimpse the truth. I become so engrossed in solitude that it deadens all my sense of human relationships and makes me incapable of tolerating or responding to any tenderness. Cilia, for me, was not an obstacle: she simply did not exist. If I had only understood this! If I had had any idea of how much harm I was doing to myself by cutting myself off from her in this way, I should have turned to her with intense gratitude and cherished her presence as my only salvation.

But is the sight of another's suffering ever enough to open a man's eyes? Instead, it takes the sweat of agony, the bitter pain that comes as we awake, lives with us as we walk the streets, lies beside us through sleepless nights, always raw and pitiless, covering us with shame.

Dawn broke wet and cloudy. The avenue was still deserted as I wandered back to the hotel. I saw Cilia and the landlady quarrelling on the stairs, both in their nightclothes. Cilia was crying. The landlady, in a dressing gown, gave a shriek as I went in. Cilia stood motionless, leaning on the handrail. Her face was white with shock, her hair and her clothes in wild disorder.

'Here he is!'

'Whatever's going on here, at this time in the morning?' I asked harshly.

The landlady, clutching her bosom, started shouting that she had been disturbed in the middle of the night because of a missing husband; there had been tears, handkerchiefs ripped to shreds, telephone calls, police enquiries. Was that the way to behave? Where did I come from?

I was so weary I could hardly stand. I gave her a listless glance of disgust. Cilia had not moved. She stood there breathing deeply through her open mouth, her face red and distorted. 'Cilia,' I cried, 'haven't you been to sleep?'

She still did not reply. She just stood there, motionless, making no attempt to wipe away the tears that streamed from her eyes. Her hands were clasped at her waist, tearing at her handkerchief.

'I went for a walk,' I said in a hollow voice. 'I stopped by the harbour.' The landlady seemed about to interrupt me, then shrugged her shoulders. 'Anyway, I'm alive, and dying for the want of sleep. Let me throw myself on the bed.'

I slept until two, heavily as a drunkard, then I awoke with a start. The light in the room was dim, but I could hear noises in the street. Instinctively I did not move. Cilia was there, sitting in a corner, looking at me, staring at the walls, examining her fingers, jumping up now and then. After a while I whispered cautiously: 'Cilia, are you watching me?' Swiftly she raised her eyes. The shattered look I had seen earlier now seemed engraved on her face. She moved her lips to speak, but no sound came.

'Cilia, a husband shouldn't be watched,' I said in a playful voice like a child's. 'Have you had anything to eat today?' The poor girl shook her head. I jumped out of bed and looked at the clock. 'The train goes at half past three,' I cried. 'Come on, Cilia, hurry! Let's try to look happy in front of the landlady.' She did not move, so I went over and pulled her up by her cheeks.

'Listen,' I went on. 'Is it because of last night?' Her eyes filled with tears. 'I could have lied, said I had got lost, smoothed things over. I didn't do that, because I hate lies. Cheer up! I have always liked to be alone. Still, even I,' and I felt her give a start, 'even I haven't enjoyed myself much at Genoa. Yet I'm not crying.'

'Viaggio di nozze'

This story was written between 24 November and 6 December 1936. It was first published shortly after Pavese's death, in the magazine *Comunità* (IV, no. 9, September–October 1950) and then included in the collection *Notte di festa* (Einaudi, 1953).

GOFFREDO PARISE
1929–86

'Melancholy' is part of Parise's *Sillabari*, an ingenious work of literature consisting of fifty-four relatively brief, essential stories, grouped according to the letters of the alphabet and dedicated to a single emotion (a *sillabario* is the Italian word for a child's spelling book, one of the first things that teaches us to read and write). The result is an artful glossary of the human heart. We begin with the letter A, for *amore* (love), and end with S, *solitudine* (solitude). Parise finished before getting to Z, explaining that he ended, in spite of his original intentions, where 'the poetry abandoned him'.[1] The writer Giuseppe Montesano compared the *Sillabari* to the work of Robert Walser and Truman Capote, and the critic Cesare Garboli called them 'virtual novels'. Indeed, each contains a universe, suggestive of much larger dimensions, yet each is a marvel of concision that, like Johann Sebastian Bach's *Goldberg Variations*, constitutes a series of interlocking yet autonomous texts, orderly yet emotionally anarchic. Parise worked as a journalist and screenwriter and also wrote several novels, but the *Sillabari* (there were originally two volumes, *Sillabario n. 1* and *Sillabario n. 2*, published in 1972 and 1982, and published, respectively, in English, as *Abecedary* and *Solitudes*) are considered his finest achievement. He received the Strega Prize for the second volume. In a letter from that period, he writes about striving to achieve 'a sort of limbo, a light and suffused exaltation in which, all told, you like life and at the same time feel nostalgic about it'. The structure of Parise's sentences – fluid, multi-faceted, associative – have a characteristic looseness that permits one thought to always make room for another, infusing this story with profound ambivalence. Parise, an illegitimate child, never knew his father, and was the long-time companion of the painter Giosetta Fioroni, celebrated for her pop-art portraits of women.

Melancholy

Translated by Jhumpa Lahiri

Every day that cool and distant summer, the children of the Bedin-Alighieri Colony, a camp for the poor managed by the equally poor Sisters of Saint Dorothy, were woken up bright and early and taken immediately on to the meadows or into the pine grove at the crest of the hill. Two young nuns watched over them, dressed all in white for summer instead of the black habit and bonnet; they too were quite young, and nearly as small as the children. There were boys and girls, and among the girls was a 'guest' named Silvia, referred to as a 'guest' because she was the granddaughter of one of the founders, a Socialist who was hardly poor.

This is why Silvia – unlike everyone else, who wore the grey, collarless smock the camp required, made from cheap cotton – was able to choose, from her little trunk, her normal clothes every day: the shoes she always wore (and not the red rubber sandals that were part of the uniform), and even her own dolls or toys that she'd brought from home. She slept, however, in the dormitory with all the other girls, and so the rest of Silvia's day was just like the others': the same small breakfast, same lunch, same snack in the afternoon, same dinner. Even the white enamelled bed and the coarse sheets with thick stitching down the middle were the same as everyone else's.

It was the first time Silvia was among other children in a camp and not alone, as usual, with her grandfather and the maid with whom she lived year round. Her grandfather had brought her there on the crossbar of his bike, which had a seat just for her. He was dressed, as always, in black: a black alpaca cape, floppy bow tie, big black hat and tall boots, also black, made of goatskin, with buttons up the side. He had entrusted her to the nuns, who seemed quite happy to receive her, treating her like a special guest.

The great discovery for Silvia during her stay at the camp were the smells: she could clearly detect, in the meadows, the smells of various herbs and plants, without knowing the names of one from the other: wild mint, sage, rosemary or else simple weeds, dandelion or fern or crab grass or other weeds that stank instead, which the boys stuck under her nose on purpose. The grove of fir and larch trees at the crest of the hill, where they went in the afternoons, contained other, entirely different smells: pine cones, pine nuts, pine needles and certain bell-shaped berries that Silvia called 'The Dead', much to the children's delight.

Even the insects had a distinct smell: the grasshoppers Silvia expertly caught smelled of verbena, while certain bugs or stag beetles smelled of celluloid, or emanated this scent once trapped in little cages that one of the nuns had taught them to make from strands of grass. One of Silvia's favourites was the smell of her bed and of the sheets that saturated the whole dormitory: it smelled like a thunderstorm, and mixed up with it at times was a faint smell of baby sweat and pee that she liked a great deal.

Silvia thought of her grandfather now and then, but in a fleeting way, and she didn't think she missed him. She thought of him in the late afternoons right after dinner, after the rosary in the small chapel when, still seated outside on the grass, she looked and, most of all, listened to the swallows who cried and flew quite low over their heads and over the camp while the oldest of the children sounded the bell. At dusk the swallows stood out sharply against the sky which was pale purple and yellow on the horizon, while a faint smell of incense emerged from the chapel door, and this, together with the damp smell that rose from the fields of tall grass just at the base of the chapel, aroused in Silvia an emotion she'd never felt and didn't know what to call. And it was clear that this emotion, aroused by those smells rendered chilly at dusk, closed up her throat and made her want to cry.

Silvia asked a nun if she could dress like all the others: in the grey canvas smock and red rubber sandals. But the nun, to Silvia's astonishment, said No.

'Did somebody say something to you about your clothes or your toys?' the Mother Superior asked her. 'Did they tease you, or scold you?' Silvia said No. No one had said a thing, but without knowing how to explain it to the nun (she was only seven years old), Silvia felt estranged from the

others, and in some sense she was ashamed of her dolls and toys as well
as her clothes: in fact, she let the others take her toys, she didn't care about
them. Silvia felt estranged: but this didn't mean that the other children
treated her differently or excluded her from their games. No, on the contrary, she was always invited or coaxed or urged to do something, to play
some role, even an important one, in their games and in building their
little huts. Silvia didn't feel estranged on account of her family – maybe
precisely because, apart from her grandfather, she had no family – but on
account of her birth. The other children were utterly amazed to hear this
and, instead of considering her different, as she thought they would, they
were filled with curiosity and questions that Silvia couldn't answer.

No, she had never met her father; her mother, maybe; she remembered,
thanks to certain minor details, certain gifts, a young woman who must
have been her mother: a little gold chain with a coral pendant, a young
woman with blonde hair she'd seen two or three times. No brothers or
sisters. At that point in the questioning, however, she spoke at length and
with enthusiasm about her grandfather, whom all the other children had
seen, since he had inspected the whole camp on the day of their arrival.
They knew he was one of the founders.

'Is your grandfather rich?' one of the kids asked. He was the oldest one
in the colony, a veteran who had been coming for a few years, and had
scaly skin that smelled like fish and eggs.

'I don't know,' Silvia replied.

'But what does he do?'

'He owns a bicycle factory.'

'That means he's rich,' the boys and girls all said at the same time.
'That's why you have nicer clothes than we do.'

Silvia didn't like having a rich grandfather, or being better dressed than
them. Not because the other children were poor, much poorer than she
was, or because her grandfather's presumed wealth or her different clothes
made her an object of curiosity and questions, but because she felt estranged.
And she mainly felt estranged because of her great sensitivity to smells
which, furthermore, stirred up great excitement among the other children,
who stuck weeds under her nose, a bay leaf, a butterfly, and she, blind-
folded, could recognize everything, never once making a mistake. But she
also felt estranged for another reason, and this reason, which was closely

connected to her sensitivity to smells, was that twilight feeling, only now she felt it at other times, even during the day, and at night. She could only describe the feeling by saying to herself, 'I feel like crying.'

August arrived, and the 'I feel like crying' feeling got stronger, for some reasons that were quite clear and others that accumulated with the passing of days; in fact the smells had turned slightly colder, different from before. In some sense they were changing: maybe the sun warmed things less, and besides, it seemed to her that the cicadas and crickets no longer chirped as much. This evolution in the quality and substance of the smells and in the timbre of sounds and murmurs was more pronounced and perceptible at dusk, always at the same time, after the brief service in the chapel, and at that hour even the colours in the sky were no longer the same. For a few days Silvia was allowed to wear the clothes and sandals the others did, but – and this was something she would never have expected – her sense of estrangement grew. Dressed like the others, she felt even more different, and the 'crying' feeling increased. She went back to her own clothes. One day a thunderstorm turned the camp cold, then the sun returned, but it only occasionally poked through quickly moving clouds, grey and pink and beige. In those days of fluctuating weather Silvia wanted to cry very much and sometimes she went to cry in the lavatory.

Photos were taken of the group: Silvia dressed in her clothes, her eyes hidden behind her bushy red hair, in the middle of all the others who were dressed the same way. The nuns explained that souvenir pictures were taken every year and Silvia asked to see the ones from previous years. The Mother Superior took her into her office, where other pictures like the one they'd just taken were hanging on the wall: she saw a group of boys and girls wearing the camp uniform, with the same nuns, against the same background. A few of the same children were in the camp that year too.

'And the others?' Silvia asked the Mother Superior.

'The others have grown up,' the Mother Superior said. 'They don't come to the camp any more.'

Even this response, and those photos, each the same as the others, also the same as the one that they'd taken a few days before in the same corner of the big square under the flagpole, plunged Silvia into that 'crying' mood, which got worse day by day, so much so that Silvia had to go and cry in the lavatory. It was a moment; then it passed.

August came to an end, and her grandfather came to get her. The children wanted to see him and clung to his trousers as he passed out sweets to everyone. Silvia's suitcase was packed and they said goodbye to the Mother Superior in her office, along with all the other nuns. Naturally her grandfather asked the nuns how Silvia had liked her summer, and how she'd behaved.

'I'd say she liked it very much, am I right?' the Mother Superior asked, looking over at Silvia.

'Oh yes, very much,' Silvia replied.

'Are you sad to go back home?' her grandfather asked.

Silvia said No. She listened to what the nun and her grandfather were saying, and the Mother Superior, speaking of Silvia's character, said a word Silvia didn't understand: she said that she was a very good girl, very bright, and said many other kind things among which was the word melancholy, melancholic.

Silvia didn't say anything, but a little later, as her grandfather was pushing his bicycle towards the big gate next to the pine grove, between two high mossy walls, she asked him what melancholy meant.

Her grandfather stopped to catch his breath (he was a bit winded) and waited before answering. Then he looked up at the sky here and there.

'Melancholy? Let's see now . . .' and then paused at length.

'The passage of time causes melancholy,' he said. 'Why? Did you feel melancholic?'

Silvia hopped on to her seat on the crossbar. Now they were going downhill.

'Sometimes,' she replied.

'Malinconia'

First published as part of a series in *Corriere della Sera* (23 July 1978). It was later included in *Sillabario no. 2* (Mondadori, 1982), republished along with *Sillabario no. 1* under the title *Sillabari* (Mondadori, 1984, then Adelphi, 2004).

ALDO PALAZZESCHI

1885–1974

The Futurist movement, founded by the poet F. T. Marinetti in 1909, sought to break with the past by dismantling syntax, grammar and punctuation and by setting words free. It embraced speed, immediacy, a spirit of aggression, military strength and war. It was thus bound up with the Fascist vision also gathering force in those years; the two movements, one cultural, the other political, were to be strange bedfellows. Palazzeschi, born Aldo Giurlani in Florence, adopted his grandmother's surname, began publishing in Marinetti's magazine, *Poesia*, and went on to become one of Futurism's foremost literary protagonists. But he subsequently broke with that movement and all others; during his long and prolific writing life, he avoided any one style or trend. His earliest poetry was considered '*crepuscolare*' (derived from the word '*crepusculo*', which means 'sunset' in Italian) – a poetic school in turn-of-the-century Italy that celebrated free verse and eschewed sentimentality. Palazzeschi embraced freedom and avoided sentimentality in all his work, which consists of two stylistically distant poles, shifting from poetry to prose, from avant-garde writing to more traditional narrative forms, though always steeped in ambiguity and enigma. He divided his time between two cities, shuttling for decades between Venice and Rome. Always contradicting himself, Palazzeschi, whose homosexuality was an open secret, maintained a playful distance even from himself; in his poem '*Chi sono?*' ('Who am I?') he describes himself as '*il saltimbanco dell'anima mia*' ('the acrobat of my soul'). He wrote shrewdly about isolated figures – often widows, bachelors and spinsters – perhaps most memorably in *Sorelle Materassi* (*The Sisters Materassi*), published in 1934 but significantly revised and re-released, in its definitive version, in 1960. This story, from his later phase, is novelistic in scope, with the theme of communication – or rather, the emphatic lack of it – at its centre. It is the tale of an unconventional coupling that transmits, elegantly and harrowingly, an ineluctable state of solitude.

Silence

Translated by Erica Segre and Simon Carnell

Benedetto Vai, who for more than twenty years had been living with his housekeeper, Leonia, was reputed to be a man of many faults and of unsound mind: selfish, lazy, stingy, arrogant; prone to mischief and eccentric to the nth degree: unique. In reality he had only one defect: he was misanthropic and in full possession of his mental faculties. Instead of trying to mitigate, or at least to conceal his supposed shortcoming, as is usual in such cases, he had chosen to bravely embrace it – and to do so, perhaps, with a pleasure as acute as his blameworthiness was deep, pushing him to the most extreme of consequences as if it were the achievement of an ideal, or the fulfilment of a dream. Following a long and arduous process, an immeasurably harsh one requiring constant, lifelong effort, he had managed to establish complete silence in his home, and while outside it to utter never a word to anyone.

It is worth emphasizing the fact that Benedetto Vai, who was well-to-do by birth, lived with Leonia: it would have been impossible for him to cope with the practicalities of everyday life by himself.

The situation had reached such a point that if a word, or even a syllable, had escaped unwittingly or by mistake in Benedetto Vai's home, it would have been tantamount to an apocalyptic event: the end of an epoch, the collapse of an entire world.

Outside of his domestic shell, Benedetto Vai adopted such extreme reserve that no one would have dared to approach him with a greeting, or any other word for that matter; and if on occasion some inconsiderate or ignorant soul did so, he would squeeze his lips together and widen his large blue eyes to fix the culprit with such a look as to induce them to lower their gaze and seal their lips. And if by chance anyone should happen to ask him for directions in the street, they would surely conclude that they had spoken to a deaf person.

Leonia, too, would play her part. If someone stopped and looked as if he was about to say something, she would raise an index finger in a solemn gesture and place it over her lips, like a bar across her mouth and face.

Nor should we assume that she had ended up going to such lengths easily, though we choose not to pursue here the intimate reasons behind her willing acceptance of what, for a woman, was a most inhuman sacrifice. She had met her master when he was young and handsome. And Benedetto Vai had been an exceptionally handsome young man, with his blond hair and big eyes that seemed to mirror the sky. Now he was a distinguished elderly gent: tall, slim, with an athletic, straight-backed body and eyes that were still like those of a child. She was unacquainted with any echo of the voice he had kept locked within himself, and his irascibility had fascinated her from the start. To have followed him to the very limit of his desperate plan was an act of extraordinary devotion to duty – as well as, subconsciously, an act of passionate love.

On one occasion, to force him to speak, she had added four times the usual amount of salt to his soup. As soon as he raised the spoon to his lips, he returned the bowl to her with such a heartfelt look that she bitterly regretted what she'd done. Another time, to force him to utter something – even a scream – she had stuck a needle in the seat of his chair. Once again the look that the master gave – so pure and doleful, though not on account of being pricked by a needle – caused her to lower her head, full of shame and remorse, to plead for his forgiveness. He seemed to understand the harshness of the trial this woman was being subjected to; he showed that he understood her and pitied her, and was on hand to support her through moments of weakness or doubt. Many were the times when, subjected to temptations like those which saints must endure, she was on the verge of breaking the spell; of giving, after so much constraint, free rein to a torrent of shouting, laughing and singing. She remembered an old rhyming proverb that fitted her case exactly, and would have justified such behaviour to the entire neighbourhood. Yet she was pleased, afterwards, to have conquered the urge. If it had been a woman demanding such a sacrifice from her, however, it was clear that Leonia's tongue would have worked like a windmill, like the propeller of a plane.

For her master, on the other hand, that absolute dedication represented indispensable control over the only person in the world that he needed.

Leonia too had been a beauty in her day: age had given her a matronly air, and silence had had no effect other than to fill her out, to make her look solemn and somewhat mysterious. And so it was that the two silent ones enjoyed excellent health, and appeared to be thriving and satisfied with their lot.

The concierge of their building would limit himself to remarking that each of the occupants of apartment number seven was no less cracked than the other. The one who couldn't seem to get over their behaviour was his wife, poor thing: never in a thousand years could she have been persuaded that a phenomenon such as this was acceptable. 'The Lord gave us the gift of speech,' she would always repeat: 'Why refuse it?' She was speaking as one who honoured this divine gift to the full. And the other residents, on encountering the silent ones, would turn their heads and scrutinize them from head to foot, in an eloquent mutism of their own.

There had been certain panic-inducing occurrences in the apartment building: a small fire that had been brought quickly under control, a theft, or rather two; gas leaks, and a flood caused by a burst water pipe – together with instances of more serious, collective panic. It had been impossible by any means to gain access to that apartment, or in any way to persuade its residents to come out of it. In addition to the standard lock, Benedetto Vai's door was reinforced by another with twelve pins, a chain and three enormous bolts – and further defended by two buttresses that made it as solid as the wall in which it was set.

There was something heroic as well as ascetic in this bizarre hermeticism.

If we were to trace back to his birth all that a man's character has become, we would have in Benedetto Vai's case to say immediately that he was an excessively tranquil and smiling child. And we have a more telling clue: he was inclined, from infancy, to substitute words with a smile: a smile that with age had become extinguished from his lips, but which had seemed so sweet and gentle as to signify to others an eloquent contentment, and to provide its wearer with an infallible means of isolating himself.

In the vastness and depths of life one is sometimes compelled to follow a strange turning, as when a masterpiece is revealed and shaped.

He tended not to speak with his father, but rather more with his mother, whose only son was the source of all of her joy and happiness. 'My darling Betto,' she would say, with infinite tenderness: 'my golden-haired Bettino, my golden boy'.

At school his taciturn character had become more pronounced. He would often resort to a companion to distance himself from and ward off the others en masse, at the same time maintaining extremely cold relations with him, and a sense of mystery to his own smiling appearance, so as not to prompt or encourage any of that spontaneous intimacy or friendship which in the ardour of youth often wells up and escapes unchecked. In the end he managed to alienate every single one of them.

He loathed the poetic, the literary, the picturesque, the fantastic. He could recite dates in history with impressive promptness and accuracy, and reduce the essence of facts to a few words. His manner when uttering them suggested that they were still too many. And he would pen certain compositions that seemed designed to be sent by telegram. Adjectives were completely excluded from his vocabulary, and verbs in the infinitive used as much as possible. The professor of rhetoric felt at a loss before him. To throw away so much God-given grace, and to reduce to capsules what for him represented the light, the splendour, the greatness and the richness of the universe . . . The topic would be developed, albeit with a disdainful aridity, and just so that it would pass, his work would be awarded a chronic mark of 'Six'.

In the exact sciences Benedetto Vai was a prodigy. The maths teacher would remain perplexed by the ability and rapidity with which his young pupil could solve the most difficult problems. And his classmates would crane their necks for a glimpse of his open exercise book, rest their chin on his shoulder from behind when passing, or, hoping for some shaft of illumination when in trouble, would wink at him from across the class-room. At such times he would let his smile spread to hide the disappointment that such antics provoked in him, becoming as mute as a fish to discourage them from trying to use him in this way. They were all intimidated by him, and yet at the same time attracted.

His father determined to make an electrical engineer of him, but as soon as he had obtained his degree, with top marks, there was no more talk of engineering in the Vai household.

As a young man Benedetto Vai was in possession of a rather crude, forceful and domineering virility: but he looked for the kind of love that completely excludes an entrancing prelude of any kind, or any trembling and corroborating comment at the point of action, woven from sweet nothings but nevertheless so expressive. It is hardly surprising that liaisons such as these survived in his memory as little more than statistics.

As the years passed he began to withdraw from his family, and when relatives, acquaintances or friends showed up he was increasingly less visible. 'Bettino is out with a friend . . .' his mother would mutter, uncertainly. But which one? He didn't have any. Or she would say, with little conviction: 'He's in his room: his poor head was hurting a little.' This was an affliction unknown to Bettino. 'My Bettino is a bit of a hermit, and a bit of a mole,' she added, laughing, 'and he's getting worse, he runs away the moment he catches sight of anyone.' And gradually she managed to avoid the subject, allowing Bettino, now a fully grown man, to exercise his right not to be seen at all by anyone.

The death of the mother ushered in a fatal cooling of the atmosphere in the Vai family home, due to which our hero's nature underwent a very marked development. For five years, father and son sat facing each other without moving. The father had become taciturn due to the void, impossible to fill, that had been created within himself by the death of his companion, and taking advantage of this sorry state of affairs, Bettino had been able to indulge his temperament without encountering the slightest obstacle. Eventually all conversation between father and son was reduced to 'Goodnight' and 'Good morning'. And the ever-faithful Leonia would only intervene for those daily practicalities of everyday living which required the eternal recourse to a 'Yes' or a 'No', within a household where everything functioned with the regularity and monotony of clockwork.

When his father died, Benedetto Vai, already fifty years old, was momentarily overcome with emotion that touched him to the very depths of his soul: with emotion and grandeur the moment the old man, with a strength unexpected in a dying person, grabbed his son's wrist before breathing his last. And he felt, after that brief, fleeting moment, as if his whole being were slipping free from a bond: after that last squeeze of the hand he alone was responsible for his own actions and for himself, as if it was only then that he had actually become a grown man.

For over twenty years the house of Benedetto Vai dwelt in the silence he had imposed on it as if fulfilling a most exacting duty.

He had ended up living in one spacious room, where he had his childhood bed, a chest of drawers, a cupboard and, in the middle of it, a large round table. Three times a day Leonia would serve his meals on it, and on that table every Monday the master would leave her the money for the weekly shopping, almost as if a little angel had conveniently deposited it there during the night. Leonia had to manage this money with all the cunning and resourcefulness of her station, since it was impossible for her to ask for any additional amount. Sometimes the master would attempt to leave a little less on the table, but fearing that this might give the woman occasion to open her mouth, the next time he would end up leaving a little more.

If in that house, where an old gentleman lived with his equally elderly housekeeper, there had occurred between yawns the usual discussions relating to everyday life; the endless chatter and the most conventional, inevitable squabbling over every domestic chore, the unseasonable weather and the shopping bills, the increases in the price of milk, vegetables and pasta; the gossip of the concierge about petty news of the neighbourhood that was as old as the hills, subjects of a stagnant life that was absurdly vacuous, entirely vegetative and insulated against the slightest vibration or shock – then the house would have seemed cold and empty. Instead it was full, brimming, swollen, at boiling point with that silence, like a boiler threatening daily to explode. There was not a moment in the day when silence did not fill the place entirely; there was not a single nook or cranny that the silence had not filled with the imposing solemnity of its presence.

The Vai family linen was dwindling by the day; Leonia had to repair the repairs, to patch and to sew, to make do and mend in order to prolong its life. Even the undergarments of the master, along with the rest of his wardrobe, were only kept going by this woman's incessant ministrations, allowing him to cut a still respectable figure in public.

The family tableware had also gradually diminished: plates, trays, glasses, jugs . . . In the course of many years, as a result of moments of distraction or carelessness, the inevitable breakages had occurred, no matter how vigilant Leonia had tried to be. Now she was left with just a single bowl for herself: one which she had to use for everything, from soup to fruit. As for the master, he had two plates and a bowl at his disposal.

Leonia was frequently obliged to wash one of these items during the course of a meal. There was a single glass: the very last, so she drank straight from the bottle. She feared for that glass more than anything: it was the source of an anxiety that disturbed her sleep. One night she dreamt that she had broken it, that it had slipped from her grasp, that the last glass of the Vai household had shattered into pieces – and woke with a start, thanking the Lord that it was only a dream. And a few days later, as luck would have it, the glass really had fallen on to the floor, without breaking or receiving a single scratch. Divine providence had intervened, surely it was on her side: there could be no doubt about it. Leonia silently recited a prayer, and considered the fall of the glass to be both a miraculous event and a warning from on high.

Then something extraordinary and unexpected happened.

Arriving home one lunchtime after a morning walk, Benedetto Vai appeared with an enormous bundle under his arm and deposited it with great care on the table in his room.

At this unprecedented, astonishing sight, Leonia gave a start.

For over twenty years the master had not once returned home with something in his hands. What on earth could the package contain? What was the meaning of an event such as this?

Having removed his hat and coat, Benedetto Vai devoted himself, beneath her gaze, to unfurling the bundle with the most extreme care. It contained twelve exquisitely beautiful antique glasses of remarkable thinness. They were engraved with hunting motifs, encircled and interwoven with infinitely graceful, delicate garlands of flowers and fronds, and were the product of sophisticated eighteenth-century Venetian craftsmanship.

What could such an acquisition mean? With whom had he negotiated their purchase? Where had he got them from? Who was going to use these twelve glasses? The silent one had evidently decided to open his mouth, and the spell was broken. And was he now on the verge of deciding to open up the house to someone else? To shatter the tragic solitude and the silence? Would the superhuman effort that the sacrifice had cost end up in nothing but a clinking of glasses? Perhaps even an extremely vulgar affair. Twenty years of silence would have been concluded with a bit of rowdiness: with a bit of merry-making. A real drinking session, perhaps, with some of those present ending up under the table. The woman felt like she was falling into a void. She felt tricked, deeply violated. And for the first time she felt like the victim of a madman. It had not been a deep-seated necessity arising from his nature and spirit that had led him to such extremes after all, but an intriguing experience, the caprice of a lazy man, a game conjured up by an empty mind, a joke in very bad taste. Who would turn up for a drink at the house of a misanthropist? And who, anyway, would someone like him have invited?

Having looked for a good while at the incomparably beautiful glasses, with an admiration and gratification that appeared to be inexhaustible and which provoked in the mind of the woman an unbearable anguish, Benedetto Vai began to dedicate himself to emptying his cupboard of the thousands of useless things that had accumulated there. He threw everything away with disdain, and after having dusted the shelves he arranged the glasses in a row on the topmost one, deriving great joy from the sight of them, looking and looking again at them once they were inside, as if he were reluctant to lose sight of them by closing the cupboard door. And he would carry one with him to the window so as to examine it against the light, to savour the fragility of its material, its ingenious design, the exquisite workmanship. They really were exceptionally beautiful: execution, form and material coming together in a harmonious and perfect whole.

Glowering like a beast about to pounce on its prey, while he delighted in admiring his glasses, Leonia paced around him.

Some time later, at the same hour, Benedetto Vai arrived home with a second bundle, this time an extremely heavy one which he also placed, as was his habit, on the table in the bedroom.

When he began to unwrap it, it revealed twelve antique plates of a most prestigious make, magnificently gilded, with stunning hand-painted miniature flowers. He could not get enough of looking at them, of placing them in every possible light and in every possible position so as to be able to enjoy them to the full.

So the drinking was going to be accompanied by something solid – drink naturally goes with something to nibble on – a dessert probably, those plates undoubtedly suggested nothing less than a full entertainment. The arrival of a third package, a few days later, caused the woman to be even more taken aback. Was he hosting a lunch? The new dinner plates were splendid, the quality of the painting and gilding seemed exceptional.

A lunch for whom? She wanted to look into the faces of those who would come to eat in a house where for twenty years an iron rule of silence had reigned. Leonia continued to glower, and became ever more sullen. The matter could not end there. At the right moment she too would open the floodgates, to make up for having stayed silent for so long. The neighbours had been right all along, and if everyone said so it had to be true: the master she had so recklessly loved, and followed blindly in every respect, was nothing other than a madman, a mental case fit for an asylum who just happened to be living in normal society.

The master brought still more packages to the house. Twelve small glasses no less elegant than the others, engraved with images of flying doves. How delightful, what miraculous craftsmanship: prodigious; a dream.

Nowadays the master did nothing else during the day but open and close his cupboard in order to admire, dust and rearrange to their advantage the extraordinarily beautiful objects that could be found inside: to accord each one an appropriate place, always more apposite, so as to facilitate and reduce the risk of removing and returning them.

The mockery was becoming brutal. Leonia felt that she was being ignominiously mocked, with utter impunity. When would the great day arrive? She was out of practice as a cook, having been reduced to repeating the same old dishes year in, year out, with the accuracy of a chronometer. She felt out of sorts, offended and worried at the same time.

More plates, and more glasses were brought to the house by the master: two large silver-handled carafes engraved with foxes, a little jug of eccentric design, a baroque soup tureen, a small vegetable dish and a pale-violet sauce boat in the shape of a tulip. It was immediately obvious that the master harboured a particular weakness for this trinket; a predilection, a favouritism, a genuine tenderness: holding it gently on his fingers he seemed as if he wished to play with it; bringing it close to his face he seemed inclined to kiss it, or even to eat it, he liked it that much. One day he seemed about to drop it, but with an agile twisting of his whole body managed at the last moment to catch it again. If only it *had* fallen: what joy! To see it shatter into smithereens: what satisfaction – what happiness! She would never agree to serve mayonnaise in a tulip.

The pleasure of taking these objects in and out of the cupboard seemed to exude from this man's every pore.

And some time later he brought home a box so heavy that he came in panting, bathed in sweat, exhausted. Leonia did not rush to help him.

The box contained a gilded silver cutlery service fit for a prince. Followed by a tablecloth as fine as butterfly wings, and twelve dainty napkins of cloth so thin and delicate they seemed to have been cut from the air itself: in his hands they seemed on the point of floating away, and were covered with posies of flowers so delicate in colour and design that they regaled the eye with all the freshness and vitality of a garden. And then, with a final flourish, a great bunch of roses made in mother-of-pearl and another in silver, obviously intended to complete a sumptuous table for a feast.

The cupboard was completely full. Benedetto Vai was constantly coming and going, opening and closing it, in order to arrange, dust and admire each object, with an insatiable pleasure and exacting touch. Every so often he would extract one to admire it particularly and comprehensively. He would carry the piece to the window, only deciding with tiresome slowness to return it to its place again.

Leonia watched him with a look that seemed to be getting more rebellious by the day. She would track him with the suspicious glare of a wild animal, and circle around him.

Benedetto Vai, who throughout his long existence had enjoyed exceptionally robust health, began to feel unwell. He had retained the physique and complexion of his youth, but succumbed now to an unforeseen and sudden collapse.

Leonia cared for him assiduously, lovingly, with complete dedication, and when he became confined to his bed she never left his side: at night she would stretch out beside him on an improvised cot placed close to his. She would prepare certain delicious drinks with which to refresh him, and concoct purees that were both nutritious and delectable.

The doctor came, and respecting the rules of the house expressed his verdict with a mere shrug of his shoulders, as if to say: 'When you're old there's nothing left to do but to die.' The priest came too, and with a supplicant's invocation before the speechless patient, spread his arms towards the heavens: 'The Lord will forgive. His quarrel was not with God, but with the world.'

In May, during a lukewarm sunset, the sun's rays gradually invaded the room, during this period finding their way in every evening, as if bringing a greeting.

Benedetto Vai had had a restless night, and his agitation had grown throughout the day. He was overcome by a sense of disquiet that he was only able to rein in through a superhuman effort of will: through a real and genuine act of heroism. His mind was still lucid, his will still his own. Only certain involuntary movements of his head betrayed the presence of his illness. Leonia would arrange the pillows under his head, clasp his hands, moisten his lips, wipe the sweat from his brow. In the face of the old man, pinched with suffering, the big blue eyes still gave to him a semblance of vitality and innocence. Those lovely eyes were even larger than usual, and his shipwrecked gaze drifted about the room constantly, searching for a point of reference he could not manage to locate. Leonia's eyes were also beautiful, brimming with passion and sorrow, following the unmoored glances of her master. Then one day it was as if lightning had struck. She suddenly jumped up, as one does when remembering something important that has been overlooked. She rushed to the cupboard and flung it open. She brought out the tablecloth and carefully spread it over the round table that stood in the centre of the room. She took out twelve plates and arranged them around it in perfect order. The glasses followed. This corpulent woman now moved quickly and athletically, from the table to the cupboard, from the cupboard to the table, as if in setting it she had transcended her body and become weightless.

Benedetto Vai watched her avidly, fixing his gaze on her with all his remaining strength, his whole life concentrated into that point, into staring at the woman as she worked. And every so often he would glance fleetingly at the door. His blue eyes were still large and clear, like those of a boy's.

Next to the plates, between the plates and the glasses, Leonia precisely arranged the elegant gilt cutlery; calmly, serenely – and continued to move around that table lightly, with expansive gestures, almost as if in setting it she was performing a choreographed dance. In the middle of the table she created a large bushy display with the mother-of-pearl and silver roses, and ran through the shuttered, deserted house looking for twelve chairs. As soon as her task had been completed she stood back to admire her handiwork, and smiled with her entire being.

The sun, which had invaded the room at dusk, rendered the princely table even more resplendent, glittering in its violet light.

The master looked at Leonia, who was staring tenaciously at the table, and every so often he would become distracted and glance in the direction of the door instead.

Someone came in as lightly as mist, and so white as to be indistinguishable from the air. Only Benedetto Vai was able to make out the pale apparition that advanced from the door to the festively laid table which was being fixed for all eternity in those wide blue eyes.

'Silenzio'
First published in the weekly magazine *L'Europeo* (IV, no. 51, 19 December 1948). Later included in *Tutte le novelle* (Mondadori, 1957).

ANNA MARIA ORTESE
1914–98

Ortese, who had little more than an elementary school education, was born to a poor family in Rome, spent three years in Libya as a child, and based herself, at eighteen, in Naples. One of her brothers drowned when she was nineteen – a trauma that inspired her first writing – and both her parents died by the time she was forty. She lived the rest of her years with her sister, who followed her from place to place as Ortese cobbled together writing-related work. Massimo Bontempelli was an early fan, and her first collection was published in 1937. She would go on to publish ten others, and six novels. This story, about a child's perception of poverty, is now considered a touchstone of Italian short fiction, and opens *Il mare non bagna Napoli* (recently published in English under the title *Neapolitan Chronicles*), a collection published in 1953 in Vittorini's *Gettoni* series (see Chronology). A great fresco cycle that depicts Naples, shattered, after the Second World War, it garnered Ortese the Viareggio Prize. But the last chapter, an attack on the city's literary establishment, alienated influential critics and forced her to leave the city. She became an increasingly solitary literary figure who compared herself to a castaway and a cat. Economic difficulties plagued her; though she won the Strega Prize in 1967 she was forced to ask for help from the Legge Bacchelli, an organization created by the Italian government to support illustrious artists in need. Ortese both rejected reality and documented it. Her writing, she observed, 'has something of the exalted and the feverish; it tends towards the high-pitched, encroaches on the hallucinatory, and at almost every point on the page displays, even in its precision, something of the too much'.[1] She wrote a trilogy of novels in which animals were the main characters.

A Pair of Eyeglasses

Translated by Ann Goldstein and Jenny McPhee

'As long as there's the sun . . . the sun!' the voice of Don Peppino Quaglia crooned softly near the doorway of the low, dark basement apartment. 'Leave it to God,' answered the humble and faintly cheerful voice of his wife, Rosa, from inside; she was in bed, moaning in pain from arthritis, complicated by heart disease, and, addressing her sister-in-law, who was in the bathroom, she added: 'You know what I'll do, Nunziata? Later I'll get up and take the clothes out of the water.'

'Do as you like, to me it seems real madness,' replied the curt, sad voice of Nunziata from that den. 'With the pain you have, one more day in bed wouldn't hurt you!' A silence. 'We've got to put out some more poison, I found a cockroach in my sleeve this morning.'

From the cot at the back of the room, which was really a cave, with a low vault of dangling spiderwebs, rose the small, calm voice of Eugenia:

'Mamma, today I'm putting on the eyeglasses.'

There was a kind of secret joy in the modest voice of the child, Don Peppino's third-born. (The first two, Carmela and Luisella, were with the nuns and would soon take the veil, having been persuaded that this life is a punishment; and the two little ones, Pasqualino and Teresella, were still snoring, as they slept feet to head, in their mother's bed.)

'Yes, and no doubt you'll break them right away,' the voice of her aunt, still irritated, insisted, from behind the door of the little room. She made everyone suffer for the disappointments of her life, first among them that she wasn't married and had to be subject, as she told it, to the charity of her sister-in-law, although she didn't fail to add that she dedicated this humiliation to God. She had something of her own set aside, however, and wasn't a bad person, since she had offered to have glasses made for Eugenia when

173

at home they had realized that the child couldn't see. 'With what they cost! A grand total of a good eight thousand lire!' she added. Then they heard the water running in the basin. She was washing her face, squeezing her eyes, which were full of soap, and Eugenia gave up answering.

Besides, she was too, too pleased.

A week earlier, she had gone with her aunt to an optician on Via Roma. There, in that elegant shop, with its polished tables and a marvellous green reflection pouring in through a blind, the doctor had measured her sight, making her read many times, through certain lenses that he kept changing, entire columns of letters of the alphabet, printed on a card, some as big as boxes, others as tiny as pins. 'This poor girl is almost blind,' he had said then, with a kind of pity, to her aunt, 'she should no longer be deprived of lenses.' And right away, while Eugenia, sitting on a stool, waited anxiously, he had placed over her eyes another pair of lenses, with a white metal frame, and had said: 'Now look into the street.' Eugenia stood up, her legs trembling with emotion, and was unable to suppress a little cry of joy. On the pavement, so many well-dressed people were passing, slightly smaller than normal but very distinct: ladies in silk dresses with powdered faces, young men with long hair and bright-coloured sweaters, white-bearded old men with pink hands resting on silver-handled canes; and, in the middle of the street, some beautiful automobiles that looked like toys, their bodies painted red or teal, all shiny; green trolleys as big as houses, with their windows lowered, and behind the windows so many people in elegant clothes. Across the street, on the opposite pavement, were beautiful shops, with windows like mirrors, full of things so fine they roused a kind of longing; some shop boys in black aprons were polishing the windows from the street. At a café with red and yellow tables, some golden-haired girls were sitting outside, legs crossed. They laughed and drank from big coloured glasses. Above the café, because it was already spring, the balcony windows were open and embroidered curtains swayed, and behind the curtains were fragments of blue and gilded paintings, and heavy, sparkling chandeliers of gold and crystal, like baskets of artificial fruit. A marvel. Transported by all that splendour, she hadn't followed the conversation between the doctor and her aunt. Her aunt, in the brown dress she wore to Mass, and standing back from the glass counter with a timidity unnatural to her, now broached the question of the cost: 'Doctor, please, give us a good price . . . we're poor folk . . .' and when she heard 'eight thousand lire' she nearly fainted.

'Two lenses! What are you saying! Jesus Mary!'

'Look, ignorant people . . .' the doctor answered, replacing the other lenses after polishing them with the glove, 'don't calculate anything. And when you give the child two lenses, you'll be able to tell me if she sees better. She takes nine diopters on one side, and ten on the other, if you want to know . . . she's almost blind.'

While the doctor was writing the child's first and last name – 'Eugenia Quaglia, Vicolo della Cupa, at Santa Maria in Portico' – Nunziata had gone over to Eugenia, who, standing in the doorway of the shop and, holding up the glasses in her small, sweaty hands, was not at all tired of gazing through them: 'Look, look, my dear! See what your consolation costs! Eight thousand lire, did you hear? A grand total of a good eight thousand lire!' She was almost suffocating. Eugenia had turned all red, not so much because of the rebuke as because the young woman at the cash register was looking at her, while her aunt was making that observation which declared the family's poverty. She took off the glasses.

'But how is it, so young and already so near-sighted?' the young woman had asked Nunziata, while she signed the receipt for the deposit. 'And so shabby, too!' she added.

'Young lady, in our house we all have good eyes, this is a misfortune that came upon us . . . along with the rest. God rubs salt in the wound.'

'Come back in eight days,' the doctor had said. 'I'll have them for you.'

Leaving, Eugenia had tripped on the step.

'Thank you, Aunt Nunzia,' she had said after a while. 'I'm always rude to you. I talk back to you, and you are so kind, buying me eyeglasses.'

Her voice trembled.

'My child, it's better not to see the world than to see it,' Nunziata had responded with sudden melancholy.

Eugenia hadn't answered her that time, either. Aunt Nunzia was often so strange, she wept and shouted for no good reason, she said so many bad words, and yet she went to Mass regularly, she was a good Christian, and when it came to helping someone in trouble she always volunteered, wholeheartedly. One didn't have to watch over her.

Since that day, Eugenia had lived in a kind of rapture, waiting for the blessed glasses that would allow her to see all people and things in their tiny details. Until then, she had been wrapped in a fog: the room where she lived, the courtyard always full of hanging laundry, the alley overflowing with colours and cries, everything for her was covered by a thin veil: she knew well only the faces of her family, especially her mother and her siblings, because often she slept with them, and sometimes she woke at night and, in the light of the oil lamp, looked at them. Her mother slept with her mouth open, her broken yellow teeth visible; her brother and sister, Pasqualino and Teresella, were always dirty and snot-nosed and covered with boils: when they slept, they made a strange noise, as if they had wild animals inside them. Sometimes Eugenia surprised herself by staring at them, without understanding, however, what she was thinking. She had a confused feeling that beyond that room always full of wet laundry, with broken chairs and a stinking toilet, there was light, sounds, beautiful things, and in that moment when she had put on the glasses she had had a true revelation: the world outside was beautiful, very beautiful.

'Marchesa, my respects.'

That was the voice of her father. Covered by a ragged shirt, his back, which until that moment had been framed by the doorway of the basement apartment, could no longer be seen. The voice of the marchesa, a placid and indifferent voice, now said:

'You must do me a favour, Don Peppino.'

'At your service . . . your wish is my command.'

Silently, Eugenia slid out of bed, put on her dress, and, still barefoot, went to the door. The pure and marvellous early morning sun, entering the ugly courtyard through a crack between the buildings, greeted her, lit up her little old lady's face, her stubbly, dishevelled hair, her rough, hard small hands, with their long, dirty nails. Oh, if only at that moment she could have had the eyeglasses! The marchesa was there, in her black silk dress with its white lace neckpiece. Her imposing yet benign appearance enchanted Eugenia, along with her bejewelled white hands; but she couldn't see her face very well – it was a whitish oval patch. Above it, some purple feathers quivered.

'Listen, you have to redo the child's mattress. Can you come up around ten-thirty?'

'With all my heart, but I'm only available in the afternoon, Signora Marchesa.'

'No, Don Peppino, it has to be this morning. In the afternoon people are coming. Set yourself up on the terrace and work. Don't play hard to get . . . do me this favour . . . Now it's time for Mass. At ten-thirty, call me.'

And without waiting for an answer, she left, astutely avoiding a trickle of yellow water that was dripping down from a terrace and had made a puddle on the ground.

'Papa,' said Eugenia, following her father, as he went back inside, 'how good the marchesa is! She treats you like a gentleman. God should reward her for it.'

'A good Christian, that one is,' Don Peppino answered, with a meaning completely different from what might have been understood. With the excuse that she was the owner of the house, the Marchesa D'Avanzo constantly had the people in the courtyard serving her: to Don Peppino, she gave a wretched sum for the mattresses; and Rosa was always available for the big sheets; even if her bones were burning, she had to get up to serve the marchesa. It's true that the marchesa had placed Rosa's daughters in the convent, and so had saved two souls from the dangers of this world, which for the poor are many, but for that basement space, where everyone was sick, she collected three thousand lire, not one less. 'The heart is there, it's the money that's lacking,' she loved to repeat, with a certain imperturbability. 'Today, dear Don Peppino, you are the nobility, you have no worries . . . Thank . . . thank Providence, which has put you in such a condition . . . which wanted to save you.' Donna Rosa had a kind of adoration for the marchesa, for her religious sentiments; when they saw each other, they always talked about the afterlife. The marchesa didn't much believe in it, but she didn't say so, and urged this mother to be patient and to hope.

From the bed, Donna Rosa asked, a little worried: 'Did you talk to her?'

'She wants me to redo the mattress for her grandson,' said Don Peppino, in annoyance. He brought out the burner on a tripod to warm up some coffee, a gift of the nuns, and went back inside to fetch water in a small pot. 'I won't do it for less than five hundred,' he said.

'It's a fair price.'

'And then who will go and pick up Eugenia's glasses?' Aunt Nunzia asked, coming out of the bathroom. Over her nightgown, she wore a torn skirt, and on her feet, slippers. Her bony shoulders emerged from the nightgown, grey as stones. She was drying her face with a napkin. 'I can't go, and Rosa is ill.'

Without anyone noticing, Eugenia's large, almost blind eyes filled with tears. Now maybe another day would pass without her eyeglasses. She went up to her mother's bed, and in a pitiful manner, flung her arms and forehead on the blanket. Donna Rosa stretched out a hand to caress her.

'I'll go, Nunzia, don't get worked up . . . In fact, going out will do me good.'

'Mamma . . .'

Eugenia kissed her hand.

Around eight o'clock there was a great commotion in the courtyard. At that moment Rosa had come out of the doorway: a tall, lanky figure, in a short, stained black coat, without shoulder pads, that exposed her legs, like wooden sticks. Under her arm, she carried a shopping bag for the bread she would buy on her way home from the optician. Don Peppino was pushing the water out of the middle of the courtyard with a long-handled broom, a vain task because the tub was continually leaking, like an open vein. In it were the clothes of two families: the Greborio sisters, on the second floor, and the wife of Cavaliere Amodio, who had given birth two days earlier. The Greborios' servant, Lina Tarallo, was beating the carpets on a balcony, making a terrible ruckus. The dust, mixed with garbage, descended gradually like a cloud on those poor people, but no one paid attention. Sharp screams and cries of complaint could be heard from the basement, where Aunt Nunzia was calling on all the saints as witnesses to confirm that she was unfortunate, and the cause of all this was Pasqualino, who wept and shouted like a condemned man because he wanted to go with his mamma. 'Look at him, this scoundrel,' cried Aunt Nunzia. '*Madonna bella*, do me a favour, let me die, but immediately, if you're there, since in this life only thieves and whores thrive.' Teresella, born the year the king went away and so younger than her brother, was sitting in the doorway, smiling, and every so often she licked a crust of bread she had found under a chair.

Eugenia was sitting on the step of another basement room, where Mariuccia the porter lived, looking at a section of a children's comic, with lots of bright-coloured figures, which had fallen from the fourth floor. She held it right up to her face, because otherwise she couldn't read the words. There was a small blue river in a vast meadow and a red boat going . . . going . . . who knows where. It was written in proper Italian, and so she didn't understand much, but every so often, for no reason, she laughed.

'So, today you'll put on your glasses?' said Mariuccia, looking out from behind her. Everyone in the courtyard knew, partly because Eugenia hadn't resisted the temptation to talk about it, and partly because Aunt Nunzia had found it necessary to let it be understood that in that family she was spending her own . . . and well, in short . . .

'Your aunt got them for you, eh?' Mariuccia added, smiling good-humouredly. She was a small woman, almost a dwarf, with a face like a man's, covered with whiskers. At the moment she was combing her long black hair, which came to her knees: one of the few features that showed she was a woman. She was combing it slowly, smiling with her sly but kind little mouse eyes.

'Mamma went to get them on Via Roma,' said Eugenia with a look of gratitude. 'We paid a grand total of a good eight thousand lire, you know? Really . . . my aunt is . . .' she was about to add 'truly a good person', when Aunt Nunzia, looking out of the basement room, called angrily: 'Eugenia!'

'Here I am, Aunt!' and she scampered away like a dog.

Behind their aunt, Pasqualino, all red-faced and bewildered, with a terrible expression somewhere between disdain and surprise, was waiting.

'Go and buy two candies for three lire each, from Don Vincenzo at the tobacco store. Come back immediately!'

'Yes, Aunt.'

She clutched the money in her fist, paying no more attention to the comic, and hurried out of the courtyard.

By a true miracle she avoided a towering vegetable cart drawn by two horses, which was coming towards her, right outside the main entrance. The carter, with his whip unsheathed, seemed to be singing, and from his mouth came these words: 'Lovely . . . Fresh,' drawn out and full of sweetness, like a love song. When the cart was behind her, Eugenia, raising her protruding eyes, basked in that warm blue glow that was the sky, and heard the great hubbub all around her, without, however, seeing it clearly. Carts, one behind the other, big trucks with Americans dressed in yellow hanging out of the windows, bicycles that seemed to be tumbling over. High up, all the balconies were cluttered with flower crates, and over the railings, like flags or saddle blankets, hung yellow-and-red quilts, ragged blue children's clothes, sheets, pillows and mattresses exposed to the air, while at the end of the alley ropes uncoiled, lowering baskets to pick up the vegetables or fish offered by peddlers. Although the sun touched only the highest balconies (the street a crack in the disorderly mass of buildings) and the rest was only shadow and garbage, one could sense, behind it, the enormous celebration of spring. And even Eugenia, so small and pale, bound like a mouse to the mud of her courtyard, began to breathe rapidly, as if that air, that celebration and all that blue suspended over the neighbourhood of the poor were also hers. The yellow basket of the Amodios' maid, Rosaria Buonincontri, grazed her as she went into the tobacco shop. Rosaria was a fat woman in black, with white legs and a flushed, placid face.

'Tell your mamma if she can come upstairs a moment today, Signora Amodio needs her to deliver a message.'

Eugenia recognized her by her voice. 'She's not here now. She went to Via Roma to get my glasses.'

'I should wear them, too, but my boyfriend doesn't want me to.'

Eugenia didn't grasp the meaning of that prohibition. She answered only, ingenuously: 'They cost a great amount; you have to take very good care of them.'

They entered Don Vincenzo's hole-in-the-wall together. There was a crowd. Eugenia kept being pushed back. 'Go on . . . you really are blind,' observed the Amodios' maid, with a kind smile.

'But now Aunt Nunzia's gotten you some eyeglasses,' Don Vincenzo, who had heard her, broke in, winking, with an air of teasing comprehension. He, too, wore glasses.

'At your age,' he said, handing her the candies, 'I could see like a cat, I could thread needles at night, my grandmother always wanted me nearby . . . but now I'm old.'

Eugenia nodded vaguely. 'My friends . . . none of them have glasses,' she said. Then, turning to the servant Rosaria, but speaking also for Don Vincenzo's benefit: 'Just me . . . Nine diopters on one side and ten on the other . . . I am almost blind!' she said emphatically, sweetly.

'See how lucky you are,' said Don Vincenzo, smiling, and to Rosaria: 'How much salt?'

'Poor child!' the Amodios' maid commented as Eugenia left, happily. 'It's the dampness that's ruined her. In that building it rains on us. Now Donna Rosa's bones ache. Give me a kilo of coarse salt and a packet of fine . . .'

'There you are.'

'What a morning, eh, today, Don Vincenzo? It seems like summer already.'

Walking more slowly than she had on the way there, Eugenia, without even realizing it, began to unwrap one of the two candies, and then put it in her mouth. It tasted of lemon. 'I'll tell Aunt Nunzia that I lost it on the way,' she proposed to herself. She was happy, it didn't matter to her if her aunt, good as she was, got angry. She felt someone take her hand, and recognized Luigino.

'You are really blind!' the boy said, laughing. 'And the glasses?'

'Mamma went to Via Roma to get them.'

'I didn't go to school; it's a beautiful day, why don't we take a little walk?'

'You're crazy! Today I have to be good.'

Luigino looked at her and laughed, with his mouth like a money box, stretching to his ears, contemptuous.

'What a rat's nest.'

Instinctively Eugenia brought a hand to her hair.

'I can't see well, and Mamma doesn't have time,' she answered meekly.

'What are the glasses like? With gold frames?' Luigino asked.

'All gold!' Eugenia answered, lying. 'Bright and shiny!'

'Old women wear glasses,' said Luigino.

'Also ladies, I saw them on Via Roma.'

'Those are dark glasses, for sunbathing,' Luigino insisted.

'You're just jealous. They cost eight thousand lire.'

'When you have them, let me see them,' said Luigino. 'I want to see if the frame's really gold. You're such a liar,' and he went off on his own business, whistling.

Re-entering the courtyard, Eugenia wondered anxiously if her glasses would have gold frames or not. In the negative case, what could she say to Luigino to convince him that they were a thing of value? But what a beautiful day! Maybe Mamma was about to return with the glasses wrapped in a package. Soon she would have them on her face. She would have . . . A frenzy of blows fell on her head. A real fury. She seemed to collapse; in vain she defended herself with her hands. It was Aunt Nunzia, of course, furious because of her delay, and behind Aunt Nunzia was Pasqualino, like a madman, because he didn't believe her story about the candies. 'Bloodsucker! You ugly little blind girl! And I gave my life for this ingratitude . . . You'll come to a bad end! Eight thousand lire, no less. They bleed me dry, these scoundrels.'

She let her hands fall, only to burst into a great lament. 'Our Lady of Sorrows, Holy Jesus, by the wounds in your ribs let me die!'

Eugenia wept, too, in torrents.

'Aunt, forgive me. Aunt . . .'

'Uh . . . uh . . . uh . . .' said Pasqualino, his mouth wide open.

'Poor child,' said Donna Mariuccia, coming over to Eugenia, who didn't know where to hide her face, now streaked with red and tears at her aunt's rage. 'She didn't do it on purpose, Nunzia, calm down,' and to Eugenia: 'Where've you got the candies?'

Eugenia answered softly, hopelessly, holding out one in her dirty hand: 'I ate the other. I was hungry.'

Before her aunt could move again, to attack the child, the voice of the marchesa could be heard, from the fourth floor, where there was sun, calling softly, placidly, sweetly:

'Nunziata!'

Aunt Nunzia looked up, her face pained as that of the Madonna of the Seven Sorrows, which was at the head of her bed.

'Today is the first Friday of the month. Dedicate it to God.'

'Marchesa, how good you are! These kids make me commit so many sins, I'm losing my mind, I . . .' And she collapsed her face between her paw-like hands, the hands of a worker, with brown, scaly skin.

'Is your brother not there?'

'Poor Aunt, she got you the eyeglasses, and that's how you thank her,' said Mariuccia meanwhile to Eugenia, who was trembling.

'Yes, Signora, here I am,' answered Don Peppino, who until that moment had been half hidden behind the door of the basement room, waving a piece of cardboard in front of the stove where the beans for lunch were cooking.

'Can you come up?'

'My wife went to get the eyeglasses for Eugenia. I'm watching the beans. Would you wait, if you don't mind?'

'Then send up the child. I have a dress for Nunziata. I want to give it to her.'

'May God reward you . . . very grateful,' answered Don Peppino, with a sigh of consolation, because that was the only thing that could calm his sister. But looking at Nunziata, he realized that she wasn't at all cheered up. She continued to weep desperately, and that weeping had so stunned Pasqualino that the child had become quiet as if by magic, and was now licking the snot that dripped from his nose, with a small, sweet smile.

'Did you hear? Go up to the Signora Marchesa, she has a dress to give you,' said Don Peppino to his daughter.

Eugenia was looking at something in the void, with her eyes that couldn't see: they were staring, fixed and large. She winced, and got up immediately, obedient.

'Say to her: 'May God reward you,' and stay outside the door.'

'Yes, Papa.'

'Believe me, Mariuccia,' said Aunt Nunzia, when Eugenia had gone off, 'I love that little creature, and afterward I'm sorry, as God is my witness, for scolding her. But I feel all the blood go to my head, believe me, when I have to fight with the kids. Youth is gone, as you see –' and she touched her hollow cheeks. 'Sometimes I feel like a madwoman.'

'On the other hand, they have to vent, too,' Donna Mariuccia answered. 'They're innocent souls. They need time to weep. When I look at them, and think how they'll become just like us –' she went to get a broom and swept a cabbage leaf out of the doorway – 'I wonder what God is doing.'

'It's new, brand new! You hardly wore it!' said Eugenia, sticking her nose in the green dress lying on the sofa in the kitchen, while the marchesa went looking for an old newspaper to wrap it in.

The marchesa thought that the child really couldn't see, because otherwise she would have realized that the dress was very old and full of patches (it had belonged to her dead sister), but she refrained from commenting. Only after a moment, as she was coming in with the newspaper, she asked:

'And the eyeglasses your aunt got you? Are they new?'

'With gold frames. They cost eight thousand lire,' Eugenia answered all in one breath, becoming emotional again at the thought of the honour she had received, 'because I'm almost blind,' she added simply.

'In my opinion,' said the marchesa, carefully wrapping the dress in the newspaper, and then reopening the package because a sleeve was sticking out, 'your aunt could have saved her money. I saw some very good eyeglasses in a shop near the Church of the Ascension, for only two thousand lire.'

Eugenia blushed fiery red. She understood that the marchesa was displeased. 'Each to his own position in life. We all must know our limitations,' she had heard her say this many times, talking to Donna Rosa, when she brought her the washed clothes, and stayed to complain of her poverty.

'Maybe they weren't good enough. I have nine diopters,' she replied timidly.

The marchesa arched an eyebrow, but luckily Eugenia didn't see it.

'They were good, I'm telling you,' the marchesa said obstinately, in a slightly harsher voice. Then she was sorry. 'My dear,' she said more gently, 'I'm saying this because I know the troubles you have in your household. With that difference of six thousand lire, you could buy bread for ten days, you could buy . . . What's the use to you of seeing better? Given what's around you!' A silence. 'To read, maybe, but do you read?'

'No, Signora.'

'But sometimes I've seen you with your nose in a book. A liar as well, my dear. That is no good.'

Eugenia didn't answer again. She felt truly desperate, staring at the dress with her nearly white eyes.

'Is it silk?' she asked stupidly.

The marchesa looked at her, reflecting.

'You don't deserve it, but I want to give you a little gift,' she said suddenly, and headed towards a white wooden wardrobe. At that moment the telephone, which was in the hall, began to ring, and instead of opening the wardrobe the marchesa went to answer it. Eugenia, oppressed by those words, hadn't even heard the old woman's consoling allusion, and as soon as she was alone she began to look around as far as her poor eyes allowed her. How many fine, beautiful things! Like the store on Via Roma! And there, right in front of her, an open balcony with many small pots of flowers.

She went out on to the balcony. How much air, how much blue! The apartment buildings seemed to be covered by a blue veil, and below was the alley, like a ravine, with so many ants coming and going . . . like her relatives. What were they doing? Where were they going? They went in and out of their holes, carrying big crumbs of bread, they were doing this now, had done it yesterday, would do it tomorrow, forever, forever. So many holes, so many ants. And around them, almost invisible in the great light, the world made by God, with the wind, the sun, and out there the purifying sea, so vast . . . She was standing there, her chin planted on the iron railing, suddenly thoughtful, with an expression of sorrow, of bewilderment, that made her look ugly. She heard the sound of the marchesa's voice, calm, pious. In her hand, in her smooth ivory hand, the marchesa was holding a small book covered in black paper with gilt letters.

'It's the thoughts of the saints, my dear. The youth of today don't read anything, and so the world has changed course. Take it, I'm giving it to you. But you must promise to read a little every evening, now that you've got your glasses.'

'Yes, Signora,' said Eugenia, in a hurry, blushing again because the marchesa had found her on the balcony, and she took the book. Signora D'Avanzo regarded her with satisfaction.

'God wished to save you, my dear!' she said, going to get the package with the dress and placing it in her hands. 'You're not pretty, anything but, and you already appear to be an old lady. God favours you, because looking like that you won't have opportunities for evil. He wants you to be holy, like your sisters!'

Although the words didn't really wound her, because she had long been unconsciously prepared for a life without joy, Eugenia was nevertheless disturbed by them. And it seemed to her, if only for a moment, that the sun no longer shone as before, and even the thought of the eyeglasses no longer cheered her. She looked vaguely, with her nearly dead eyes, at a point on the sea, where the Posillipo peninsula extended like a faded green lizard. 'Tell Papà,' the marchesa continued, meanwhile, 'that we won't do anything about the child's mattress today. My cousin telephoned, and I'll be in Posillipo all day.'

'I was there once, too . . .' Eugenia began, reviving at the name of that place and she looked, spellbound, in that direction.

'Yes? Is that so?' Signora D'Avanzo was indifferent; the name of the place meant nothing special to her. In her magisterial fashion, she accompanied the child, who was still looking towards that luminous point, to the door, closing it slowly behind her.

As Eugenia came down the last step and out into the courtyard, the shadow that had been darkening her forehead for a while disappeared, and her mouth opened in a joyful laugh, because she had seen her mother arriving. It wasn't hard to recognize that worn, familiar figure. She threw the dress on a chair and ran towards her.

'Mamma! The eyeglasses!'

'Gently, my dear, you'll knock me over!'

Immediately, a small crowd formed. Donna Mariuccia, Don Peppino, one of the Greborios, who had stopped to rest on a chair before starting up the stairs, the Amodios' maid, who was just then returning, and, of course, Pasqualino and Teresella, who wanted to see, too, and yelled, holding out their hands. Nunziata, for her part, was observing the dress that she had taken out of the newspaper, with a disappointed expression.

'Look, Mariuccia, it's an old rag . . . all worn out under the arms!' she said, approaching the group. But who was paying attention to her? At that moment, Donna Rosa was extracting from a pocket in her dress the eyeglasses case, and with infinite care, she opened it. On her long red hand, a kind of very shiny insect with two giant eyes and two curving antennae glittered in a pale ray of sun amid those poor people, full of admiration.

'Eight thousand lire . . . a thing like that!' said Donna Rosa, gazing at the eyeglasses religiously, and yet with a kind of rebuke.

Then, in silence, she placed them on Eugenia's face, as the child ecstatically held out her hands, and carefully arranged the two antennae behind her ears. 'Now can you see?' Donna Rosa asked with great emotion.

Gripping the eyeglasses with her hands, as if fearful that they would be taken away from her, her eyes half closed and her mouth half open in a rapt smile, Eugenia took two steps backward, and stumbled on a chair.

'Good luck!' said the Amodios' maid.

'Good luck!' said the Greborio sister.

'She looks like a schoolteacher, doesn't she?' Don Peppino observed with satisfaction.

'Not even a thank you!' said Aunt Nunzia, looking bitterly at the dress. 'With all that, good luck!'

'She's afraid, my little girl!' murmured Donna Rosa, heading towards the door of the basement room to put down her things. 'She's wearing the eyeglasses for the first time!' she said, looking up at the first-floor balcony, where the other Greborio sister was looking out.

'I see everything very tiny,' said Eugenia, in a strange voice, as if she were speaking from under a chair. 'Black, very black.'

'Of course: the lenses are double. But do you see clearly?' asked Don Peppino. 'That's the important thing. She's wearing the glasses for the first time,' he, too, said, addressing Cavaliere Amodio, who was passing by, holding an open newspaper.

'I'm warning you,' the cavaliere said to Mariuccia, after staring at Eugenia for a moment, as if she were merely a cat, 'that stairway hasn't been swept. I found some fish bones in front of the door!' And he went on, bent over, almost enfolded in his newspaper, reading an article about a proposal for a new pension law that interested him.

Eugenia, still holding on to the eyeglasses with her hands, went to the entrance to the courtyard to look outside into Vicolo della Cupa. Her legs were trembling, her head was spinning, and she no longer felt any joy. With her white lips she wished to smile, but that smile became a moronic grimace. Suddenly the balconies began to multiply, two thousand, a hundred thousand; the carts piled with vegetables were falling on her; the voices filling the air, the cries, the lashes, struck her head as if she were ill; she turned, swaying, towards the courtyard, and that terrible impression intensified. The courtyard was like a sticky funnel, with the narrow end towards the sky, its leprous walls crowded with derelict balconies; the arches of the basement dwellings black, with the lights bright in a circle around Our Lady of Sorrows; the pavement white with soapy water; the cabbage leaves, the scraps of paper, the garbage and, in the middle of the courtyard, that group of ragged, deformed souls, faces pocked by poverty and resignation, who looked at her lovingly. They began to writhe, to become mixed up, to grow larger.

They all came towards her, in the two bewitched circles of the eyeglasses. It was Mariuccia who first realized that the child was sick, and she tore off the glasses, because Eugenia, doubled over and moaning, was throwing up.

'They've gone to her stomach!' cried Mariuccia, holding her forehead. 'Bring a coffee bean, Nunziata!'

'A grand total of a good eight thousand lire!' cried Aunt Nunzia, her eyes popping out of her head, running into the basement room to get a coffee bean from a can in the cupboard; and she held up the new eyeglasses, as if to ask God for an explanation. 'And now they're wrong, too!'

'It's always like that, the first time,' said the Amodios' maid to Donna Rosa calmly. 'You mustn't be shocked; little by little one gets used to them.'

'It's nothing, child, nothing, don't be scared!' But Donna Rosa felt her heart constrict at the thought of how unlucky they were.

Aunt Nunzia returned with the coffee bean, still crying: 'A grand total of a good eight thousand lire!' while Eugenia, pale as death, tried in vain to throw up, because she had nothing left inside her. Her bulging eyes were almost crossed with suffering, and her old lady's face was bathed in tears, as if stupefied. She leaned on her mother and trembled.

'Mamma, where are we?'

'We're in the courtyard, my child,' said Donna Rosa patiently; and the delicate smile, between pity and wonder, that illuminated her eyes, suddenly lit up the faces of all those wretched people.

'She's half blind!'

'She's a halfwit, she is!'

'Leave her alone, poor child, she's dazed,' said Donna Mariuccia, and her face was grim with pity, as she went back into the basement apartment that seemed to her darker than usual.

Only Aunt Nunzia was wringing her hands:

'A grand total of a good eight thousand lire!'

'*Un paio di occhiali*'

First published under the title '*Ottomila lire per gli occhi di Eugenia*' in the magazine *Omnibus* (May 1949). Later included in *Il mare non bagna Napoli* in the *Gettoni* series (Einaudi, 1953).

ALBERTO MORAVIA

1907–90

A quintessentially Roman writer, Moravia, born Alberto Pincherle, wrote more works about that city's people, streets and soul than any other. His 1952 collection, called simply *I racconti* (Stories), won the Strega Prize. His complete *Racconti romani* (published in English as *Roman Tales* and *More Roman Tales*) collected in 1954 and then in 1959, number well over one hundred. This story comes from a lesser-known collection, published in 1976, called *Boh* (an untranslatable expression one often hears in Rome, to express a general state of befuddlement). All are told in the first person from the female point of view. Together, these snapshots form a collective portrait of Roman women on the threshold of something new, like the protagonist of this selection, caught between traditional roles and a nascent feminist consciousness. The collection, coming as it did after Moravia had settled into his reputation as a celebrated man of letters and author of iconic novels like *La noia* (*Boredom*), represents another side to the author. But Moravia, at once a classical and subversive writer, embodied a spirit of contradiction from the very start. He had little formal schooling. A childhood illness confined him to bed and books, an experience fundamental to his becoming a writer. His early efforts included stories written in French for Bontempelli's magazine, *900*, and his first novel, *Gli indifferenti* (translated as *The Time of Indifference*), a scathing portrait of a bourgeois family that enraged Fascist critics, published when he was just twenty, is still considered by many to be his best. He wrote with equal facility about working-class and middle-class characters, about shop-keepers and bank clerks. Moravia was the founding editor of *Nuovi Argomenti*, one of Italy's most prestigious literary journals and still a forum for short stories. Involved romantically with literary women, he was the husband of Elsa Morante, and the companion for many years of the writer Dacia Maraini.

The Other Side of the Moon

Translated by Michael F. Moore

I am two persons in one or, if you prefer, a double-faced person, with two sides, like the moon. And like the moon, I have one side that everyone knows, always the same, and a side unknown not only to others but also, in a sense, to myself. This second completely unknown side might not even exist: if you think about it, the things we ignore do not exist. But they do. Even if I don't know it or allow it to be known, the other side of the moon is something I 'sense'. And this obscure sense that the other side exists, invisible and different, behind my apparent face, at the back of my head, and is looking at the world behind me, means that in everyday life I am always scrupulously, dutifully occupied and, at the same time – how how can I put this? – 'unglued'. Yes, unglued. That is to say, detached from the things I am doing at the very moment that I'm doing them. Have you ever seen an antique table from which a piece becomes suddenly unglued? A piece that until then had seemed to belong to the whole? When you look at it you see that on the surface of the old dry wood there is a kind of dull sheen of old glue. The table was damaged who knows how many centuries ago. Someone, who has likewise been dead for centuries, glued it back together. But one fine day, the glue no longer holds and the broken piece becomes unglued. Now it needs a new application of glue, as good as the former one, but who knows what kind? Well, in everyday life, I am that fragment that seems to stick but, in actuality, is detached.

Unglued and diligent, from eight in the evening until six in the morning I am the perfect beautiful young wife of an older judge; from six in the evening until nine at night the perfect stepmother to the judge's two children by his first wife; and from eight-thirty until one-thirty the perfect bank clerk. Why do I keep this schedule? Because there is no time in my life except for the time I see on my watch; all the other times are off-limits to me. Every day I get up at six, wash and dress myself, wake the children, help them to wash and get dressed, and I then prepare breakfast for everyone. After that my husband leaves in his car. First he'll drop the children off at school, with the nuns, where they are day students. Then he'll drive to the courthouse. I walk to the bank, not far from home. At the bank, so serious and diligent that my colleagues jokingly call me Miss Dutiful, I keep myself busy until one-thirty. Then I walk back home. The part-time maid has already done the shopping from a list that I prepare every night before turning in. I go to the kitchen, open up bags and boxes, turn on the burners, and prepare a light lunch for my husband and me. My husband arrives. We sit down at the table. After eating I wash the dishes and put everything back in its place. Then we move to the bedroom. It's time to make love, and my husband likes it at that hour because at night he's too tired. At four o'clock he leaves and a few minutes later the children arrive. Without taking a break, I prepare a snack for them, watch TV with them, help them do their homework, cook them dinner, put them to bed. By now it's eight o'clock and my husband arrives home. He sits down to read the newspaper. I run to the bedroom, put on a fancy dress, put on my make-up, fix my hair, and then we go out to dinner at a restaurant or a friend's house, and then to the cinema. At this point, however, I collapse because, for years, I've been losing about two hours of sleep a day. So I doze off wherever I happen to be: at the dinner table, at a restaurant, in my seat at the cinema, next to my husband while he's driving the car. Do I love my husband? Let's just say that I'm fond of him. Besides, I don't have time for thoughts like this.

And yet, despite this life as Miss Dutiful, I don't stick to the things I do. I always feel, as I said, unglued. By the way, I said that my other side of the moon is unknown not only to others, but also to me. That's not exactly true: if you know how to read it, this unknown side can be inferred from my facial features. I'll describe myself, you be the judge. I'm blonde, tall and thin, with a slightly Germanic face, like the ones that peer out from the niches of old gothic churches. I have a triangular face, with the wide part that is my forehead, hard and bony, and the pointed part, my chin, which is fleshy and soft. I have an aquiline nose and thin lips, both of noble design. But my ugly eyes, a washed-out blue, counter the severe nobility of my face, with a gaze so sullen it's frightening. My eyes have a fleeting, furtive, cold expression, as if lying in wait, like the gaze of an animal that will bite at the first chance.

'That opportunity arose, finally, in the fourth year of my marriage. One November morning, on my way to work beneath a pelting grey rain, I saw a man at the wheel of a big black car, parked in front of my bank, taking photographs. I had already seen him from a distance: he would hold a tiny camera to his eye and snap the pictures – three, four, five at a time – with a calm and expert fury. After this he would hide his hand and, for a few moments, stare into space. But all of a sudden he would start snapping pictures again. What was he taking pictures of? It was obvious: the entrance to the bank. I came a little closer and got a better look at him. From behind, he seemed to be a man of short stature. He had a broad forehead, a hook nose, and a well-drawn mouth. He reminded me of certain prints portraying the young Napoleon. Then I passed him. He put his hand down and looked at me, as if waiting for me to disappear. Then, inexplicably, I don't know what impulse made me wink at him. He saw the wink and nodded, to show me that he'd noticed. I crossed the avenue with a determined step, wrapped in my bright red trench coat. I joined the group of employees at the entrance to the bank. When I turned around, the car was gone.

Fifteen days went by. One morning I came out of the bank to go home. While walking, I realized that I did not feel any part of the relief and joy that swept through the streets in waves, like on Sundays, as the offices and schools emptied out for the day and the people who had been holed up in them, forced to work or study, were leaving, emancipated, and hurrying home. I felt no relief or joy: I was already thinking of the lunch I would cook, the dishes I would wash, the love-making I would perform. Then, suddenly, I looked up and saw, right next to me, the photographer who, at the wheel of his car, was following me step by step. Our eyes met. And then he propositioned me with a short sentence of an unrepeatable obscenity. I didn't hesitate. I nodded yes. He stopped the car, opened the door, and I got in.

We went a short way, to a deserted spot on the Lungotevere, parked, and he immediately tried to kiss me, as if he were following a pre-established plan. When he wasn't moving, as I said, he resembled a young

Napoleon. But as soon as his face lit up in any expression, it immediately revealed the vulgarity, though not without grace, of a small-town gangster. I pushed him away and said, 'Quit pawing me, there's time for that. Now tell me what you want from me.'

Undeterred, he answered, 'I want you.'

'No, you don't want me. If you wanted only me, then it would mean that you're a fetishist.'

'A fetishist? What's that supposed to mean?'

'Someone who, like you, loves not only the person but also the things around her. For example, the door of the bank where I work.'

'What are you talking about?'

'I'll tell you what. Two weeks ago, at eight-thirty in the morning. How many pictures did you take? I'd say at least twenty.'

'I can't hide anything from you. Who are you? The devil?'

So began our story that, in the end, filled the newspapers with bold headlines. There's no sense in my telling you how the robbery took place. It was a 'classic' of the genre, according to reporters. If you want to know how it went, you can check the crime pages of that year's newspapers. Nor do I want to tell you the prominent part that I played. It would be dangerous for me, since there's been no further mention of it in the papers. For my colleagues at the bank, I am still the same old Miss Dutiful. The only thing I'd like to add is that the robbery took place in the early afternoon, when there are only a few employees and the bank is closed to customers. It was about four o'clock and I had escaped from home, right after the usual love-making with my husband. And with just an hour to spare before the children came home from school. I had to wait, at the wheel of the classic stolen car, on a solitary street, for my gangster and his buddy to arrive right after the robbery. Well, wouldn't you know it? Despite my palpitations, the usual fatigue made me fall asleep at the wheel, in an amazing, invincible, blessed sleep. In sleep I took part in the robbery in my own way. I dreamt I was locked in the vault of the bank and then, all of a sudden, my gangster opened it and I, with a cry of joy, fell into his arms. But at that same moment, *voilà*, he was waking me up, shaking me by the arm, cursing between his teeth. Immediately, like a robot, without even looking around, I started the car and we took off.

After the robbery we didn't see each other again for six months. He didn't want us to. He said that the police were definitely enquiring into the life of every employee of the bank. We did, however, agree that after these six months, I would go and live with him, turning myself from Miss Dutiful to Machine-Gun Mama, or a similar moniker that, without a doubt, my former co-workers would give me, with a snicker, as soon as they found out.

So I resumed my usual life, shuttling between home and the bank. On one such day, I realized I had run out of cologne. That same afternoon I drove my husband to the airport. He was going to Cagliari on a business trip. On my way back I remembered the cologne and so I stopped the car on a suburban street, in front of a cosmetics shop named after the Parisian perfume house that made my cologne. The moment I entered, I was bedazzled by the gleaming of the many decanters, phials and teardrop-shaped bottles of eau de toilette and lotions lined up in glass cabinets against every wall. So for a moment I didn't notice my gangster. Standing behind the counter, he was helping a middle-aged customer who wanted some rare shade of lipstick. My gangster had various little tubes scattered on the counter between himself and the customer. And as he gradually uncapped one and then the other, and rubbed a tiny smudge on the back of his hand, he enlarged the mark with his thumb and then showed it to the customer, speaking with her at length all the while, softly, gently, patiently. But the customer would look and then shake her head: it still wasn't the shade she was looking for.

My gangster hadn't told me that he owned this magnificent shop. The only thing I knew about him was that he lived with his elderly mother and two children, and that his wife had left him and was living in Milan with another man. But then I realized he had been a cosmetics salesman for a while, maybe years, because his conversation with the customer was that of a professional; you can't improvise it. For me the precision of his speech was like a flash of lightning in the night, illuminating the tiniest details of a landscape, even if just for a moment. I realized, in other words, that I had been wrong. I had mistaken him for a predatory falcon. He was instead a sly mole. So in that flash of awareness, I made a quick calculation and realized that he was no better than my husband. He, too, had two children that I would have to take care of. He, too, would expect me to slave away in the house. As for work, it was better to be a bank clerk than a cosmetics saleslady, if for no other reason than that I only had to work at the bank in the morning. There was love, it's true. But I realized now, after discovering the shop, that I felt just as unglued around him as I did around my husband. So I didn't wait for the customer to find the right lipstick. I did an about-face and walked out. At the door, however, I glanced back. Now he was looking at me from over his customer's shoulders, and I shook my head no. He wasn't stupid, and he must have understood, because he never came looking for me after that. Maybe, who knows, he didn't trust me as a cosmetics saleslady. After all, there's no difference between a shop and a bank. He must have feared that I, incorrigible, would repeat the robbery, but this time against him, and maybe in cahoots with a genuine gangster, the kind that holds up a bank to commit a real crime and not to buy a cosmetics shop.

'*L'altra faccia della luna*'
Part of the collection *Boh* (Bompiani, 1976).

ELSA MORANTE

1912–85

A photo of Elsa Morante from the 1960s shows her seated at Caffè Rosati in Rome's Piazza del Popolo, with her then husband, Alberto Moravia, and the writer Pier Paolo Pasolini, a close friend. Caught in profile, she seems to be saying something, and looks like she may be scratching a mosquito bite on her arm. Morante, too poor to finish her university degree, remains the literary queen of that city. Her mother was a Jewish school teacher, and her biological father – her mother would marry another man, who raised her – worked in a post office. One of five children, she grew up in the neighbourhood of Testaccio and left home at eighteen to support herself. Her first novel, *Menzogna e sortilegio* (Lies and Sorcery, which was published in English under the title *House of Liars*), is a sprawling masterpiece, demonic in its energy. It was typical of her complex, choral novels, including *La storia* (*History*), but she made her literary debut with a collection of short stories called *Il gioco segreto* (The Secret Game) in 1941. Among her most revered works is a novel called *L'Isola di Arturo* (*Arturo's Island*). It won the Strega Prize in 1957. Active in cultural and literary delegations, she visited the Soviet Union, China, India, the United States and Brazil, often in Moravia's company. But by 1960 she had set up a separate home for herself, while still married, and had befriended Bill Morrow, a young American painter whom she took under her wing. She was laid low following Morrow's suicide in 1962 (he jumped from a skyscraper). In 1983, Morante herself attempted suicide. She remains a major writer who had tiny penmanship and a grand, tragic vision. She wrote with particular power about parent–child relationships, a theme central to the selection here. Posthumously published, it demonstrates her wit and her dense, virtuosic prose.

The Ambitious Ones

Translated by Erica Segre and Simon Carnell

When I first met the Donato women, a few years ago now, the falling-out between the mother and her eldest daughter was already well advanced. Angela Donato, the widowed mother, had three daughters, and of these, Concetta, the eldest, was by far the most beautiful as well as the one who resembled her most. In those southern Italian villages women mature early; sweet and languorous humours run through their veins, and their bodies bloom with the fleshy elegance of a tuberose, while the primitive ardour in their eyes is concealed with a veil of tenderness. Concetta was still an adolescent, radiant in her litheness; Angela was already in decline, and above her majestic matronly corpulence her face with its clear-cut, determined features was languidly fading. But mother and daughter shared a similar smile, at once flirtatious and fervid; similar too was the shape of their eyes, in which an inclination to affection mingled with what one might venture to call ferocity; also similar was the shape of their lips, which when they weren't laughing revealed a proud determination. And similar, finally, were their hands: white, plump and soft; so beautiful as to resemble the hands of aristocratic women. Both mother and daughter took loving care of their hands, delegating the roughest tasks to Concetta's younger sisters. Mother and daughter, evidently, were both vain, especially with regard to these exquisitely beautiful hands of theirs. The mother would habitually kiss her daughter's hands, I recall, giving a kiss to every dimple, and one to every finger – and in response the daughter would kiss the hands of her mother.

Both mother and daughter had clear, high singing voices, and among their ambitions was the ambition, precisely, to sing: but whereas the mother had dreamt of a career on the stage, her daughter yearned to sing sacred motets, in church, with choirs of nuns and organ accompaniment. Both

Concetta and Angela loved festivities and the pomp of an occasion; but whereas Angela fantasized about crowded avenues, carriages, balls, carnivals in the piazzas, Concetta had a predilection for solemn ceremony in cathedrals; the lilies, the candle flames, the stories illuminated in stained glass. Angela liked elegant clothes, earrings and necklaces; Concetta would go into ecstasies over embroidered chasubles, golden tabernacles, splendid stoles. It was here that the source of the difference between mother and daughter was to be found. To which we must add that when Concetta turned fifteen her mother had begun to promise herself a grand marriage for her daughter: one that would bring to the family all the distinction and elegance that she'd always yearned for in vain. Instead Concetta, having talked with her nuns about their heavenly spouse, never wanted to hear about any other kind of husband again.

Even as a young girl, at times, when she'd found herself alone in a room, the sound of the gentle smack of her particularly resonant kisses could be heard in the next room; and if you hovered at the door to spy on what she was up to, you would catch sight of her blowing kisses into thin air and smiling, enraptured. Kisses that were directed, of course, to her intended: that is to say, the Lord. Her mother would shake her by the arm and say: 'So this is what I have to put up with, you silly, stupid girl!' – and Concetta, eyes blazing with fury, would free herself from the maternal grasp and run.

The four women lived in the centre of the village, on Piazza Garibaldi to be precise, in an apartment with two small rooms and a kitchen, with a little balcony overlooking the square. The rooms were decorated with those tapestries peddled at fairs by travelling salesmen, depicting the Madonna of the Chair, or the Discovery of America, or the Landing of the Thousand in Sicily. In addition to this the walls were adorned with cuttings from magazines, with old photographs and postcards. On the beds were covers of fake scarlet damask. There were no maids, and they lunched in the kitchen, beneath a beaded paper lampshade, at a table covered with oilcloth.

When I first met the Donato women, Concetta's hand in marriage had been asked for by the son of the most important hotelier in the city; and this offer, coming from such a suitor as this, in every way so very flattering, had electrified Angela. She could already see Concetta installed in the entrance of the hotel, in a velvet wedding dress, with a brooch of rubies, welcoming the guests with sovereign affability; and herself wearing a fur stole, feathers and bracelets, visiting her daughter, fanning herself in the drawing room

But instead Concetta rejected the offer made by the hotelier's son. And she repudiated that offer as if it were obviously out of the question – with a promptness so offensive that the young man had sworn eternal enmity towards the Donatos. If he crossed paths with the widow in the street he would ostentatiously overtake her with a martial gait, without acknowledging her, while she in turn would snub him with a disdain worthy of an empress. Soon this suitor was engaged to another young lady, and would deliberately parade with her beneath the windows of the Donato household, showing them how elegantly turned out his new fiancée was, and what heels and what necklaces she sported. Her eyes darkened with envy, an indifferent smile on her lips, the widow Donato would peer at him from behind the windowpanes. 'Well, it's something rather better than him that my daughter deserves!' she would tell me, with supreme disdain: 'My daughter was born to live in style – to drive around in a luxury car, with a chauffeur, a nanny and a pram!'

It was frequently the case at this time that Concetta's dainty shoes, and those of her sisters as well, were down-at-heel. I would notice this when she was kneeling in church. I could not see her eyes, but I knew that they would be directed towards the altar like two tiny larks taking flight towards the sun. Concetta had numerous sacred images, given to her by the nuns, and she would spend all day in contemplation of them. One of these showed a graceful young novice, no longer wearing the habit of a nun but bedecked in exquisitely brocaded vestments, extending her hand towards an affable-looking, chubby-cheeked infant who, given the golden aura that crowned his head, was none other than the Baby Jesus. With a loving smile he was placing a gold wedding ring on her plump index finger; while, suspended above them, an angel in a tunic covered in precious gems was depositing a garland on her head. In another image there was an extremely tall colonnade covered with unfolding edifying scenes, in front of which a humble nun was holding the hand of the Lord of Heaven. A venerable old man dressed as splendidly as a Pope was witnessing these nuptials, gently urging the little virgin with a gesture towards her spouse. The nuns would explain to Concetta that the precious colonnade in the background was nothing less than the entrance to the 'mansion' (for they were prone to express themselves in such terms) – the mansion into which she would be welcomed as a young bride. Churches, explained the nuns – even those cathedrals glittering with mosaics – are merely God's houses on earth. Imagine then what His heavenly mansions must be like in comparison. The floors are carpeted with meadows of flowers, but these flowers are made of precious stones. In the gardens, angels with the wingspan of eagles fly about instead of birds, producing a melodious sound with the beating of their wings. Life passes there with continuous music, dances and smiles of love. Angels hidden amongst the trees, like shepherds, sing the praises of the young bride. Others bring her regal vestments, others still slip elaborately decorated sandals on to her feet. She needs only to raise a finger and the whole of paradise will fall silent and listen to her.

Concetta glowed with pride on hearing such promises; every day she would flee her home to visit the nuns, and as soon as she came of age she entered the convent. I was out of town at the time, so was not present when she took her vows, in a ceremony that her mother and sisters refused to attend. When I returned, her sisters whispered to me a warning that she was never to be spoken of again in front of her mother; Angela had sworn that, as far as she was concerned, her daughter had ceased to exist. She did mention her to me, on just one occasion. She placed a hand on her heart, and with dark eyes and the portentous tone of someone about to pronounce an anathema, she said: 'My whole heart was devoted to that daughter of mine; and now, where my heart used to be, *there is nothing but stone.*' Then she flung a glance of haughty commiseration in the direction of her other two daughters, who were both short and stout, with lank hair and thick, coarse hands.

Meanwhile, from the convent, Concetta was attempting to pay court, so to speak, to her mother. She would frequently send her gifts, such as sweet pizzas, topped with confectionery, that her mother refused to taste and passed on to us; or strips of white silk on which a red heart pierced by an arrow had been embroidered. These bits of embroidery transported to the house a redolence of the domesticity and piety of a monastic enclosure, and the mother would throw them into a corner with a gesture of ironic contempt. At Easter a cardboard box arrived, containing a figurine of a nun made of sweet pastry, more than forty centimetres tall, wearing a habit made of chocolate. It was the product of a collective effort by the whole convent, and they had not failed to include such realistic details as the thin rope around her waist from which a minuscule cross was hanging, done in red sweets. At the sight of this nun the mother was overcome with sheer, cold fury, and ordered that it should be thrown into the fire. Her other two daughters obeyed, though not without a pang of regret.

In the evening, behind the grates of the convent, Concetta would hold a cross in her hands and look at the star-studded sky. She would fantasize that the stars were the lit windows of her future abode, trying to imagine which one of them belonged to her future spouse's room. Concetta had reached the age of twenty-three. And it was at this time that she fell ill with typhus and died.

The sisters rushed to inform me breathlessly that Concetta was in her final agony, and to beg me to persuade her mother to visit her at least this one last time. I ran to the widow's home, but quickly realized that Angela had already made up her mind to go, and that she only pretended to need to be begged to do so. With pupils sparkling, and two vermilion stains on her cheeks, she walked ahead of me towards the convent, and without even stopping to acknowledge the nun who acted as doorkeeper, swept upstairs to her daughter's cell with the proprietorial air of a mistress. To the murmuring nuns who came to her side it seemed that she was saying, 'Out of my way, she's my daughter and mine alone; I'm the only one with any right to cry for her.' She approached the bed, and in the theatrical, passionate manner that my female compatriots assume when afflicted, she exclaimed: 'Ah, my little Concetta, my own Concetta!', and kneeling down by the side of the bed she grasped her daughter's hands and showered them with a flurry of kisses.

So as not to weigh down her weary head, Concetta's nun's bands had been removed. Her short hair was thick with curls, like a child's. But although her face had become more gaunt, it was clear that the illness had struck her at the point when her beauty was maturing and expanding, as you regularly see in brides in those parts. Her big healthy chest heaved beneath the sheet; her face, with its languishing gaze and dark circles beneath her eyes, had the warm, richly hued pallor of jasmine flowers;

with every breath from between her blanched lips her small beautiful teeth were revealed, with an animal grace but now shadowed by her illness. 'She's dying like a saint,' the Mother Superior told me, shaking her head. Angela overheard this and darted a vitriolic look at the Mother Superior: the look of a rival. Then she grabbed hold of that basic iron bedstead, and with a strident voice, shaken by sobbing, she began to scold her daughter thus: 'Oh, how beautiful you used to be, my little daughter!' she said, 'Oh, how beautiful you were! You were like a garden of roses. You should have married a gentleman, instead of dying in this garret. Ah, daughter of my flesh, my own flesh and blood, who has murdered you? You should have stayed with your mother, who kissed your lovely mouth and would not have let you die. Everything about you was beautiful, such lovely small feet, such precious little hands. Concetta, Concetta, come back to your mother!'

All of those standing around her were silent, as if watching a show. But Concetta gave no sign of being aware of her mother's presence. She parted her lips slightly in an exhausted and ecstatic smile that still had an irrepressible trace of flirtatiousness. And with a childish and almost extinguished voice, as frail as a spiderweb, she began to utter: 'I see, I see . . .'

All of those around her held their breath. She was lowering her eyelashes, with an amorous demeanour, and her voice could barely be heard, sighing out: 'I see a meadow, of lilies, I see saints, and angels. This beautiful palace, it's mine, Lord! What a beautiful palace, how many crowns, for me . . .' She seemed to pause as if searching for words with which to express her gratitude. Her mouth was still half open, but she was quiet now. I noticed that her fellow nuns who had gathered around her seemed to have assumed a triumphant air, as if in victory. I looked at Concetta's graceful hand, lying lifeless now on the sheet, and realized that her elegantly oval nails had turned violet. Angela looked devastated: her silent face was as bloodless as her daughter's, but it was wet with dense, heavy tears. She let go of Concetta's hand and covered her face. When she looked up again, her eyes were dry and she had assumed a dignified, set expression.

Soon after, she was giving orders in the convent relating to Concetta's funeral, which she imagined would be a sumptuous affair: 'My daughter was a real lady!' she declared, haughtily, to the nuns, who, in that convent, were almost all daughters of peasants and artisans. They listened with lowered heads, and nodded humbly, almost as if they were in the presence of the Abbess herself.

And so we retired, leaving to the nuns of the convent, according to established custom, the task of keeping vigil over their sister. She was dressed again in the clothes that identified her as belonging to God: the black skirt; the wooden crucifix; the wimple, black wings on her head. The next day, having stayed at Angela's home so as not to leave the mother on her own, I saw, from the window, Concetta's procession towards her longed-for mansion. Despite any efforts to the contrary, the funeral was a modest one. The coffin was carried to the cemetery, with just three small wreaths, followed by chanting priests, and then the nuns. Bringing up the rear were the Daughters of Mary, wearing their immaculate bridal veils, beneath which their everyday, brightly coloured felt dresses and their down-at-heel ankle boots could be glimpsed.

Angela was watching the cortège with a fixed look. At a certain point, shaking her fist, she said: 'She didn't even spare a last word for her poor mother!' And she turned her face to one side, with a sob of bitter jealousy, then resumed her careful scrutiny of the wreaths, the procession, the Daughters of Mary bearing long candles in their hands. From behind the glassy veil of her tears a mundane curiosity peered, and her lips formed a childish pout that culminated in a lachrymose outburst: 'Ah, my beautiful daughter,' she cried, with desperate vanity, 'look how they're taking her! She deserved a send-off worthy of a queen! And she was a queen, that wretched girl!' And with disdain she withdrew from the window, while the short procession disappeared behind Piazza Garibaldi.

'Le ambiziose'
First published in the magazine *Oggi* (6 December 1941), and posthumously published in *Racconti dimenticati* (Einaudi, 2004).

GIORGIO MANGANELLI

1922–90

Manganelli, who detested Realism and conventional narrative, was a member of the 'Gruppo 63', a neo-avant-garde literary movement founded in Palermo in 1963. In opposition to the intellectual mainstream and the post-war vision of writers such as Carlo Cassola, the group, which never wrote a manifesto, insisted on experimental writing with a strong linguistic focus. Born in Milan, Manganelli, a gifted student, joined the Partisan War in 1944. Captured and condemned to die a year later, he was set free by his executioner after being beaten with a rifle. He began his literary career by translating Henry James' *Confidence* and also translated the works of T. S. Eliot, Edgar Allan Poe and W. B. Yeats. He worked as an editor for various publishing houses and taught English literature at La Sapienza University, in Rome, but grew bitterly disillusioned with academia. He was a passionate traveller and wrote perceptively about India. A Jungian analysand for many years, he had a tormented relationship with his possessive mother and incorporated mythic archetypes into his work. Notes from his psychoanalysis inspired his first book, a linguistically ornate, brazenly stylized monologue called *Hilarotragoedia*, published when he was over forty, after his mother's death. *Centuria* (published in English as *Centuria: One Hundred Ouroboric Novels*), which received the Viareggio Prize in 1979, is a volume of one hundred extremely short, anguished, trenchant tales – the same number contained in Boccaccio's *Decameron*. They are recondite and relentless, rigorously on the edge. Each segment is to be savoured slowly and, given their intricately wrought nature, not necessarily all at once. Here are a few examples of his refined register, his experimental sensibility, his aspect at once audacious and kempt.

Sixteen, Twenty-one, Twenty-eight and Thirty-seven from Centuria

Translated by Henry Martin

Sixteen

The gentleman dressed in a linen suit, with loafers and short socks, looks at the clock. It is two minutes to eight. He is at home, seated, slightly uneasy, on the edge of a stiff and demanding chair. He is alone. In two minutes – by now no more than ninety seconds – he will have to begin. He got up a little early in order to be truly ready. He washed carefully, attentively urinated, patiently evacuated, meticulously shaved. All of his underwear is new, never worn before, and this suit was tailored more than a year ago for this morning. For a whole year he has not dared. He has frequently got up very early – in general, moreover, he's an early riser – but at the moment when all preparations were completed and he took his place on the chair, his courage had always failed him. But now he is about to begin. Fifty seconds remain before eight o'clock. Properly speaking, there is absolutely nothing he must begin. From another point of view, he stands at the beginning of absolutely everything. In any case, there is nothing he must 'do'. He must simply go from eight o'clock to nine o'clock. Nothing more: traverse the space of an hour, a space he has traversed innumerable times, but now he must traverse it as pure and simple time, nothing else, absolutely. Eight o'clock has already passed, by a little more than a minute. He is calm, but feels a slight tremor gather within his body. At the seventh minute, his heart begins little by little to accelerate. At the tenth minute, his throat begins to close, while his heart pulses at the brink of panic. With the fifteenth minute, his whole body douses itself in sweat, almost instantaneously; three minutes later, the saliva in his mouth begins to dry; his lips grow white. At the twenty-first minute, his teeth begin to chatter, as though he were laughing; his eyes dilate, their lids cease to beat. He feels his sphincter open, and all his body hairs erect, immobile in a chill. Suddenly, his heart slows, his vision clouds. At the twenty-fifth minute, a furious tremor shakes him through and through for twenty seconds; when it stops, his diaphragm begins to move: his diaphragm now grips his heart. Tears flow, though he does not cry. A roar deafens his ears. The gentleman dressed in a linen suit would like to explain, but the twenty-eighth minute deals him a blow on the temple, and he falls from the chair; upon striking the floor, absolutely without a sound, he disintegrates.

Twenty-one

At every awakening, every morning – a reluctant awakening, which might also be described as lazy – this gentleman begins the day with a rapid inventory of the world. He realized some time ago that he always awakens in a different point of the cosmos, even if the earth, the capsule in which he dwells, does not look extrinsically modified. As a child he was convinced that the movements of the earth through space direct it from time to time into the near vicinity or even through the interior of hell, whereas it is never permitted to pass through paradise, since that experience would render all further continuance of the world impossible, superfluous and ridiculous. So paradise must avoid the earth at all cost, so as not to wound Creation's plans, which are meticulous and incomprehensible. Even now – as an adult man who drives and owns an automobile – something of that childhood hypothesis has remained with him. By now he has cast it in slightly more secular terms, and the question he asks himself is more metaphoric and apparently detached: he knows that while he sleeps the whole world moves – as dreams demonstrate – and that every morning the pieces of the world, no matter if involved in a game or not, are arrayed differently on the board. He claims no right to know what this shift may mean, but he knows that at times he can feel the presence of abysses, the temptations of sheer cliffs, or rare, long plains on which he'd like to roll – there are times when he comes to see himself as a spherical celestial body – on and on. There are moments, too, of confused impressions of grasses, and as well of the exciting but not infrequently unpleasant sensation of being illumined by several suns, suns not always reciprocally friendly. At other times, he clearly hears the sound of waves, sent by either storm or calm; and on occasion he is brutally reminded of his own position in the world: for example, when cruel and attentive jaws take him by the back of the neck, as must have happened countless times to doomed and exhausted forebears between the teeth of beasts whose faces they never saw. He learned some time ago that you never wake up in your own room: he has concluded in fact that there are no such things as rooms, that walls and sheets are illusions, a fakery; he knows that he is suspended in the void; that he, like every other person, is the centre of the world, from which infinite infinities radiate. He knows he could not hold his own in the face of so much horror, and that the room, and even the abyss and hell, are inventions intended to defend him.

Twenty-eight

Excited by a strange and senseless design of the clouds at dawn, the Emperor arrived in Cornwall. But the voyage had been so strenuous, so tortuous and errant, as to leave him with a very unclear memory of the place from which he had first set out. He had departed with three squires and a menial. The first squire had run off with a gypsy woman, after a desperate discussion with the Emperor during a night charged with strokes of lightning. The second squire had fallen in love with the plague, and would hear no reason to abandon a village devastated by advancing death. The third squire had enrolled into the troops of the following emperor, and had tried to assassinate him. The Emperor was forced to consider him condemned to death, and pretended to carry out the sentence by cutting his throat with his little finger; they both had laughed, and bade farewell to one another. The menial had remained with the Emperor. Both of them were silent, melancholy men, aware of pursuing a goal which was not so much improbable as irrelevant; they both had metaphysical notions which were highly imprecise, and whenever they came to a temple, a church, a sanctuary, they did not enter, since both of them were certain, for different reasons, that inside such places they could only encounter lies, equivocations, disinformation. Once they had arrived in Cornwall, the Emperor made no secret of his discomfort: he did not understand the language, he did not know what to do, his coins were examined with suspicious care by diffident villagers. He wanted to write to the Palace, but did not remember the address. An emperor is the only man who can, or must, be ignorant of his own address. The menial had no problems: remaining with the disoriented Emperor was his only way of establishing orientation. As time passed, Cornwall opened to merchant traffic and the tourist trade. And a history professor from Samarkand, Ohio, recognized the Emperor's profile: by now he passed his days at the pub, served by his taciturn drudge. News of the Emperor's presence in Cornwall spread rapidly, and even though no one knew what an emperor might be, nor with respect to what part of the world, the locals found it flattering. Beer was served to him for free. The village in which he resided put one of his coins in its coat of arms. The menial was given a generic noble title, and the Emperor, who speaks by now a little of the local language, is in a few days time to marry the beautiful daughter of a depressed warrior; he now has a watch and eats apple pie; they say that at the next elections he'll be a candidate for the liberals; and he will lose with honour.

Thirty-seven

The woman for whom he was waiting has not come to the appointment. He, all the same – the man attired more youthfully than suits him – does not feel offended. Indeed, it does not bother him at all. If he were more observant, he would have to admit to feeling a slight but indubitable pleasure. He can shape a number of hypotheses on the reasons why the woman has not appeared at their rendezvous. As he sounds out these reasons, he does not desert their meeting's appointed place, but only steps off slightly to one side of it, as though it were a den in which some part of her, or the whole of her, sat concealed. Perhaps she has forgotten. Since he likes to think of himself as an insignificant person, he is pleased with such a hypothesis, which would mean that she too has identified him as exiguous, aleatory and thus of such a kind that forgetting him is the only way to remember him. She might have reached her decision in a moment of caprice – or perhaps of pique – since she is an impetuous woman; and in that case she will have recognized his function as a nuisance, as a minuscule bother, surely no longing of the heart, but something no longer removable from her life, or at least from a few of the days of it. She may have mistaken the hour of the appointment, and in that moment he realizes that he is not clear, he himself, as to what that hour may have been. But this realization does not disturb him: he finds it natural for the hour to be imprecise, since he sees himself as having a perpetual appointment with the woman who has not arrived. Or has there perhaps been an error of place? He smiles. Might that not mean that she has taken repair, gone into hiding in some secret place, and that her absence is therefore fear, flight or even a game, a summons? Or that the appointment was everywhere, so that neither one, in reality, could fail the other, for either the place or the time? So he might conclude that in fact the appointment has been not only respected, but obeyed with absolute precision, indeed has been interpreted, understood, consummated. His slight feeling of pleasure is beginning to transmute into an overture of joy. He decides, indeed, that the appointment has been so thoroughly experienced that now he has nothing higher or more total to give of himself. Brusquely, he turns his back on the meeting place and tenderly whispers 'Adieu' to the woman he is preparing to meet.

'Sixteen', 'Twenty-one', 'Twenty-eight' and 'Thirty-seven' from *Centuria*. (Rizzoli, 1979).

PRIMO LEVI

1919–87

Levi hated labels. Throughout *Il sistema periodico* (*The Periodic Table*), a work of literature impossible to define, he talks about the Germans' love for classifying things. Levi survived Auschwitz, and he resists classification. He was a human polyhedron who contemplated the act of transformation throughout his life: the conversion of elements, and the double nature of things. He was a writer who worked in multiple genres and a chemist who worked for years at a paint factory. Born to a Jewish family in Turin, Levi was a young man of letters long before his deportation in 1943 – a lover of adventure stories, of Herman Melville, of François Rabelais. The story included here, at once cruel and magical, features a centaur as a character and celebrates life, desire and the animal aspect of man. It comes from *Storie naturali* (*Natural Histories*), published in 1966. The collection was dismissed as science fiction, and Levi published it under the pseudonym, Damiano Malabaila, perhaps to evade the label which had been affixed to him as a 'Holocaust writer' after the publication of *Se questo è un uomo* (*If This Is a Man*), an account of his time in Auschwitz. Poorly received when first published, *Se questo è un uomo* was reprinted and widely appreciated only in 1958, with the flap copy anonymously written by Calvino, and is now required reading for every high-school student in Italy. The flap copy of *Storie naturali*, which Levi composed himself, was also anonymous, but more or less reveals his identity: 'I would not publish them if I had not noticed (not immediately, to tell the truth) that a continuity – a bridge – existed between the Lager [camp] and these inventions.' Levi received the Strega Prize in 1979 for *La chiave a stella* (published in English as both *The Wrench* and

The Monkey's Wrench), a novel in the form of interlinked stories featuring a manual labourer as one of its main characters and incorporating Torinese dialect. He ended his life eight years later, throwing himself down the stairwell of the apartment building where he had been born.

Quaestio de Centauris

Translated by Jenny McPhee

et quae sit iis potandi, comedendi et nubendi ratio. Et fuit debatuta per X
hebdomadas inter vesanum auctorem et ejusdem sodales perpetuos G.L. et L.N.

My father kept him in a stall, because he didn't know where else to keep
him. He had been given to him by a friend, a sea captain, who said he
had bought him in Salonika: I, however, learned from him directly that
he was born in Colophon.

They had strictly forbidden me to go anywhere near him because, they
said, he was easily angered and would kick. But from my direct experience
I can confirm that this was an old superstition; so from adolescence I never
paid much attention to the prohibition and, actually, especially in the winter, I spent many memorable hours with him, and other wonderful times
in the summer, when Trachi (this was his name) put me on his back with
his own hands and took off at a mad gallop towards the woods on the hills.

He had learned our language fairly easily, but retained a slight Levan-
tine accent. Despite his two hundred and sixty years, his appearance was
youthful, both in his human aspects and in those equine. What I will
relate here is the fruit of our long conversations.

The centaurs' origins are legendary; but the legends that they pass down
among themselves are very different from those we consider to be classic.

Remarkably, their traditions also begin with a highly intelligent man, a
Noah-like inventor and saviour, whom they call Cutnofeset. But there were
no centaurs on Cutnofeset's ark. Nor, by the way, were there 'seven pairs of
every species of clean beast, and a pair of every species of the beasts that
are not clean'. The centaurian tradition is more rational than the biblical,

recounting that only the archetypal animals, the key species, were saved: man but not the monkey; the horse but not the donkey or the wild ass; the rooster and the crow but not the vulture or the hoopoe or the gyrfalcon.

How, then, did these species come about? Immediately afterward, legend says. When the waters retreated, a deep layer of warm mud covered the earth. Now, this mud, which harboured in its decay all the enzymes from what had perished in the flood, was extraordinarily fertile: as soon as it was touched by the sun, it was immediately covered in shoots from which grasses and plants of every type sprang forth; and even more, within its soft and moist bosom, it was host to the marriages of all the species saved in the ark. It was a time, never again to be repeated, of wild, ecstatic fecundity in which the entire universe felt love, so much so that it nearly returned to chaos.

Those were the days in which the earth itself fornicated with the sky, in which everything germinated and everything was fruitful. Not only every marriage but every union, every contact, every encounter, even fleeting, even between different species, even between beasts and stones, even between plants and stones, was fertile, and produced offspring, not in a few months, but in a few days. The sea of warm mud, which concealed the cold and prudish face of the earth, was a single immense nuptial bed, boiling over with desire in all its recesses, and teeming with jubilant germs.

This second creation was the true Creation; because, according to what is passed down among the centaurs, there is no other way to explain certain analogies, certain convergences observed by all. Why is the dolphin similar to the fish, and yet gives birth and nurses its offspring? Because it's the child of a tuna fish and a cow. Where do the delicate colours of butterflies and their ability to fly come from? They are the children of a flower and a fly. And tortoises are the children of a frog and a rock. And bats of an owl and a mouse. And conchs of a snail and a polished pebble. And hippopotami of a horse and a river. And vultures of a worm and an owl. And the big whales, the leviathans, how else to explain their immense mass? Their wooden bones, their black and oily skin and their fiery breath are living testimony to a venerable union in which this same primordial mud got greedy hold of the ark's feminine keel, made of gopher wood and covered inside and out with shiny pitch, when the end of all flesh had been decreed.

Such was the origin of every form, whether living today or extinct:

dragons and chameleons, chimeras and harpies, crocodiles and minotaurs, elephants and giants, whose petrified bones are still found today, to our amazement, in the heart of the mountains. And so it was for the centaurs themselves, since in this festival of origins, in this panspermia, the few survivors of the human family had also taken part.

Notably, Cam, the profligate son, took part: the first generation of centaurs originated in his wild passion for a Thessalian horse. From the beginning, their progeny were noble and strong, preserving the best of both human nature and equine. They were at once wise and courageous, generous and shrewd, good at hunting and at singing, at waging war and at observing the heavens. It seemed, in fact, as happens with the most felicitous unions, that the virtues of the parents were magnified in their progeny, since, at least in the beginning, they were more powerful and faster racers than their Thessalian mothers, and a good deal wiser and more cunning than black Cam and their other human fathers. This would also explain, according to some, their longevity; though others have instead attributed this to their eating habits, which I will come to in a moment. Or it could simply be a projection across time of their great vitality, and this I, too, believe resolutely (and the story I am about to tell attests to it): that in hereditary terms the herbivore power of the horse does not count as much as the red blindness of the bloody and forbidden spasm, the moment of human-feral fullness in which they were conceived.

Whatever we may think of this, anyone who has carefully considered the centaurs' classical traditions cannot help noticing that centauresses are never mentioned. As I learned from Trachi, they do not in fact exist.

The man–mare union, today, moreover, fertile only in rare cases, produces and only ever has produced male centaurs, for which there must be a fundamental reason, though at present it eludes us. As for the inverse of the unions, between stallions and women, these occur very rarely at any point in time, and furthermore come about through the solicitation of dissolute women, who by nature are not particularly inclined to procreate.

In the exceptional cases in which fertilization is successful in these very rare unions, a female bi-part offspring is produced: her two natures, however, inversely assembled. The creatures have the head, neck and front feet of a horse, but their back and stomach are those of a human female, and the hind legs are human.

During his long life Trachi encountered very few of them, and he assured me that he felt no attraction to these squalid monsters. They are not 'proud and nimble', but insufficiently vital; they are infertile, idle and transient; they do not become familiar with man or learn to obey his commands, but live miserably in the densest forests, not in herds but in rural solitude. They feed on grass and berries, and when they are surprised by a man they have the curious habit of always presenting themselves to him head first, as if embarrassed by their human half.

Trachi was born in Colophon of a secret union between a man and one of the numerous Thessalian horses that are still wild on the island. I am afraid that among the readers of these notes some may refuse to believe these assertions, since official science, permeated as it is still today with Aristotelianism, denies the possibility of a fertile union between different species. But official science often lacks humility: such unions are, indeed, generally infertile; but – how often has evidence been sought? Not more than a few dozen times. And has it been sought among all the innumerable possible couplings? Certainly not. Since I have no reason to doubt what Trachi has told me about himself, I must therefore encourage the incredulous to consider that there are more things in heaven and on earth than are dreamt of in our philosophy.

He lived mostly in solitude, left to himself, which was the common destiny of all like him. He slept in the open, standing on all four hooves, with his head on his arms, which he would lean against a low branch or a rock. He grazed in the island's fields and glades, or gathered fruit from branches; on the hottest days he would go down to one of the deserted beaches, and there he would bathe, swimming like a horse, with his chest and head erect, and then would gallop for a long while, violently churning up the wet sand.

But the bulk of his time, in every season, was devoted to food: in fact, during the forays that Trachi frequently undertook in the vigour of his youth among the barren cliffs and gorges of his native island, he always, following an instinct for prudence, brought along, tucked under his arms, two large bundles of grass or foliage, gathered in times of rest.

Even if centaurs are limited to a strictly vegetarian diet by their predominantly equine constitution, it must be remembered that they have a torso and head like a man's: this structure obliges them to introduce through a small human mouth the considerable quantity of grass, straw or grain necessary to the sustenance of their large bodies. These foods, notably of limited nutritional value, also require long mastication, since human teeth are badly adapted to the grinding of forage.

In conclusion, the centaurs' nourishment is a laborious process; by physical necessity, they are required to spend three-quarters of their time chewing. This fact is not lacking in authoritative testimonials, first and foremost that of Ucalegon of Samos (Dig. Phil., XXIV, II–8 and XLIII *passim*), who attributes the centaurs' proverbial wisdom to their alimentary regimen, consisting of one continuous meal from dawn to dusk; this would deter them from other vain or baleful activities, such as avidity for riches or gossip, and would contribute to their usual self-restraint. Nor was this unknown to Bede, who mentions it in his *Historia ecclesiastica gentis Anglorum*.

It is rather strange that the classical mythological tradition neglected this characteristic of centaurs. The truth of the fact, however, rests on reliable evidence, and moreover, as we have shown, it can be deduced by a simple consideration of natural philosophy.

To return to Trachi: his education was, by our criteria, strangely fragmentary. He learned Greek from the island's shepherds, whose company he sought out now and again, despite his taciturn and shy nature. From his own observations he also learned many subtle and intimate things about grasses, plants, forest animals, water, clouds, stars and planets; and I myself noticed that, even after his capture and under a foreign sky, he could feel the approach of a gale or the imminence of a snowstorm many hours before it actually arrived. Though I couldn't describe how, nor could he do so himself, he also felt the grain growing in the fields, he felt the pulse of water in underground streams, and he sensed the erosion of flooded rivers. When De Simone's cow gave birth two hundred metres away from us, he felt a reflex in his own gut; the same thing happened when the tenant farmer's daughter gave birth. In fact, on a spring evening he indicated to me that a birth must be taking place and, more precisely, in a particular corner of the hayloft; we went there and found that a bat had just brought into the world six blind little monsters, and was feeding them minuscule portions of her milk.

All centaurs are made this way, he told me, feeling every germination, animal, human or vegetable, as a wave of joy running through their veins. They also perceive, on a precordial level, and in the form of anxiety and tremulous tension, every desire and every sexual encounter that occurs in their vicinity; therefore, even though usually chaste, they enter into a state of vivid agitation during the season of love.

We lived together for a long time: in some ways, it could be said that we grew up together. Despite his advanced age, he was actually a young creature in everything he said and did, and he learned things so easily that it seemed useless (not to mention awkward) to send him to school. I educated him myself, almost without realizing it or wanting to, passing on to him in turn the knowledge that I learned from my teachers day after day.

We kept him hidden as much as possible, owing, in part, to his own explicit desire and, in part, to a form of exclusive and jealous affection that we all felt for him, and, in yet another part, a combination of rationality and intuition that advised us to shield him from all unnecessary contact with our human world.

Naturally, his presence among us had leaked out among the neighbours. At first, they asked a lot of questions, some not very discreet, but then, as will happen, their curiosity diminished from lack of nourishment. A few of our intimate friends were admitted into his presence, the first of whom were the De Simones, and they swiftly became his friends, too. Only once, when a horsefly bite provoked a painful abscess in his rump, did we require the skill of a veterinarian; but he was an understanding and discreet man, who most scrupulously promised to keep this professional secret and, as far as I know, kept his promise.

Things went differently with the blacksmith. Nowadays, blacksmiths are unfortunately very rare: we found one two hours away by foot and he was a yokel, stupid and brutish. My father tried in vain to persuade him to maintain a certain reserve, which included paying him tenfold as much as was due for his services. It made no difference; every Sunday at the tavern he gathered a crowd around him and told the entire village about his strange client. Luckily, he liked his wine, and was in the habit of telling tall tales when he was drunk, so he wasn't taken too seriously.

It pains me to write this story. It is a story from my youth, and I feel as if in writing it I were expelling it from myself, and that later I will feel deprived of something strong and pure.

One summer Teresa De Simone, my childhood friend and cohort, returned to her parents' house. She had gone to the city to study; I hadn't seen her for many years, I found her changed, and the change troubled me. Maybe I had fallen in love, but with little consciousness of it: what I mean is, I did not admit it to myself, not even hypothetically. She was rather lovely, shy, calm and serene.

As I have already mentioned, the De Simones were among the few neighbours whom we saw with some regularity. They knew Trachi and loved him.

After Teresa's return, we spent a long evening together, just the three of us. It was one of those rare evenings never to be forgotten: the moon, the crickets, the intense smell of hay, the air still and warm. We heard singing in the distance, and suddenly Trachi began to sing, without looking at us, as if in a dream. It was a long song, its rhythm bold and strong, with words I didn't know. A Greek song, Trachi said; but when we asked him to translate it, he turned his head away and became silent.

We were all silent for a long time; then Teresa went home. The following morning, Trachi drew me aside and said this:

'Oh, my dearest friend, my hour has come: I have fallen in love. That woman has got inside of me, and possesses me. I desire to see her and hear her, perhaps even touch her, and nothing else; I therefore desire something impossible. I am reduced to one point: there is nothing left of me except for this desire. I am changing, I have changed, I have become another.'

He told me other things as well, which I hesitate to write, because I feel it's very unlikely that my words will do him justice. He told me that, since the previous night, he felt that he had become 'a battlefield'; that he understood, as he never had understood before, the exploits of his violent ancestors, Nessus, Pholus; that his entire human half was crammed with dreams, with noble, courtly, and vain fantasies, and he wanted to perform reckless feats, to do justice with the strength of his own arms, raze to the ground the densest forests with his vehemence, run to the edges of the earth, discover and conquer new lands, and create there the works of a fertile civilization. All of this, in a way that was obscure even to himself, he wanted to perform before the eyes of Teresa De Simone: to do it for her, to dedicate it to her. Finally, he realized the vanity of his dreams in the very act of dreaming them, and this was the content of the song of the previous evening, a song he had learned long ago during his adolescence in Colophon, and which he had never understood and never sung until now.

For many weeks nothing else happened; we saw the De Simones every so often, but Trachi's behaviour revealed nothing of the storm that raged inside him. It was I, and none other, who provoked the breakdown.

One October evening, Trachi was at the blacksmith's. I met Teresa, and we went for a walk together in the woods. We talked, and of who else but Trachi? I didn't betray my friend's confidence; but I did worse.

I quickly realized that Teresa was not as shy as she initially appeared to be: she chose, as if by chance, a narrow path that led into the thickest part of the woods; I knew it was a dead end, and knew that Teresa knew. Where the path came to an end, she sat down on dry leaves and I did the same. The valley bell-tower rang out seven times, and she pressed up against me in a way that rid me of all doubt. By the time we got home night had fallen, but Trachi hadn't yet returned.

I realized immediately that I had behaved badly; actually, I realized it during the act itself, and still today it pains me. Yet I also know that the fault is not all mine, nor is it Teresa's. Trachi was with us: we had immersed ourselves in his aura, we had gravitated into his field. I know this because I myself had seen that wherever he passed flowers bloomed before their time, and their pollen flew in the wind of his wake as he ran.

Trachi didn't return. Over the following days, we laboriously reconstructed the rest of his story based upon witnesses' accounts and his tracks.

After a night of anxious waiting for all of us, and for me of secret torment, I went to look for him myself at the blacksmith's. The blacksmith wasn't at home: he was at the hospital with a cracked skull; he was unable to speak. I found his assistant. He told me that Trachi had come at about six o'clock to get shoed. He was silent and sad, but tranquil. Without showing any impatience, he let himself be chained as usual (the uncivilized practice of this particular blacksmith: years earlier he had had a bad experience with a skittish horse, and we had, in vain, tried to convince him that this precaution was in every way absurd with regard to Trachi). Three of his hooves had already been shod when a long and violent shudder coursed through him. The blacksmith turned upon him with that harsh tone often used on horses; as Trachi's agitation seemed to increase, the blacksmith struck him with a whip.

Trachi seemed to calm down, 'But his eyes were rolling around as if he were mad; and he seemed to be hearing voices.' Suddenly, with a furious tug, Trachi pulled the chains from their wall mounts, and the end of one hit the blacksmith in the head, sending him to the floor in a faint. Trachi then threw himself against the door with all his weight, head first, his arms crossed over his head, and galloped off towards the hills while the four chains, still constricting his legs, whirled around, wounding him repeatedly.

'What time did this happen?' I asked, disturbed by a presentiment.

The assistant hesitated: it was not yet night, but he couldn't say precisely. But then, yes, now he remembered: just a few seconds before Trachi pulled the chains from the wall the time had rung from the bell-tower, and the boss said to him, in dialect so that Trachi wouldn't understand: 'It's already seven o'clock! If all my clients were as currish as this one . . .'

Seven o'clock!

It wasn't difficult, unfortunately, to follow Trachi's furious flight; even if no one had seen him, there were conspicuous traces of the blood he had lost, and the scrapes made by the chains on tree trunks and on rocks by the side of the road. He hadn't headed towards home, or towards the De Simones': he had cleared the two-metre wooden fence that surrounds the Chiapasso property, and crossed the vineyards in a blind fury, making a path for himself through the rows of vines, in a straight line, knocking down stakes and vines, breaking the thick iron wires that held up the vine branches.

He reached the barnyard and found the barn door bolted shut from the outside. He easily could have opened it with his hands; instead, he picked up an old thresher, weighing well over fifty kilos, and hurled it against the door, reducing it to splinters. Only six cows, a calf, chickens and rabbits were in the barn. Trachi left immediately and, still in a mad gallop, headed towards Baron Caglieris's estate.

It was at least six and a half kilometres away, on the other side of the valley, but Trachi got there in a matter of minutes. He looked for the stable: he didn't find it with his first blow, but only after he used his hooves and shoulders to knock down many doors. What he did in the stable we know from an eyewitness, a stable boy, who, at the sound of the door shattering, had had the good sense to hide in the hay, and from there he had seen everything.

Trachi hesitated for a moment on the threshold, panting and bloody. The horses, unsettled, shook their heads; tugging on their halters. Trachi pounced on a three-year-old white mare; in one blow he broke the chain that bound her to the trough, and dragging her by this same chain led her outside. The mare didn't put up any resistance; strange, the stable boy told me, since she had a rather skittish and reluctant character, nor was she in heat.

They galloped together as far as the river: here Trachi was seen to stop, cup his hands, dip them into the water, and drink repeatedly. They then proceeded side by side into the woods. Yes, I followed their tracks: into those same woods and along that same path, to that same place where Teresa had asked me to take her.

And it was right there, for that entire night, that Trachi must have celebrated his monstrous nuptials. There I found the ground dug up, broken branches, brown and white horsehair, human hair and more blood. Not far away, drawn by the sound of her troubled breathing, I found the mare. She lay on the ground on her side, gasping, her noble coat covered with dirt and grass. Hearing my footsteps she lifted her head a little, and followed me with the terrible stare of a spooked horse. She was not wounded, but exhausted. She gave birth eight months later to a foal: in every way normal, I was told.

Here Trachi's direct traces vanish. But, as perhaps some may remember, over the following days the newspapers reported on a strange series of horse-rustlings, all perpetrated with the same technique: a door knocked down, the halter undone or ripped off, the animal (always a mare, and always alone) led into some nearby wood, and then found exhausted. Only once did the abductor seem to meet with any resistance: his chance companion of that night was found dying, her neck broken.

There were six of these episodes, and they were reported in various places on the peninsula, occurring one after the other from north to south. In Voghera, in Lucca, near Lake Bracciano, in Sulmona, in Cerignola. The last happened near Lecce. Then nothing else; but perhaps this story is linked to a strange report made to the press by a fishing crew from

Puglia: just off Corfu they had come upon 'a man riding a dolphin'. This odd apparition swam vigorously towards the east; the sailors shouted at it, at which point the man and the grey rump sank under the water, disappearing from view.

'Quaestio de Centauris'
First published in *Il Mondo* (4 April 1961) under the title '*Il centauro di Trachi*'. It was then included in the collection *Storie naturali* (Einaudi, 1966).

TOMMASO LANDOLFI
1908–79

Landolfi was an aristocrat from the province of Caserta, once home to the Bourbon kings of Naples. He loved gambling and hated being photographed. He avoided literary events, granted very few interviews and insisted that his books' flaps – precious commercial real-estate for most authors – be left blank. His work was just as eccentric; he eventually abandoned conventional forms altogether and played rigorously with language, manufacturing his own idiosyncratic lexicon. For this reason Landolfi can be grouped, in this anthology, along with authors like Gadda and Savinio: iconoclastic, verbally precocious, linked to Surrealism and experimentation. Landolfi's writing, filled with archaic terms, can be challenging today even for an Italian reader. His creative output can be divided roughly into two phases, evolving from traditional narrative to deeply metaphysical texts, invented diaries and dialogues. An undisciplined student who nearly failed to finish high school, he excelled at learning languages and was a collector of grammars and dictionaries. A reader in French, Spanish, German and English, he also studied Arabic, Polish, Hungarian, Japanese, Swedish and was a lover in particular of the Russian language and its literature, writing his university thesis on the poetry of Anna Akhmatova. He also wrote a celebrated essay about the time Nikolai Gogol spent in Rome. The female protagonist of his first, fantastic novel, *La pietra lunare* (*The Moonstone*), published in 1939, is half-human, half-goat. His short stories are long, blasphemous, bitter, attuned to mystery and chance. This story, outlandish on every level, epitomizes Landolfi's fascination for the circuitous and the irrational. It is an unreal and hyper-real commentary on the writing of literary biography and our ongoing obsession with writers' lives. Landolfi received the Strega Prize in 1975 for a collection of short stories called *A caso* (At Random) and won the Viareggio Prize both in fiction and poetry.

Gogol's Wife

Translated by Wayland Young

At this point, confronted with the whole complicated affair of Nikolai Vassilevitch's wife, I am overcome by hesitation. Have I any right to disclose something which is unknown to the whole world, which my unforgettable friend himself kept hidden from the world (and he had his reasons), and which I am sure will give rise to all sorts of malicious and stupid misunderstandings? Something, moreover, which will very probably offend the sensibilities of all sorts of base, hypocritical people, and possibly of some honest people too, if there are any left? And finally, have I any right to disclose something before which my own spirit recoils, and even tends towards a more or less open disapproval?

But the fact remains that, as a biographer, I have certain firm obligations. Believing as I do that every bit of information about so lofty a genius will turn out to be of value to us and to future generations, I cannot conceal something which in any case has no hope of being judged fairly and wisely until the end of time. Moreover, what right have we to condemn? Is it given to us to know, not only what intimate needs, but even what higher and wider ends may have been served by those very deeds of a lofty genius which perchance may appear to us vile? No indeed, for we understand so little of these privileged natures. 'It is true,' a great man once said, 'that I also have to pee, but for quite different reasons.'

But without more ado I will come to what I know beyond doubt, and can prove beyond question, about this controversial matter, which will now – I dare to hope – no longer be so. I will not trouble to recapitulate what is already known of it, since I do not think this should be necessary at the present stage of development of Gogol studies.

Let me say it at once: Nikolai Vassilevitch's wife was not a woman. Nor

231

was she any sort of human being, nor any sort of living creature at all, whether animal or vegetable (although something of the sort has sometimes been hinted). She was quite simply a balloon. Yes, a balloon; and this will explain the perplexity, or even indignation, of certain biographers who were also the personal friends of the Master, and who complained that, although they often went to his house, they never saw her and 'never even heard her voice'. From this they deduced all sorts of dark and disgraceful complications – yes, and criminal ones too. No, gentlemen, everything is always simpler than it appears. You did not hear her voice simply because she could not speak, or to be more exact, she could only speak in certain conditions, as we shall see. And it was always, except once, in tête-à-tête with Nikolai Vassilevitch. So let us not waste time with any cheap or empty refutations but come at once to as exact and complete a description as possible of the being or object in question.

Gogol's so-called wife was an ordinary dummy made of thick rubber, naked at all seasons, buff in tint, or as is more commonly said, flesh-coloured. But since women's skins are not all of the same colour, I should specify that hers was a light-coloured, polished skin, like that of certain brunettes. It, or she, was, it is hardly necessary to add, of feminine sex. Perhaps I should say at once that she was capable of very wide alterations of her attributes without, of course, being able to alter her sex itself. She could sometimes appear to be thin, with hardly any breasts and with narrow hips more like a young lad than a woman, and at other times to be excessively well endowed or – let us not mince matters – fat. And she often changed the colour of her hair, both on her head and elsewhere on her body, though not necessarily at the same time. She could also seem to change in all sorts of other tiny particulars, such as the position of moles, the vitality of the mucous membranes and so forth. She could even to a certain extent change the very colour of her skin. One is faced with the necessity of asking oneself who she really was, or whether it would be proper to speak of a single 'person' – and in fact we shall see that it would be imprudent to press this point.

The cause of these changes, as my readers will already have understood, was nothing else but the will of Nikolai Vassilevitch himself. He would inflate her to a greater or lesser degree, would change her wig and her other tufts of hair, would grease her with ointments and touch her up in various ways so as to obtain more or less the type of woman which suited him at that moment. Following the natural inclinations of his fancy, he even amused himself sometimes by producing grotesque or monstrous forms; as will be readily understood, she became deformed when inflated beyond a certain point or if she remained below a certain pressure.

But Gogol soon tired of these experiments, which he held to be 'after all, not very respectful' to his wife, whom he loved in his own way – however inscrutable it may remain to us: he loved her, but which of these incarnations, we may ask ourselves, did he love? Alas, I have already indicated that the end of the present account will furnish some sort of an answer. And how can I have stated above that it was Nikolai Vassilevitch's will which ruled that woman? In a certain sense, yes, it is true; but it is equally certain that she soon became no longer his slave but his tyrant. And here yawns the abyss, or if you prefer it, the Jaws of Tartarus. But let us not anticipate.

I have said that Gogol obtained with his manipulations more or less the type of woman which he needed from time to time. I should add that when, in rare cases, the form he obtained perfectly incarnated his desire, Nikolai Vassilevitch fell in love with it 'exclusively', as he said in his own words, and that this was enough to render 'her' stable for a certain time – until he fell out of love with 'her'. I counted no more than three or four of these violent passions – or, as I suppose they would be called today, infatuations – in the life (dare I say in the conjugal life?) of the great writer. It will be convenient to add here that a few years after what one may call his marriage, Gogol had even given a name to his wife. It was Caracas, which is, unless I am mistaken, the capital of Venezuela. I have never been able to discover the reason for this choice: great minds are so capricious!

Speaking only of her normal appearance, Caracas was what is called a fine woman – well built and proportioned in every part. She had every smallest attribute of her sex properly disposed in the proper location. Particularly worthy of attention were her genital organs (if the adjective is permissible in such a context). They were formed by means of ingenious folds in the rubber. Nothing was forgotten, and their operation was rendered easy by various devices, as well as by the internal pressure of the air.

Caracas also had a skeleton, even though a rudimentary one. Perhaps it was made of whalebone. Special care had been devoted to the construction of the thoracic cage, of the pelvic basin and of the cranium. The first two systems were more or less visible in accordance with the thickness of the fatty layer, if I may so describe it, which covered them. It is a great pity that Gogol never let me know the name of the creator of such a fine piece of work. There was an obstinacy in his refusal which was never quite clear to me.

Nikolai Vassilevitch blew his wife up through the anal sphincter with a pump of his own invention, rather like those which you hold down with your two feet and which are used today in all sorts of mechanical workshops. Situated in the anus was a little one-way valve, or whatever the correct technical description would be, like the mitral valve of the heart, which, once the body was inflated, allowed more air to come in but none to go out. To deflate, one unscrewed a stopper in the mouth, at the back of the throat.

And that, I think, exhausts the description of the most noteworthy peculiarities of this being. Unless perhaps I should mention the splendid rows of white teeth which adorned her mouth and the dark eyes which, in spite of their immobility, perfectly simulated life. Did I say simulate? Good heavens, simulate is not the word! Nothing seems to be the word, when one is speaking of Caracas! Even these eyes could undergo a change of colour, by means of a special process to which, since it was long and tiresome, Gogol seldom had recourse. Finally, I should speak of her voice, which it was only once given to me to hear. But I cannot do that without going more fully into the relationship between husband and wife, and in this I shall no longer be able to answer to the truth of everything with absolute certitude. On my conscience I could not – so confused, both in itself and in my memory, is that which I now have to tell.

Here, then, as they occur to me, are some of my memories.

The first and, as I said, the last time I ever heard Caracas speak to Nikolai Vassilevitch was one evening when we were absolutely alone. We were in the room where the woman, if I may be allowed the expression, lived. Entrance to this room was strictly forbidden to everybody. It was furnished more or less in the Oriental manner, had no windows and was situated in the most inaccessible part of the house. I did know that she could talk, but Gogol had never explained to me the circumstances under which this happened. There were only the two of us, or three, in there. Nikolai Vassilevitch and I were drinking vodka and discussing Butkov's novel. I remember that we left this topic, and he was maintaining the necessity for radical reforms in the laws of inheritance. We had almost forgotten her. It was then that, with a husky and submissive voice, like Venus on the nuptial couch, she said point-blank: 'I want to go poo poo.'

I jumped, thinking I had misheard, and looked across at her. She was sitting on a pile of cushions against the wall; that evening she was a soft, blonde beauty, rather well covered. Her expression seemed commingled of shrewdness and slyness, childishness and irresponsibility. As for Gogol, he blushed violently and, leaping on her, stuck two fingers down her throat. She immediately began to shrink and to turn pale; she took on once again that lost and astonished air which was especially hers, and was in the end reduced to no more than a flabby skin on a perfunctory bony armature. Since, for practical reasons which will readily be divined, she had an extraordinarily flexible backbone, she folded up almost in two, and for the rest of the evening she looked up at us from where she had slithered to the floor, in utter abjection.

All Gogol said was: 'She only does it for a joke, or to annoy me, because as a matter of fact she does not have such needs.' In the presence of other people, that is to say of me, he generally made a point of treating her with a certain disdain.

We went on drinking and talking, but Nikolai Vassilevitch seemed very much disturbed and absent in spirit. Once he suddenly interrupted what he was saying, seized my hand in his and burst into tears. 'What can I do now?' he exclaimed.

'You understand, Foma Paskalovitch, that I loved her?'

It is necessary to point out that it was impossible, except by a miracle, ever to repeat any of Caracas's forms. She was a fresh creation every time, and it would have been wasted effort to seek to find again the exact proportions, the exact pressure, and so forth, of a former Caracas. Therefore the plumpish blonde of that evening was lost to Gogol from that time forth forever; this was in fact the tragic end of one of those few loves of Nikolai Vassilevitch, which I described above. He gave me no explanation; he sadly rejected my proffered comfort, and that evening we parted early. But his heart had been laid bare to me in that outburst. He was no longer so reticent with me, and soon had hardly any secrets left. And this, I may say in parenthesis, caused me very great pride.

It seems that things had gone well for the 'couple' at the beginning of their life together. Nikolai Vassilevitch had been content with Caracas and slept regularly with her in the same bed. He continued to observe this custom till the end, saying with a timid smile that no companion could be quieter or less importunate than she. But I soon began to doubt this, especially judging by the state he was sometimes in when he woke up. Then, after several years, their relationship began strangely to deteriorate.

All this, let it be said once and for all, is no more than a schematic attempt at an explanation. About that time the woman actually began to show signs of independence or, as one might say, of autonomy. Nikolai Vassilevitch had the extraordinary impression that she was acquiring a personality of her own, indecipherable perhaps, but still distinct from his, and one which slipped through his fingers. It is certain that some sort of continuity was established between each of her appearances – between all those brunettes, those blondes, those redheads and auburn-headed girls, between those plump, those slim, those dusky or snowy or golden beauties, there was a certain something in common. At the beginning of this chapter I cast some doubt on the propriety of considering Caracas as a unitary personality; nevertheless I myself could not quite, whenever I saw her, free myself of the impression that, however unheard of it may seem, this was fundamentally the same woman. And it may be that this was why Gogol felt he had to give her a name.

An attempt to establish in what precisely subsisted the common attributes of the different forms would be quite another thing. Perhaps it was no more and no less than the creative afflatus of Nikolai Vassilevitch himself. But no, it would have been too singular and strange if he had been so much divided off from himself, so much averse to himself. Because whoever she was, Caracas was a disturbing presence and even – it is better to be quite clear – a hostile one. Yet neither Gogol nor I ever succeeded in formulating a remotely tenable hypothesis as to her true nature; when I say formulate, I mean in terms which would be at once rational and accessible to all. But I cannot pass over an extraordinary event which took place at this time.

Caracas fell ill of a shameful disease – or rather Gogol did – though he was not then having, nor had he ever had, any contact with other women. I will not even try to describe how this happened, or where the filthy complaint came from; all I know is that it happened. And that my great, unhappy friend would say to me: 'So, Foma Paskalovitch, you see what lay at the heart of Caracas; it was the spirit of syphilis.'

Sometimes he would even blame himself in a quite absurd manner; he was always prone to self-accusation. This incident was a real catastrophe as far as the already obscure relationship between husband and wife, and the hostile feelings of Nikolai Vassilevitch himself, were concerned. He was compelled to undergo long-drawn-out and painful treatment – the treatment of those days – and the situation was aggravated by the fact that the disease in the woman did not seem to be easily curable. Gogol deluded himself for some time that, by blowing his wife up and down and furnishing her with the most widely divergent aspects, he could obtain a woman immune from the contagion, but he was forced to desist when no results were forthcoming.

I shall be brief, seeking not to tire my readers, and also because what I remember seems to become more and more confused. I shall therefore hasten to the tragic conclusion. As to this last, however, let there be no mistake. I must once again make it clear that I am very sure of my ground. I was an eyewitness. Would that I had not been!

The years went by. Nikolai Vassilevitch's distaste for his wife became stronger, though his love for her did not show any signs of diminishing. Towards the end, aversion and attachment struggled so fiercely with each other in his heart that he became quite stricken, almost broken up. His restless eyes, which habitually assumed so many different expressions and sometimes spoke so sweetly to the heart of his interlocutor, now almost always shone with a fevered light, as if he were under the effect of a drug. The strangest impulses arose in him, accompanied by the most senseless fears. He spoke to me of Caracas more and more often, accusing her of unthinkable and amazing things. In these regions I could not follow him, since I had but a sketchy acquaintance with his wife, and hardly any intimacy – and above all since my sensibility was so limited compared with his. I shall accordingly restrict myself to reporting some of his accusations, without reference to my personal impressions.

'Believe it or not, Foma Paskalovitch,' he would, for example, often say to me: 'Believe it or not, she's ageing!' Then, unspeakably moved, he would, as was his way, take my hands in his. He also accused Caracas of giving herself up to solitary pleasures, which he had expressly forbidden. He even went so far as to charge her with betraying him, but the things he said became so extremely obscure that I must excuse myself from any further account of them.

One thing that appears certain is that towards the end Caracas, whether aged or not, had turned into a bitter creature, querulous, hypocritical and subject to religious excess. I do not exclude the possibility that she may have had an influence on Gogol's moral position during the last period of his life, a position which is sufficiently well known. The tragic climax came one night quite unexpectedly when Nikolai Vassilevitch and I were celebrating his silver wedding – one of the last evenings we were to spend together. I neither can nor should attempt to set down what it was that led to his decision, at a time when to all appearances he was resigned to tolerating his consort. I know not what new events had taken place that day. I shall confine myself to the facts; my readers must make what they can of them.

That evening Nikolai Vassilevitch was unusually agitated. His distaste for Caracas seemed to have reached an unprecedented intensity. The famous 'pyre of vanities' – the burning of his manuscripts – had already taken place; I should not like to say whether or not at the instigation of his wife. His state of mind had been further inflamed by other causes. As to his physical condition, this was ever more pitiful, and strengthened my impression that he took drugs. All the same, he began to talk in a more or less normal way about Belinsky, who was giving him some trouble with his attacks on the *Selected Correspondence*. Then suddenly, tears rising to his eyes, he interrupted himself and cried out: 'No. No. It's too much; too much. I can't go on any longer,' as well as other obscure and disconnected phrases which he would not clarify. He seemed to be talking to himself. He wrung his hands, shook his head, got up and sat down again after having taken four or five anxious steps round the room. When Caracas appeared; or rather when we went in to her later in the evening in her Oriental chamber, he controlled himself no longer and began to behave like an old man, if I may so express myself, in his second childhood, quite giving way to his absurd impulses. For instance, he kept nudging me and winking and senselessly repeating: 'There she is, Foma Paskalovitch; there she is!' Meanwhile she seemed to look up at us with a disdainful attention. But behind these 'mannerisms' one could feel in him a real repugnance, a repugnance which had, I suppose, now reached the limits of the endurable. Indeed . . .

After a certain time Nikolai Vassilevitch seemed to pluck up courage. He burst into tears, but somehow they were more manly tears. He wrung his hands again, seized mine in his, and walked up and down, muttering: 'That's enough! We can't have any more of this. This is an unheard-of thing. How can such a thing be happening to me? How can a man be expected to put up with this?'

He then leapt furiously upon the pump, the existence of which he seemed just to have remembered, and, with it in his hand, dashed like a whirlwind to Caracas. He inserted the tube in her anus and began to inflate her . . . Weeping the while, he shouted like one possessed: 'Oh, how I love her, how I love her, my poor, poor darling! . . . But she's going to burst! Unhappy Caracas, most pitiable of God's creatures! But die she must!'

Caracas was swelling up. Nikolai Vassilevitch sweated, wept and pumped. I wished to stop him but, I know not why, I had not the courage. She began to become deformed and shortly assumed the most monstrous aspect; and yet she had not given any signs of alarm – she was used to these jokes. But when she began to feel unbearably full, or perhaps when Nikolai Vassilevitch's intentions became plain to her, she took on an expression of bestial amazement, even a little beseeching, but still without losing that disdainful look. She was afraid, she was even committing herself to his mercy, but still she could not believe in the immediate approach of her fate; she could not believe in the frightful audacity of her husband. He could not see her face because he was behind her. But I looked at her with fascination, and did not move a finger.

At last the internal pressure came through the fragile bones at the base of her skull, and printed on her face an indescribable rictus. Her belly, her thighs, her lips, her breasts and what I could see of her buttocks had swollen to incredible proportions. All of a sudden she belched, and gave a long hissing groan; both these phenomena one could explain by the increase in pressure, which had suddenly forced a way out through the valve in her throat. Then her eyes bulged frantically, threatening to jump out of their sockets. Her ribs flared wide apart and were no longer attached to the sternum, and she resembled a python digesting a donkey. A donkey, did I say? An ox! An elephant! At this point I believed her already dead, but Nikolai Vassilevitch, sweating, weeping and repeating: 'My dearest! My beloved! My best!' continued to pump.

She went off unexpectedly and, as it were, all of a piece. It was not one part of her skin which gave way and the rest which followed, but her whole surface at the same instant. She scattered in the air. The pieces fell more or less slowly, according to their size, which was in no case above a very restricted one. I distinctly remember a piece of her cheek, with some lip attached, hanging on the corner of the mantelpiece. Nikolai Vassilevitch stared at me like a madman. Then he pulled himself together and, once more with furious determination, he began carefully to collect those poor rags which once had been the shining skin of Caracas, and all of her.

'Goodbye, Caracas,' I thought I heard him murmur, 'Goodbye! You were too pitiable!' And then suddenly and quite audibly: 'The fire! The fire! She too must end up in the fire.' He crossed himself – with his left hand, of course. Then, when he had picked up all those shrivelled rags, even climbing on the furniture so as not to miss any, he threw them straight on the fire in the hearth, where they began to burn slowly and with an excessively unpleasant smell. Nikolai Vassilevitch, like all Russians, had a passion for throwing important things in the fire.

Red in the face, with an inexpressible look of despair, and yet of sinister triumph too, he gazed on the pyre of those miserable remains. He had seized my arm and was squeezing it convulsively. But those traces of what had once been a being were hardly well alight when he seemed yet again to pull himself together, as if he were suddenly remembering something or taking a painful decision. In one bound he was out of the room.

A few seconds later I heard him speaking to me through the door in a broken, plaintive voice: 'Foma Paskalovitch, I want you to promise not to look. Golubchik, promise not to look at me when I come in.'

I don't know what I answered, or whether I tried to reassure him in any way. But he insisted, and I had to promise him, as if he were a child, to hide my face against the wall and only turn round when he said I might.

The door then opened violently and Nikolai Vassilevitch burst into the room and ran to the fireplace.

And here I must confess my weakness, though I consider it justified by the extraordinary circumstances. I looked round before Nikolai Vassilevitch told me I could; it was stronger than me. I was just in time to see him carrying something in his arms, something which he threw on the fire with all the rest, so that it suddenly flared up. At that, since the desire to see had entirely mastered every other thought in me, I dashed to the fireplace. But Nikolai Vassilevitch placed himself between me and it and pushed me back with a strength of which I had not believed him capable. Meanwhile the object was burning and giving off clouds of smoke. And before he showed any sign of calming down there was nothing left but a heap of silent ashes.

The true reason why I wished to see was because I had already glimpsed. But it was only a glimpse, and perhaps I should not allow myself to introduce even the slightest element of uncertainty into this true story. And yet, an eyewitness account is not complete without a mention of that which the witness knows with less than complete certainty. To cut a long story short, that something was a baby. Not a flesh-and-blood baby, of course, but more something in the line of a rubber doll or a model. Something, which, to judge by its appearance, could have been called Caracas' son.

Was I mad too? That I do not know, but I do know that this was what I saw, not clearly, but with my own eyes. And I wonder why it was that when I was writing this just now I didn't mention that when Nikolai Vassilevitch came back into the room he was muttering between his clenched teeth: 'Him too! Him too!'

And that is the sum of my knowledge of Nikolai Vassilevitch's wife. In the next chapter I shall tell what happened to him afterwards, and that will be the last chapter of his life. But to give an interpretation of his feelings for his wife, or indeed for anything, is quite another and more difficult matter, though I have attempted it elsewhere in this volume, and refer the reader to that modest effort. I hope I have thrown sufficient light on a most controversial question and that I have unveiled the mystery, if not of Gogol, then at least of his wife. In the course of this I have implicitly given the lie to the insensate accusation that he ill-treated or even beat his wife, as well as other like absurdities. And what else can be the goal of a humble biographer such as the present writer but to serve the memory of that lofty genius who is the object of his study?

'La moglie di Gogol'
First published in the magazine *Città* (14 December 1944), later included in *Ombre* (Vallecchi, 1954) and then in *Racconti* (Vallecchi, 1961).

NATALIA GINZBURG

1916–91

Ginzburg was a young bride and recent mother when she left Turin, where she was raised, to follow her husband, an anti-fascist dissident, who had been interned in a small village in Abruzzo. It was there, in a place she both loved and detested, that she wrote several short stories which she published under a false name, Alessandra Tornimparte, necessary protection for a Jewish writer at the time. After the fall of Mussolini and the liberation of Italy, Einaudi published a volume called *La strada che va in città* (*The Road to the City*) under her real name. This story comes from that book. Ginzburg wrote it at night, as her children slept. In 1943, her daughter Alessandra was born, named after the pseudonym that had protected and in some sense 'given birth' to Ginzburg the writer. Her most famous work, *Lessico famigliare* (the most recent English version is called *Family Lexicon*), which received the Strega Prize in 1963, is an amalgam of truth and invention that both anticipates the literary memoir and surpasses it. Reading Ginzburg, one understands that all memory is constructed. In 1937, she was approached by Einaudi, where Leone was among the first and most prominent editors, to join the group of writers entrusted to translate the complete works of Marcel Proust (she translated the first volume, *Swann's Way*). Ginzburg also worked for years as an editor at Einaudi (where she famously rejected Levi's manuscript of *Se questo è un uomo*). This tale, characteristic of Ginzburg's delicate, unblinking style, and her love of first-person narration, is composed with a placidity that contains violent emotional currents. It was Natalia's daughter Alessandra who suggested I include this particular story in this volume.

My Husband

Translated by Paul Lewis

Let every man give his wife what is her due: and every woman do the same
by her husband.

(I Corinthians 7:3)

I was twenty-five years old when I got married. I had always wanted to
get married but had often thought, with a sort of gloomy resignation, that
there was not much prospect of it happening. I was orphaned as a child
and lived with an elderly aunt and my sister in the country. Our existence
was monotonous; besides keeping the house clean and embroidering large
tablecloths, which we didn't know what to do with once they were finished,
we didn't have much to keep us occupied. Ladies would come to visit us
sometimes and we would all talk all day about those tablecloths.

The man who wanted to marry me came to our house by chance. He had
come to buy a farm which my aunt owned. I don't know how he came to
know about this farm. He was just a local district doctor for a little village
out in the country, but he was fairly well off as he had private means. He
came in his car, and as it was raining, my aunt told him to stay for lunch.
He came a few more times and in the end asked me to marry him. It was
pointed out to him that I was not rich, but he said this did not matter.

My husband was thirty-seven years old. He was tall and quite smart,
his hair was going a little grey, and he wore gold-rimmed glasses. He had
a stern, reserved and efficient manner; one could recognize in him a man
accustomed to prescribing treatments for his patients. He was incredibly
self-assured. He liked to stand motionless in a room, his hand resting
underneath his jacket collar, silently surveying everything around him.

I had barely spoken to him at all when we got married. He had never kissed me or brought me flowers; indeed he had done none of the things which fiancés usually do. All I knew was that he lived in the country with a rough young male servant and an elderly female one called Felicetta in a very old big house surrounded by a large garden. Whether something in my personality had attracted or interested him or whether he had suddenly fallen in love with me, I had no idea. After we had taken leave of my aunt, he helped me into his car, which was covered in mud, and started to drive. The level road, flanked by trees, would take us to our home. I took the opportunity to study him. I looked at him for a long time with some curiosity, and perhaps even a certain impertinence, my eyes wide open underneath my felt hat. Then he turned towards me and smiled. He squeezed my bare, cold hand and said, 'We'll have to get to know each other a little.'

We spent our first wedding night in a hotel in a village not very far from our own. We were to continue on the following morning. I went up to the room while my husband took care of the petrol. I took off my hat and looked at myself in the big mirror which reflected everything. I was not beautiful – I knew that – but I did have a bright, lively expression and a tall, pleasant figure in my tailored dress. I felt ready to love that man, if he would only help me. He had to help me. I had to make him do this.

Yet when we left the next day nothing had changed at all. We barely said a word to each other, and nothing happened to suggest there was any kind of understanding between us. As a young girl, I had always thought that an event of the kind we had experienced would transform two people, bring them closer or drive them apart forever. I now knew it was possible for neither of these things to happen. I huddled up, chilled inside my overcoat. I had not become a new person.

We arrived home at midday, and Felicetta was waiting for us at the gate. She was a little hunched woman with grey hair and sly, servile ways. The house, the garden, and Felicetta were just as I had imagined them. In the house nothing looked gloomy, as is often the way in old houses. It was roomy and light, with white curtains and cane chairs. Ivy and rose plants climbed on the walls and all along the fence.

Once Felicetta had given me the keys, stealing round the rooms behind me to show me every minute detail, I felt happy and ready to prove to my husband and everybody else that I was competent. I was not an educated woman and perhaps I was not very intelligent, but I did know how to keep a well-organized and orderly house. My aunt had taught me. I would apply myself diligently to this task and, in so doing, show my husband what I was really capable of.

That was how my new life started. My husband would spend the whole day away while I busied myself around the house, took care of lunch, made desserts and prepared jams; I also liked working in the vegetable garden with the male servant. Though I squabbled with Felicetta, I got on well with the male servant. When he tossed his hair back and winked at me, there was something in his wholesome face which made me smile. Sometimes I would go for long walks in the village and talk to the peasants. I asked them questions, and they asked me questions too. But when I came home in the evenings and sat down next to the majolica stove, I felt lonely; I missed my aunt and sister and wanted to be back with them again. I thought about the time when my sister and I would get ready for bed; I remembered our bedsteads, and the balcony looking over the road where we would sit and relax on Sundays.

One evening I started crying. All of a sudden my husband came in. He was pale and very tired. When he saw my dishevelled hair and tear-stained cheeks, he said to me, 'What's the matter?' I stayed silent, my head lowered. He sat next to me and caressed me a little. 'Are you sad?' he asked. I nodded. He pressed me to his shoulder. Then all of a sudden he got up and went to lock the door. 'I've been wanting to talk to you for a while,' he said. 'I find it difficult, that's why it's taken me so long. Every day I've thought, 'Today will be the day,' and every day I've put it off; it was as if I was tongue-tied, I was scared of you. A woman who gets married is scared of her man, but she doesn't realize how much a man is also scared of a woman; she has no idea how much. There are lots of things I want to talk to you about. If we can talk to each other, get to know each other bit by bit, then perhaps we can love each other, and we'll no longer feel sad. When I saw you for the first time, I thought, 'I like this woman, I want to love her, I want her to love me and help me, and I want to be happy with her.' Perhaps it seems strange to you that I should need help, but that's the way it is.'

He crumpled the pleats of my skirt in his fingers. 'There is a woman in this village whom I have loved very much. It's ridiculous to call her a woman; she's not a woman, she's just a child, nothing but a scruffy little animal. She's the daughter of a local peasant. Two years ago I cured her of a bad bout of pleurisy. She was fifteen at the time. Her family is poor; not just poor but mean too; they have a dozen children and wouldn't dream of buying medicine for her. So I paid for the medicine, and after she got better, I would go and look for her in the woods where she would go to gather wood and I would give her a little money, so that she could buy herself something to eat. At home she had nothing but bread and salted potatoes; she didn't see anything unusual in this – her brothers and sisters, her mother and father, and most of their neighbours all lived like this. If I'd given her mother money, she would have quickly hidden it away in her mattress and wouldn't have bought a thing. But I soon saw that the girl was ashamed of buying things, afraid that her mother would find out what was happening, and I realized that she too was tempted to hide the money away in her mattress as she had always seen her mother do, even though I told her that if she did not eat properly, she could get ill again and die.

'I started taking food to her myself every day. To begin with she was ashamed to eat in front of me, but she soon got used to it and she would eat and eat, and when she was full she would stretch out in the sun, and we would spend hours like that, just the two of us. I got an extraordinary pleasure from watching her eat – it was what I most looked forward to during my day – and later when I was alone, I would think about what she had eaten and what I would bring her the next day. It was like this that I started making love to her. Whenever I could I would go to the woods and wait for her, and she would come; I didn't even know why she came, whether it was to eat or to make love, or out of fear that I would get angry with her. Oh how I waited for her! When passion is penetrated by pity and remorse you're done for; it becomes an obsession. I would wake up at night and think about what would happen if I made her pregnant and had to marry her, and the idea of having to share the rest of my life with her filled me with horror. Yet at the same time I couldn't bear to imagine her married to another person, in somebody else's house, and the love that I felt for her was unbearable, it took all my strength away. When I saw you I thought that by tying myself to you I would be freeing myself from her, maybe I would forget her because I didn't want her. I didn't want

Mariuccia; it was a woman like you that I wanted, a woman like me, who was mature and responsible. I could see something in you that made me think you might forgive me, that you would agree to help me, and so it seemed to me that if I behaved badly with you, it wouldn't matter, because we would learn to love each other, and all this would go away.'

'But how will it go away?' I said. 'I don't know,' he said, 'I don't know. Since we got married I don't think of her any more in the way I did before, and if I see her I say hello calmly, and she laughs and goes all red, and so I tell myself that in a few years I'll see her married to some peasant, weighed down with children and disfigured by hard work. But then something stirs inside me when I meet her, and I want to follow her to the woods again and hear her laugh and speak in her dialect, and watch her while she collects branches for the fire.' 'I want to meet her,' I said. 'You must show her to me. Tomorrow we'll go for a walk and you can show her to me when she goes by.' It was my first decisive act and it gave me a sense of satisfaction. 'But don't you feel bitter towards me?' he asked. I shook my head. I didn't feel bitter. I didn't know what I felt. I was happy and sad at the same time. It was late, and when we went to have dinner we found all the food was cold: but we didn't feel like eating anyway. We went down to the garden. It was dark and we walked for a long time on the grass. He took my arm and said, 'I knew you would understand.' He woke several times during the night and pulled me close, repeating, 'You've understood everything!'

When I saw Mariuccia for the first time she was coming back from the fountain, carrying a bucket of water. She was wearing a faded blue dress and black socks and she was stumbling along with a huge pair of men's shoes on her feet. When she saw me red blushes appeared on her dark face, and she spilled a little water on the steps of the house as she turned to look at me. I was so overwhelmed by this meeting that I asked my husband if we could stop, and we sat down on the stone bench in front of the church. However, just at that moment he was called away and I was left there alone. A deep discomfort came over me at the thought that perhaps I would see Mariuccia every day and that I would never be able to walk around those roads freely again. I had believed that the village where I had come to live would become dear to me, that I would belong in every part of it; now it seemed this had been taken away from me forever. And it was true. Every time I went out I would see her, either rinsing her laundry at the fountain or carrying buckets or holding one of her grubby little siblings in her arms. One day her mother, a fat peasant, invited me into their kitchen; Mariuccia stood by the door with her hands tucked into her apron; she gave me the odd sly and inquisitive look and then disappeared. When I got home I would say to my husband, 'I saw Mariuccia today.' He would ignore me and look the other way until one day he said to me in an irritated voice, 'So what if you saw her? It's all in the past, there's no reason to discuss it any more.'

In the end, I stopped venturing beyond the confines of our garden. I was pregnant, and I had become big and heavy. I sat in the garden sewing, and everything around me was calm; the plants were rustling and giving out shadows, the male servant hoed the vegetable garden, and Felicetta went back and forth in the kitchen polishing the copper. Sometimes I would think with amazement about the child that would be born. He belonged to two people who had nothing in common, who had nothing to say to each other and who sat beside each other for long periods of time in silence. Since that evening when my husband had spoken about Mariuccia he had stopped trying to come near me and had shut himself off in silence; sometimes when I spoke to him he would look at me in an empty, almost offended kind of way, as if I had disturbed him from some important thought with my ill-chosen words. Then I would tell myself that our relationship needed to change before the arrival of our baby. Otherwise what would the child think of us? But then I would be moved to laughter: as if a little baby would be able to think.

The child was born in August. My sister and aunt came to stay, a party was organized for the christening, and there was a great deal of coming and going in the house. The child slept in his crib next to my bed. He looked quite red, with his fists closed and a patch of dark hair sticking out under his cap. My husband came to see him all the time; he was cheerful and smiling, and spoke about the child to everybody. One afternoon we found ourselves alone. I had lain down on the pillow, wearied and weakened by the heat. He looked at the child and smiled, stroking his hair and ribbons. 'I didn't know that you liked children,' I said all of a sudden. He gave a start and he turned to me. 'I don't like children,' he replied, 'but I like this one, because he is ours.' 'Ours?' I said to him. 'He's important to you because he is ours, you mean yours and mine? Do I mean something to you then?' 'Yes,' he said as if lost in thought, and he came to sit on my bed. 'When I come home and know that I will find you here, it gives me a feeling of pleasure and warmth.' 'Then what happens?' I asked quietly, looking him in the eye. 'Then, when I'm in front of you, and I want to tell you about what I have done during the day, what I have thought, and I just can't do it, I don't know why. Or maybe I do know why. It's because there is something in my day, in my thoughts, that I have to hide from you, and so I can't talk to you any more.' 'What is it?' 'It's this,' he said, 'I've been meeting with Mariuccia in the woods again.' 'I knew it,' I said. 'I've known for a long time.' He knelt down in front of me and kissed my bare arms. 'Help me, I'm begging you,' he said. 'What am I going to do if you won't help me?' 'But how can I possibly help you?' I screamed, pushing him away, and burst into tears. Then my husband picked up Giorgio, kissed him, gave him to me and said, 'Everything will be easier now, you'll see.'

Since I did not have any milk, a wet nurse was summoned from a nearby village. My sister and aunt left us and we went back to our old routine; I got up and went down to the garden and gradually took up my familiar old tasks again. But the house was transformed by the presence of the child; little white nappies hung in the garden and on the terraces, the velvet dress of the wet nurse swished through the corridors, and her singing echoed throughout the rooms. No longer a young woman, she was a rather fat and proud person who liked to talk a lot about the aristocratic houses where she had worked in the past. We had to buy her new embroidered aprons every month or pins for her handkerchief. When my husband came home I would go to meet him at the gate, and we would go up to Giorgio's room together to watch him sleep; after this we would have dinner and I would tell him about how the wet nurse had bickered with Felicetta, and we would talk for a while about the baby, the coming winter, the supply of wood, and I would tell him about a novel I had read and what I thought about it. He would put his arm around my waist and stroke me while I rested my head on his shoulder. Truly the birth of the child had changed our relationship. Nonetheless, I still sometimes felt that there was something strained in our conversations and in his goodness and affection, although I couldn't focus properly on the feeling. The child was growing up; he had started toddling and putting on weight, and I liked watching him, but at times I wondered if I really loved him. At times I didn't feel like climbing the stairs to go to him. It seemed to me that he belonged to other people, to Felicetta or to the wet nurse maybe, but not to me.

One day I learned that Mariuccia's father had died. My husband had said nothing about it to me. I took my coat and went out. It was snowing. The body had been taken away in the morning. Surrounded by their neighbours in their dark kitchen, Mariuccia and her mother held their heads in their hands, rocking back and forth and letting out shrill cries, as is the custom in the country when a close relative dies; the children, dressed in their best clothes, warmed their cold blue hands against the fire. When I went in, Mariuccia stared at me for a moment with her familiar look of amazement, lit up by a sudden animation. But she quickly recovered herself and began mourning again.

She now wore a black shawl when she walked around the village. Meeting her was still very difficult for me. I would return home unhappy: I could still see her dark eyes in front of me, those big white teeth which stuck out over her lips. But I hardly ever thought about her if we did not happen to meet.

The following year I gave birth to another child. It was a boy again, and we called him Luigi. My sister had got married and gone to live in a city far away and my aunt never left her home, so nobody helped me when I gave birth except for my husband. The wet nurse who had fed the first child left and so a new one came – she was a tall and shy girl who got on well with us and stayed even after Luigi had been weaned. My husband was very happy to have the children. When he came home they were the first thing he asked about, and he would run to see them and play with them until it was bedtime. He loved them, and no doubt thought that I loved them too. It was true that I did love them, but not in the way that once upon a time I had thought a mother ought to love her children. There was something subdued inside me when I held them on my lap. They tugged my hair, pulled on my necklace, wanted to search through my little workbox, and I would get irritated and call the wet nurse. Sometimes I thought that maybe I was too sad to have the children. 'But why am I sad?' I asked myself. 'What's the matter with me? I don't have any reason to feel this sad.'

One sunny autumn afternoon my husband and I were sitting on the leather sofa in the study. 'We've been married now for three years already,' I said to him. 'Yes, you're right,' he said, 'and it's been just as I thought it would be, hasn't it? We have learned to live together, haven't we?' I remained silent and stroked his lifeless hand. Then he kissed me and left. After a few hours I went out as well, crossing the village roads and taking the path that ran alongside the river. I wanted to walk a little beside the water. Leaning on the wooden parapet of the bridge I watched the water run, still and dark, between the grass and the stones, and the sound made me feel a little sleepy. I was getting cold and was about to leave when all of a sudden I spotted my husband scrambling up the grassy ridge of the slope, heading for the woods. I realized that he had seen me as well. He stopped for a moment, uncertain, and then carried on climbing, grasping at the branches of the bushes as he went, until he disappeared in the trees. I returned home and went to the study. I sat on the sofa where just a little while ago he had told me that we had learned to live together. I understood now what he had meant by this. He had learned to lie to me, and it didn't bother him any more. My presence in his house had made him worse, and I too had got worse by living with him. I had become dried up and lifeless. I wasn't suffering, and I didn't feel any pain. I too was lying to him: I was living by his side as if I loved him, when really I didn't love him; I felt nothing for him.

All of a sudden the stairs resounded under his heavy steps. He came into the study, took off his jacket without even looking at me, and put on his old corduroy jacket which he wore around the house. 'I want us to leave this place,' I said. 'I will ask to be moved to another practice, if you want me to,' he replied. 'But it's you who should want it,' I screamed. I realized then that it wasn't true to say that I wasn't suffering; I was suffering unbearably and I was shaking all over. 'Once you said to me that I must help you, and that was why you married me; but why did you marry me?' I sobbed. 'Yes, why indeed? What a mistake it has been!' he said, and sat down, covering his face with his hands. 'I don't want you to go on seeing her. You mustn't see her again,' I said, bending over him. He pushed me away with an angry gesture, 'What do I care about you?' he said. 'You're nothing new for me; there's nothing about you which interests me. You're like my mother and my mother's mother, and all the women who have ever lived in this house. You weren't beaten as a child. You didn't have to go hungry. They didn't make you work in the fields from dawn till dusk under the back-breaking sun. Your presence, yes, it gives me peace and quiet, but that's all. I don't know what to do about it, but I can't love you.' He took his pipe, filled it meticulously, and lit it, suddenly calm again. 'Anyway, all this talk is useless; these things don't matter. Mariuccia is pregnant,' he said.

A few days later I went to the coast with the children and the wet nurse. We had planned this trip for a long time, as the children had been ill and they both needed the sea air; my husband was going to accompany us and stay there with us for a month. But, without needing to mention it, it was now understood that he would not come. We stayed by the sea for the whole winter. I wrote to my husband once a week and received a punctual response from him each time. Our letters contained just a few short and rather cold sentences.

We returned at the beginning of spring. My husband was waiting for us at the station. While we travelled through the village in the car I saw Mariuccia pass us with a swollen belly. She walked lightly in spite of the weight of her belly, and the pregnancy had not changed her childish smile. But there was something new in her expression, some sense of submission and shame, and she blushed when she saw me, but not in the same way as she used to blush, with that happy impudence. I thought that soon I would see her carrying a dirty child in her arms, wearing the long clothes which all peasant children have, and that child would be my husband's son, the brother of Luigi and Giorgio. I thought that it would be unbearable to see that child with the long clothes. I wouldn't have been able to continue living with my husband or carry on living in the village. I would leave.

My husband was extremely dispirited. Days and days passed during which he barely uttered a word. He didn't even enjoy being with the children any more. I saw he had grown old and his clothes had become scruffy; his cheeks were covered in bristly hair. He came home very late at night and sometimes went straight to bed without eating. Sometimes he didn't sleep at all and spent the entire night in the study.

On our return I found the house in complete chaos. Felicetta had grown old; she couldn't remember anything, and argued with the male servant, accusing him of drinking too much. They would exchange violent insults and often I had to intervene to calm them down.

For several days I had a lot to do. The house had to be put in order so that it would be ready for the coming summer. The woollen blankets and cloaks needed to be put away in the cupboards, the armchairs covered in white linen, the curtains taken out on the terrace; the vegetable garden needed sowing, and the roses in the garden needed pruning. I remembered the pride and energy I had given to all these tasks in the early days after we had got married. I had imagined that every simple job was of the highest importance. Since then hardly four years had passed, but how I now saw myself changed! Even physically I looked more like an older woman now. I brushed my hair without a parting, with the bun low down on my neck. Looking at myself in the mirror, I sometimes thought that having my hair combed like that didn't suit me, and it made me look older. But I didn't care about looking pretty any more. I didn't care about anything.

One evening I was sitting in the dining room with the wet nurse, who was teaching me a knitting stitch. The children were sleeping and my husband had gone to a village a few miles away where somebody had fallen seriously ill. All of a sudden the bell rang and the servant went barefoot to see who it was. I went downstairs as well: it was a boy of about fourteen, and I recognized him as one of Mariuccia's brothers. 'They sent me to call the doctor; my sister is not well,' he said. 'But the doctor isn't here.' He shrugged his shoulders and went away. After a while, he came back again. 'Hasn't the doctor returned yet?' he asked. 'No,' I told him, 'but I'll let him know.' The male servant had already gone to bed, so I told him to get dressed and go and call for the doctor on his bicycle. I went up to my room and started to undress, but I was too anxious and on edge; I felt that I should do something as well. I covered my head with a shawl and went out. I walked through the empty, dark village. In the kitchen Mariuccia's brothers were dozing with their heads resting on the table. The neighbours were huddled by the door talking among themselves. In the room next door Mariuccia was pacing up and down in the small space between the bed and the door; she was crying and walking, leaning against the wall as she went. She went on walking and screaming, and stared at me but didn't seem to recognize who I was. Her mother gave me a resentful and hostile look. I sat on the bed. 'The doctor won't be long, will he, Signora?' the midwife asked me. 'The girl has been in labour for some hours now. She had already lost a lot of blood. The delivery is not going well.' 'I've sent for him to be called. He should be here soon,' I said.

Then Mariuccia fainted and we carried her on to the bed. They needed something from the chemist's and I offered to go myself. When I returned she had come round and had started screaming again. Her cheeks were hot and she struggled around, throwing off the covers. She clung to the headboard of the bed and screamed. The midwife came and went with fresh bottles of water. 'It's a terrible business,' she said in a loud, calm voice. 'But we must do something,' I said to her. 'If my husband is late, we must alert another doctor.' 'Doctors know lots of clever words, but not much else,' her mother said, and she gave me another resentful look, clutching the rosary to her breast. 'Women always scream when the baby is about to come,' one of the women said.

Mariuccia was writhing on the bed and her hair was all dishevelled. Suddenly, she grabbed hold of me, squeezing me with her dark, bare arms. 'Mother of God,' she kept saying. The sheets were stained with blood; there was even blood on the ground. The midwife did not leave her side now. 'Be strong,' she said to her from time to time. Now she was making hoarse sobbing noises. She had bags under her eyes, and her face was dark and covered in sweat: 'It's not good, it's not good,' the midwife kept repeating. Finally, she received the baby in her hands, lifted it, and shook it. 'It's dead,' she said, and she threw it down into a corner of the bed. I saw a wrinkled face. It looked like a little Chinese person. The women took it away, bound up in a wollen rag.

Now Mariuccia had stopped screaming; she lay there looking extremely pale, and the blood continued to flow from her body. I saw that there was a little mark of blood on my blouse. 'It'll come out with some water,' the midwife said to me. 'It doesn't matter,' I said. 'You've helped me a lot tonight,' she said. 'You're a very courageous lady – truly the wife of a doctor.'

One of the neighbours insisted that I should have a little coffee. I followed her into the kitchen and drank a cup of weak, tepid coffee from a glass. When I returned Mariuccia was dead. They told me she had died like that, without having come round from her drowsiness.

They plaited her hair and straightened up the blankets around her. At last my husband arrived. He was holding his leather briefcase; he looked pale and out of breath, and his overcoat was open. I was sitting next to the bed, but he did not look at me. He stood in the middle of the room. The mother stood in front of him, tore the briefcase from his hands, and threw it to the ground. 'You didn't even come to see her die,' she said to him.

I gathered up his briefcase and took my husband's hand. 'Let's go,' I said to him. He let me lead him across the kitchen, through the murmuring women, and he followed me out. All of a sudden I stopped; it seemed to me right that he should see the little Chinese-looking baby. But where was he? God knows where they had taken him.

As we walked I held him tight, but he did not respond to me in any way, and his arm swung lifelessly by my side. I realized that he was not taking any notice of me and I understood that I mustn't speak, and that I had to be extremely careful with him. He came upstairs with me to the door of our room but then left me and went off to the study, as he had done recently.

It was already nearly light outside; I heard the birds singing in the trees. I went to bed. All of a sudden I realized that I was overcome with a feeling of immense joy. I had no idea that somebody's death could make you so happy, yet I didn't feel guilty for it at all. I had not been happy for some time, and for me this was a completely new feeling, which amazed and transformed me. I also felt full of foolish pride for the way I had conducted myself that night. I knew that my husband could not think of it now, but one day, when he had composed himself a little, he would think of it again, and perhaps he would realize that I had performed well.

All of a sudden a shot rang out through the silence of the house. I got up from my bed screaming and went down the stairs, screaming all the way. I burst into the study and shook his large body, which lay motionless on the armchair; his arms were hanging down lifelessly. There was a little blood on the cheeks and lips of that face I knew so well.

Afterwards the house filled up with people. I had to speak and answer every question. The children were taken away. Two days later I accompanied my husband to the cemetery. When I came home I wandered around the rooms in a daze. That house had become dear to me, but I felt as though I didn't have the right to live there, because it didn't belong to me, because I had shared it with a man who had died without uttering a single word to me. Yet, I didn't know where I should go. There wasn't a single place in the world where I wanted to go.

'*Mio marito*'
Written in 1941 and first published (under the pseudonym A. Tornimparte) in 1942 in the journal *Lettere d'oggi* (IV, 2–3, March–April), then included in *La strada che va in città e altri racconti* (Einaudi, 1945).

CARLO EMILIO GADDA
1893–1973

Gadda both intimidates and exasperates; those who don't worship him tend to throw up their hands, as if he were the later Henry James or the Joyce of *Finnegans Wake*. For those not reading him in Italian, he also poses a particular challenge, in that many claim he is untranslatable (I disagree). He began his professional life as an electrical engineer, but imprisonment as a soldier in the First World War, which killed his brother, inspired him to start writing. The word 'macaronic' is key to appreciating Gadda – it stems from a poetic genre that combined Latin metres with vernacular words, and found its most famous interpreter in Teofilo Folengo, whose *Baldus* was to inspire Rabelais. Gadda, too, kneaded together high and low registers, mixing dialect with literary language, and this collision is central to his aesthetic. The result was a voice, quintessentially unique, that never ceased to confound, to challenge, to upend. His approach to genre was equally playful; story, novella, novel were restrictive terms Gadda rejected. Like Pasolini, Gadda learned Roman dialect and worked with it; he also shared, with Pasolini, a homosexual identity and themes of prostitution and life on the urban periphery (most famously explored in the novel *Quer pasticciaccio brutto de via Merulana*; in English, *That Awful Mess on the Via Merulana*). Gadda lived briefly in Argentina, and translated the work of the New Spanish dramatist Juan Ruiz de Alarcón, who wrote during the sixteenth and seventeenth centuries. He had a difficult relationship with his mother and lost his father when he was sixteen. This story – plotless, careening, terrifying – appears both in a short-story collection and as a chapter in the autobiographical novel, *La cognizione del dolore* (most recently published as *The Experience of Pain*). Set in an invented South American country, it is a marriage of chaos and coherence. Gadda began writing it after his mother's death, and it was left intentionally unfinished. The author's footnotes form an integral part of the story. Indeed, they are not really footnotes at all, but digressions.

The Mother

Translated by Richard Dixon

She wandered about, alone, in the house. And those walls, that copper: were they all she had left? of a life. They had told her the exact name, cruel and black, of the mountain: where he had fallen: and the other name, desolately serene, of the ground where they had taken and left him, with face restored to peace and oblivion, devoid of any response, for ever. The son who had smiled at her, brief springtimes!, who had so sweetly, passionately, hugged, kissed her. A year later, at Pastrufazio, a military non-commissioned officer* had presented her with a diploma, had given her some kind of book, asking her to sign her name in another register: and on doing so he handed her a copying pencil. First he had asked her: 'Are you Señora Adelaide François?' Turning pale on hearing mention of her name, the name that tormented her, she had replied: 'Yes, I am she'. Trembling, as if at the savage harshening of a sentence. To which, after the first hideous cry, that dark voice of eternity continued calling her.

Before he left, when with a clink of the chain he picked up the register and then the gleaming sword, she had asked as if to detain him: 'May I offer you a glass of Nevado?', clasping her bony hands together. But he didn't want to accept. She thought he strangely resembled the person who had occupied the brief splendour of time: of time consumed. The beating of her heart told her so: and with a quiver of the lips she felt the need to love once more the re-emergent presence: but she knew well that no one, no one ever returns.

She drifted about the house: and sometimes unlatched the shutters of a window, to let the sun in, into the main room. The light then met her

* A military non-commissioned officer: From the district gendarmerie.

261

modest, almost shabby clothing: the small expedients she had managed
to repair them with, holding back the tears, the mean dress of her old age.
But what was the sun? What day did it bring? over the baying of the darkness. She knew its sizes and its essence, its distance from the earth, from
all the other planets: and their movement and orbit; she had learned and
had taught many things: and Kepler's formulations and squarings that
pursue the ellipse of our desperate pain into the vacuity of senseless space.*

She drifted about, in the house, as though searching for the mysterious
path that would have taken her to meet someone: or perhaps just to solitude,
devoid of any pity and of any image. From the kitchen, now fireless, to the
rooms where voices were no longer heard: occupied by just a few flies. And
surrounding the house she still saw the countryside, the sunshine.

Sometimes the sky, so vast over vanished time, was overshadowed by
its ominous clouds; which flowed plump and white from the mountains
and gathered and then blackened, and suddenly seemed to threaten the
person alone in the house, her sons far, terribly far, away. This occurred
once again at the close of that summer, one afternoon in early September,
after the long heatwave that everyone said would never end: ten days after
she had called for the keeper, with the keys: and had wanted to go down,
with her, to the cemetery. That menace hurt her deeply. It was the clash,
it was the scorn of powers or of beings unknown, and yet bent on persecu-
tion: the evil that rises again, again and for ever, after the clear mornings
of hope. What always upset her most was the unexpected malevolence of
those who had no reason to hate her, or to insult her: of those to whom
her trust, so pure, was so unreservedly given, as to equals and to kindred
beings in a superior society of souls. Then every consoling experience and
memory, value and labour, and support from the city and the people, was
suddenly cancelled by the devastation of mortified instinct, the inner
strength of awareness was lost: like a child struck by the crowd, knocked
down. The barbarized crowd of lost ages, the darkness of things and souls,
were a grim enigma, before which she wondered anxiously – (ignorant
like a lost child) – why, why?

The storm, that very day, would drive with long howls through the
dreadful mountain gorges, and then flow out into the open against

* Senseless space: Devoid of sensory apparatus and therefore of sensitivity.

people's homes and factories. After each sombre build-up of its bitter spite, it unleashed its thunderbolts through the whole sky, like the havoc and pillage of a marauding corsair among sinister flashes and shots. The wind, which had carried her son away towards forgetting cypresses, seemed to be searching at every window for her as well, for her as well, inside the house. From the small window over the staircase, a gust of wind, breaking in, had snatched her by the hair: the creaking floors and their wooden beams seemed about to collapse: like planking, like a ship in a tempest: and its hatches closed, battened down, swollen by that fury outside. And she, like a wounded animal, if it hears the barbarous hunting horns above it again and again, does what it can in its exhausted state to find a refuge, below, beneath the staircase: going down, step by step: into a corner. Timidly overcoming that emptiness of each step, trying them one after the other with her foot, clinging to the banister with her hands that could hardly grip, step by step, down, down, towards the darkness and dampness below. There, a small ledge.

And the gloom nevertheless allowed her to feel her way to a candle, softened, a saucer with some matches, left there for the night hours, for anyone coming home late. No one came home. She struck a match several times, another, on the glass-paper: and here, at last, in the yellowness of that tremulous recognition of the brick floor, here a sliver of horrific darkness, fleeing further, but then suddenly recovering in the stillness of a snare: the blackness of a scorpion. She drew back, shut her eyes, in her final solitude: raising her head, like one who knows there's no point pleading for kindness. And she shrank within herself, close to annihilation, a painful spark of time: and in time she had been a woman, a wife and a mother. She stopped now, terror-stricken, before the faithless weapon that still she used to push back the darkness. And the blasts and the rampaging glory of the storm followed her there, where she had gone down, down, into the dark depth of every memory, and savagely they hurled themselves at her. The repugnant snare of obscurity: the blackest stain, born from dampness and from evil.

She thought she no longer knew why, why! forgetting, in her extreme distress, that a plea, or love, is possible from the charity of the peoples:* she no longer recalled anything: all previous help from her people was long gone, distant. In vain she had given birth to infants, had given them her milk: no one would realize it in the sulphurous glory of the storms, and of the chaos, no one gave it any further thought: other events had fallen across those distant visceral years, across the torment, across the forgotten tenderness: and the clamour of victory, and the rhetoric and the pomp of victory: and, for her, old age: this last solitude to close the final heavens of the spirit.

Molten wax dripped on to her trembling hand, burning it: the icy breath of the storm, from the window of the staircase inflected and laminated the flame, making it flicker over the pool and over the grease of the wax: that glimmer of the wick grew dim, in a deathly farewell.

She no longer saw anything. Everything was horror, hatred. Thunder loomed over everything and electric flashes plummeted in anger, gridded repeatedly by the slats of the closed shutters, high up. And here the scorpion, awake, had moved on, as if to one side, as if to outwit her, and she, trembling, had drawn back inside her lone being, stretching out a gelid and weary hand, as though wanting to stop it. Her hair hung over her brow: she dared not say a thing, with lips dry, bloodless: no one, no one would have heard her, beneath the clamour. And who could she call, in these altered times, when, after so many years, there was now so much hatred towards her? If those same infants, over the years, had been a pointless suffering, pride of cemeteries: lost! . . . in the vanity of the earth . . .

Why? Why?

* Peoples: The word 'people', 'peoples' is still used today in certain better areas of Lombardy to mean, more or less, 'civilized progeny, ancestry of Roman origin, community of beings instructed in the Gospel and Roman teachings'. Sometimes 'good people' = 'bona gens'. A reverse process to that for which the Romans and Pagans were called 'gentiles', which meant 'idolatrous foreigners', by the Hebrews and by Paul: in the somewhat drawling violence with which the word emerges from the throats of fellow countrymen in such a way as to induce a wealth of meanings and a visceral memory of centuries and events long past, and the trauma of a whole Ambrosian-Tridentine 'civilization': namely of a conversion, of a collective baptism during the years of Theodelinda, who founded churches and temples dedicated to John the Baptist (Monza, Florence), and of a gradual acquisition of the new language and ritual. The 'fara', a Lombard family or community established in a specific village or area, gradually become 'gens', 'bona gens'.

From the dark depth of the staircase she looked up from time to time, and even during those hours, to distinguish silent interludes in the storm, the surprised nullity of the space: and of the intervening evening, from the eaves outside, drops, like tears, or the compassionate silence. She imagined that the sudden thrusts of each blast, having hurtled through each room, had left almost like a tardy tribe to regroup towards the plain and the night, where they rejoined their migrant flock. A shutter* was banging, striking the wall of the house. The trees, outside, she heard, gave off light droplets, towards night-time, cleansed as if from weeping.

No one saw her, in the depth of fear, down there, alone, where the yellow light of the wick flickered, paled into the shadows, from the shelf, slowly dying in its liquefied wax. But if someone had happened to see her, oh! even a landsknecht! he would have felt in his heart that this face looking up, petrified, was not even attempting to plead, from vanished distance. Her loose hair rose from her brow, like a breath of horror. Her face barely emerged from the sombre swathe, her cheeks were a trough to the impossibility of tears. Her hooked fingers of old age seemed to be pressing down, down, into the plasma of the dark, the features of someone drawn to solitude. That face, like a spectre, turned away from the underground darkness† to the supernal society of living beings, looking perhaps, without hope, for some assistance, for the voice of a man, of a son.

This name rested lightly on her mind: and was a cherished presence, a suggestion almost of morning and of a dream, a wing that flew high above, a light. Yes: there was her son, in the time, in the certainty and in the experience of the living: and even after the transformation, after the precipitation of the years. He walked among the living. He walked along the paths of men. Her first son. The one in whose young body she had yearned to see, oh! days!, the proof of nature's deficiency, a failed experiment of the womb after the accepted fraud of the seed, reluctant to have suffered, to have generated something not its own: in a long and untreatable eclipse of her whole being, in the weariness of the mind, of the womb

---

* [Historical]: A shutter: The house had ordinary folding shutters: and some shutters 'à coulisse'.
† Underground darkness: The house was built on a slope, where the land falls away: and the foot of the staircase was therefore below the level of the ground above it.

opened then to the slow disgrace of birth, in the derision of shrewd traffickers and merchants, under the constriction of the duties they impose, so nobly promoting the common good, to the suffering and misery of honest people. And now there was the son: just the one son. He wandered the parched roads along the fleeing elms, after the dust towards the evenings and the trains. Her first son. Oh! Only the raincloud – whistling skies lashing over the bent trees of the countryside – only terror could have separated her in such a way from the truth, from the sound security of memory. Her son: Gonzalo. Gonzalo, no, no!, he had not been awarded the funerary honours of darkness; his mother recoiled at the memory: away, away!, from the empty funeral, the dirges, the vile tears, the wailing: no candles had burnt down from on high, for him, between the pillars of the cold nave and arches darkened by the centuries. When the song of the abyss, among the candles, calls for those sacrificed to go down, down, into the verminous pomp of eternity.

The sound of a horn, from the highway: and emptiness. All went silent, at last. The cats, at the usual time, of course, had come here into the house, from where only they could enter: velvet presences were staring at her from halfway down the staircase, with eyes like topaz in the dark, but cleaved with a cut, their pupils lined with hunger: and, meowing, they gave her a timid greeting, a cry: 'It's time'. Domestic order and charity urged her up. And she, forgetting her own suffering, concerned herself immediately, as always, with that of others: she went back upstairs. The clomping stride of the peasant sounded on the brick floor above: back from buying tobacco, and perhaps, she hoped, some salt: he called out to her in the darkness, told her about the provisions and the fire, told her what time it was, how the crops were ruined: he moved around, still jabbering, opening the shutters, the windows. Consoled, once again she saw the sweet and distant resplendence of the village, and those everlasting words blossomed in her sweet memory: 'Open the balconies – open the family terraces and loggias': almost as though the reconstituted society of men had reappeared to her after a long night. And the faithful retainer, here, in front of the cats, was moving about the house: from his own hearth to another, so spacious and gelid: carrying flares, thyrsi; and then on the stairs; doors and windows banged behind the quadrupedal flight of clogs. And twigs and branches dropping more or less everywhere along the man's route. And the wind had lost itself towards the plain, in the direction of Pequeño.

From the terrace, on summer evenings, she could see smoke from the houses on the far horizon, which she imagined populated, each one, with the wife keeping house, the husband in the cattle shed, and the children. Girls were returning, in droves, from the factory, the looms, or winding rooms, or dying-vats at the silk mill: bicycles had brought apprentices back from the anvil: or they had returned behind their father with swaying oxen from the field, and he guiding and controlling his low cart by the shaft: a cart with short, sloping, open sides, with small wheels on slick, silent axles, piled up with implements and with labour, with logs and with hay: on which tired scythes lay, as though forgotten, in the evening shadow.

Rustic offspring back numberless from work to the hearth, to a spoon: to the poor chipped bowls that compensated their day.

Far-off gleams of light, and song, reached her from outside the house. As if a housewife had taken her copper pot outside to dry in the yard, to reflect, glinting, the sunset. Perhaps to greet her, the Señora!, who herself had once, like them, been a woman, a wife and a mother. She envied no one. She wished all of them, all of them, the joy and calm strength of sons, that they would have work, health, peace: good marches in morning where the captain commands them: that they would soon find their bride, once back from the regiment, in the fragrant throng of girls.

And so, each day, she found some reason or excuse to call for the washerwoman, the baker's daughter, the woman who sold lemons or sometimes a rare Tierra Caliente orange, the retainer's eighty-six-year-old mother, or the fishmonger's wife. (She had reason to think the last of these didn't have a complete set of clothes on her person.) They were poor, dark pikes, whose gloomy noses were pointed with the wants of poor people; pikes that had swum and swum through green dearth towards the silvery flash of Durendal; or tench, large, yellow lake fish with a greasy and vapid slime, which, even with carrots and celery, still had a muddy taste; harpooned up by line from the Seegrün after the hour of sunset, or from that other valley, most sweet in autumn, of the abbé-poet, or that other valley still further away, of the painter disciple, when it mirrors, beneath liquefied clouds, the upturned indentation of the mountain.

With carrots and celery, on a slow flame, in the long pike kettle; she stirred that sludge with a wooden spoon: out of which came something full of bones, of celery, but fairly appetizing. Once cooked, all that remained was to taste it; she was happy, offered it all to the women. The women praised her for her wonderful cooking, repaid her for her kindness.

She envied no one. Perhaps, after so much courage and concern, after having striven and suffered, and having produced her offspring without tears, so that they, the strategists of the republic,* might have her finest blood at their disposal!, to do whatever they commanded; perhaps after the fiery haste of every day, and of the years, tired ellipses, perhaps the time was right: gentle assuager of every sacrifice: oh! it would take her to the place where people forget and are forgotten, beyond the houses and the walls, along the path attended by cypresses.

Rustic progeny, raising perpetual bread: let them grow up, let them love. She considered her story to be at its end. The sacrifice had been performed. In purity; of which God alone is knowledge. She was happy that other men and women might gather the vital sense of the tale, deluded still, with their hot blood, in regarding it as necessary truth. The smoke rose from the houses on the far horizon. No one would have kept her spirit, or her cheer, for so long in the empty days.

But Gonzalo? Oh, the marvel of life! A continuity fulfilled. Once again, from the terrace, she seemed aware of the curve of the world: the sphere of lights, revolving; they vanished in a mist the colour of periwinkle towards the quietness of the night. On the world, bringer of grain, and of song, the tranquil lights of midsummer. She felt herself still watching it, from the terrace of her life, oh! still, for a moment, to be part of the calm evening. A sweet lightness. And, high in the sky, the sapphire of the ocean: which Alvise had contemplated, in trepidation, and Antoniotto of Noli, rounding capes of nameless reality towards the emergent dream of archipelagos. She felt drawn into the event, into the ancient flow of possibility, of continuation: like all, close to all. She had overcome the darkness through her thought, her sons, giving herself: gifts of good works and hopes for the sanctity of the future. Her consummate labour took her back on to the path of souls. She had learned, taught. Late chimes: and

---

* The strategists of the republic: South American Republic, 1916.

silence had drunk the slow-burning wick of the vigils. Dawn crept in between the lines: noble paragraphs! and she, in sleep, repeated its sentence. Generations, chirruping of springtime, game of perpetual life beneath the gaze of the towers. Thoughts had stirred thoughts, souls had stirred souls. Grieving nations ferried them towards the shores of knowledge, ships by the Dark Sea. Perhaps in this way the atrocity of her pain, to God, would not be without purpose.

She put her hands together.

Gonzalo, with his work, made enough to live on. Recently, he had been to Modetia,* the seamstress at Modetia was to make him some plain woven shirts: she had, indeed, written: she would cut them with the greatest care, so obliged she felt, dear Señora, for her kindness and courtesy.

Gonzalo! Her older son had no state pension, except for a trifle, for a paltry medal: the last and most ludicrous of medals. (But this is what the experts might believe, not his mother's certainty.) There was, in any case, no reason for him to have a state pension. His eardrums were affected, now, by an ailment other than some traumatic wound – ruined, it could be said, by some other tedium that was not the impenetrable mist of deafness. She couldn't say how he had reappeared to her, oh!, in an ashen dawn: among the commerce and the mire of Pastrufazio, and the indomitable motor cars. He was unscathed, with few years inside the grey epaulettes he wore on his return. Perhaps his war had not been hazardous for him. He told no stories, never: he never spoke about it to anyone: certainly not to the children, when they gathered round him during a moment's rest, warriors or admirals, grazed, hot, with tin bayonets: nor to the ladies in the villas who were, he said, among the choicest women of Pastrufazio, those most thirsty for epic sagas: and consequently the most enthusiastic imbibers of tall stories.

There again, it seemed he had a loathing for children. A glum severity came over his face on finding even a single one of them in the house, like that poor dimwit – the mother smiled – of the caillou, bijou. Oh! 'her' Gonzalo! It was quite obvious that the arsenal of glory had refused to take

* Recently, he had been to Modetia: Founded in 1695 below the last undulating moraines of Mount Serruchón, by several immigrants from Monza; who named the new city with the Latin name of the city they had left behind.

care of him. In him, Plautus wouldn't find his character, perhaps Molière. The poor mother, without wishing it, saw once again the distant figures of Le Misanthrope and L'Avare, all lace and frills to the knees, in the old book, in two columns, of her adolescent mornings, of her so fervid wakenings: when the circle of the small oil lamp, on the table, was the orb of thought and clarity in the security of the silence. In the old book, smelling of old French ink, with bonnets, lace and Maître Corbeau.* It was clear. After salvaged victories, the printers of funereal glory no longer had enough of their mortuary wood-cuts for a veteran's verses without hendecasyllables: funerary lamps and phrases and flames and perennis ardee: all used up for the wood-cuts, on the covers of cadaverous poems. Never, never would he, Gonzalo, have used his dead comrades for such glorious poetizing, his brother, a distant smile! The name, the desperate memory, closed up inside him.

The haberdashers had no frills at any price that they could sell him, nor caballero braid, nor ribbon, nor buckles, for his quiet existence. The hidalgo kept away from salons, from the opinions of patriotic ladies. To weak tea, if that were not enough, he preferred the solitary Recoleta road. After such regrettable observations, serious people began indeed to form the view that he should be avoided. And one fine day, indeed, having completed his courses in humanities, and in engineering, his native city of Pastrufazio couldn't wait to be rid of him.

But these considerations lay beyond his mother's love, as also her language: in the misery of her dull days she had never taken part in the conversations, in the tinkling conglomerations of fine society.

She thought sweetly of this elder son of hers, seeing him as a child again, intent and studious. And now already hunched, bored of wandering the footpaths. She returned, from the terrace, into the main room. The flies were back, now that the storm was over, buzzing over the table: where the newspapers lay, with new events, that had given way to others. And likewise from year to year, from day to day; for the whole succession of years, of days. And the pages, soon, turned yellow. When the flies ceased their merry-go-round, for a moment, and even the fat green fly, for an

* In the old book, smelling of old French ink, with bonnets, lace and Maître Corbeau: One volume for Molière and La Fontaine, the other for Corneille and Racine.

instant; then in the fleeting cosmos of that unexpected suspension she could hear the woodworm more distinctly crunching, crunching laboriously, in short spurts, in the old walnut secrétaire that she could no longer unlock. The key had lost its play over successive attempts, or, perhaps, in the painful shadows of memory. The portrait must be there . . . the portraits . . . the mother-of-pearl cufflinks . . . two letters, perhaps, as well . . . the last ones! . . . her work scissors, the black lace fan . . . The one they'd given her in the marshes, a farewell present from colleagues, from the few girls she had taught . . . several of them excited, all wanting a kiss from her . . . but she had no shortage, por suerte, of spare scissors: three pairs, in fact.

And there had been the wedding.

If her thoughts moved down, from the recollection of those two children, to recent years, to today . . . the cruelty seemed to her too great: akin, savagely, to scorn.

Why? Why? Her face, in those intervals, petrified her in anguish: no stirring of the soul was any longer possible: perhaps she was no longer the mother, as in the distant, lacerated, howls of childbirth: she was no longer a person, but a shadow. She paused like that, in the room, with eyes blind to every compassionate return, fleshless immobility of old age, for long swathes of time. And the cloak of poverty and of old age was like an extreme sign of existence brought before the faces of portraits, where fatuous flying insects, in the emptiness, will orbit inside what is left of tomorrow. Then, almost a seasonal rite, all of a sudden, the hour struck from the tower; liberating its lost, equal chimes into the emptiness. And it seemed to her an unnecessary, cruel reminder. In the finished time of every summer, across the world that had forsaken her in this way. The flies traced a few circles in the main room, in front of the portraits, beneath the horizontal rays of the evening. Then, with one weary hand, she tidied her hair, whitened by the years, spilling over her forehead, unstroked like the hair of King Lear. Survivor of every fate. And now in the silence, as dusk came down, the storms of possibility vanished. She had learned so much, read so many books! By the small oil-lamp, Shakespeare: and she still recited several verses, like forgotten syllables scattered from a shattered stele, once a light of knowledge, and now the horror of the night.

In the sky the vapour, the smoke, had vanished from above the fireplaces, beneath cooking pots, of people's frugal suppers. They had vanished like a bounty of the earth: towards the evening star, through the bluish September air: up, up, to the golden light, from the black chimneys; which rise with the strength of towers beyond the shadows and the blue-tinted hills, behind trees, above the distant chimney pots of the houses.

She had heard the rolling of the train . . . the arriving whistle . . . She would have liked someone to be near, as darkness approached.

But her child appeared only rarely at the doorway of the house.

'*La mamma*'

Originally published as part of *La cognizione del dolore* in *Letteratura* (IV, no.1. January–March 1940). As the original project was temporarily abandoned, Gadda included the short story in *Novelle dal ducato in fiamme* (Valecchi, 1953) and in *Accoppiamenti giudiziosi* (Garzanti, 1963). It then appeared as the fifth chapter of *La cognizione del dolore* (Einaudi, 1963).

ENNIO FLAIANO

1910–72

Flaiano was born in Pescara, on the same street as the writer Gabriele D'Annunzio. He came to Rome in his teens and later planned to get a degree in architecture. Instead he wrote about the city's café culture, its vulgarity, its paparazzi-driven vapidity. In the process he captured, with a gimlet eye, the cultural zeitgeist of the 1950s. His perspective was laconic, pessimistic, at times nihilistic. A great enthusiast of Thomas Mann and Charlie Chaplin, Flaiano started out as a theatre critic. In October 1935, he went to fight in Mussolini's invasion of Ethiopia, and his post-colonial debut novel *Tempo di uccidere* (*A Time to Kill*, also published under the title *The Short Cut*) won the Strega Prize in 1947, but much of his subsequent energy was devoted to writing screenplays for some of the classics of post-war Italian cinema, including Federico Fellini's *La Dolce Vita* and *8½*, and Michelangelo Antonioni's *La Notte*. He collaborated extensively with Fellini and married the sister of Nino Rota, who composed the music for Fellini's films. Flaiano was also a master of the aphorism, and wrote a column called *Diario notturno* (Nocturnal Diary) for the magazine *Il Mondo*. 'A Martian in Rome' was the piece which inaugurated that column, and it was collected, along with the other pieces he wrote, into a volume by the same name. The story, written in the form of a diary, is set in Rome and incorporates, in cameo roles, a series of actual cultural figures, including some of the authors in this anthology. Long considered a classic portrait of Roman life, Flaiano's take on how 'aliens' arriving from afar are perceived and received continues to strike a chord. A book called *Diario degli errori* (Diary of Errors), an omnibus of acerbic observations and travel writing, was published a few years after he died.

A Martian in Rome

Translated by Philip Balma and Fabio Benincasa[1]

October 12 – Today a Martian descended in his spaceship upon Villa Borghese, in the race-track lawn. So I will try to maintain, in writing these notes, the calm that I completely lost at the announcement of this incredible event, to repress the anxiety that immediately pushed me into the streets to mingle with the crowd. The entire suburban population poured into the city's centre, blocking traffic completely. I must say that everyone's joy and curiosity is mixed with a hope that yesterday could have seemed absurd, and is instead growing more intense with every passing hour. The hope that 'now everything will change'. Rome immediately assumed the slovenly and homely appearance of grand occasions. There's something in the air that is reminiscent of July 25th, of 1943; the same people hugging; the same old commoner women that walk by heading towards imaginary barricades, shouting the praises of freedom; the same army reserve officers that wore their uniforms, convinced they would be able, in their get-up, to make their way through the crowd and reach the riding track: which is instead guarded by police tanks and two regiments in fighting trim.

You already can't get through Piazza Fiume: the packed crowd, swaying, waits, sings, shouts, improvises dances. I saw the first drunks. The roofs of the buses (stuck in the streets like ships surprised by winter in a glacial sea) were swarming with young people and screaming children who were waving large dirty flags. The stores have lowered their rolling shutters. At times the blowing wind brings a distant burst of applause that reignites curiosity and causes disorientation, a greater and more cheerful confusion.

Around seven I met my friend Fellini, pale and devastated by emotion. He was at the Pincio when the spaceship landed and at first he thought he was having a hallucination. When he saw people running and yelling and heard sharp orders being shouted from the spaceship in a somewhat cold, scholastic Italian, Fellini understood. Immediately stampeded and stepped on by the crowd, he woke up without shoes on, his jacket in shreds. He wandered around the park like a dolt, barefoot, trying to find any exit whatsoever. I was the first friendly face he met. He cried while embracing me, shaken by an emotion that was communicated to me soon enough. He then described the spaceship to me: a saucer of enormous dimensions, yellow and bright like a sun. And the unforgettable rustling, the rustling of a silk foulard, upon its landing! And the silence which followed that moment! In that brief instant he felt that a new period was beginning for humanity. The prospects are, he tells me, immense and inscrutable. Maybe everything: religion and laws, art and our very lives, will soon appear to us illogical and meagre. If the solitary traveller who descended from the spaceship is really – and by now after the official communiqué it would be foolish to doubt it – the ambassador from another planet where everything is known about ours, this is a sign that 'things are more simple' elsewhere. The fact that the Martian came alone proves that he possesses means of self-defence which are unknown to us; and such knowledge that could radically alter our system of living and our conception of the world.

At the Policlinico, where I take him to treat the wounds on his feet, I meet Giovannino Russo and Carletto Mazzarella among the injured. The first one had lost his glasses and does not recognize me, the second one lost his shoes and I don't recognize him. They are still devastated by their emotions. Before the crowd let loose in its enthusiasm, they had enough time to see the Martian! Hence, it is true! Their irony (they suspected a publicity stunt) suddenly desisted when they saw the blond pilot of the ship disembark. Russo describes him as a tall man, of noble appearance, a bit melancholic. He dresses like anyone, like a Swede might dress – Mazzarella added. He spoke in perfect Italian. Two women fainted when he passed, smiling, through the police cordon to reach the police commissioner's car. No one dared get too close to him. Only a child ran towards him. The scene that followed caused shouting and tears among those present. The Martian spoke to the child, softly, caressing him. Nothing else. He smiled and was tired.

Mazzarella is particularly enthused about the Martian. He deduces that Martian girls are surely better than Spanish girls, and maybe even better than American ones. He hopes the Martian has brought the poetic texts of Martian literature with him.

October 13 – The Martian was received by the President of the Republic, last night. Around 2 a.m. Via Veneto was swarming with people like on a Sunday morning. Small groups were forming around the fortunate ones who saw the Martian up close. It seems that the Martian knows our economic, social and political situation well. He is a man of simple, but polite ways. He does not offer many explanations, and he requests none. When they asked him why he chose Rome in particular for his visit, he smiled subtly. It also seems that he will stay in Rome for quite some time, maybe six months. Around two-thirty I met Mario Pannunzio with the usual group from *Il Mondo*. They spoke of the Martian, but with a certain scepticism which surprised me. 'There still is no official news –' said Sandro De Feo '– the communiqué has been disproved.' To which Pannunzio added: 'I won't believe it even if I see him.'

At three the special editions of the newspapers, forbidden by the authorities up to that point for reasons of public safety, were made available. The Martian is called Koont. He has peaceful intentions, even though, he claims, other spaceships are cruising the stratosphere. The voyage from Mars to earth lasts no longer than three days. There is no information on the exchanges taking place between the Martian and the authorities. This is all. While returning home I stopped to read a poster for a political party, full of insults for another party. Suddenly everything seemed ridiculous to me. I felt the need to scream. I believe in the Martian, and I especially believe in his good faith! I was deranged. And who do I run into? The old man who looks after the cars on Via Sicilia, the one with the hat that says *Journaux Suisses*. I gave him all the money I had on me, not much, I kissed his hands, begging him to forgive me, like a good Christian. The scene did not appear at all strange to two or three people who witnessed it and hurried to give the old man money. At home I collapsed on the bed and fell asleep all of a sudden, happy and weightless as a child. Great and terrible days are to come.

October 14 – The authorities had the spaceship fenced off, and from now on one will be able to see it upon payment of a fee to certain Catholic charity services. The Martian gave his approval. The fee was fixed at one hundred lire, to allow even people of modest means to see the spaceship.

Nevertheless, injured veterans, officials from the Ministry of Internal Affairs, card-carrying members of the press can enter for free. Members of ENAL, schools and large groups can obtain a discount.

October 15 – We walk around Rome like crazed ants, seeking some friends to communicate our inebriating happiness to. Everything appears to us in a new dimension. What is our future? Will we be able to prolong our lives, combat diseases, avoid wars, give food to all? We speak of nothing else. Even more so than in the preceding days we feel that something new is to come. It's not the end of the world, but the beginning of the world. There's the wait before the curtain is raised, made harsher by a play we do not know. This wait is only disturbed by predictable prophecies, told by those who had always said so and now are ready for the new challenge; by the Communists, who have already tried to secure the Martian for themselves, by the Fascists, who raise the question of his race.

October 18 – I finally managed to see the spaceship. It is impressive. The police guards are kind, they speak softly, almost as if to have their presence forgiven. After all, no one commits the slightest disrespectful act. A child who tried to write something in chalk on the shiny surface of the spaceship has been spanked by his parents. I too, like everyone, touched the spaceship, and in that metallic warmth I felt a profound sweetness I had never experienced before. A stranger and I were smiling, looking at each other, and in the end we shook hands, moved by the same fraternal impulse; and later on I did not feel embarrassed by my state of commotion. It seems that the spaceship has already performed two miracles, but there is no proof, even though some women have insisted on leaving memorial marble tablets on the ground, with their thanks. A municipal employee has already been contracted to sell candles, but it seems that the proceeds will benefit a Catholic charity.

Leaving the enclosure I see Mario Soldati. He's there, sitting on the grass, his tie undone, wearing a shirt and vest. He was sighing, actually devastated by the reality that was a few steps away. 'It's over!' he said when he saw me. He held my hands and I felt that his emotion was sincere. '*C'est la fin!*' he added then in French, and he repeated the phrase many times, until both of us lost track of its meaning: we looked at each other bewildered, not knowing what else to say. We then went to have a drink instead, in one of the many improvised kiosks which popped up illegally in the riding track. Soldati wanted a soda, the kind that used to be sold at fairs, with a ball floating inside, and he insisted in vain. They don't make them any more. The curious incident caused by a young thief who had managed to make his way into the spaceship distracted us from our extremely favourable considerations on the Martian. Recognized by a guard as one of those guys who steal from foreigners' cars, he tried to escape feigning an epileptic seizure. He has an opaque face, suspicious and hardened by his work. Fear made him a savage.

October 19 – The reception at the Campidoglio had some great moments, they tell me. I was not even able to get to Piazza Venezia because of the crowd. There was a calmer curiosity in the air which I liked. This calm degenerated perhaps into indifference in the bus drivers and ticket salesmen, who looked tired and nervous. Trapped for hours, always hoping that the crowds would disperse, they did not abandon their vehicles. A few idiots were already getting mad at the Martian: 'What the heck did he come here for?' said a ticket salesman. A colleague of his answered: 'Do you think that life on Mars can measure up to life in Rome? Would you live on Mars?' 'I'd sooner die,' replied the first one. A bit later, walking by again, I heard the same two talking about football. Next Sunday there will be a fairly important match.

At the Campidoglio, the mayor made a fool of himself speaking of Rome, master of civilization. There were a few coughs, the gaffe was unfixable by now, and the mayor did not insist on the subject, limiting himself to praising the planetary system, the discovery of which was aided by Galileo, with his telescope and his studies on the sun. The Martian was smiling, and at a certain point it seems that he leaned in close to the ear of a cardinal sitting beside him to tell him something. The cardinal smiled paternally. When they offered him a certificate of honorary citizenship, the Martian said a few words. The loudspeakers broadcasted them, but not clearly. The press reports them, it's nothing special, maybe we expected more effort out of him; but you must also keep the delicate situation of the Martian in mind, he feels he's a guest.

October 21 – The first photograph of the Martian, they say, was sold the very evening of his arrival for three million to an American news agency. The fortunate photographer could have made more, but he gave in real quick at the sight of the banknotes.

The political life seems to have come to a halt. Today the Martian attended a session of the Chamber of Deputies. The speakers stuttered. A proposed law to increase certain customs tariffs has been unanimously approved, euphorically. The deputies were all dressed in black tie, and they gave way to each other with courteous detachment. 'It seemed –' Vittorio Gorresio told me – 'like the last day of school.' Everyone pretended not to look at the Martian, well knowing that the Martian was observing everyone. It seems that the Martian had a good impression of it all.

October 27 – What is the Martian doing? We await new information, and hope there is big news. For now the papers limit themselves to informing us on how he spends his time. One could point out that he participates in too many receptions, banquets and cocktail parties: but he does have some diplomatic obligations, and he's the only one to fulfil them. Perhaps there is a conspiracy of silence concerning his intentions, which he may have clearly expressed to the government. The Communists already say so, albeit covertly. There were rumours of his decision to leave, and an evening paper sold a hundred thousand copies publishing the news, refuted later on, that the Martian had left. Many photographs of the Martian are still published. They say that the aristocracy, however, has abandoned him. But these are inevitable tall tales. And already some shady bon mots, some atrocious witticisms are repeated. I won't relate them, as they are very humiliating to the human race.

November 3 – Life in Rome is almost back to normal. The police have re-established the usual closing time for the bars, and major raids take place during night-time hours, in the public parks that by now had become the meeting place for lovers. Nine films about the Martian are in preparation, one with the comedian Totò.

November 5 – The Martian has been received by the Pope. The *Roman Observer* gives news of this, however without publishing photographs, in the column 'Our Information'. In this column, as it is known, the names of the people to whom the Holy Father granted a private audience are recorded in order of importance. The Martian is among the last, and is so mentioned: Mr Koont from Mars.

November 8 – Today the Martian suddenly agreed to be part of a jury of artists and writers for the crowning of Miss Vie Nuove. When they pointed out to him that the jury was made up of leftist artists and writers, the Martian showed a certain disappointment: but he had already given his word. The evening was marked by a very joyful atmosphere, and the Communists did not conceal their satisfaction for this first victory. The Martian, seated between Carlo Levi and Alberto Moravia, did not say a word. The photographers literally blinded him with their flashes. The competing beauties went unnoticed. Alberto Moravia broke his chair by nervously shifting around.

That evening, I met Carlo Levi with other friends. I joined them to hear his impressions on the Martian. Favourable. The Martian knows about the southern question, certainly not like Levi himself. He's an intelligent man, even though his upbringing is affected by the flaws of Martian education. All in all, Carlo Levi finds him very likeable, and he'll go far if he follows Levi's advice. Levi gave him some books to read, and, among them, *Christ Stopped at Eboli*, that the Martian was already familiar with in the American edition.

November 19 – I meet Amerigo Bartoli. We talk about the weather. He shows me some red wool socks which he bought in a store downtown at a good price. Then he asks me if I received his postcard. – 'What postcard?' – 'I had sent you a postcard to ask you for a cigarette, did you not receive it?' He tells me that now, with the cold, he's forced to go to bed early because he has to get up late in the morning. In the end, he confesses that he's looking for an idea for a humorous sketch of the Martian. In truth, the topic is a bit passé: everything has been done. Mino Maccari conceived a good sketch, in *Il Mondo*. It shows some old imperialist Fascists in uniform shouting 'O Roma o Marte!' Bartoli wants to do something literary, not political. I advise him to try this drawing: the Martian looks at his little, distant, native planet from the terrace of the Pincio. 'It's not funny,' observes Bartoli. 'It's not supposed to be funny –' I reply – 'but rather, it's supposed to move you.' Bartoli does not answer and we speak of other things. Bartoli will never understand the Martian.

November 20 – As of today the Martian has received around two hundred thousand letters. A team of secretaries is at work reading them. They are, for the most part, from misunderstood inventors, dissatisfied women, good children. In a letter, postmarked from Catania, they found a single word: cuckold. But letters also arrive in which the Martian is asked to act, soon, and he's reproached for wasting precious time. Disappointment is already rife. Mario Soldati, whom I met today in a bookstore, whispered in my ear: 'Treason!' And he went away, bent forward under the weight of his thoughts, like a conspirator pondering his resignation.

November 27 – The scene which took place the other night at the Cisterna, in Trastevere, between the drunk Martian and a popular film actor disgusted me. It seems that the actor insisted on the Martian agreeing to eat some spaghetti at his table. Naturally the paparazzi did not miss this chance to photograph the Martian wolfing down spaghetti, hand fed by the actor. The afternoon papers publish the photographs. The meaning of the vulgar comments is this: the Martian appreciates Roman cuisine very much, and is happy to be living in Rome, where life is undoubtedly better than in every other city on the planet.

November 28 – I stop by the offices of *Il Mondo* to say hello to my friends. The photographer arrives with the package full of new stuff. They reprimand him because he brings many photographs of the Martian. It seems that Pannunzio has decided to no longer publish photographs of the Martian. Enough!

December 2 – F. calls me to invite me to a cocktail party he's throwing today in honour of the Martian. I respond, imitating the voice of the maid, saying that I'm not home. Meeting the Martian seems useless to me, among people who want to get their hands on him, some to tell him how things really are in Italy, some to invite him to another cocktail party, some to involve him in a literary prize.

December 6 – Finally I saw the Martian. It was last night, at 2 a.m., Pierino Accolti-Gil and I were quietly smoking when we saw him coming, in the company of two girls, tall, leggy, maybe two chorus-girls. He was laughing and speaking in English. He quit laughing when he passed by, even though we were purposefully not watching him. Near the news stands in Via Lombardia the Martian ran into the ex-King Faruk, who was walking slowly, bored. They did not greet each other. The ex-King Faruk was looking for some cigarettes, and he gestured at the old man who was there selling them. 'Here you are!' answered the old man, running towards his client.

We later passed by two prostitutes who were muttering. One was saying: 'Will you go with the Martian? Come on, already!' The other appeared nervous and put out: 'Not me. You go with him. I'm not going with the Martian.' I did not understand if her refusal was due to a fear of the unknown, or only misguided nationalism.

December 7 – Ercole Patti tells me that the Martian, invited to the Ciampino airport to welcome a movie star, was asked by the photographers to get out of the way. It seems, in fact, that his presence in a photograph may prevent their sale to magazines. 'Hey, Mr Mars, will you move your ass?' they said to him, laughing, but resolutely. And the Martian, sweet, smiling, without fully understanding what was being said to him, was shaking his head and his hands, waving hello.

December 18 – Vittorio Ivella and I, the other night, were speaking about Italy, when Ivella shared his hypothesis with me. I don't know why it really amused me. He said: 'But for what reasons would he have landed here of all places? I say he didn't come on purpose, he fell here!' The thought of the Martian forced to make an emergency landing, then behaving like a discoverer of new worlds, was, I repeat, very amusing to me. All night I did nothing but laugh thinking about it. Attilio Ricci claims, instead, that the Martian is a typical case of idolization of the unknown. He predicts that the Martian will end up lynched.

They also say, and I take notice of it as a matter of record, that the Martian has fallen in love with a ballerina, who plays hard to get, and speaks of him in despicable terms.

December 20 – Today for the first time I spoke with the Martian. I was in Fregene, and I recognized him immediately. He was walking along the sunny, but windy beach. He was watching the sea and stopping to pick up sea shells: some he put in his pocket. Since we were alone on the beach, he walked up to me to ask for a match. I pretended not to recognize him, so as not to offend him with my curiosity, and also because in that moment I wanted to be alone with my thoughts. It was he who told me, pointing a finger at his chest: 'Me, Martian.' I feigned surprise. Then the idea popped into my head that I should interview him. I intended to jot down an interview different from the rest, something a bit literary, if you know what I mean, to coax him into broader reflections than usual, which could have been justified by the proximity of the sea, if it's true what Flaubert says that the sea inspires deep thoughts in the bourgeois. Then laziness stopped me. I should have asked questions, insisted, explained.

No – I told myself – let's content ourselves to watch him up close. His excessive height struck me in a bad way. He's too tall, so much that he appears defenceless, like certain elderly men from the north who look younger than their real age, but who, in their childish smile, reveal an existence led without great pains and far from sin, or rather, totally uninteresting to my eyes. I invited him to get a drink. At the bar he asked for a whisky and, certainly to thank me, he placed a hand on my shoulder, smiling. For just a moment, a fleeting and slight impression, I was certain that he was unhappy.

December 21 – Last night, in a café in Via Veneto, a table of young pederasts were talking about the Martian: so audibly that one could not avoid hearing what they said. Thus it seems that the Martian has befriended a young and unknown film actor. But it also seems that the Martian lives in the preoccupation of appearing politically orthodox to the (invisible) eyes of his fellow planetsmen, who certainly monitor him with the means they possess which we cannot even imagine. Maybe some remote-controlled microphones? All hypotheses are possible. Hence, the Martian, locked in his hotel room with the young actor, after having amused himself at length, would have got up and, with the attitude of someone who intends to address a visible listener, would have said aloud, articulating his words clearly: 'But why don't you come live on Mars, Home of True Democracy?'

December 22 – The Martian agreed to play a small role as a Martian in a film, which would be directed by Roberto Rossellini, who is pushing for the participation of a Martian company in the financing of the film. Mario Soldati, whom I saw today at Rossetti's, spoke to me about the new book he wants to write before beginning his new film. It's a story that takes place in Turin, in 1932. He was very happy, Soldati, telling me the plot. He left because he was rushing to get shaved. He had purchased some paper goods. I saw him disappear like a butterfly.

January 6 – The Christmas holidays went by, as usual, melancholically. And it's hot! I was out a little late last night in Via Veneto, because I was not sleepy. At a table at Rosati's, there were Pannunzio, Libonati, Saragat, Barzini and other political journalists. They were speaking about proportional representation. At another table, the Martian with Mino Guerrini, Talarico and Accolti-Gil. It was obvious that they were mocking him in good humour. A bus boy was already dumping sawdust on the floor, and when I walked by I heard Accolti-Gil saying this to the Martian: 'If you come to Capri for Easter, I will introduce you to Malaparte. Great brain, more than Levi. Insightful connoisseur, central and northern question.' The Martian was nodding, courteous and distracted. Because a waiter, quite rudely, made it clear that it was closing time, everyone stood up. Even the Martian exited, and said goodbye to us from the doorway, then headed towards the Hotel Excelsior. Sitting at the last table, next to the gas pump at the corner of Via Lombardia, there was Faruk. He was whistling, watching the sky filled with pink clouds, he too absorbed in a melancholic thought of his own. Leaning his elbows on the wicker chair, he held his hands together in front of his mouth; he fidgeted slowly with his fingers and whistled. But softly, like a king in exile might whistle, or a Muslim who imagines the notion of pleasure. Two tables away, some taxi drivers were discussing football; and further down the old cigarette guy was bouncing around, waiting for someone to call on him. This is, for me, such a familiar picture that it never fails to move me, and in fact I smiled, thinking of this sweet Rome that mixes the most distinct destinies in a maternal, implacable whirl.

To this picture the Martian has been added, who walked past the drivers and Faruk, happily ignoring them, but sticking his chest out a bit. At the Excelsior he stopped and retraced his steps. He did not feel like going to sleep, I understood this well. The boredom of the night, the fear of the bed, the horror of an unfriendly room that repulses you, were now keeping him glued to a display window full of toys, now in front of a flower-shop window. It seems that beautiful flowers like ours do not grow on Mars . . . he decided finally to cross the street, and, at this point, in the grey silence, someone yelled out 'Hey, Martian! . . .' The Martian turned around immediately, but once again the silence was broken, and this time by a long sound, lacerating, vulgar. The Martian remained still and scanned the darkness. But there was nobody there, or rather, no one to be seen. He resumed his walk; an even louder sound, multiple, roaring, nailed him to the pavement: the night seemed to be ripped open by a concert of devils.

'Scoundrels!' yelled the Martian.

An outburst of sounds, prolonged, crackling like an atrocious firework, which later extinguished itself in a flowery vibrato only when the Martian managed to blend in with the small crowd which loitered in front of the Caffé Strega. We were able to deduce that the youngsters were in a big group, hiding behind the news stand in Via Boncompagni.

Later on, returning home, I saw Koont, heading alone towards Villa Borghese with long, soft steps. Above the tips of the pine trees the red dot of Mars was shining, almost solitary in the sky. Koont stopped to look at it. There is, in fact, talk of an imminent departure, if only he will be able to get his spaceship back from the hotel owners who, they say, had it distrained.

'Un marziano a Roma'
First published in the weekly magazine *Il Mondo* (2 November 1954) and then included in *Diario notturno* (Bompiani, 1956).

BEPPE FENOGLIO

1922–63

Fenoglio created two literary alter egos: 'Johnny' and 'Milton'. Together, the names of these protagonists, Italian characters who are stand-ins for Fenoglio, add up to an Americanized version of John Milton. The seventeenth-century English poet (who also composed in Italian) was a touchstone for Fenoglio, who never graduated from university, served in the Partisan Army, and wrote about the Resistance in an unsparing key. But perhaps Fenoglio's first act of literary resistance was to not write at all: when required, in school, to write an essay celebrating Mussolini's March on Rome, he left the page blank. Apart from his years in the military, Fenoglio lived in the Piedmontese city of Alba, in the Langhe, where he was born. This isolated region and its peasant culture provided him with inspiration for his work. 'The Smell of Death' is one of twelve stories in his debut collection, *I ventitré giorni della città di Alba* (*The Twenty-three Days of the City of Alba*), published in 1952 in Vittorini's *Gettoni* series. The collection, widely considered a quintessential work of literature about the Italian Resistance, describes the trauma of the partisan struggle without rhetoric, and with exceptional acuity. It was deemed a political betrayal by the Left, given that it was more truthful than ideological. Fenoglio's knowledge of English, a language he fell passionately in love with as a teenager, was strong enough to translate Samuel Taylor Coleridge and Gerard Manley Hopkins. He also conceived and drafted his own work directly in English, saying that the last novel published in his lifetime, *Primavera di bellezza* (Beautiful Spring), was a 'mere translation' for the Italian reader. The novels *Una questione privata* (most recently published as *A Private Affair*) and *Il partigiano Johnny* (*Johnny the Partisan*) perhaps his most powerful, were published after his death from lung cancer at forty. The first draft of *Il partigiano Johnny* was composed in an anomalous blend of English and Italian dubbed 'Fenglish' by Italian literary critics.

The Smell of Death

Translated by John Shepley

If you rub the fingers of one hand on the back of the other long and hard, and then smell your skin, what you smell is the smell of death.

Carlo had learned this as a child, maybe from his mother's conversations with other women in the courtyard, or more likely in those gatherings of children on summer nights, in that interval that falls between the last game and the first job, where from slightly older companions one learns so many things about life in general and about the relations between men and women in particular.

He smelled a definite odour one evening in another summer, when he was already a man, and that it was precisely the smell of death was demonstrated by the facts.

That evening Carlo was waiting at the end of the street where the San Lazzaro Hospital stands and opposite the grade crossing just outside the railroad station. The last train for T. left, puffing its black smoke into the evening sky and giving off a fine odour of coal and steel under friction; from its windows came a yellow light, as soft and soothing as the light from the windows of one's home. Eight-fifteen, he said to himself, as he excitedly watched the dispatcher turning the crank to raise the barrier.

Inside the house against whose corner he was leaning, a woman, who from her voice seemed to be his mother's age, started singing a song of her youth:

> *Mamma mia, dammi cento lire,*
> *Che in America voglio andare . . .*
> Mamma mia, gimme a hundred lire,
> 'Cause I wanna go to America . . .

It would be nice to be in America, he thought – especially in Hollywood. But not tonight, tonight I want to make love in my own country. And he stuck his fists in the pockets of his trousers.

Carlo was waiting for his eighteen-year-old girlfriend, to take her out towards the fields, and there is no need to dwell on his desire, nor on the way time went by on the illuminated face of the station clock. And still she didn't come. But it should be said that her body represented Carlo's only riches at this harsh moment in his life, and if she didn't show up this evening he would have to live another whole week of tension and constraint to have her again.

Thus, even when her usual hour had passed, he was reluctant to discard all hope and go away, and remained standing there superstitiously, almost as though she could not fail to come if he held out long enough. But now it was eight-forty, and looking around he saw the old people sitting on benches in the public park, half obscured by the darkness, but those who were smoking were all pointing the red tips of their cigars at him. And that woman who had been singing before – she was surely the one who had been singing before – was now out on her balcony and for some time had been gazing down at the top of his head.

From the city's bell-towers the stroke of nine o'clock came to his ears, and so he set out for the centre of town, where other young men stroll in the piazza or sit in cafés, trying to brush women from their minds like flies from their noses.

He kept walking and every five paces he turned around to look back at that corner. He met two or three very young couples, swaying from side to side on the pavement like little drunkards, and clasping each other or separating depending on whether they were in or out of the areas of shadow between the street lamps. Carlo envied these boys with their girls, but then he said to himself: I wonder if they're going to do what we would have done if only she'd come. Otherwise there's no reason to envy them.

He made a slight detour to drink from the fountain in the park. He drank deeply then, raising his head, looked back one last time at that corner and saw a tall girl appear, as tall as she, with a canary-yellow jacket – then a fashionable colour and she had the same kind of jacket – and she was walking quickly towards the grade crossing.

He dashed away from the fountain, giving a long whistle in the girl's direction as he ran along the path in the park. The old people, their legs comfortably outstretched on the gravel, hastily drew them back under the benches as he ran past whistling again.

The girl did not turn around nor slow her pace; he ran faster, almost bumping into the dispatcher, who was about to lower the barriers for the last arriving train. He jumped across the tracks and came up behind the girl.

She was walking stiffly and rapidly past the gasworks, and he stopped, for he had just realized that it wasn't she, but another girl with more or less the same build and wearing the same kind of jacket. But by the time he realized this, he had already whistled a third time and the girl, hearing him, looked back over her shoulder without stopping and saw him standing in the middle of the street, his arms drooping at his sides. She turned her head and proceeded still more rapidly towards the dark end of the street.

He was out of breath and failed to see the man whom the dispatcher saw bend down to pass under the barriers and run up behind Carlo. But instead of hitting Carlo from behind, the man circled halfway around until he was ahead of him and with bony fingers clutched Carlo's biceps – all this without saying a word.

At that moment Carlo knew nothing about him except that his name was Attilio, that he had been a soldier in Greece, then a prisoner in Germany, and people said he had come back with TB.

Carlo in his turn clutched the other man's arms and they began to struggle. Looking over Attilio's shoulder, he had a brief glimpse of the girl, who had shrunk into a doorway in an effort to hide but was betrayed by the exposed edge of her yellow jacket.

Attilio had attacked him but didn't look him in the face; indeed, he had lowered his head on Carlo's chest and his hair kept brushing his chin. He squeezed the muscles of Carlo's arm and Carlo squeezed his, but Carlo was unable to open his mouth and cry out: What the hell's the matter with you? For now he smelled – he saw it enter his nostrils like dirty white smoke – the smell of death, that smell that can be reproduced, if much too lightly, by doing what we said at the beginning. So he kept his mouth clamped shut, and when at the height of his exertions he could no longer breathe enough air with his nose, he twisted his head away until his neck bone creaked. It was while twisting his head that he saw the dispatcher, standing there watching and making no move to intervene. Couldn't he understand that they were fighting, when the two of them looked like a couple of drunkards leaning on each other for support? But what the dispatcher couldn't imagine was how they were gripping each other's muscles. Carlo was wondering how Attilio's frightfully skinny arms were able to resist his grasp and not turn into pulp. But Attilio's grip was terribly strong too, and if he hadn't had to keep himself from swallowing the smell of death, Carlo would have cried out in pain.

He had already realized why Attilio had confronted him this way, and oddly enough it didn't seem at all absurd or bestial to him. Carlo understood Attilio even while the man was trying to break his arms.

Now Attilio raised his head again and held it to one side, and Carlo saw his tight-shut eyes, his sharp cheekbones shining as though smeared with wax, and his mouth wide open to emit the smell of death. He too closed his eyes, no longer able to bear looking at that open mouth, and concentrated only on keeping his feet firmly planted on the ground and not loosening his hold.

Although the station bell had begun ringing insistently, he could distinctly hear Attilio's heartbeat banging against his ribs as though to break through and burst on Carlo like a projectile.

He decided to put an end to it. That smell, he now smelled it everywhere inside him; it had passed through his nostrils, his mouth, his pores, as relentless as the very power that gave it off; already it must have enveloped his brain, for he felt crazed. He raised one leg and brought it forward to trip his opponent and knock him down into the gutter. But just then Attilio's head slid slowly down Carlo's belly, his hands too loosened their hold and came down along Carlo's arms, now they grasped only his wrists, and gasping 'Mhuuuh! Mhuuuh!' he also let go of the wrists, and without Carlo even giving him a push, he ended up sitting on the ground. Then, toppled by the weight of his upturned head, he fell backward full length on the pavement.

Carlo made no move to pull him up and prop him in a sitting position against the wall of the gasworks, for he couldn't stand the smell. With Attilio lying on the ground, he forgot that he had understood him and opened his mouth to yell: What the hell's the matter with you? But he remembered in time that he had understood and closed his mouth again.

The train was near – judging by the sound it made, it was passing over the bridge. He looked down the street in search of the girl. She had left the shelter of the doorway and was standing in the middle of the street, looking from a distance at that heap of black-and-white rags that was Attilio lying on the pavement; then very slowly and cautiously she approached the two of them.

Now Carlo could leave; he turned his back on Attilio and went to the grade crossing. The dispatcher was looking intently at the track where the train would arrive, but Carlo could see that he was watching him out of the corner of his eye. The dispatcher said nothing to him, and anyway he would have had to yell. The train went by with all its lights falling on Carlo; the passengers at the windows saw the expression on his face, and who knows what they may have thought.

He walked away. With his arms crossed over his chest, he felt his muscles, which ached as though still encircled by iron rings, while before his eyes was Attilio's pale, infected skin, and he was thinking that he would never again be the same as he was before this struggle. He stayed out of the light as he walked, his eyelids, mouth and knees trembling. An attack of nerves, and yet he felt that never again would he be able to feel nervous tension, since his nerves had been broken by clasping Attilio's skinny arms.

And still before his eyes the whiteness of that skin. To drive it away, he concentrated on imagining in the void his girlfriend's body, naked, healthy and beneficent, but it refused to take shape and remained a white cloud added to and extending Attilio's skin.

He went to the bar of the railroad station but did not go inside; he signalled to the bartender from the doorway and ordered a brandy, a medicinal brandy if they had any.

While he waits for them to bring him the brandy, he sees a yellow jacket appear from the path in the park. It is Attilio's girl, walking much more slowly than before. She sees him, stops to think of something, and then comes up to him, still looking at the ground and with a guarded step. So Carlo has time to study her body, a very ordinary body but one that aspires to be possessed only by a healthy man.

Now here she is. She looks at him with blue eyes and says in a disagreeable voice, 'It was good of you not to hit him with your fists.'

'Brandy,' says the bartender behind him. He does not turn around and hears the sound of the saucer being set down on the open-air table.

The girl says to him, 'You've already figured it all out, haven't you?'

He says to her, 'I think you'd already realized yourself that I'd made a mistake, that I took you for someone else. What's sad is that he didn't realize it.'

She twists her hands and looks down and away. He says to her, 'Excuse me, but how did he get the idea that someone wants to take you away from him?'

'Because there is someone.'

'Someone . . . healthy?'

'Yes, someone healthy. We're right, aren't we? He wants me to be like before, but he's the one who's no longer like before. And besides, my family no longer approves.'

'How is he now? Did you take him home?'

Yes, but he's in very bad shape, he's having an attack, Attilio's mother has sent her to get the doctor in a hurry, but Carlo can see she's not the type to run through streets where the evening promenade is in full swing.

She asks him, 'Where does Dr Manzone live? Isn't he in Via Cavour?'

'Yes, at the beginning of Via Cavour.'

The girl takes a step back; she has already thanked him and is about to turn when a horrible curiosity comes over him, and he puts out a hand to stop her. He would like to say: Excuse me, you are, you've often been, close to him – have you smelled that smell on him . . . ? But then his hand drops and he only says goodnight, and she goes slowly away.

He drank his brandy and went home. At home he stripped naked and washed himself under the tap, so long and energetically that his mother woke up and from her room cried not to use so much soap, which cost a lot of money.

That night he dreamt of his struggle with Attilio, and in the morning at the employment office he heard that he'd been admitted to the infectious ward of the hospital.

'Germany,' said another jobless man like Carlo.

'Who are you talking about?' said someone who had just arrived. 'Who's this Attilio? Someone you know?' he asked Carlo.

'Me? I smelled the smell of death on him,' Carlo replied, and the other drew back his head to look him in the face, but then he had to turn around to answer 'Here!' to the clerk who had begun the roll call.

He dreamt again of his struggle with Attilio three weeks later, and in the morning, on his way as always to the employment office, he stopped at a wall along the street to strike a kitchen match, since he didn't have enough money to buy the little wax ones, and saw Attilio's name in big black letters on a funeral poster.

'*L'odore della morte*'
Part of the collection *I ventitré giorni della città di Alba* in the *Gettoni* series (Einaudi, 1952).

LUCE D'ERAMO

1925–2001

She is buried in Rome, along with John Keats, Percy Bysshe Shelley and
Antonio Gramsci, in the non-Catholic cemetery. She was born Lucette
Mangione in Reims, raised in a Fascist family living in Paris and moved
to Rome to attend high school. At nineteen, against her family's wishes,
determined to learn the truth about the Second World War, she volunteered to work in a German labour camp, and became an active member
of the Resistance. Shirking family connections when she was arrested, she
ended up imprisoned in Dachau. She escaped and got as far as the city of
Mainz, Germany, where, in the act of rescuing victims of a bombing, a
wall fell on to her legs, partially paralysing her for the rest of her life. Upon
return to Rome, she met writers like Moravia and Morante, began publishing in *Nuovi Argomenti*, and became a close friend of Amelia Rosselli,
a trilingual poet whose life spanned Italy, France, Switzerland, England
and the United States. D'Eramo's best-known work is an autobiographical
novel, *Deviazione* (*Deviation*), published in 1979 and made into a film in
Germany. She wrote frequently about foreigners, about those displaced by
the Second World War and its aftermath; *Io sono un'aliena* (I Am an Alien),
the title of one of her collections of essays, is the thematic underpinning
of all her work. The author of three story collections, D'Eramo's writing
is impeccably clean, stripped down to its essentials. '*Vivere in due*' is a tight
shot of a literary couple, a masterful monologue that is also in some sense
a dialogue. It opens slowly, lingering on the particulars and rhythms of a
shared domestic interior, then shifts register, incorporating Rome, a sense
of history and what lies beyond this mortal coil.

Life as a Couple

Translated by Howard Curtis

He'll be back at one again tonight, or two, or maybe even three. And I daren't even tell him he's wasting his time with all those meetings and discussions, because he gets so annoyed . . .

Who said anything about being a hermit? It's precisely because I have a social sense that I tell him to ease off if he doesn't want his talking to get in the way of his doing. And what's it got to do with being superior? There's no way he can say that, he knows perfectly well it's all about restraint.

This world of couples. You end up by closing in on the person you're talking to, from both sides. And at home? At home it's different: we receive visitors together, but we have distinct roles; when we go out to see friends we go together, but as individuals, and once there we lose sight of each other, then bump into each other by chance. But when a discussion starts up, you just have to join in, you get heated, and then it's hard to avoid ending up shoulder to shoulder, presenting a united front, which isn't very nice. Or else you get into an argument you might as well be having in private.

Wait a minute, you're the one who's always saying: 'Respect is what matters, respect is everything.'

Right now, though, I need to get some sleep. I have to get up early, I have a class first thing. He never feels sleepy in the evening, and in the morning, by the time he's up, his coffee has gone cold . . . 'Have you stirred the sugar?' he mutters, making himself even more comfortable. He drives me up the wall. I have to tell him about the electricity bill, twelve thousand lire for two people is too much, he keeps the light on all night; although according to the electrician, it's the boiler that really uses up energy . . . I stir the little spoon a dozen times at the bottom of the cup; no, I'll tell him later. Right now, he needs to make up his mind to cut out those twenty lines that don't work in the story, that monologue makes no sense, he's so fond of it, he gets so carried away with these inane flights of fancy. 'Listen,' I begin, stirring the spoon nine times, but no, why must I always wake him up with some tiresome reminder? I lean over him, his eyelids are red, there are dark, hollow rings under his eyes, his mouth is weary, I wait; even if he sleeps for just another five minutes that's something; I look at him, gently stir the spoon the number of months, years that I've known him; soon we'll be old.

He lacks judgement. The other night I wake up, the opaque whiteness of dawn is already casting stripes across the room (I've forgotten to close the blinds again, I'll get up now, in a while), and what do I see? The light's on, filtering beneath the door. 'For heaven's sake!' I cry, throw back the blankets and jump out of bed, totally roused now by my anger. I go to his study and fling open the door: he's sitting numbly behind the desk, his face haggard, green, the room foggy with smoke, the ashtrays overflowing with cigarette ends, the carton of milk balanced on the edge of the table. Of course I lay into him, and he looks at me distantly, resentfully, increasingly pale, startled in his solitude.

'If I said that,' I hesitated, 'I didn't mean . . .' (His lips have tightened in a bitter smile.) 'It's because I don't like it when –'

'You always do this: you either shoot me down or you give in.'

'Couldn't you at least –'

'Don't take that tone with me, I'm not one of your stupid pupils.' He points his finger at my chest. 'You either shoot me down or you give in. There's no middle ground. As far as you're concerned, I'm an illogical person, someone who tortures himself for no reason, isn't that what you think?' (I hear his agitated breathing; he gets up laboriously from his chair, aching all over.) 'As far as you're concerned, all I do is count ants, isn't that so? Ants!' He takes a few stiff steps towards me: 'I count ants,' he says again emphatically.

'No,' there's a pang in my heart, 'what ants?' (I caress his drawn face with my eyes.) 'Where,' I say, 'what ants?'

We look at each other and suddenly we see each other, him kneeling on the ground, pressing down on his hands, intent on counting a long column of black ants parading in front of him: 'One, two, three . . . seven hundred and twelve, seven hundred and thirteen', and me, standing there in my nightdress, my hair a mess, staring at all those little animals with their little feet, murmuring: 'What ants, no, there aren't any ants . . .'

We've burst out laughing. We're laughing so hard we've had to sit down, then I put on his slippers and we go in procession into the kitchen, to the refrigerator.

Huddled on the hard chairs, we gobble down sandwiches, like birds perching on a treetop; like those palms on the Riviera, facing the sea, with their long scaly trunks and their miserly clumps on top, ruffled by the winter wind as the waves rose and unfurled on the sand.

But what time is it? I need to sleep. God knows when he'll be back, plus it's raining so hard, it must be lashing down, it sounds like the cracking of a whip; what a downpour there was today, it sprouted like daffodils on the ground, such a shame to step on them, meadows full of silvery corollas of water on the asphalt, it was beautiful.

I wonder if he's eaten. Maybe I should have sliced some salami too: all those nice red circles on the plate, surrounded by white wedges of fennel, would have whetted his appetite, whereas the *involtini* I made are shrinking and turning brown, streaked with congealed tomato sauce; when they're kept too long, they aren't at all enticing. Yes, but what if he reprimanded me for letting the salami dry out when they should be sliced just before eating, why am I so wasteful, and so on? It's best if he doesn't drink wine. On Sundays, though, yes, we'll have half a glass together, just a little, on those slow savoured afternoons, when I wander about the house, quietly enter the study, he doesn't raise his head, stern in the shade behind the cone of light. That direct light, though, ruins his eyes, it's an obsession of his, even though he can see perfectly well that I turned the lamp upwards; I think it's less glaring, too, it softens the corners.

But then he's extreme in everything.

When he opens the refrigerator, he almost takes the door off its hinges, then stands there engrossed; his legs crossed, his elbow leaning on the open door, his forehead in his hand, which he then rubs against his cheek down to the chin, to the stubble that scratches the skin of his palm; he supports his chin, in deep meditation as he looks at the ham in greaseproof paper, the long green courgettes sleeping in the lunar glow of the fluorescent light, the bars of the iron shelves.

He pulls himself together, grabs the carton of homogenized milk and gulps it down, his head tilted back slightly. And of course he looks for the coffee. He drinks too much of it. That's why he's so on edge. He agrees, just as he agrees that he ought to smoke less, that the smoke scrapes his throat.

'And you don't eat.'

'You're obsessed with eating, you'd like to see me stuffed full.'

All right, I'm going, it's pointless, he's sitting there perched on the corner of the table with one leg dangling, does he think I haven't got the message?

I hear him fiddle with the coffee pot, strike the match. I tiptoe back into the kitchen, stop at the door and place my temple against the lacquered wood of the door-frame, looking at him in silent disapproval as, with one hand in his pocket and the other down at his side, he stands by the gas cooker, monitoring the espresso pot. We watch the crown of blue tongues licking at the steel in the half-light. The pot shakes and starts to splutter and puff, the smell of coffee spreads. He heaves a big sigh and turns off the gas. He opens the cupboard, searches in the table drawer, places cups, spoons and sugar bowl on the marble top, the porcelain and metal wobbling.

'At least put the light on,' he says, jumping up, 'why are you just standing there watching?'

I switch the light on, and at a dignified pace go back to the bedroom. I sit down at the table and place my hand on the open dictionary.

He approaches with cautious, creeping steps, and I see him standing there stiffly, his forearms held out in front of him with the two full cups, scowling at them in turn, making sure the coffee doesn't spill into the saucers.

Then he goes away again with the empty cups, quickly, flinging things about, the crockery and cutlery jangle. 'Don't leave the cups around,' I yell after him, 'put them in the sink.'

I go back to the study. He looks at me, dragging on his cigarette, he follows me with his eyes around the room. 'Stay,' he says, as I'm about to withdraw (my presence doesn't bother him, it's part of him).

Instead, he suddenly flings my door open and stands there in the middle of the room, hair in disarray. 'I'm disturbing you, aren't I?'

I turn towards him on my chair. 'Tell me.'

'It doesn't matter, I'll come back later,' and he turns his back on me.

'Tell me.'

He's so impatient.

'Why do you always have to keep the lift waiting?' he cries irritably when we go out and at the last moment I realize I forgot to check the gas, the tap, something.

I run zealously, slowly, because the lift is involved. I slip inside. He snaps the doors shut.

'Do you love me?' I ask him softly, as the coin clicks in the metal slit.

'What about you?' he says, immediately aggressive.

'Yes,' I let out.

'Hmm,' he says, mouth closed; he presses the button, the lift starts and he stands facing the door, leaving me behind.

'You haven't answered,' I mutter. 'You haven't answered,' I repeat.

We've reached the ground floor. The old lift squeals and shakes. I take advantage of the din: 'So why do you always ask me?' I say resentfully.

We walk out of the lift.

'Because I need to hear you repeat it,' and with a jerk he closes the doors and slams the little iron gate behind him.

We pass the caretaker one after the other, as stiff as two German soldiers, and wave to her with the deference of the distracted. She follows us out of the corner of her eye. Under the arch of the main entrance, his impatient voice articulates sonorously, 'You should know it by now.'

Then (but the caretaker can no longer hear him): 'You don't know,' he says to himself, 'it's a dream.'

What time is it now? This interdependence isn't right. I'd have done better to read, to do something useful, instead of being here in the warmth, idle, in this total lethargy, in the dark.

He doesn't understand that it's much healthier to go to bed early and work at dawn. The lucidity you feel in the evening, when your body is worn out, isn't the same at all, it's a tense, abstract, disembodied intellectual clarity, not the fine, full calm of the mind getting down to work in the morning, with the body relaxed, restored, responsive; there's more space. Instead of which, he does everything on the edge, he has to tire himself out, that's his temperament, feeling hassled.

He phones me from the office, someone or other has done something or other to him and he takes it out on me. Oh, yes? I think, now I'll show him, and as I answer him curtly, a warmth spreads through me, and maybe he senses it, because his voice grows softer and he can't remember what it was he wanted to tell me, he'll call me again later.

Like when he comes home. He sits down at the table, casts a hyper-critical circular glance at the dishes, unfolds his napkin, and mutters, examining the spaghetti, 'Any news?' and I tell him the events of the morning, 'Today Class 3C . . . That colleague you know . . . I didn't tell you, the father of . . .' I get excited and laugh ever more loudly.

'It's impossible to understand you when you laugh and speak at the same time,' he says, chewing with diligent haste.

He cuts the red meat, stabs his fork into the side dish of light green curly salad, pours himself a drink and breaks the bread with calculated gestures, every now and again shooting me a glance that sizes me up and stabs me like a mouthful of food and then looking down again. I feel like one of those odalisques who are there to enliven the pasha's meal as he bends over his food and peers every now and again to see if the little finger of that dancer arching her back in the third row is gracefully crooked.

The lift rises, squeaking, screaming, but no, it's stopped on the floor below. I almost get dressed again so that I can wait for him in the entrance.

This time it's definitely him, the lift jerks at every floor, now he'll come in and switch on the big light: 'Were you sleeping? Oh, I'm sorry,' he'll say. (I keep my eyes closed and hear him standing in the middle of the room, tense and tired, with his coat on.) 'I didn't mean to wake you,' he insists in a loud voice (the hypocrite); then, as if realizing that he's stand-ing there exposed, he starts to undress with the gestures that are part of my sleep, then sits on the bed, causing it to sink, crushing me a little, but I don't shift: 'You don't know,' he says softly, 'it's raining.'

'Did you get wet?' the words brush against me.

'Mmm,' he mutters. As he speaks, his sentences run over me like clouds in a dream.

It isn't him. It's someone from the apartment opposite who's come in. I could go out. When I went to pick him up from the last but one conference – another one on 'Literature and Society' or some such thing – he didn't seem annoyed with me, on the contrary, he was quite pleased,

I couldn't see him at first with all those people jammed together, I squeezed my way into the crush, and suddenly there he was, right in front of me. That evening, going home, he was cheerful; as we reached the car park, he declaimed, he speeded up so that I had to run after him, then stopped suddenly, yes, he was cheerful. But his mood changes suddenly, I don't know why, he takes offence over trifles, withdraws and freezes. It was beautiful, though, that night, we sped in the car along the deserted streets, and all at once we slowed down to a snail's pace on the Aventino, down Via dei Fori Imperiali, past those walls of dry bare brick, lapped by the golden glow of the discreet, considerate floodlights; then we got out in the crisp autumn air and sat down at the foot of the Basilica di Massenzio, in silence, motionless, until it was late.

The moon rose in an arc of night, surrounded by the vaults of clay kneaded by men, the high vaults of earth as porous as the surface of the moon, old; one day, we, too, will grow old, and then, like the arid, rough, desolate moon, all you'll have left of me will be a soft image, faded, you know how: with restraint.

'Vivere in due'
First published in the magazine *Tempo presente* (December 1966), and then included in the anthology *Voci: Antologia di testi poetici e narrativi di autori italiani iscritti all'ENAP* (1993).

ANTONIO DELFINI

1907–63

Few Italian writers intersected with the Surrealist movement, but Delfini
was one of them. He was born and died in Modena, a city he both loved
and detested. Although he wrote mostly in prose, he also produced two
collections of experimental poetry, a very short plaquette self-published at
the very beginning of his literary career and a longer volume published by
Feltrinelli two years before his death. Largely self-taught, he sketched, wrote
on matchbooks and created verbal collages from cut-up published texts. He
hand-wrote a flyer advertising his first book, a collection of very brief stories
that describe an unnamed protagonist's wanderings in an unidentified city.
An avant-garde writer to the core, Delfini's recurring theme was a ceaseless
re-elaboration of the past. His prose is synthetic, rhapsodic, idiosyncratic.
Natalia Ginzburg helped edit his diaries, which Einaudi published posthumously in 1982. In them, he confesses to having begun and abandoned
hundreds of books. He received the Viareggio Prize, a few months after he
died. His most famous collection of stories, *Il ricordo della Basca* (Memories
of the Basque Country), had various incarnations: it was first published in
1938, then republished in 1956 with an elaborate introduction: a tour de force
that straddles artistic statement, memoir and metafiction. It was renamed
Racconti (Stories) in the year of his death, published along with an unfinished fragment of a new story. This selection below, moving and despairing,
is both static and catapults by leaps and bounds, distilling the mechanism
of memory. Much of Delfini's work was openly autobiographical, but here
he presents an incisively drawn female protagonist (his father died when he
was young, and he was raised in a household of women). The public library
in Modena which bears Delfini's name, created a prize in his honour to
recognize young poets.

The Milliner

Translated by Ann Goldstein

Signora Elvira was past sixty. Sitting in a soft, flower-patterned chair, with comfortable armrests, she leaned her head back. She seemed to be lost in a place that was easy to get to but painful to return from. How many nights, in the years of her youth, had she sat, exhausted, in that chair? She looked at the wide bed with the big white lace-trimmed counterpane. The counterpane was a little shabby. But it didn't matter then. Provided Arturo returned every night! The work wasn't so important. The millinery shop she owned on the main street could easily cut back its business. All she needed was enough to live on. Arturo earned well, and she didn't have to put anything aside for him. If only she managed to keep the apartment clean, buy a new counterpane every year, with more elaborate lace, make fragrant coffee of the highest quality every evening (there was the Brasile, the big bar that stayed open all night during Carnival), life would go on in the happiest way.

Arturo was certainly a handsome man, strong, tireless. How Goldena the dressmaker envied her! She wouldn't have thought twice about leaving her husband, who was an office worker, to be Arturo's. Goldena the dressmaker, although she was a pretty woman, had never succeeded with Arturo. She, Elvira, an orphan, a self-made woman, had grabbed him and wouldn't let him go. Who rode a bicycle the way he did? Who smoked a cigar like him, inserting playful, hoarse-voiced compliments between one drag and the next? That big, raspy voice, which muddled her mind, made her spoil the shape of a hat when she thought about it. What a delight the vest (she had sewed it) that clung so nicely to his broad chest!

'If the Signora knew . . .' one of her workers said to her in the shop.

'What is it?' she asked, disturbed.

'Nothing,' she said, just to say something.

'But tell me, maybe you met him somewhere last night?'

The shop-girl burst out laughing and disappeared into the back room, humming. Elvira looked at her hands, which she had ruined by washing so many sheets and towels the day before. She was worried. She had heard from a friend of hers that Arturo was considered a man with a future and, one of these days, would be able to give up the modest position he now occupied. My God, how would she manage? She, too, would make a reputation, would build a great fashion house in Milan. There was no other way: she had to keep up with him. Not stay behind. What a surprise Marchesa Y had that night when she saw the hat with feathers arrive (the young cavalry captain would spur his horse to a little jump of pleasure, a nice hop! hop! in honour of the marchesa), which she had ordered just the day before! And how refined it was! And how it suited her! And how majestic she was! The next day, the large marchese, sitting in the café with the silver knob of his cane in his hands, saw his wife's fluttering feathers through the smoke rings from his very aromatic cigar. The gentlemen complimented him with a wink. Later, the ladies flooded into the shop: 'What a beautiful hat you made for the marchesa! We want one that's just the same but doesn't cost so much, we don't have a lot to spend.' The city was invaded by so many feathers in luscious colours, and an unusual softness flowed through it; the men, touching the gold watches in the pockets of their waistcoats, eyed the women happily. They passed by, swinging their hips slightly, just revealing an aching foot, feathers in the wind and bunches of violets pinned to their chests.

Picking violets one day in early spring, in the meadows outside the city, she had slipped, and a man with a handsome bearing had said to her: 'What nice legs, Signora!' He helped her up and between one compliment and the next squeezed her arm hard. She had let him take her home. Her old aunt, preparing dinner, observed: 'You have a big rip in your sleeve. At your age, thirty, do you have to be followed about on the street?' She blushed, thinking that someone had torn her sleeve. At thirty she wasn't yet married, and though she was an attractive woman that didn't keep others from laughing at her behind her back.

Once, at seventeen, she went for a walk alone with a young medical student. He stank of tobacco, had a nice tie and bad teeth. For seven days he had waited for her to emerge from the workshop of her first teacher: an old dressmaker, a friend from her mother's youth. The teacher was still going to the Carnival parties, in the company of a seventy-year-old senator who liked to enjoy himself or to be seen enjoying himself. On those occasions he had a little dinner prepared at home, including meat pie, aspic, fruit tart, red wine from his farm in the hills, Sassolino liqueur. The porter, who dressed as a servant for the occasion, brought the dinner basket to the theatre, and served the senator and the dressmaker in the rear of the box. Although she was old, the wine emboldened her, and she climbed over the balustrade and descended into the orchestra half undressed. For two days she didn't come to the workshop, and the girls knew that she was sobering up from the dinner.

It was on one of those days that Elvira left the workshop at an unusual time, seizing some freedom that otherwise wouldn't have been granted. The student asked permission to accompany her, and she accepted, walking with him along deserted back streets where in the evenings a gas lamp shone, very faintly (when the fellow passed to light it, they hid behind a column of the portico). It was the first time she'd gone out with a man, and the first time she'd been kissed. Maybe someone knew about her adventure, since everyone looked at her differently the next day. That evening a strong taste of someone else's saliva and a Tuscan cigar lingered in her mouth, so that when her aunt asked what was wrong, she answered: 'This food is disgusting,' and burst into tears, running to her room to lie on the bed. She didn't see the student any more. She could do without that wan youth, who spit with every word (even though he had the money to buy her a new shawl).

After that, what a long time passed before she went out with a man again! She had proposals, even suitable ones. And rich shopkeepers who would have made sacrifices just to have her as their lover. No, she couldn't, who knows why, tolerate a man. And there was an occasion when she sank quite low. One winter, a few years after the affair with the student, a cousin of hers, a dancer in the opera theatre in the city of M—, invited her to visit for a few days during Carnival. One evening in the studio of a man who pretended to paint, she, her cousin and another dancer; another evening in an apartment full of photographs of women, belonging to a young man who always paid for everyone, wherever he was. Elvira attended the orgies impassively, affecting to have fun when it was appropriate or being outraged and getting scared when her own safety was at risk. She said to the men, 'I'm not like my friends,' and they, laughing, after a few attempts gave up, and in their good humour turned to the other two, who were cheerful and amenable. After all, they just wanted to have some fun, and end the evening. The other girls got what they wanted: to have dinner paid for and receive some gifts, something that, without Elvira, wouldn't have happened, she being younger and more attractive. Her friends envied Elvira her indifference: 'Lucky you, you're so cold, you're spared a lot of suffering.'

While she waited for her friends in the dressing room of the theatre, she got the idea of making a hat, something she'd never done. Her work at the dressmaker's consisted of a little basic stitching, buttonholes, sewing on buttons, and so on . . . It turned out well: a big hat, which was the style then, with an enormous pink ribbon in a bow. When her cousin saw it she wanted it for herself, and her friend ordered one like it. Elvira made this one different: with loops of beads. She went home, in third class, and during the journey she thought of becoming a nun. She lowered her eyes and enjoyed thinking that others were looking at her: 'Sister Elvira, with well-shod ankles, if you were a lady I would have kissed you'; 'Hail Mary, forgive us our sins, Lord, Hail Mary'. And meanwhile the spiteful aunt, exasperated, waited for her niece: she hadn't succeeded in getting her into the life and being rid of her once and for all. Elvira returned: with the rosary in hand and a mad wish to run. The years passed, the aunt grew old, and the hats and the orders and the earnings made Elvira independent, free to go and pick violets one spring day in the meadows, to slip and fall, to raise her skirt. 'What nice legs, Signora!' She tore a sleeve of her dress. Tomorrow will be so much better with a new dress!

Arturo was one of the early employees of the gas company. He earned a lot. It was he who gave Elvira the initial sum necessary to set up in business. He came to the shop, content, a large man, shaking his head and his bamboo stick. She was sewing, sitting with her legs apart, and exchanged slow words in dialect with her workers, savouring each one. Every so often, lost in ecstasy, she sang a bit from *La Traviata*: 'Tonight I'll come to you, kisses': he showed up at the shop casually, opening the door slightly, and letting in a very faint smell of the elegant officers who had passed at that moment. They were returning from eating sweets at Celestina's pastry shop. Arturo disappeared, swallowed up by the seven-o'clock crowd, the hour when it's whispered how Signora Altani is having an affair with the captain of the cavalry. Finish work early and then close up, and what a delightful evening! 'Tonight I'll come to you, kisses, with lots of nice cream puffs, all for you.' She had to go to Celestina to buy the pastries, to the Brasile for coffee, to the Toscana for a bottle of sparkling white wine, and to the cigar store for the *minghetti*. Then run home to change, put on her perfume. And every pleasure passed under the domed lampshade, with its encircling fringe of multi-coloured beads. Around two, he got up from the bed. Either he had to get the train for some little matter he had to attend to, or he wanted to return to his house, because, he said, when one stays with one's lover too much, people find something to criticize; he left her alone to enjoy the warmth of the sheets and her sated pleasure. It was another hour before she'd go to sleep, letting herself be rocked by the fantasy that always ended by transporting her back to his arms. Then she fell asleep, and she slept until a beautiful feathered hat called her back to reality. 'Oh! Elvira, oh! Pretty Elvira,' the neighbourhood boys sang. She went to the shop in the morning, and her strong, resolute step echoed on the pavement. That young master who was still sleeping up there, had he wanted to listen, would have understood with anguish and delight whose legs they were. But she offered the young masters nothing, she didn't even give them a look. They could linger for hours in front of the shop window, because she would never get upset over them. What a pleasure, however, to let the sound of her own steps be heard! What strength, what line, what torment (as Arturo said), those legs! And she pounded the pavement even harder, going along proudly and saying something obscene to herself in dialect.

Sometimes in summer (Arturo being away on business) she sat in the soft flower-patterned armchair, in front of the window, and, half naked because of the intense heat, dreamt of being suspended amid the clouds with handsome Arturos around her making a breeze. And she even saw herself in Paris running a grand fashion house: Chez Arthur. Or, in the suffocating heat that came from the neighbourhood, she got lost on a paradise-like market day amid the carts of the gelato-makers; and every gelato-maker had a strange, vague, Arturo-like expression. The lovely outings in a carriage on important occasions, one day on the river, another to the villa of the Four Towers. The *bocce* players, envious, stopped and watched them pass by. One of them said: 'How I'd like that pretty kept woman, I'd take her to Milan and show her a good time, she'd have no peace with me.' And the others laughed, while he was holding her tight around the waist. One year they went to the beach in mid-August. But she didn't like it and wanted to return immediately, to see the pretty lace-trimmed counterpane on the bed again. He let his moustache grow, a black moustache. One night, as usual, he said goodbye, and told her that he would be away for two days on business. She fell asleep blissful, woke in the morning, and worked for two days without rest, since beautiful, elegant ladies were waiting for their hats. Arturo didn't return, she never saw him again, she never heard anything about him. The women of the city had to find a new milliner. Elvira's shop closed.

She drew a long sigh and rose slowly to her feet: large and heavy, in a long, full black-striped grey skirt and a dark embroidered shirt that smelled of a closed cupboard with biscuits left forgotten inside. She hobbled across the room. She managed to reach the work table, her heart beating hard and her throat constricted. She looked, from a distance and fleetingly, in the mirror on the wall: she was so tall, and such dark eyes she had! In the table drawer there was a piece of butcher paper. Something was written on it. Maybe: 'What nice legs, Signora,' or 'Tonight I'll come to you, kisses.' She read for a long time. Then slowly she went back to the soft flower-patterned chair. The white lace-trimmed counterpane on the bed was yellowed and, merely looked at, gave off a bad smell. It was suffocating. Signora Elvira couldn't go back in time.

'La modista'
First published in the magazine *Oggi* (1933, no. 11) and later included in *Il ricordo della Basca: Dieci racconti e una storia*, initially published by Parenti in 1938. The collection was reissued by Einaudi in 1982 and by Garzanti in 1992.

GRAZIA DELEDDA
1871–1936

Deledda's work combines the sublime realism of Leo Tolstoy and the moral framework of Greek tragedy. Among her running themes are arranged marriages, forbidden love, public humiliation, intergenerational conflicts, the old world clashing with the new. Her authorial domain is society and family, but she also writes blistering, haunting descriptions of the natural world. To all this one must add a gothic sensibility, given that her work is full of witches, evil spirits, malevolent winds. Deledda learned to write in Italian, as opposed to the Sardinian language that shaped her childhood and early life. She was raised in the mountainous Barbagia region of Sardinia, in the town of Nuoro, which is named for the prehistoric Nuragic structures that dot its spectacular landscape. Entirely self-taught, she never attended school. The title of one of her first published stories, in a Roman fashion magazine in 1888, is *'Sangue Sardo'* ('Sardinian Blood'), and her first novel, *Stella d'oriente* (Oriental Star), was published in instalments under the pseudonym Ilia de Saint Ismail. In 1900, after meeting her husband in the Sardinian capital of Cagliari, she moved with him to Rome, a city that traumatized her at first, and stayed there. And from that distance, from mainland Italy, she wrote most frequently about Sardinia: the overwhelming, archaic beauty of the place, its mysterious energy, its population that kept either to land or to sea, producing one of her most important novels, *Canne al vento* (*Reeds in the Wind*) in 1913. Deledda writes as Rembrandt painted: majestically, intimately, in sombre hues. She wrote over forty novels, one published nearly every year, alongside copious short stories, all while upholding her responsibilities as a wife and mother. D. H. Lawrence adored Deledda and translated some of her work into English, including the novel *La madre* (*The Mother*). The story included here has an almost pagan sensibility, and the fervently desired animal at the centre is totemic. Deledda's Nobel Prize in Literature confirms that her regional artistic focus was, in fact, of universal resonance.

The Hind

Translated by Erica Segre and Simon Carnell

'At one time,' Baldassare Mulas' servant Malafazza was saying to the cattle dealer who had come to the Mulas' place to acquire certain bullocks, 'my master was what you could call a proper gent. He used to live in that tall house with the wrought-iron balcony that's next to the church of San Baldassare, and his wife and daughter wore cloth skirts and embroidered shawls, like real ladies. The young girl was supposed to marry a nobleman, in fact, a moneybags who was so afraid of God that he hardly ever opened his mouth for fear of committing a sin. But the day before the wedding the master's wife, who was a beautiful woman and still young at the time, was seen behind the church kissing a lad of no more than twenty, a soldier home on leave. What a scandal that was! We'd never seen the like of it in these parts before. The daughter was dumped after that, and died of a broken heart. From then on, my master started to spend weeks and months and whole seasons with the sheep, not going back to town at all. He hardly ever speaks, but he's all right – a bit of a simpleton, to tell the truth! The dogs, the cat, other animals are all his friends! He even gets on with wild deer! At the moment he's befriended a young hind whose fawns were probably stolen from her soon after they were born, and who came all the way here desperately looking for them. My master is so placid that this creature comes right up to him. When she catches sight of me, though, she's off like the wind. And it's just as well, since I'd catch her if I could and sell her to some hunter or other. But here comes my master now . . .'

Baldassare Mulas advanced across the green plain wearing a cap and sporting a great white beard, as short in stature as a woodland gnome. In response to his call the lovely fat cows and still wild red bullocks approached docilely, letting him touch their flanks and open their mouths, and the fierce-looking mastiff wagged its tail as if recognizing a friend in the cattle dealer.

A deal, however, could not be concluded. For although the servant Malafazza – a filthy scoundrel, as dark as a Bedouin – had portrayed his master as a fool, the latter proved to be well enough equipped to handle his own business affairs, not budging from the high price he'd originally quoted to the dealer, and obliging him to leave empty-handed.

The servant, who was heading back to town as he did every evening, kept the dealer company for some of the way, and the master saw from a distance how he was gesturing and laughing – having some fun at his expense, perhaps – but he was past caring about what others thought of him. Left alone, he headed back to the hut, placed a bowl of milk on the grass in the clearing, and, sitting on a rock, began to cut strips from the skin of a pine marten.

All around the vast plain, green with the new grass of autumn, there was a biblical calm; the sun was setting rose-coloured above the violet line of the plateau of Goceano; the rose-coloured moon was rising from the violet woods of the lands of Nuoro. The herd was grazing tranquilly, and the hides of the heifers were lit by the sunset, as if dyed red. The silence was such that if some distant voice reverberated, it seemed as if it were coming from underground. A man of aristocratic appearance passed in front of the hut, wearing a moleskin suit, but with a Sardinian beret, leading two reddish oxen dragging an ancient plough with its silvery shares turned upwards. He was an impoverished gentleman farmer who was not above ploughing and planting the land himself. Without stopping, he greeted old Baldassare.

'So, have you seen your sweetheart today?'

'It's still too early: if she isn't hungry that little she-devil won't put in an appearance.'

'What are you doing with that pelt?'

'Making laces for my shoes. I've discovered that the skin of a marten is more durable than dogskin.'

'It can take more rain, you'll see! Well, God be with you.'

'And Mary with you.'

Once the man with his plough shining like a silver cross had vanished, everything was silent again; but as the sun was going down the old man gazed a little anxiously towards the line of scrub at the far end of the plain, and finally stopped what he was doing and remained motionless. The cows were retreating into their herds, turning first to look at the sun suspended above the line of the horizon: red and blue mists were rising, and everything, lightly veiled in them, seemed to give a shudder of sadness; the grass blades that moved despite there being no wind resembled eyelids blinking over eyes that were on the verge of tears.

The old man kept looking at the patches of invasive vegetation at the far end of the plain. It was around this hour that the hind would approach the hut. The first time he had seen her she had leapt terror-stricken out of the overgrown weeds, as if pursued by a hunter. She had paused for a moment, looking around her with big, gentle, chestnut-coloured eyes like those of a girl, before vanishing again swiftly and silently, crossing the clearing as if flying over it. She was fawn-coloured, with legs that looked like polished wood, and grey horns as delicate as the stems of dried asphodels.

The next day her visit lasted hardly longer than the first. The hind spotted the old man; looked at him, and fled. He would never forget that look, which had about it something almost human, at once pleading, tender and diffident. At night he would dream of the young deer fleeing across the plain. He would pursue her, manage to catch her by her back legs and hold her tightly in his arms, afraid and with her heart racing. Never before – not with an ailing newborn lamb, or with a calf condemned to be butchered; not with an injured marten or with a leveret – had he been moved to such burning tenderness. The palpitations of the creature connected directly with his own heart. He would return with her to his lonely hut, and it seemed to him that he was no longer alone in the world, mocked and derided by everyone, even by his own servant.

But in reality, unfortunately, things did not turn out like this. The hind came a little closer each day, but as soon as she would spot the manservant or some other stranger, or if the old man gave any sign of movement, she would launch herself into the distance like a low-flying bird, leaving in her wake a faint silver groove between the reeds on the other side of the clearing. When on the other hand the old man was sat motionless on his stone stool, she would linger, still diffident as ever, grazing on the grass but lifting her beautiful delicate head every so often, startled by every sound, turning tail and sprinting from side to side before leaping into the cover provided by the weeds – then returning, advancing and looking at the old man.

Those eyes filled the shepherd with tenderness. He smiled at her across the silence, just as the god Pan must have smiled at the hinds in mythological forests: and the creature continued to advance, treading lightly with her slim legs, as if she was actually fascinated by that smile, lowering her muzzle from time to time as if to smell the treacherous earth.

She was lured by the milk and bread that the old man would place at a certain distance. One day she took a small piece of *ricotta* and fled; on another, she reached the bowl, but no sooner had she brushed the surface of the milk with her tongue than she started, springing into the air with all four hoofs off the ground, as if it was scorching underfoot, then took flight again. But she returned immediately. A series of more frequent flights and returns followed, becoming less timorous, almost flirtatious. She would leap into the air, turn around on herself as if trying to catch her own tail between her teeth, scratch her ear with her hoof, peer at the old man giving him the impression that she had become less fearful and stressed – and that she was returning his smile.

One day he placed the bowl just a few steps' distance from his seat, almost at the threshold of the hut, shooing away the cat that was intent on getting his share of the milk. The hind soon approached calmly, drank the milk and peered inquisitively inside. He was keeping dead still, watching her, but when he saw her so close, glossy and palpitating, he was overcome by the desire to touch her and reached out his hand. She leapt, all four dainty legs leaving the ground, her muzzle dripping milk, and fled. But she came back, and from then on he refrained from attempting to lay a hand on her again.

By now he had come to know her ways, and was confident that she would eventually stay with him of her own free will. There is no more sweet-tempered and sociable creature than a young hind. As a boy he had kept one that had taken to following him around wherever he went, and to sleeping next to him at night.

So as to better attract his new friend and keep her with him all day without using force of any kind, he had the idea of searching for a litter of fawns, taking one and tying it next to the hut so that, on seeing a potential companion, she would yield more readily to being domesticated. But no matter how much he searched, his plan was not easily achieved: one needed to head towards the mountains, to the lower slopes of the Gonare itself, in order to find fawns – and he was unaccustomed to hunting. He found nothing but a crow with one damaged wing, flapping the other pitifully in a vain attempt to fly off. He took it in to look after, holding it tight to his chest; but when the hind caught sight of him with that ugly bird she fled without ever coming close. She must have been jealous. So the old man hid the crow behind the herds: his servant found it and took it to town to give to some lads who were acquaintances of his, and retorted when his master rebuked him for it – 'If you don't keep quiet, I'll lasso that hind as well, and sell it to some out-of-luck hunter.'

'If you so much as touch her, I swear on the cross I'll break every rib in your body.'

'*You?*' laughed the lout. 'You and who else? What are you good for anyway? For supping on bread and honey, that's what!'

That day, after the servant and the dealer had left, the old man waited in vain for the hind. Night was falling, and even the sound of the rustling wind made no impression on the silence of the misty evening. The old man was overcome with sadness. He had no doubt that the servant had got a rope around the creature and dragged it to town.

'You see, if you had only let yourself be caught! You see, if you had only stayed here with me!' he grumbled, sitting before the fire in his hut, while the cat lapped the milk from the bowl, oblivious to his master's sorrow. 'Now they will have tied you up, they will have butchered you. This too was your fate . . .'

And all his most bitter memories came back to him; came back horrible and deformed, like corpses washing up on a shore. The next day, and in those that followed, he began to argue with his servant, forcing him to quit.

'Get out, and may you break your legs as you must have shattered those of the poor hind.'

Malafazza sniggered scornfully.

'Yes, I broke them! I caught her with the rope, I trussed her up and carried her to a hunter. I got three francs and nine *reali*: here they are, look!'

'If you don't leave now, I'll shoot you.'

'*You?* Like you shot your wife's boyfriend! Like you shot the man who betrayed your daughter!'

With a face darker than his hood, his green eyes bloodshot with fury, he unhooked the musket and fired. Through the purple gunpowder smoke he saw the servant leap up like the hind and take to his heels, howling.

Then he sat down again in front of the hut, with the weapon across his knees, without regretting what he had done and ready to defend himself if he came back. But the hours passed and nobody came. Night fell, gloomy and still: the mist enveloped the horizon with a grey ribbon, and the cows and the bullocks lingered with their muzzles in the grass, unmoving, as if already asleep.

A rustle of the bushes startled the old man, but instead of his nemesis he saw the hind jump out, coming up close to him until her muzzle brushed against the stock of the musket. He thought he must be dreaming. He kept perfectly still, and the creature, on not seeing the milk, craned her neck to peer into the hut. Displeased, she turned tail and swiftly retreated. For a moment everything was silent again.

The cat which was sleeping next to the fire woke up, turned around himself and settled back down again like a border of black velvet trim.

Once again there was a commotion within the line of overgrown scrub, once again the hind popped out, leaping across the clearing. Immediately behind her, a buck leapt into view (the old man recognized the male by its darker skin and branching antlers), chasing and catching up with her. They leapt one on top of the other, in the most lively fashion, tumbling together, getting up again and resuming the race, the pursuit, the assault. The entire ancient landscape, pale in the autumn evening, seemed to rejoice in their coupling.

A little later the gentleman farmer passed by, with his plough covered with soot-black earth.

'Baldassà, what have you done?' he said in a voice that was grave but tinged with irony. 'The law is out looking for you.'

'Here I am!' replied the old man, calm again.

'But what made you injure your servant?' the other insisted, determined at all costs to discover the reason behind their falling-out.

'Leave me alone,' the old man said at last. 'Well if you must know, it was because of that little creature: In her eyes I saw the eyes of my poor daughter Sara.'

'La cerbiatta'
Part of the collection *Chiaroscuro* (Treves, 1912).

ALBA DE CÉSPEDES

1911–97

De Céspedes is a wonder: a Cuban citizen who married at fifteen to
become Italian, sought Mussolini's help to get an annulment and later
became a friend of Fidel Castro. Her first novel, *Nessuno torna indietro*
(published in English with the title *There's No Turning Back*), sold five
thousand copies in three days and was made into a film. Her work was
translated into nearly thirty languages before being almost entirely forgotten. Daughter of a man who was briefly president of the Republic of
Cuba, she was raised in Europe in the homes of relatives while her father
and Italian mother lived in America. In 1943 she left Rome, where she
was born, and went to Abruzzo and to Puglia where, under the name
Clorinda, she broadcast passionate Resistance messages for Radio Bari.
When she returned to a liberated Rome the following year she founded
the influential journal *Mercurio*, dedicated to art and politics. It lasted
only four years, but published the most important writers of the time,
including Alberto Moravia, Natalia Ginzburg, Corrado Alvaro and
Giuseppe Ungaretti. And yet, pigeon-holed as a 'woman writer', seeking
perhaps to redefine herself, perhaps to maintain a distance from her Italian
public, she began basing herself partly in Paris. She ended up living there,
writing in French, and dying there. She published her first novel in French
in 1973, and translated it herself back into Italian. She spent the last ten
years of her life working on an ambitious autobiographical novel, also
written in French, about her Cuban family. She was a close friend of
the writer Paola Masino, who was the companion of Bontempelli;
both women wrote critically about marriage and motherhood, institutions
idealized by Fascism in order to promote nationhood. This story, with

its brief temporal arc, encapsulates an entire period of history. Set in the home of a bourgeois Roman family, it highlights the difference between how Italy was perceived after the Second World War, and how it perceived itself.

Invitation to Dinner

Translated by Michael F. Moore

The story I am about to tell concerns an event that is not very important in itself. Nowadays, however, our lives are filled with events like this that burden our days.

It was a few nights ago. We had invited a British officer to dinner who had helped my brother-in-law Lello to come to Rome immediately after the north had been liberated. We had been very worried about Lello. We considered him a quick, intelligent boy, who could always get himself out of a jam, but we hadn't heard anything from him for twenty months. That's why my husband and I were unable to fully enjoy the pleasant spring evenings or the thrill of being back home, finally, and able to start work again, and to relax together, reading, by the window. We were always oppressed by an anxiety that kept us in a state of discontent, of agitation. So we said to each other, 'We won't be happy until we find out what happened to Lello.'

He returned unexpectedly. I went to open the door, thinking it was the doorman with the newspapers, and instead it was him, smiling, holding out his hand, as if he had just left a few hours earlier. There were big hugs, exclamations, chiding; great joy, in other words, together with regret at being caught off guard, denying us the pleasure of looking forward to his arrival. We blamed this on the sense of oppression we still felt inside even though Lello had returned. We immediately uncorked a bottle, as one does on such occasions, and then I showed my brother-in-law a new lamp we had at home and some photographs and two plants in bloom on the balcony. For some reason I couldn't find anything more to say to him after so many months of his being away and after so much had happened, but, despite myself, a feeling of uneasy melancholy crept up on me. I wanted

327

to cry, not laugh. 'I'm sorry,' I said, 'that we don't have a nice little dinner prepared for tonight. Tomorrow . . .'

At which Lello said, 'Tomorrow night, if you don't mind, I'd like to invite Captain Smith to dinner.' He explained that Smith was a British captain who had brought him, by car, from Turin to here. On the spur of the moment we agreed, as an expression of our appreciation: we rushed to the telephone and were overjoyed to hear Captain Smith accept our invitation to dinner the next night.

Our house is very big and beautiful. Once upon a time there were always flowers everywhere, matching the colour of the upholstery. Today one can no longer bother with such things, but that night we felt as if we were back in the old days. There were flowers in the sitting room and on the table we laid the sky-blue tablecloth rather than the usual straw place-mats used every day to save on soap.

We had everything ready too early. While waiting for our guest, we relaxed on the sofas, sipping vermouth as if we had stopped by for a visit, and I was pleased to observe that my husband had dressed up for dinner, as he used to do before the war. Now the war is over and I thought it would be normal for us to resume our old ways. 'He's a very nice man, Captain Smith,' Lello said, 'I think you'll like him.' I said nothing, but I was happy that our house was so luminous at that hour and I hoped that our guest wouldn't arrive too much later since the red clouds of sunset were about to fade. I imagined that the British officer, as he left his hotel on Via Veneto, would notice the boys bent over their shoe-shine boxes, certain men standing on the corners, looking around warily, their pockets filled with cigarettes, the girls with eye-catching hairdos smiling at the soldiers and strolling on cork high heels, and the streets littered with paper, orange and lemon peels, and every kind of trash. I realized, however, that to arrive at our house he would have to walk slightly uphill, as if we rose contemptuously above that pocket of misery and could even ignore it. And then, I have to confess, I was pleased with the three of us: my husband's suit was well tailored – although he had pointed out to me on numerous occasions that the shoulders were threadbare – and his tie had been purchased on Bond Street. I felt, in short, that our appearance, our house, our books and our English would leave our guest with a very pleasant impression of the people from around here.

We relaxed into a bourgeois feeling of well-being. Since Lello's return we had realized that, in the midst of the general ruin, we were a truly lucky family. We were all alive, our houses intact, not even a crack, not even a broken window. At that moment, for the first time, I no longer felt that sense of oppression inside, and my husband didn't either, I could tell, since he was so lively in his speech, he who was always so serious and taciturn. This meant that our spirits were intact, too. We were young and we could start over.

Captain Smith arrived a little late. He was a tall man with grey hair who laughed and gestured abundantly, and his cordiality smoothed over the first moments of embarrassment that always accompany encounters between people who have nothing, not even a language, in common. I accompanied him to the balcony and showed him the panorama, which is vast and serene, surrounded by undulating mountains whose names he wanted to know, one by one, with a thoroughly Anglo-Saxon meticulousness. I don't know all of them. I've been living here for many years and I never thought to ask what they were. For me it's enough to contemplate the landscape and see it change colour with the time of day. To avoid admitting my ignorance, however, I made up a few names that he wrote down in a little notebook. This gave me a childish joy. I laughed. Maliciously, among the trees below, the fireflies lit up and faded.

When we sat down to the table, I felt a little exhilarated, like a girl at her first ball. I was happy to live in this house, in this season, in this country. Beyond the window you could see the tops of the cypress trees and a dim blue light lingering in the sky. The table was lovely, decorated with short-stemmed flowers interspersed with antique Capodimonte figurines of dancing cupids. The food had been carefully prepared. We hadn't eaten this well in ages, but we wanted to celebrate the great occasion of Lello's return. We spoke about the usual things one speaks about in such circumstances. Our English, first, and then our stays in London, and finally our guest's family, who we declared we couldn't wait to meet. The moment also arrived, without fail, when he showed us, with obvious pride, the photographs of his children. They were passed around the table, each of us demanding them from the other. Lello, who was the last to get them, really had to struggle to find, in English, a new expression of admiration, after the ones my husband and I had used. Especially since the children were so ugly.

Next, the roast, with red wine, then politics came up, as it always does with the British: and I knew that this subject would entertain us until the moment the guest took his leave. I had no desire to speak about politics that night. It would have taken me back fatally to the troubles of the present. Indeed the conversation narrowed down, turned local, and by the time the fruit arrived, all we talked about was Italy. Or rather, the Italians. And our guest, who was a hearty drinker, felt so comfortable in our house that he was almost led to believe – also since he could express himself quickly in his own language – that he was among old friends. That is to say, he spoke about the Italians the same way he would once he was back home and dining at the club. Nothing he said was inexact. He really was a good man. The only thing he said was, 'You Italians are like this and like that.' And since he was filled with the best intentions and wanted above all to be courteous, every so often he would repeat, 'Do you mind,' asking if he could speak freely, and we would answer, 'Please, go right ahead.' Nothing he said was bad, I repeat. Not even a tenth of what we tend to say about ourselves. At a certain point, in a paternal and affectionate way, he said, 'You have to wait for the world to form a better opinion of you, or rather for it to regain a certain trust after the twenty years of Fascism. For the moment, it's best not to rush things. You have to work hard and demonstrate through your politics, through your civilization, that you're a people who deserve to be helped. In the meantime, the friends of Italy – and I count myself among them – will work for you, lend you a hand.' He smiled, waiting for us to thank him, to say something to him, or at least to smile ourselves. I couldn't bear it any more. Under cover of the long drop of the tablecloth, I twisted my fingers, one by one, until my knuckles cracked. I couldn't stand the idea that we were still a people to be judged, a people to whom any old Captain Smith felt obliged to deliver his opinion. At that moment he was adding that we were a population of good people, despite some of our shortcomings – Do you mind? But it's true, isn't it? Please, go right ahead – despite some of our mistakes. A people that deserved to be helped. And I lowered my eyes, humiliated at the thought that we, that all of us – all forty-five million healthy and very intelligent people – really did need the help of Captain Smith.

The men listened seriously, attentively: maybe because he was expressing himself in a foreign language and they didn't want to miss a word. It was as if they were listening to a lecture. Then they rebutted, debated, contradicted, cited facts, conditions, that should have changed Captain Smith's opinion. Lello, who had seen what had happened in the north, spoke of houses gutted by bombs, families that went from one village to the next with mattresses on their backs, seeking shelter, innocent Jews deported and stuck into ovens, alive, partisans hung from trees along the avenues and left there, dangling, their tongues black between their teeth, their mothers not allowed to cut them down from the branches and carry them away. I stared at him, hoping he would meet my gaze and realize that he should stop talking. We shouldn't speak about all that. About us, our wounds, I was gripped by a steely restraint, feminine, jealous. I couldn't allow them to be discussed like that, between one course and the other. And above all I sensed that the foreign officer wouldn't have understood the motives that had driven us to do certain things, or not to do them, that he wouldn't have been able to appreciate our efforts, our suffering. What did he know about all this? He had set his cigarettes and lighter on the tablecloth, very fine cigarettes that were sold around here on the black market, on street corners, by people risking prison every day. Ours were the events and the miseries of a poor people, of illiterate peasants that eat bread and onions, of a bitter earth that only yields fruit, flowers and children. All of this, when you read about it in books, is very picturesque. But it dug an unbridgeable divide between us and him. My brother-in-law continued to speak and I appealed to him with my eyes. I begged him: Be quiet, Lello, be quiet. How could our guest understand all this? Captain Smith had been educated at the best boarding school in the world, and he travelled across continents with nonchalance, in shorts, as if he were in a colony wherever he went. On the tablecloth I could see his arm, naked to the elbow and densely covered with red hairs. I asked myself why he had come dressed like this, while my husband would never dare, even in August, to sit down at the table with me without a jacket. And I was irritated with myself at the fact that he could take such a liberty in my home.

By now it was dark outside and from the window you could no longer see the tops of the cypress trees. The flowers on the tablecloth had started to wilt. I didn't understand why we were sitting with that stranger or why we had spent so much money on that dinner, getting all dressed up, decorating the table with those dancing cupids that, ordinarily, were kept in a curio cabinet. There were no more festive occasions for us: not even Lello's return could really be festive. I wanted to sweep away everything with a gesture, glasses flowers figurines, cross my arms over the tablecloth, bury my head and cry. It wasn't enough, as proof of civilization, to have manufactured that porcelain or to have written those books squeezed into the shelves that lined the walls of the library. We had to demonstrate once again, to prove, to pass, all forty-five million of us together, a lengthy exam. I suddenly felt great compassion for myself. And the two men of my family overwhelmed me with feelings of pity. I didn't want them to keep conversing, explaining. To me they seemed to be demeaning themselves through their honest arguments, being beaten, humiliated: maybe because they weren't very big and Captain Smith was a whole head taller than them. 'Let's go away again,' I wanted to say. 'Let's flee, abandon the house and the city once more, let's go into hiding.' Only this could be our fate, the experience of the past few years. To flee from house to house, town to town, crouched behind the thickets, watching our backs, plotting, fighting, even dying, but under fake names. How was it possible to go back to wearing nice clothes, to sitting in comfortable armchairs, reading or listening to music? We were not three people like any others who might host a visiting foreigner at their house. We were three of those poor Italians who, basically, despite many shortcomings, one was supposed to help.

We moved to the living room, continuing the conversation. But little by little, I went back to feeling the anguish that had accompanied me for many years now. It hadn't dissipated even with the return of Lello, so I realized that it would not go away any time soon. It didn't depend on a house or a person. It was everywhere, in the air. The certainty of being safe and young, and of still having books on the shelves and flowers on the table, wasn't enough to expel it: and we couldn't rejoice that the hard times were over, only that we no longer had to face them under false names.

So when the English officer took his leave and said, 'Goodnight,' it came as a great relief. He promised to come back before his return to England, which, he added with a smile, would be very soon. I knew we would never see him again. We were old enough to have already experienced many times, at home and abroad, other useless and polite encounters like this one. Captain Smith was a good man, filled with sympathy for our country and for us, as Lello had said. But as soon as the door was closed behind him I said, 'Goodnight, guys.' They did not detain me, and headed straight for their bedrooms. I watched them walking down the hall with deep tenderness. And I could not help but notice that the shoulders of my husband's navy-blue suit were threadbare, really threadbare. And he was quite right to say that, nowadays, there was no sense in getting dressed up for dinner.

'Invito a pranzo'
Written in 1945 and part of the collection *Invito a pranzo: Racconti* (Mondadori, 1955).

SILVIO D'ARZO

1920–52

Born in Reggio Emilia, traditionally a Socialist stronghold in northern Italy, Ezio Comparoni was an illegitimate son who wrote a collection of seven short stories and a volume of poetry, published under a partial pseudonym, when he was just fifteen. He studied the history of languages and graduated from the University of Bologna in 1942. The following year he was summoned by the army. Captured by Germans after Italy surrendered, he was destined for a concentration camp. He managed to escape en route and to return to Reggio Emilia. Nevertheless, endangered for his refusal to support the Salò government – an Italian puppet state set up by Adolf Hitler – he lived in and out of hiding until the war ended. During this period he wrote a series of articles which were published under different pseudonyms: critical essays on authors including Joseph Conrad, Rudyard Kipling and Robert Louis Stevenson, all of whom he adored. The story *Casa d'altri* ('The House of Others'), now regarded as his masterpiece, was published in its final form in a magazine in 1952, the year he died from leukaemia at thirty-two. It formed part of a collection of the same name that had been rejected by three major Italian publishers, one of whom complained of its 'lack of architecture', and not published until 1980. The title story was deemed by Nobel Prize-winning poet Eugenio Montale *un racconto perfetto*: a perfect story. It was also included in the first edition of Siciliano's anthology for Mondadori, exposing D'Arzo to a wider audience. This selection is a somewhat shorter story from the same volume. Here, as in all his work, is an example of his heterodox vision, his elusive rhythms, his rarified style. His invented last name, 'D'Arzo', means 'from Reggio' in Emilian dialect.

Elegy for Signora Nodier

Translated by Keith Botsford

It is said that, for a certain period at least, we live a life that is not properly our own; then, suddenly, 'our day' dawns, as might a rebirth, and only then does each of us have his own, unconfoundable life.

I have managed to observe this in more than one person. However, in the case of Signora Nodier, who owns the land next to ours, it seems to me that she always lived her own life.

An unusual case, Signora Nodier had got to the age of twenty-five, to thirty and beyond without marrying; furthermore, no one had so much as made an offer. This, despite the fact that she was distinguished and something like rich, owning land here and there throughout the province. Those who knew her when she was young still remember her expression as tending towards being beautiful, though not quite attaining beauty – and that is the only way to be seriously beautiful, and forever. To sum up, they found her disdainful. But no one was brave enough to admit it. It was a lot easier to say that she lacked 'femininity' or 'vivacity', the latter, and other such sorry tags, being the word most commonly used.

As is the way in the provinces, when she reached thirty people ceased talking about her; that lasted for five or six years. But just as she was about to reach the age at which it is vaguely said of distinguished ladies who have contacts and come from a wealthy family that they 'do good works', the city suddenly learned that she was to marry General B. D.

At the time, this seemed odd (for in the provinces even the most obvious things seem strange), though in truth no one managed to explain why. When, however, a little later, they managed to get to know the general, seeing him at meals or out hunting, it finally came to people that if she had behaved in that way for years, defying the world with invariable calm, scorn, irony and shadowy suggestions of a presumably unhappy future, it was with the certainty that what had now happened would happen.

Initially, the general was a disappointment. Then, suddenly, everyone found him to be elegant – slightly conventional, but elegant – and discovered that his elegance lay precisely in the fact that it had been noted only by chance, and after some time. From that point on, little by little it came to be acknowledged that he was a man of spirit and wit. 'Ah, but he's a man of spirit . . . But he has wit, let's face it,' they found themselves saying, as though they'd been contradicted or the matter was particularly important.

If the truth be told, the general's looks and manners had nothing of the soldier in them: his bearing was as unmilitary as one might reasonably be asked to put up with. He had been about in the world, and his assignments had been vaguely bureaucratic and political, he had taken part in campaigns only rarely and at a distance; no victory bore his name. On the other hand, he had never committed any errors or stupidities; he had never been the object of ridicule. That dispassionate irony with which he viewed his career and, at heart, all his actions, had always kept him from disaster. Be all that as it may, military figures – some of them celebrated, with names that appeared in the newspapers – often sought his advice.

He arrived among us at the beginning of October. And for a few days, like some discreet tourist, he seemed to be everywhere, with a Scottie by his side. She was often absent. But no one noted how this absence was, in its own way, a reinforcement of her presence. Then one afternoon she was seen by someone or other hunting in the neighbourhood, dressed in fustian olive-brown and reddish riding boots; and the little Scottie dog was always by her side.

By the end of the month the marriage ceremony took place and we never saw her again.

As I found out later (and I confess I did everything in my power not to lose them from sight for too long), they had gone to live in an old country house of his to which, during the hunting season, he had long been accustomed to retire. But we heard nothing more about them. For that matter, even the locals seemed not to have had much to say – admitting, that is, that the locals could find much to interest them in a couple so reasonable, so self-contained and so little given to extravagance. Only a diary might have had something to say. But diaries, in which the gaps speak louder than words, are getting rarer and rarer; and in those days, I'd be willing to swear that Signora Nodier had not yet thought of keeping one.

Every morning he went off hunting; and every morning, from the drawing-room window, she watched him disappear into the fields along with the little Scottie dog. Occasionally, she would open the window to call him back and remind him of something. On other occasions, when he had forgotten something, for instance, his knife – which happened not infrequently – she would hold up the missing object, waving her arms, and the dog would run up and carry it off in its mouth. Anyway, nothing more exciting than that happened; for such appearances, and no more, were what the servants and the gardeners could observe on any day of the week.

Later, I also found out that the pair of them never made plans of any sort for the future, and often asked themselves what the next day would bring. In the autumn, the mist rose early on the river. Along the country roads, already hard with frost, there was no one to be seen. Sometimes the only sign of life was the flight of a wild duck; or else, at dusk, a child lazily wending his way home with a goat. It was therefore natural that in the late afternoon or evening their conversations were prolonged and frequent. But all those conversations bore upon the past. She could only feel truly sure of him when she had succeeded in conquering the entirety of his past.

Once, when suddenly they had almost been without light due to a violent storm that broke over their fields, she asked him, among other things, about his old love affairs. The request was so natural that he didn't even realize how very natural it was. That evening they talked to each other at great length; and when the maid knocked to bring them light, she was told to return later.

For all that, however, she never became a personage; nor a legend, which is so easy to do in the country. She was ever lively, understanding and spirited. So sharp, in fact, that she understood perfectly well that in their behaviour there was a touch of selfishness, and that the hostility and antipathy of the people around them was therefore reasonable.

But two days came whose effect, for a time at least, brought her back into touch with the world – despite the fact that she managed, in short order, to make those days 'hers': the day on which the general, together with his Scottie, left for a colonial war; and the day, seven months later, when she was apprised of his death.

It was, I recall, in September, and the newspapers announced the event in two lines.

But we learned of it only much later, accidentally, and via a misplaced vowel.

It was (sometimes banality is inevitable) a terrible blow: the more so because she found it unjust, monstrous and alien to her natural order. 'Oh my God,' she would say, twisting handkerchief or glove, 'why did this have to happen to me, to me? It's different for other people . . . Yes it is, different, very different.' 'There's no comparison,' she added impatiently, as though overcoming some inner objection. 'Don't people forget? Don't they forget a little more every day?' And she named names; and thought that in this, above all else, people were all alike. Nor were moments lacking in which she was convinced that she was being persecuted by something more intelligent and personal than fate itself. She tried doing ill, then doing good, but both brought her poor returns, and if finally she settled on doing only good it was because, after all, that was a lot easier.

She managed that for a few consecutive months. That is, until March. Then, occasionally, she was again seen out and about. She made the odd unnecessary purchase; sometimes she spoke briefly with someone. It was during this period that she began to keep a diary. 'Ah, I'm no longer the same woman. I've become so good,' she wrote a few days later, 'that I now manage to look with a good heart on the happiness of others close to me. I am no longer offended. Is this possible? I don't even feel envy . . .' And then, four pages later: 'I am seriously worried. I really don't know what to do: I could give away half of myself . . .' And more of the same.

She was indeed disposed to yield half of her all: but certainly not to accept the other half that people necessarily wanted to give her in return. She soon had to realize that her gift could never be accepted unless she, in turn, accepted her reward. This was asking too much from her. To tell the truth, it was beyond her strength.

Furthermore, her peasants no longer showed the respect they had in the old days; they looked at her with a certain expression, as though she had some obscure guilt. For instance, the way in which she smiled at certain things, and at problems by which they swore; the way she was serene and distant, and offered them, fundamentally, little more than maternal irony, perhaps that of her own presence. 'The general, well, he understood,' she almost felt them thinking. 'He realized that he had no time left . . . He went away just in time . . . He understood . . . But as for her, what's she waiting for?'

Thus it came about that she reduced herself to spending all her time in the house; and, because the grounds included an old chapel which she undertook to restore, she no longer went out even to go to church. This little island was, in fact, her definitive salvation and, little by little, the general's death was slowly transmuted into a bearable unhappiness – into, I can only guess, a sort of eternal evening. She might not have withstood a further shock; certainly she wouldn't have survived the extinction of her unhappiness. It was an unhappiness that she had constructed day by day, as others build, day by day, their own illusions. In its own way, that unhappiness was an illusion too: as to the past and as to the future. Yet it was absolutely necessary to her; it was, in fact, her self. The villa now constantly spoke of the general and what he had, in his day, meant to her: the old ways, serenity, good manners and more. But she took marvellous care to avoid anything or anyone who could bring back to life, or make vivid, those memories. Had this happened, grief would again have supplanted this gentle unhappiness of hers, and that she did not want. For instance, she refused to go to a memorial service for the general; nor would she read a speech that recalled his death. One day, certainly, those two events would have become memories, and she would have discovered them bit by bit. Now, however, they were part of life; they spoke of a day barely past; and life was too much for her.

However, when she learned that a lady found herself in the area, a lady of whom many years before it had been said that she was an old flame of the general's, she did not fail to invite her to visit. It must have been a strange encounter: highly refined, serious and at the same time faintly ridiculous, with the kind of absurdity that makes everything human. That day they, too, spoke at length. They spoke until, beyond the windows, the garden took on a certain violet tinge. Then, somewhat surprised, her visitor rose. At that point she was able to make out, beyond the ploughed field and the vineyards, fleeting trails of smoke.

'Ah, his old ducks,' she said suddenly, looking out on that rural squalor.

She said it with a smile, as someone looking at an old childhood portrait discovers in that image the little defects of a person to whom one wishes well.

'What's that? You mean to say even 'then' he went hunting?' asked Signora Nodier, she too coming to the windows. And looked at her with a smile, for her visitor too was a little failing of the general's.

'Yes, but a dreadful hunter, then,' her visitor said, laughing. 'Not everyone wanted him around. They even found excuses to avoid him. Once they went so far as to invite him on the wrong day . . . Luckily, he never found out.'

'He never confessed as much to me,' Signora Nodier brought out, after briefly consulting her memories. 'But I think I always suspected that was the case.' And she added, as if to herself, 'He took it too seriously to be good at it.'

'Almost solemnly,' her visitor added.

'True, true,' agreed Signora Nodier, almost grateful for a conclusion that made the general come alive. 'Absolutely true, solemn.'

And the pair of them began to talk of his defects: in such a way that they didn't seem to be speaking of one who was dead or alive, but of a myth, of the presence of one who combined a little of each, of life and death. Neither did either of them realize that the death, as well as other even sadder events, had taken place barely half a year earlier.

Signora Nodier considered that day one of the most important, and most 'hers'.

She was to know another such, and more important still.

One evening two years later, as the oldest of the maids was ironing, there was a ring at the gate. Against the garden lamp one could see snowflakes falling, and in between, rain. It was deep winter. After looking out the window, she said, turning to the young maid, 'You go, Agata,' and the other returned to the other ironing.

She had to get up a few moments later, however, for though panting from her run across the garden, and though her feet were wet and a few flakes of snow clung to her hair, Agata reappeared smiling and excited, chattering about someone who stood outside the door. Then a soldier came in. Then a dog. The old woman immediately recognized the dog as the general's Scottie.

The soldier stood there looking around, bewildered. He knew nothing: only that, thanks to an old dog he'd never seen before, handed over to him by another soldier, he'd had to take a huge detour; that he was tired, it was raining and his feet were wet. He found the whole thing exceedingly strange.

He found it even stranger when the young maid returned more than a half-hour later to tell him that her mistress thanked him profusely, found his gesture in bringing back the dog splendid, but on that evening couldn't possibly receive him – 'in no way could receive him' – and accompanied him back to the gate.

'Giovanna,' she said on her return, 'I'm taking the dog over to the farmhouse.'

'In this weather?' the old woman said, startled. 'Can't he sleep next to the fire? And what if 'she' wants to see him? Is she supposed to go over there?'

'No, not in the house. Not here,' the young maid said, standing with the dog at the open door. Outside you could still see snow and rain, and a row of dripping hedges. She looked for something to put over her head, but found nothing better than an old newspaper, which she took, and left. From the top step she turned once more to the old woman. 'Be ready,' she said. 'She'll call you to give you a note.'

But no note came from Signora Nodier the whole of the next day. Nor the day after. She stayed in her room, and the only time she came down was to ask the gardener something. But on the third day the note was on the table, addressed to Quintilio, the oldest of the peasants on her land.

I had access to it only many years later.

My dear Quintilio,

You won't mind, after so many years in which we haven't seen each other, if I ask you to do me a last favour? It's a big favour, but it is the last I will ask. You can be sure of that. I beg above all, if you come, not to question me, don't ask me twice to explain myself, as if you hadn't understood the first time. The stranger this request seems to you, the better you'll have understood. But how silly I am! You're doing me a favour (you'll do it, won't you, Quintilio?) and it is I who impose conditions. I really no longer understand myself. With friendly greetings, to you, to old Maria, to the old Tromps and to the old Felicità. All old, now. How sad!

There was a postscript: 'Don't refuse me this favour, Quintilio. If for some reason you think you can't do me this favour, do it for the little girl you once taught to fish.'

The old peasant accepted on the spot.

A week later, I happened to be passing nearby and paid her a visit.

As always, she received me well, and I had the impression that my conversation was not displeasing to her. I remember that at one point she rose and left me alone for a moment, so I was able to look around the room. To do that in her presence would have struck me as offensive.

Thus I could see paintings, portraits, a few sticks of queer furniture, a few old magazines and an infinity of tasteful objects: the whole of it looking like someone who suddenly, of her own free will, without dying, has stopped. Last, because it was partly hidden in the shadow of a curtain, I saw the embalmed figure of a little Scottie dog. This, too, I remember as partaking of myth, but also of the present – somewhat more than a memory, almost a pale memory.

Then she came back, apologized and began to talk again. From time to time I picked up noises from the road, and I kept my eyes fixed on her; strange as it may sound, she seemed nearly happy.

This is a true story.

'Elegia alla signora Nodier'

Published under the pseudonym Sandro Nardi in the journal *Cronache* (18 January 1947), and later included in *Casa d'altri e altri racconti* (Einaudi, 1980).

FAUSTA CIALENTE
1898–1994

Cialente is a writer who is hard to track down. Practically out of print in Italy, her work seldom appears in anthologies. And yet she won the Strega Prize, at the age of seventy-eight, for a novel called *Le quattro ragazze Wiesleberger* (The Four Wiesleberger Girls). Both celebrated and ignored by critics, Cialente herself declared that she was 'everywhere a foreigner'. But this condition, combined with her nomadic, cosmopolitan perspective, fuelled her artistry. She was born in Cagliari, but, given that during her childhood her family moved around Italy, is not regarded a Sardinian writer. After marrying Enrico Terni, a Jewish composer, she moved to Alexandria, in Egypt, where she lived until 1947, and started writing. Her first novel, *Natalia*, published in 1930, was banned by Fascist censors because it portrayed a lesbian relationship. An outspoken anti-Fascist, Cialente wrote no fiction after the war, turning to journalism. In describing her stories, set both in Egypt and in Italy, she noted that her characters were almost always either ordinary people or children. The premise of '*Malpasso*', set in an obscure mountain town, is about a stranger who interacts with an established community. An evocative portrait of place, it is at heart a story about storytelling itself and, ever pertinently for our times, about the truth as stated from a woman's point of view as opposed to a man's. Cialente's stories were gathered together and published only after she became a finalist for the Strega Prize in 1961. A translator of Henry James' *The Turn of the Screw* and Louisa May Alcott's *Little Women*, she remained rootless throughout her life, and died in a small English village at the age of ninety-five.

Malpasso

Translated by Jenny McPhee

Malpasso is the name of the road that winds up the side of the mountain. It's carved into the same rock to which the houses cling and cast their reflections in the river far below. Built, it seems, one on top of the other, the houses resemble a tower, and beneath them is a low portico that shields the Malpasso from the rain and sun in both winter and summer. Gusts of blazing heat burst off the rock in summer, and in winter, the snow and the north wind dance upon it in a whistling swirl.

From that height, looking down at the river is like peering into a well, and at that juncture the river curves sharply to create a wide clear mirror reflecting the houses. Farther off, among the gently rising and expanding hills – neatly organized like the wings of a theatre – one sees other, milder curves where the water flows languidly and shimmers brightly. This is the town's most beautiful view and so, long ago, there under the portico they had built the Malpasso Caffè, its large windows shutterless even in winter. The main street begins there, rounds a bend and culminates in a more sheltered piazza. The Malpasso's clientele is always the same. The veterinarian, the pharmacist and the bailiff frequent the Malpasso, while the doctor, the captain and the lawyer all go to the Theatre Caffè.

The old fellow was considered one of the newest customers, even if he had been coming to the Malpasso every day at the same time for two years now, always sitting in the same spot by the window. The red velvet upholstery covering the seats along the walls was shabby, the planks in the wooden floor were loose, the mirrors foggy. But the town was beautiful and, in the spring, the mild sky was further softened by the clouds, while mists rising off the river drifted across the hills. In winter, the river froze between banks of hardened snow, and at night one heard the ice cracking.

Initially the old man was given a measured, if not actually hostile, welcome. No one knew where he had come from – a retired bureaucrat, but this became known only later. He lived behind the church and was somewhat bothered by the bells (however – and this is what the neighbours said – the bells drowned out the shrieks of an angry wife who used her bitter voice to yell incessantly). Instead, at the Malpasso he was happy; no wife, no bells. Contented, he licked his lips, leaving them a little moist. He stayed for as long as he could at the Malpasso, together with people who had increasingly shown themselves to be kind, talkative and polite. At certain times, when the young people came to play billiards and turned on the radio, it could get a bit boisterous. The elderly played interminable games of cards, dominoes and dice. Every day, the old man showed up looking as if he had run away from home, his wool scarf wrapped around his neck, his bowler hat pulled down to his ears. Having scooted along the walls in a near-sprint, he arrived completely out of breath and went to sit in his usual place, where he loved to look out at the river and hills. That landscape was a privilege. He always talked about it while gesturing with his hands, inserting a Latin phrase here and there. After a while everyone began to call him 'The Professor'.

At the first hint of winter he put on an old coat with a red fur collar, yet he still managed to come down with a cough that lasted for weeks. Whenever he was overcome by a coughing fit, he shook like a twig, then dried his eyes on a handkerchief before having a glass of steaming grog. He was happy at the Malpasso. The young veterinarian, who had taken a shine to the old man, gave him a prescription, and the others, laid-back and light-hearted, had teased him: 'How well you take care of him. Isn't it animals you look after?'

Even the old man laughed. He was certainly an animal. He had a wife. And what a wife! Feeling a bit more at ease, he began to talk, even if reluctantly, but the others had been needling him to tell his story. He was an amusing old man and the idea of that scarecrow-wife amused them too.

No one had ever seen her, but everyone knew that she was spiteful and ruled with a stick. He couldn't stay in his house even if he sat in a corner and said nothing, nor did it do any good to pretend to be asleep or sick. It was simply an impossible life, years of never being able to swallow a bite of food in peace with that ugly, poisonous, aggressive woman around. When he managed to enter the house without being seen, he would sneak into the kitchen, lift the lid off a pot, get himself a cup of soup, then fish some meatballs out of a casserole dish. Later, his wife would make one of her scenes, but eventually her outbursts stopped upsetting his stomach so much. For a long spell afterward she would, like a dragon, stand guard, and she locked everything away in the cupboards, keeping the key in her pocket.

When she felt hot, she removed the bed covers, and when she felt cold, she put them back on. But because she was fat and always sweating, the old man's teeth chattered through the night in April and November; after the lights went off he would put on his winter coat so that his wife wouldn't yell at him. Avaricious, she could squeeze blood from a sardine, and she caressed her coins so often, they sparkled when leaving her hands.

Finally someone said to him, 'But why did you marry her?' and the old man became sad and confused. For a few days afterward, he didn't mention his wife, and he went back to expressing his passion for the landscape and praising the Malpasso. Other confessions ensued, hesitantly, as if he had to fight against a melancholic modesty. When she was in her thirties, his wife had suffered from a grave illness. Before that, oh, she had been a darling woman, a sweet, beautiful bride. In the rush of his words, he seemed to want to excuse himself for keeping her the way she was now, spiteful and tempestuous, but he had married a different woman, and, well, everyone knows about the heart's memory . . . No one could have detected in that woman her old self, but he could, he who had been very happy with her for a few years. He then became dazed and pathetic. As a result of all the questions and answers, he weaved a new pleasurable plot in which the gold of youth shimmered while a white, wispy ghost sailed like a swan through the Malpasso's smoky atmosphere.

Everyone was listening to him, especially the young people – a beautiful young bride, gentle and fresh-faced, with a velvety voice and chaste abandon. Those first years – what a beautiful young thing! – she had a long braid that fell down over her sky-blue dress and she sang. He lifted up his hands as he did when quoting Latin: *She sang!* It was as if by some sorcery the door to a fairy kingdom had been sealed off forever. The young people urged him on. Despite the passage of time, the intimacy they were witnessing was still an exciting elixir. They loved the beautiful woman, her white arms, her gracious devotion, her sweet perspiration. She had sweated even then, but this wasn't what had motivated her to take the blankets off her husband. And she was often in the kitchen then too, but joyfully, shelling peas with her caressing pink fingers.

This beautiful ghost reigned over the Malpasso clientele for some time. Every day there was a new touch: a flower in her hair, a delicate ring on her finger, some lace, a feather. By now, everyone knew how the beautiful woman had once stood at the window-sill with a geranium over her ear. What a lucky old man!

This entertainment, however, soon came to an end. One day when the old people were sitting, as they usually did, around a table with their noses in their tattered cards, occasionally shouting peevishly at those playing billiards to stop their ruckus, a tall, massive woman dressed in black came cautiously in through the glass door. A clump of celery stalks protruded out of her shopping bag. She wore an ugly shapeless hat and brittle, grey, unkempt locks of hair framed a sour yellow face. She didn't go near the bar, moving slowly about the room until she stopped in front of the table of old men, remaining perfectly still as she stared at them, her two large hands clutching the shopping bag. The old man turned white, holding his breath, and pulled his head down further into the collar of his coat. He appeared to want to slide off of his seat and under the table. The onlookers understood that she must be his wife.

They had imagined her to be ugly, but not this ugly! They were indignant, and since they'd chased after a beautiful ghost for all this time, the reality of her now disturbed them and they too looked at her suspiciously. But the woman paid no attention to either their glares or their words, nor did she notice when the veterinarian stood up to offer her his seat. The shopping bag she held in her gnarled hands swayed slightly as she held her husband in a fixed and threatening stare.

Finally, her lips barely moving, she began to interrogate him. One question followed another without his having a chance to answer even one of them. So this was his headquarters, right? She knew it was here that he came to spin his tall tales, the old fool. Oh, she knew everything. And she didn't much care, to tell the truth. But why was he the one that came off looking good in the story? Marriage notoriously doesn't always work out, and he might not be happy, but neither was she. Fate! In any case, these 'gentlemen' had no business interfering.

As she spoke she didn't look at anyone else, as if the 'gentlemen' were not there. Her glare was reserved for her husband, who continued to shrink down in his chair, sliding down slowly and stretching his legs ever deeper under the table. What they needed to know, she went on, was that she had always been like this, had never suffered any illness. She was as healthy as an ox. She had always been ugly and tough, it was useless to pretend otherwise. Everyone is born with a destiny, and he married her as she was, only a little younger and with quite a bit of money. The money was still there and so was the wife. Life isn't rosy. And had never been rosy, nor any better than it was now.

She noticed the empty chair next to her. A large foot emerged from beneath the hem of her long skirt and kicked it away. The men's eyes widened noticeably. What a foot that bride has! Even the young men, holding their long billiards sticks, gathered closer. The woman continued to speak quietly. She hadn't come to make a scene. She wanted to show what she knew herself to be – a civil woman. However, she also wanted to set the story straight. When one had such an enormous imagination, one never knew how far a story would go, and the old man still read all those books that had ruined his brain. She wouldn't want for him to one day boast about having abducted and seduced her at eighteen, when instead she had married him at over thirty, but honourably so, accompanied by a healthy prenuptial agreement in which her husband was given access to very little of her money to squander. He had, of course, always resented this. Ah, so he had invented a cute little bride with geraniums in her hair? She didn't like this, nor did she find it convenient. The gentlemen were embarrassing themselves by sitting there listening to all his drivel.

She smiled nastily, flashing her rotten teeth, then turned and left without saying goodbye to anyone. The creaking floorboards accompanied her all the way to the door, which she slammed behind her, the glass tinkling for a good while afterward. In front of the Malpasso, she was hit by a gust of wind and they saw her raise her hands and the shopping bag in order to keep her hat on. She then disappeared, that bunch of celery bouncing on top of her head.

*

At sunset the wind died down. Leaning against a railing near the river, the old man paused to look at the landscape. How much better it would have been if he had just contented himself with the view instead of letting himself be dominated by his usual weaknesses! Life is what it is, his wife is what she is, the river and hills are what they are. Instead, they had made a mockery of him . . . And who knew how long those who surely believed they too had been ridiculed would hold it against him?

Out of pity, the veterinarian, who had accompanied him, said: 'Let's try not to talk about it any more . . . But you made a mistake. The hours are long at the Malpasso and things last.'

The old man blinked his eyes and swallowed now and again. Finally he mumbled, 'It's just that . . . by now I was convinced of it myself. And it . . . did me good. Almost as if it had really happened.'

The other man took his arm and they made their way to the bridge. Ghosts are a private thing and should be cultivated in silence. Someone as old as he is should have known this. Ghosts can't be used to remedy what others see as our mistakes, the compromises we once made.

'Now he is suffering like a widower,' the young man thought, and walking beside him he stole a glance at his face. Instead, the old man still appeared to be entirely transported by that landscape. And it is right that old people experience nature so intensely, because when they are gone, it remains eternally, and the unwavering certainty of this reassures them.

'Malpasso'
First published in the magazine *Le grandi firme* (27 January 1938). Later included in *Pamela o la bella estate* (Mondadori, 1962).

CARLO CASSOLA

1917–87

'I love the periphery more than the city. I love everything in the margins.'
This declaration more or less sums up Cassola's aesthetic. Always an outsider, he would reformulate his approach to writing throughout his life.
He was born in Rome, but loved Tuscany, thanks to summers spent in
Volterra and Cecina. He pursued a law degree and worked for many years
teaching history and philosophy in local high schools. He suffered severe
personal losses; his first wife died at thirty-one, and he had to bury a
daughter from his second marriage, born with a congenital disease, when
she was only six months old. *Il taglio del bosco* (Timber Cutting), a long
autobiographical story about a young widower published in 1950, echoes
the plaintive tones of Joyce's *Dubliners*. Cassola's enthusiasm for the Irish
writer inspired him to write a story about discovering Joyce at a young
age. In the 1970s, he curated Thomas Hardy's works for Mondadori in
order to revive interest for Hardy in Italy. His novel *La Ragazza di Bube*
(*Bebo's Girl*) was nominated for the Strega Prize in 1960, but in the weeks
leading up to the vote, was publicly attacked by Pasolini, who called it a
betrayal of the neoRealist movement. Cassola won anyway, and the novel
was made into a film starring Claudia Cardinale. Cassola responded to
widespread literary fame by reverting to an existential phase of writing;
his final works were about the extinction of mankind. This story appears
in a collection called *La visita* (The Visit), early work that showcases his
signature elements: limited characters, spare prose, charged emotional
subtext. Drawing attention to one of life's interstitial moments, it illuminates, fleetingly but trenchantly, the traditional lot of married women.

At the Station

Translated by Jhumpa Lahiri

The train was already half an hour behind schedule, and a railway man said it would be later still.

– It's nice here, said the mother. Let's hope Dad isn't waiting.

– If he goes to the station, they'll tell him it's running late, Mum.

– But you know how Dad is.

They walked in silence along the pavement, stopping at the far end of the station building. The tangle of tracks ahead of them gradually narrowed. The grey air, cold and dense, hung heavily over the countryside.

– Who knows why it's late, said Adriana.

Her mother glanced at her without replying.

– It's usually right on time, Adriana added.

She stopped talking and lowered her eyes. The silence and her mother's gaze made her uncomfortable.

– Adriana, you're not pregnant, are you?

The daughter denied it emphatically.

– All the better, the mother said. At least you two can have a little fun. There's time to have kids. You're both so young.

Two men were talking a few feet away: one standing, the other seated on a stack of railroad ties. Adriana studied their gestures, muted by twilight. Her mother was also looking in their direction. The one standing up nodded goodbye to the other and came towards them, swinging a lantern. Passing by, he stared at Adriana. Adriana turned to her mother.

– Promise you'll come back soon, she said.

– My dear girl, it's not easy, with that man. I can't leave him on his own.

– That's what you think, Mum.

– Maybe, the mother replied. After a pause she added: But newlyweds

355

should be left alone. I'm not one of those women always at their daughters' house for every trifling thing.

– But in our case . . . Mario likes your coming now and then, the daughter said.

– And now and then, as you can see, I'll pop over to see you. But not like women who install themselves for months in their daughters' homes, or in their sons', like your poor grandmother, God bless her soul. When she passed away I heaved a sigh of relief.

– Mum, the daughter scolded.

– Believe me, Adriana, it had become torture in the end. And since then I've told myself: When your daughter gets married, each of you will live in her own house, with her own husband. I learned the hard way, I can assure you, she added after a pause.

All at once the station lights turned on. Casting a last look at the countryside around the station, the two women realized it had turned dark.

– The days are getting shorter, the mother said.

They turned back. Bursts of laughter came from the station master's room, and then the station master appeared in the doorway, smiling, with a cigar in his mouth, his cap at an angle. Adriana wished him a good evening.

– Good evening, the station master replied, without looking at her.

– Will it be much longer? Adriana asked.

The station master turned towards the room and made an enquiry.

– At least another ten minutes, he replied.

In the middle of the station a small crowd had gathered, composed mostly of labourers. They'd formed several small groups. Their discussion was lively, they were laughing: no one seemed bothered by the delay.

– Adriana, the mother said abruptly. Tell me the truth, you're not fighting with Mario, are you?

– Of course not, Mum. What gave you that idea?

– I don't know . . . I just got the sense . . . her mother said.

She glanced at her wristwatch, and then at the station clock.

– It's just that Mario's so busy, Adriana said. He never gets home before seven-thirty, eight o'clock. And after dinner he goes out, he always has.

– They're all the same, all men, her mother said. They're one big selfish lot. I remember when I was nursing . . .

The bell began to ring. A collective 'Ah' of satisfaction was heard.

– Finally, Adriana said.

– But I hoped women today were better off, the mother said. I've lived like a slave.

Adriana started laughing.

– I'm not exaggerating, the mother went on. If you think it's funny, good for you. But think about it, Adriana: what pleasures do we women get out of life? At times I think I'd have been better off not being born.

They were silent, listening to the conversations around them. Then, suddenly, they had to move out of the way to avoid a collision with a railway man who rushed past shouting:

– Step back, everyone! Step back!

The two red eyes of the train sprang out of the dark countryside. For a moment it seemed immobile, then it seemed to race towards them at breakneck speed, and finally it passed by slowly, stopping at the last minute with a tremendous jerk, while people calmly gathered up their things.

Mother and daughter embraced. The mother was one of the first to board and, looking out, she called to Adriana, who was standing in front of the window.

– We've still got a little time, Adriana said. It always stops for a few minutes.

– Get going if you need to, the mother said.

– Dinner's ready in any case, Adriana replied.

– It's seven-thirty, the mother said. Who knows what that man will make a fuss about? I can almost hear him. He's always done what he's wanted, unlike me . . .

Their separation now looming, the conversation broke apart.

– Give everyone my best, Adriana said.

– I will, the mother replied.

The station had emptied out. Three or four people had lingered to say goodbye to those leaving.

– Ready to go, Adriana said.

She'd seen the captain raise his paddle.

– Thank goodness, the mother said.

The train started to move.

– Say hi to Mario. Tell him I'm sorry not to have said goodbye.

– Lots of kisses to Dad! Ariana shouted out.

She stood there waving her handkerchief for as long as she could see something, or thought she did.

'Alla stazione'

Written in 1945 and likely to have been published in a local newspaper. Later included in the collection *La visita* (Einaudi, 1962), updated by the author to include his early stories.

CRISTINA CAMPO

1923–77

A writer's writer who published very little in her lifetime, Campo, who came from an aristocratic family, was the daughter of an openly Fascist composer. She was born with a grave heart condition, inoperable at the time, which prevented her from playing vigorously with other children and from attending school. This sense of solitude characterizes her project as a writer, which mines a consistently interior, spiritual vein. Her creativity was a vocation in the truest sense; always at a remove, indifferent to attention or success. Her real name was Vittoria Guerrini; the name Cristina Campo was invented when she was around thirty years old. Educated by tutors but largely self-taught, she learned to read in French, German, Spanish and Latin. Katherine Mansfield was one of the first authors she translated. She also translated the work of Emily Dickinson, John Donne, William Carlos Williams and Simone Weil, introducing the latter's writing to Italy. Campo lived for most of her life in Rome, on a secluded piazza dominated by an enormous abbey, and was openly involved for twenty years with Elémire Zolla, a married man who was a scholar and philosopher of esoteric doctrine and mysticism. She wrote criticism about fairy tales and turned emphatically to religion towards the end of her life. Perfection was her theme, aesthetic as well as moral. This autobiographical story, isolated in the appendix of a volume of her essays, introductions and translator's notes, is a hallucinatory remembrance of an unconventional, encumbered childhood. It is about the enchantment of reading, the enigmas of adulthood and the slippery border between literature and life. The book's title is *Sotto falso nome* (Under a False Name). She left behind several volumes of magnificent letters, all of them signed Cristina Campo.

The Golden Nut

Translated by Jenny Mcphee

Ave, viaticum meae peregrinationis.

Cicero

Children born on Sunday have the gift of being able to see the fairies who preside over their baptism.

Karl Felix Wolff

Over a string of long and glorious summers, every afternoon at half past four, the watered-down gravel on the driveway crackled furtively, almost ceremoniously, under the tyres of the blue Dilambda. The car had driven up along the ancient Via Cavaliera's scalding, dusky portico, flashed beneath the light-splattered leaves of the linden trees lining the Via dei Cappuccini, passed by the inane patrician gates surrounding the Villa Revedin, in order to arrive at the top of our hill. Reacting to the cold roar of the tyres, combined with the midday heat and cicadas, I threw my tricycle on to the lawn, and Luigi, priest-like in his red jacket, flung open the small glass door wreathed in bronzed ivy, while my beautiful older cousins, Zarina and Maria Sofia, fluttered forth from the car like birds. The pure white of the last bridal-wreath spirea, the petals already strewn over the gravel, instantly mirrored the new whites – my cousins' long gloves, their little sectional cloche hats, the freshly washed fur of their old Sealyham terrier, and above all, their bags, those deep sacks made of linen or canvas in which, afternoon upon afternoon, from the gloomy and oppressive rooms on Via Cavaliera, their old toys made their way up to me.

The days of agitated cries of What-did-you-bring-me associated with those bags were over for me. Now, smiling silently, my heart in tumult, I walked hand in hand between my older cousins as we headed towards the small green iron table surrounded by tall wooden chairs, these also green and dotted with hard little bubbles of paint, ready to drink our tea under the Cedar of Lebanon. My mother came down, having recently awoken, wearing a violet kimono and carrying two or three pillows, a yellow-rose print on their thick cotton cases. Kisses and minor exclamations ensued: 'But why have you come down so soon?' 'Goodness, I've been up for over an hour.' 'Didn't you sleep?' 'And yet how beautiful you are, a rose.' 'Oh, but you needn't say so, I hardly sleep any more.' 'But what a splendid afternoon.' 'Oh, yes, it seems like a dream to be here once again.' Then my mother would see me, a smile slipping across her lips, and on the round table, amidst polite laughter, the beautiful bags opened up like corollas beneath glowing faces. Two of those faces, my mother's and Maria Sofia's, were velvet-smooth and peach-brown and they looked identical, even though Maria Sofia was younger. Zarina's face, covered in golden freckles, had a Japanese look. Her real name was Maria Cesarina, but she had called herself Zarina in honour of the unfortunate Russian empress. And in the silence, thick with midday heat and cicadas, small objects emerged from the bags and were placed in a circle on the table.

It is, perhaps, perverse, but maybe also useful, for a child to be brought up among people who are older than she is by at least twenty or thirty years. It is certain, in any case, that my childhood, in many ways already asymmetrical, was, in an indescribably peaceful manner, superimposed upon by another, already lived – that of my older cousins and their brothers, the last children to wear straw hats with wide blue ribbons, the last children whose childhoods hadn't, in fact, been stolen from them. I do not want to dwell excessively on those austere and bewitching toys I was in the process of inheriting on those afternoons – the dark walnut dolls' house, its rooms so warm and sweet and solemn; the bed with the ornate headboard; the stout little rocking chair; the goblet-flower basin with the tiny blue jug in the shape of a closed flower bud. And the minuscule green wool carpets, the quilted bedspreads and that incongruous bench, sturdy on its corrugated legs, which belonged to the dolls' house, but evoked those long periods outdoors when I had been inspired to create a string of miniature vegetable patches in the darkest corners of the garden, patiently girding them with twigs from the spirea shrubs. These toys had made it through a war, having crossed, with a heroic and immeasurable leap, the abyss that had split apart the century, in order to come to rest on the fragile edge of the last ridge where we still endured – but for how long? The last toys, the dying proof of an era when, in relationship to childhood, the wink did not yet exist, a time when play was both a prophecy of, and a preparation for, that singular and always insufficient *répétition générale de la vie*, which is, in fact, childhood: the carriage which is only a smaller carriage, the wooden horse a miniature of a real horse, the doll who is a little woman or girl – but never an ambiguous, symbolic puppet. Just like the three-year-old toddler in jewels and ribbons holding a rose, framed on a wall in my bedroom, looked more like a plump little grandmother, and was, in any case, the only creature I yearned for in that adult-filled childhood of mine. ('It's an old portrait of the Princess of Linguaglossa, the daughter of Prime Minister Crispi. Poor thing, she is no longer of this world,' I heard it said, enigmatically, at home.)

During one of those summers when they brought me back to the house on the hill, I learned to read. In the city where we spent our winters, while taking walks through the streets with my young father – who carried his walking stick straight up as if it were a sabre, the handle tucked into the pocket of his coat – I would follow the tip of that walking stick which brusquely directed itself towards signs indicating antique or pastry shops, and I quickly figured out the relationship, the gravitational law, that brought letters together. The news reached my godmother, the solitary Gladys Vucetich, and she, too, came up that summer from her house on Via dei Cappuccini. She appeared to be in the permanent shadow not only of those enormous cedar trees but of her entire family line of military heroes, for whom she remained in a state of mourning. She came up in her black veils, oppressed by an almost mythological illness (which hadn't kept her from 'spending the entire war with the Red Cross'), her heavy step lightened by the striking of her black cane, her head covered by a rubber rain bonnet. Her very light-blue eyes – so light that her eyelids seemed transparent – were fixed in a slightly maniacal stare, one that held a persistent presentiment of disaster. Gladys Vucetich had herself once discovered in that huge impenetrable house (where the silence was such that at the very far end of the gloomy dining room one could hear the taps dripping in the distant kitchen filled with cookware from Carnia), the books of her childhood. And she came now too, with her oracular gift, no less prophetic than the gold pendant she had placed around my neck the day I was baptized, inscribed with all four of my names: Vittoria, Maria Angelica, Marcella, Cristina.

The books had very durable covers with lovely faded colours, and some looked quite gothic. On the cover of one, I recall a tall solemn female figure wearing a yellow headband ushering forward a young girl, her hands on her shoulders. Where to? The small space allocated to these two figures didn't afford an answer. A kind of sweet horror transpired there, above all, in the face of the little child, who was a miniature replica of the woman – the same headband, hers greenish, her hair a little blonder, the same long peaked sleeves. Her eyes wide with astonishment, the child leaned back against the person standing over her, the anguished reluctance of her action revealing, like a mirror does, extreme fascination. Written underneath in eight large gothic letters was: FAIRY NIX. Nothing else about that feminine image of life's journey hinted at its mysteries.

As was true for toy designers in that prediluvian era, the book illustrators would never even have understood if someone had suggested that they 'assist the child' in accepting the mystical characters she encountered (thereby, inevitably, ensuring she wouldn't believe in them). Later, incorporated into that same vile pretext was the irreversible, rigid and programmatic distortion of figures that came about with the advent of cartoons: the smirks on the faces of the fake-baby-animal-like gnomes; the ogres' wide-open eyes ('Come now, don't you see he's not real? Can't you see that even he doesn't believe he's real?'); iridescent inconsistency, from beetles to princes and princesses ('In place of these characters here, who don't have faces, you can put whomever you want, yourselves, for example').

Gladys Vucetich's books belonged to an era of her childhood at the turn of the century known as the 'Liberty' period and the artists had illustrated the fairy tales extremely seriously, using Liberty-style figures. Their hands had been guided by the same delicate excitement evident, for example, in the creation of the scenery for *The Tempest*, the same deliberate, meticulous black-and-white designs dedicated to the novel *Demetrio*

Pianelli or to *The Crime of Sylvestre Bonnard*. The result was an adorably gloomy jumble of girls who looked like Anna Pavlova. They wore gauze wings and star-studded crowns as if attending a Spanish-style tea party at a Hapsburg court in 1880. It was a mildly lugubrious atmosphere, in which wasp-waisted princesses, likely to be wearing corsets and wigs, dwelled in enormous sombre-grey palaces, filled with potted palms, balconies, curtains with heavy silk tassels and thick bannisters. Those fateful places and people, I discovered at the time, with a shiver, were really no different from the disturbing, yellowed cabinet card photographs of my young grandmother and other dead relatives. My mother always carried these around with her in green leather cases whenever she travelled. Those photographs of terribly distant smiles always made me so anxious, because behind the lady standing there, brittle under her mass of hair, beyond the open curtains, beyond the haze and foliage, there was the constant oppressive threat of a thunderstorm.

Instead of a feathered toque, the princess in the book once owned by Gladys Vucetich wore a crown on her head, but that threat behind her fragile shoulders also culminated in stupendous and sorrowful secrets. From the ornate double-arched window, she could vertiginously whizz into the room with a large black-and-white swallow in her arms, a tiny King of the Elves riding on the bird's back. And from under the raised curtains, slowly, tragically, in creeped nothing less than the Monster, that desolate and amorous nightmare, the nocturnal visitor who exposed the slim and pale Belinda (representing, for me, my grandmother's childhood) to the horror. And the Monster, as those sombre and virtuous artists had depicted him, was nothing other than a Monster – a pathetic and unmentionable chimaera, half-griffin, half-serpent, drawn with maniacal precision, scale by scale, coil by coil. And because of this mad loyalty to his name, it tormented me to no end to see huge tears flowing from his eyes as he lay on the floor, poor Monster, wearing his crown – and Belinda sitting at the table at that ceremonial hour, the dinner and music hour, alone, unmoving, dauntless.

This figure, together with another, and for an entirely different reason, illustrated in the fairy tale of the 'Twelve Dancing Princesses', occupied a special place for me. In this one, a soldier of fortune guarded the bedroom of twelve princesses who had caused the king, their father, to become suspicious, because the soles of his daughters' shoes were always pristine. This soldier, shrewdly pouring into his beard the drugged wine the girls offered him each evening, managed to discover the lake-filled underground realms where the princesses descended at midnight, through a trapdoor and down a swirling spiral staircase, in order to go dancing on an island with their young lovers. And those twelve, revealing their naked shoulders to the soldier, their abundant hair pulled up, were no less fascinating and palpable than the most beautiful of my older cousins who in that moment – shoulders, hips, delicate chest, all transparent as the sunlight penetrated her white dress – was heading towards the spigot concealed beneath a small iron hatch, which magically liberated, as if from the centre of the earth, a fountain of water gushing on to the lawn. There with my cousins it was easy to believe in every word of the story, to comprehend almost a parallel version, hearing those delectable creatures with their silken skin, their almond eyes, whispering as they drank their tea under the Cedar of Lebanon, with their ladyfingers and their *langues de chat* biscuits, sitting in their green chairs covered in paint bubbles, (certain, in their naivety, that no one would understand what they were saying): 'We had fun last night, didn't we?' 'Oh, how amusing it is to sneak behind the back of that poor soldier!' 'Let's hope Papa doesn't suspect anything!' 'Don't be silly, he has no idea . . .' In the book, of course, they sounded completely different, breathed a different air; certainly the real life of my beautiful cousins was a life of fun until the midnight curfew, the hour at which, like the poor drugged sentinel, I had to go to sleep between the two high rails of my brass bed; the hour of provocation and delirium, which I didn't get a real taste of until the following day, when I would spell out the words, my finger on the page, while seated at the edge of a bed of rust-coloured zinnias, so engrossed a stream of saliva fell from the corner of my mouth. I was following the twelve princesses as they made their way down the twists and turns of the spiral staircase towards the centre of the earth, like the twelve hours that head towards the dark and fluid midnight of life . . . But suddenly from the garden I heard my mother's voice meekly questioning the cook who was standing at the kitchen window: 'Cook, have you done the shopping? You know how important it is that the professor . . .' I imagined her large, dazzling and anxious eyes, while I, without distinguishing one woe from another, listened to that other sweet, bewitched creature, Anatrella of 'The Three Oranges', floating in the castle moat beneath the windows of the royal kitchens:

'Cook, my cook, in the castle do they sleep?'
'Anatrella, my dear, I don't hear a peep.'
'Cook, my cook, you must not slack,
One more day and I'll never come back.'

And what were the royal kitchens if they weren't our kitchen, with the deep dark pantry and the great red-brick oven into which Fernanda was just at that moment placing a *timbale* of *maccheroni*, and into which a little while later, her hands and feet bound, the nasty Queen Mother would be tossed? As I read, beneath our kitchen windows, the zinnia bed and the spirea shrub were replaced with flowing water. It was so real to me that to this day when I return for a moment to that long-gone kitchen, the zinnias and the bridal-wreath spirea under the windows still appear so out of place, as if I were seeing them suddenly sprout up in the middle of a Venetian canal. And during those summer mornings kissed by a liquid sun, a stitching-together of Riccardo's shears clicking among the box-woods, of puppy paws pattering on the gravel, of the turtle doves' gilded cooing from the Cedar of Lebanon, a voice would call to me from a French door that suddenly opened, causing me to jump like a gun, explode in my own skin, the golden skin that was my book. And having fallen to the ground, it lay there like the skin of the Serpent King when the spell is broken – and now the hatch in the middle of the lawn leading to lakes and subterranean islands and the moat beneath the kitchen windows – now the hatch and the kitchen were suddenly brutally severed from the book, robbed of their coat of arms, their secret noble weapons.

At the time, I began to think that any incredible thing could befall my relatives while living their undeniable double lives. My thinking on the matter was such that soon, the entire house, already mysterious in and of itself, became twice as full of enigmas. Small things, such as the prohibition on speaking at the dinner table – above all, in the presence of my uncle, my mother's silent, handsome brother around whom the whole house gravitated as if circulating around a black sun – shrouded our hours and encounters with a magic veil of restriction. Above the white oval of the table, during the summer evenings when the French doors were open on to the garden, the silence assumed its true value, which was the hoarding of power. And when my uncle, often exhausted from the many surgeries he had performed throughout the day, fell into a light reverie that no one dared disturb, and his beautiful hand, his pinky finger sporting a golden serpent ring with a tiny emerald eye, rested distractedly on the Baccarat bowl, another finger tracing the bowl's rim and making a high-pitched sound similar to the groaning of a trapped spirit, the sweet atmosphere of the room transformed into a cavern in which a wizard, the Wizard of Latemar, for example, was lifting his lantern to the faces of prisoners in order to indicate if they had been pardoned or condemned. In reality, this was something that my uncle did every day and many times a day, the impenetrable implications of which only I, in those silences consumed by the crystal's whine and refined by the glint of the serpentine ring, could predict. On the table, the glint from other rings resonated: the four pearls forming a kind of lunar bee on my mother's ring finger, and the braided gold of my father's ring that shone in the long sunsets as he silently tapped his pencil on the wide pages of music covered in the black marks of another language, more silent and impenetrable still.

Among Gladys Vucetich's books there was one slightly more modern than *Fairy Nix* and it was illustrated by a brilliant artist who drew his characters' eyes without eyelids, leaving in those empty orbs a watery and funereal light so that they resembled the eyes of a mermaid or statue. The very presence of Gladys Vucetich, whose eyes were so light as to appear empty, was laden with new mysteries, as was her appellation of 'Godmother' – 'Who is Gladys Vucetich, Mama?' 'She is your godmother.' This nomenclature immediately evoked that horoscopic baptismal scene, occurring so often in fairy tales, in which each of the twelve fairies – indeed, the Fairy Godmother – brings her gift to the cradle of the newborn princess. However, the gift alluded to by the fairy tale was not, of course, the dolls given to me by Gladys Vucetich, but rather to be found within certain surprising phrases that escaped her while her watery eyes stared at me without batting an eyelash, her cane clearing the street like the Fairy Gambero's wand in the magic forest Brocéliande on the night of the Secular Council: 'You know you were born on a Sunday? You will see many things that others don't.' And placing a hard finger on the tiny blue vein that was still visible between my eyes, she said: 'You are lucky, my little one. You have Solomon's knot.'

There were scenes, however, from fairy tales that, according to those illustrations, took place under the immense vaults of a crypt, decorated with palms and drapes, but they were really too monumental for me to remember any particular figure. Inserted behind these images, like a second slide in a magic lantern, was the great town, the great walled-in territory of the Certosa, the metropolitan cemetery to which I had been taken for several years on All Saints' Day. It was an impressive landscape of graves, and the fact that it had once been a vast seventeenth-century monastery made it a cemetery like no other. The sombre structure encompassed great porticoes, corridors and courtyards, suggesting a scene out of a Spanish tragedy during the era of Alfieri – all romantic madness dedicated to exquisite malice, forbidden loves and redemptive wars, but for me it was eternally and exclusively a gloomy fairy palace.

In the great noble chapels flanked by porticoes, in the immense covered passages stretching from cloister to cloister, wing to wing, pleading marble hands reached out from sepulchral monuments, their garlands still deteriorating, their flowers still dying. The hands of pale, crying women gripped truncated columns and stone medallions, their heads veiled by their arms or by the corner of a shroud. Oh, how I knew those hands. Palms lifted in prohibition: 'Never sit on the edge of a fountain, don't ever buy condemned meat . . .' – fingers that sealed lips – 'And you shouldn't speak or laugh for seven years, seven months, and seven days . . .' Tall figures stooped over, often holding a child, bringing the child reluctantly, shielding the child with great wings, like the unknown figure with the yellow headband – Fairy Nix, the godmother, leading the child, the little neophyte, fascinated and terrified, towards arcane places, her eyes empty, like those of Gladys Vucetich.

Here too, however, one was not supposed to stop or ask questions. My mother was always in a hurry, speeding through the arches of the portico, through the pure winter air, shiny with hoarfrost and blue – the only colour in that world of greys. Her veil fell on to the collar of her fur coat, and she whispered to the bouquet of tea roses clutched in her hands: 'Soon, in this place, we will be at the end, on the far side of the last cloister.' It was impossible to understand those words exactly. All that was clear was that our destination was somewhere else, at the end of something, beyond the vaults and the gardens, beyond the great mossy arches and the distant relatives whom I never knew, each renowned in the sciences, literature and the military. They lay beneath enormous sepulchral statues – 'Grief' with her cracked zither; the 'Ululaters' who were pure wail wrapped in drapery; black 'Time', with his raised hourglass (like the Wizard of Latemar who lifted his fatal lantern to one's face) – some of these statues having been sculpted by my relatives themselves.

At a certain point, we would meet up with my older cousins, their lively little noses, Zarina's laughing Japanese eyes, their kisses and perfume mixing oddly with the smell of fresh coffee, a smell everyone seemed to carry about them in that city. All of it was woven into an even more agonizing intrigue in that realm of dark angels, that enormous stony horror with its icy breath, and the marvellous gaiety of a morning beyond the city, the fragrance exuding from their bouquets of white carnations, the recollection of the large, shadowy rooms from which they had come and to which we would return for breakfast, with a charming table covered with flowers, where cupids dived into small silver bowls, and the deep walnut cupboards surely still contained treasures . . . My mother, arm in arm with my older cousins, forgot I was there. And the great hurry we had been in to get there, also forgotten.

Every so often we passed a particularly large tomb and we stopped for a minute to read the inscription – *Laudomiae Rizzoli, spe lachrymata; Federicus Comes Isolani sibe ipse et suis aedificavit: Vale, cara anima!* – which inspired neither greater or lesser dread than other harrowing recitatives and declamations:

> Farewell, Falada, who ascends,
> Farewell, Queen, who descends,
> If your mother were to know
> Her pain would be her end . . .

or:

> I wait, I wait in the night's dark,
> And open the door if one knocks,
> Good luck follows bad,
> And comes without art . . .

And everything took on terrifying life in the brief comments around me, behind the veils and furs: 'Anna Pepoli, poor unhappy thing! How much suffering she endured for that scoundrel . . .' Or: 'Fabrizio and Bianca . . . a tragedy for the entire family, a moment of insanity', and before my eyes spread abstract visions of classic massacres – Bluebeard, his seven wives immersed in their own blood, and Anna, sister Anna, who scans the horizon from the tower sadly and in vain.

And suddenly, that world of arcane sayings, of petrifying acts that froze the heart (those acts that, I knew, if one day we had really gone to the end, in silence, without ever turning back, we might have been able to undo, thus freeing the entire place from its spell, making it into a huge illuminated ballroom), that world opened abruptly, turned a corner and in a well-lit courtyard, and then in the semicircle of a chapel closed off by a wrought-iron gate, and then on a white wall, blind and conclusive like the end of a horizon – there, a miracle happened. Suddenly substituted upon the delicate marble in the place of encoded names, of hieroglyphic inscriptions, were their names – and my very own, those which I myself had worn around my neck since birth on Gladys Vucetich's gold pendant: Vittoria, Maria Angelica, Marcella, Cristina . . . That little chapel where the carnations and the roses added a freshness that was still more dazzling, like adding morning to morning, that was the true and only enigma, the crux of everything, not only of the great Certosa, but of everything – of the damsel led by the shoulders to the secret ball; of the room that transformed into a canal; of the empty eyes, the serpent ring, the underground caves; and of the blood, the silence and the prohibition. Of the girl with the rose in whom childhood and old age silently entwined their shared secret . . .

My mother uttered her soft, habitual, bloodcurdling words: 'There is

Grandmother, and over there is Grandfather, pray for them . . .' and I read, under the name of she whom I had seen so defenceless in her portrait as a girl – the great, heavy drapes ready to let monstrous love creep in, to let the Divine Prince force his way in to her – I read under her name, which was also mine, Maria Angelica, two words: '*suavis anima*' and next to that, under the name of my grandfather, Marcello, a name which was also mine: '*anima fortis*'. 'Pray for them,' my mother repeated, with the look of someone compelled simply by the force of her heart to liberate the imprisoned couple, the heroic, bewitched love. And at those abstract and reverential words, the great velvet curtain of filial compassion closed over me too, a cloud of tears obscuring my eyes. That was the fairy tale, terrible and radiant, resolved one moment and unresolvable: the eternal, ever-returning in dreams, the provisions for a pilgrimage, the golden nut to conserve in your mouth, to crack between your teeth in a moment of extreme danger. I looked for my small handkerchief and muffled my sobs while my mother, her eyes remote, placed her gloved hand on the back of my neck.

'*La noce d'oro*'
Submitted for the Teramo Prize in 1964. Posthumously published in *Sotto falso nome* (Adelphi, 1998).

ITALO CALVINO

1923–85

It is a particular challenge to introduce Calvino, an author who consummately introduced the works of innumerable authors, including his own. The copy he wrote in his many years working as an editor at Einaudi are capsules of literary criticism that turned editorial promotion into an art. Along with Umberto Eco, he remains the most widely read twentieth-century Italian author in English whose body of work yokes together folklore, neoRealism and postmodern literature. Almost all his writing, groundbreaking and intensely experimental, has been translated by the late, great William Weaver. This piece, one exception, was omitted from the novel *Palomar* (entitled, in English, *Mr Palomar*), published in 1983, in which the eponymous protagonist, who shares his name with a famous astronomical observatory in San Diego, California, describes the world with a philosopher's detachment and a taxonomist's precision. In the novel, the tortoise is described in the act of copulation, in an unforgettable chapter called 'Mr Palomar in the Garden'. In this out-take, the same creature assumes a decidedly sagacious role, speaking for himself. This text is typical of Calvino's double register: ironic and formal, phenomenological and playful, abstract and concrete. Structured as a formal dialogue that nods and winks both at Plato and Leopardi, it is about language, perception and point of view. It is also the only story in this volume that talks explicitly about translation. Calvino, who was born in Cuba, raised in San Remo and lived for thirteen years in France, was rooted to no single place or language. Obsessed with scientific lexicon, he looked repeatedly at the idiom of animals as a counterpart, and perhaps as an alternative, to human communication. One of the foremost literary luminaries of his time, he was invited to give the prestigious Norton Lectures in 1984 for Harvard University, posthumously published as *Lezioni americane* (in English as *Six Memos for the Next Millennium*), but died of a cerebral haemorrhage before he could deliver them.

Dialogue with a Tortoise

Translated by Jhumpa Lahiri and Sara Teardo

When leaving or returning home, Mr Palomar often bumps into a tortoise. At the sight of this tortoise crossing the lawn, Mr Palomar, always keen to entertain any possible objection to his line of reasoning, momentarily halts his stream of thoughts, correcting or clarifying certain points, or in any case calling them into question and assessing their validity.

Not that the tortoise ever objects to anything that Mr Palomar opines: the creature minds his own business and isn't bothered by anything else. But the mere fact of his showing up on the lawn, trudging with claws that thrust his shell forward like the oars of a barge, amounts to asserting: 'I am a tortoise' or rather: 'There is an I that is a tortoise', or better still: 'The I is also a tortoise', and finally: 'Nothing you think that purports to be universal is so unless it is equally valid for you, Man, and for me, Tortoise.' It follows that, every time they meet, the tortoise enters Mr Palomar's mind, crossing it with its steady stride. Mr Palomar continues to ponder his previous thoughts, but now they contain a tortoise, a tortoise who is perhaps sharing those thoughts, thus putting those previous thoughts to an end.

Mr Palomar's first move is defensive. He declares: 'But I've never claimed to have a universal thought. I regard what I think as forming a part of thinkable things, for the simple fact that I am thinking it. Period.'

But the tortoise – the tortoise in his head – replies: 'That's not true. You are inclined to attribute general validity to your reasoning, not because you choose to, but because the *forma mentis* that moulds your thoughts demands it.'

Then Mr Palomar: 'You're not taking into consideration the fact that I have learned to distinguish, in what I happen to think, various levels of truth, and to recognize what is motivated either by particular points of view or the prejudices I hold. For example, what I think as a member of the fortunate class, that someone less privileged would not; or as someone who belongs to one geographical area, tradition or culture as opposed to another; or what is presumed to be exclusive to the male sex, which a woman would confute.'

'In so doing,' the tortoise interjects, 'you attempt to distil, from biased and partial motivations, a quintessential I valid for all possible forms of I, and not just a portion of them.'

'Let's say that you're right, and that this is the conclusion I'm after. What would your objection be, Tortoise?'

'That even if you managed to identify with the totality of the human race, you would still be a prisoner of a partial, petty and – if I may say so – provincial point of view with respect to the totality of existence.'

'Do you mean that I should assume responsibility, in all its presumed truth, not only for the entire human race, past, present and future, but also for all species of mammals, birds, reptiles and fish, not to mention crustaceans, molluscs, arachnids, insects, echinoderms, annelids and even protozoans?'

'Yes, because there is no reason for the world's reason to identify with yours rather than mine; with a man's reason and not a tortoise's.'

'There could be a reason, one whose objective certainty cannot be cast into doubt: namely, that language is one of the faculties specific to man; consequently, human thought, based on the mechanisms of language, cannot compare to the mute thought of you tortoises.'

'Admit it, Man: you think that I don't think.'

'I can neither confirm nor deny this. But even if we could prove that thought exists inside your retractable head, I must take the liberty of translating it into words to allow it to exist for others as well, besides yourself. Just as I am doing at this moment: lending you a language so that you can think your thoughts.'

'I take it you manage effortlessly. Is it because you are generous, or because you are convinced that a tortoise's capacity to think is inferior to your own?'

'Let's just say it's different. Thanks to language, Man can conceive of things that are not present, things he hasn't seen and never will, abstract concepts. Animals, one assumes, are imprisoned by a horizon of imme-diate sensations.'

'Nothing could be further from the truth. The most basic of mental functions, the one governing the search for food, is triggered by a lack, by absence. Every thought rises from what's not there, by comparing something seen or heard with a mental representation of what is feared or desired. What do you think the difference is between you and me?'

'There is nothing more disagreeable or in poor taste than resorting to quantitative and physiological arguments, but you force my hand. Man is the living being with the most significant brain, with the greatest number of circumvolutions, billions of neurons, internal connections, nerve end-ings. The human brain, consequently, in its capacity to think, is unrivalled in this world. I'm sorry, but these are facts.'

The tortoise: 'If we are going to boast, I could bring up my record longevity, which gives me a sense of time you can't imagine; or even my shell, a product that, in endurance and perfection of design, surpasses human works of art and industry. But this is beside the point, which is that Man, who bears a special brain, and is the exclusive user of language, still forms part of a greater whole, an entirety of living beings, each inter-dependent, like the organs of a single organism. Within that whole, the function of the human mind appears to be a natural device at the service of all species, responsible for interpreting and expressing the accumulated thoughts of other beings more steadfast in their reasoning, such as the ancient and harmonious tortoise.'

Mr Palomar: 'I would be quite proud of this. But I'll go even further. Why stop at the animal kingdom? Why not annex the plant kingdom into the I? Would Man be expected to think and speak for the sequoias, the thousand-year-old cryptomeria, the lichens, the fungi, the heather bush into which you, hounded by my arguments, now rush to hide?'

'Not only do I not object, I'll go a step further. Beyond the Man–fauna–flora continuum, any discourse presumed to be universal must include metals, salts, rocks, beryl, feldspar, sulphur, rare gases and all the non-living matter that constitutes the near-totality of the universe.'

'That's just where I wanted to take you, Tortoise! Watching your little snout poke in and out of all that shell, I've always thought you were unable to determine where your subjectivity ends and where the outside world begins: if you have an I that lives inside the shell, or if that shell is the I, an I that contains the outside world within it, then the inert matter becomes part of you. Now that I am thinking your thoughts, I realize we don't have a problem: for you there's no difference between the I and the shell, that is to say, between the I and the world.'

'The same applies to you, Man. Goodbye.'

'Dialogo con una tartaruga'
Written in 1977 and posthumously included in *Romanzi e racconti*, vol. 3: *Racconti sparsi e altri scritti d'invenzione* in the *Meridiani* series (Mondadori, 1994).

DINO BUZZATI

1906–72

Buzzati's stories, preoccupied with death and pervaded by the absurd, play out on the hinterlands of reality. Critics likened him to Edgar Allan Poe, Søren Kierkegaard and, to his eventual exasperation, to Franz Kafka, but Buzzati's blend of the real and the fantastic, in parts sinister and playful, is entirely his own. He isolates moments of acute panic, peril, the collapse of norms. The titles of his stories – 'Catastrophe', and 'The End of the World' are two examples – locate calamity at the forefront of human experience. Like Savinio and Romano, Buzzati, raised predominantly in Milan, was an accomplished visual artist, and he greatly admired the work of the painter Francis Bacon. He began his long collaboration with the newspaper *Corriere della Sera* when he was twenty-two, working as a journalist and also publishing many of his stories in its literary supplement, *La lettura*. He was a war correspondent during the Second World War and later became the art critic for the newspaper. *Poema a fumetti* (*Poem Strip*), an amalgam of text and image that stymied critics, is now regarded as the first Italian graphic novel, and *Il grande ritratto* (published in English under the title *Larger than Life*), is considered to be among Italy's first works of science fiction. Buzzati wrote many novels in addition to his stories. His most famous is *Il deserto dei tartari* (*The Tartar Steppe*), set in an imaginary country. Born in Belluno, part of the Dolomites, Buzzati was an avid alpinist who wove mountains into much of his work. 'Sette Piani' ('Seven Floors'), among his best-known stories, is widely anthologized, so I have chosen another, in which the supernatural and the domestic savagely converge. He received the Strega Prize in 1958 for his definitive collection of short stories, *Sessanta racconti* (Sixty Stories).

And Yet They Are Knocking at Your Door

Translated by Judith Landry

Signora Maria Gron entered the ground-floor drawing room with her workbasket. She glanced round to see that everything was exactly as usual, put the workbasket down on a table and went up to a vase of roses, sniffing delicately. The other people in the room were her husband, Stefano, her son, Federico, known as Fedri, both sitting by the fireplace, her daughter, Giorgina, who was reading, and an old friend of the family, Eugenio Martora, who was concentrating on his cigar.

'They're all *fanées*, finished,' she murmured to herself, drawing one hand lovingly over the flowers. Several petals fell on the table.

'Mother!' called Giorgina from the armchair where she was sitting reading.

It was already evening, and the great shutters had been bolted as usual. Yet the sound of the heavy, endless rain could still be heard. At the back of the room, towards the hall, an impressive red curtain hung from the wide arch that formed the entrance: at that time of day there was so little light that it looked black.

'Mother!' said Giorgina. 'You know those two stone dogs at the bottom of the avenue of oaks, in the park?'

'Well, what about them, my dear?' replied her mother, politely uninterested, taking up her basket and sitting down in her usual place near a shaded lamp. 'This morning,' the young girl went on, 'when I was coming back in the car, I saw them on a peasant's cart, just near the bridge.'

Giorgina's slight voice broke sharply across the silence of the room. Signora Gron, who was glancing through a newspaper, set her lips in a smile of warning and glanced towards her husband, apparently hoping he had not heard.

'Wonderful!' exclaimed Martora. 'Peasants robbing statues now. That's wonderful – art collectors!'

'And then what?' enquired her father, encouraging the girl to go on.

'So I told Berto to stop the car and go and ask . . .'

Signora Gron screwed up her nose a little; she always did this when anyone brought up unpleasant topics necessitating some sort of retreat. The affair of the two statues implied something else, something hidden, therefore something which would have to be hushed up.

'Now, really – it was I who said they were to be taken away,' she said, trying to close the subject. 'I think they're simply horrible.'

Her husband's voice was heard from over by the fireplace, deep and tremulous with either old age or anxiety: 'You what? But why did you have them taken away, dear? They were very old, found during some excavations . . .'

'I didn't express myself very well,' said Signora Gron, trying to sound pleasant. (How stupid am I, she thought at the same time, that I couldn't think of anything better to say?) 'I did say I wanted them moved, but only in the vaguest terms – of course I was really only joking . . .'

'But please listen, Mummy,' the girl insisted. 'Berto asked the peasant and he said that he'd found the dog down on the riverbank . . .'

She was suddenly silent, thinking that the rain had stopped. But in the silence they could hear its deep, unwavering hiss (depressing, too, though no one had really noticed).

'Why "the dog"?' enquired Fedri, without even turning his head. 'Didn't you say you saw them both?'

'Goodness, what a pedant,' retorted Giorgina laughing. 'I only saw one, but probably they were both there.'

Fedri said: 'I don't see the logic of that.' Martora laughed too.

'Tell me, Giorgina,' said Signora Gron, promptly taking advantage of the pause. 'What book are you reading? Is it that last novel by Massin you were telling me about? I'd like to read it when you've finished it. If I don't mention it right away you'd immediately lend it to your friends, and then we'd never see it again. I'm very fond of Massin, he's so different, so strange . . . Today Frida promised me –'

But her husband broke in: 'Giorgina,' he said, 'what did you do then? Presumably you asked the man's name, at least? I'm sorry, Maria,' he added, referring to the interruption.

'You didn't expect me to start arguing then and there in the middle of the road, I trust?' she replied. 'It was one of the Dall'Ocas. He said he knew nothing about it, he'd found the statue by the river.'

'And are you certain it was one of our dogs?'

'Rather too certain. Don't you remember how Fedri and I once painted their ears green?'

'And this one had green ears too?' pursued her father, who was sometimes rather slow-thinking.

'Yes, green ears,' replied Giorgina. 'Of course the colour's faded a bit by now.'

Once more her mother interrupted. 'But listen,' she said with exaggerated politeness, 'do you really find these stone dogs so interesting? Excuse me for saying so, Stefano, but I really can't see that there's any need to make such a fuss about it . . .'

From outside – just behind the curtain, it almost seemed – there sounded a prolonged and muffled roar, mingling with the sound of the rain.

'Did you hear that?' exclaimed Signor Gron promptly. 'Did you hear it?'

'Thunder, what else? Just thunder. It's no good, Stefano, you're always so jumpy on rainy days,' his wife hastened to explain.

They were all quiet, but the silence could not last long. Some unfamiliar thought, foreign to that aristocratic household, seemed to have crept into the dimly lit room and settled there.

'Found it down by the river,' commented the father, returning to the subject of the dogs. 'How could it have got there? It couldn't have flown.'

'And why not?' enquired Martora jovially.

'Why not what, doctor?' asked Signora Maria, nervously, since she did not usually like the pleasantries their old friend tended to make.

'I meant: why should the statue not have flown? The river flows about twenty yards below it, that's all.'

'What a world we live in,' sighed Maria Gron, trying once again to change the subject, as though the dogs were a cover for something more unpalatable. 'First we have flying statues, and then do you know what the paper says here: 'a new breed of talking fish discovered off the island of Java'.'

'It also says: 'Save time',' Fedri added rather foolishly – he too was looking at a paper.

'What, what did you say?' asked his father, who had not understood, but was generally apprehensive.

'Yes, it says here: 'Save time! Time too should figure on the budget sheet of every good businessman, on the credit or debit side, as the case may be.''

'I think you might have saved your own in this case,' murmured Martora, though plainly amused.

At this point, somewhere beyond the curtain, a bell rang: so someone had braved this treacherous night, had broken the barrier of rain that was pouring down, hammering on the roofs, devouring great chunks out of the riverbanks; for fine trees were falling noisily from these banks with their great pedestals of earth attached, to emerge for a moment a hundred yards downstream and be sucked down again by whirlpools: by that river which was swallowing up the edges of the old park, with its eighteenth-century wrought-iron railings and seats and its two stone dogs.

'Now who will that be?' said Signor Gron, taking off his gold-rimmed spectacles. 'Callers even at this time of night? I dare say it's about the subscription, that man from the parish council has been a perfect nuisance these last few days. Flood victims! Where are they all, anyway? They keep asking for money but I haven't seen one victim, not a single one. As though . . . Who's there? Who is it?' he enquired in a low voice as the butler appeared from behind the curtain.

'Signor Massigher,' replied the butler.

Martora was delighted: 'Oh, your charming friend! We had such a wonderful discussion the other day . . . there's a young man who knows what he wants.'

'He may be as intelligent as you like, my dear Martora,' said Signora Gron, 'but I find that quite the least affecting of all qualities. These people who do nothing but argue . . . I don't say Massigher isn't a fine boy . . . You, Giorgina,' she added quietly, 'when you've said hello, be a good girl and go to bed. It's getting late, you know.'

'If you liked Massigher better,' retorted her daughter boldly, though trying to speak jokingly, 'if you liked him better I bet it wouldn't be late just yet.'

'That's enough nonsense, Giorgina . . . Oh, good evening, Massigher. We hardly expected to see you tonight . . . you're usually earlier than this . . .'

The young man, his hair ruffled, stopped short on the threshold and looked at the family in horror. 'But – don't you know?' He moved forward, slightly embarrassed.

'Good evening, Signora Maria,' he went on, ignoring the reproach. 'Good evening, Signor Gron, Giorgina, Fedri, excuse me, doctor, I didn't notice you there in the shadow . . .'

He was plainly very nervous, pacing around from one person to the next as if bursting with some important news.

'Have you heard?' he began at last, since the others gave him no encouragement. 'Have you heard that the riverbank –'

'Quite,' interrupted Signora Gron with masterly calm. 'Terrible weather, isn't it?' And she smiled, half-closing her eyes, trying to transmit some kind of understanding to her guest. (Almost impossible, she thought to herself while doing so: a sense of occasion really isn't his strong point.) But the father had already risen from his chair. 'Tell me, what have you heard? Something new?'

'What do you mean, new?' interrupted his wife quickly. 'I really don't understand, my dear, you're so nervous this evening . . .'

Massigher was puzzled. 'Quite,' he admitted, casting around for a way out, 'nothing new that I know of. Except that from the bridge you can see –'

'Well, naturally, the river in flood!' interrupted Signora Gron, helping him out. 'Most impressive, I should think. You remember the Niagara, Stefano? So many years ago . . .' At this point Massigher moved closer to the Signora and whispered, choosing a moment when Giorgina and Fedri were speaking to one another: 'But Signora, Signora,' his eyes sparkled, 'the river is right below the house, it's most unwise to stay, can't you hear the –'

'Do you remember, Stefano?' she went on, as though she hadn't heard him, 'do you remember how frightened the two Dutchmen were? They wouldn't go anywhere near it, they said it was an absurd risk, that one might get carried away . . .'

'Well,' retorted her husband, 'it has sometimes happened, apparently, people leaning too far over, getting dizzy perhaps . . .'

He seemed to have recovered his calm, put on his glasses and sat down by the hearth again, stretching out his hands towards the fire to warm them.

Now for the second time they heard the disturbing muffled roar. It seemed to come from deep in the earth below them, from the farthest recesses of the cellars. Despite herself, Signora Gron stopped to listen.

'Did you hear that, Giorgina?' exclaimed her father, puckering his forehead. 'Did you?'

'Yes, I did. I can't imagine what it is,' she replied, the colour gone from her face.

'Thunder, of course!' retorted her mother in a tone that admitted of no argument. 'Just thunder . . . what do you think it is? . . . not ghosts, by any chance?'

'Thunder doesn't sound like that, Maria,' remarked her husband, shaking his head. 'It seemed to come from right beneath us.'

'You know quite well how it is, my dear: every time there's a storm it feels as if the house is going to collapse,' insisted his wife. 'Then you hear the strangest noises in this house. All you heard was thunder, wasn't it, Massigher?' she concluded, certain that he, a guest, would not dare to contradict her.

He smiled with polite resignation and answered evasively: 'You mentioned ghosts, Signora . . . this evening, as I was crossing the garden, I had the curious sensation of being followed . . . I heard footsteps, as if . . . quite definite footsteps on the gravel in the main avenue . . .'

'And rattling bones, and groans as well, of course?' suggested Signora Gron.

'No, just footsteps, probably my own,' he replied, 'you sometimes get strange echoes.'

'Quite right, my dear boy . . . or mice, that's far more likely, isn't it? It's certainly not a good idea to be as imaginative as you are, or goodness knows what one might hear . . .'

'Signora,' he began again in a low voice, 'surely you can hear it? The river is right below us, can't you hear?'

'No, I hear nothing,' she said curtly, replying in an equally low voice. Then, louder: 'You're not at all amusing with these anecdotes, you know.'

The boy could think of nothing to reply. He tried to laugh, amazed at the woman's obstinacy. So you don't want to believe it, Signora Gron? he thought bitterly. (Even in his thoughts he addressed her just as in real life, using the polite form.) Unpleasant things don't concern you, do they? You think it's uncouth to talk about them. Your precious world has always withdrawn from them, hasn't it? Well, let's see where your ivory tower viewpoint gets you in the end.

'Just listen to this, Stefano,' she went on with sudden eagerness, addressing him across the whole room. 'Massigher claims to have seen ghosts out in the park and he's not joking . . . these young people certainly set a fine example.'

'Signor Gron, don't believe a word of it,' and he laughed effortfully. 'I didn't say that at all, I . . .'

He broke off to listen. In the ensuing silence, above the sound of the rain, he thought he heard another sound swelling, threatening and ominous. He was standing in an arc of light from a slightly blue-tinted lamp, his lips parted a little; not frightened, but throbbing with life, strangely unlike the people and objects surrounding him. Giorgina watched him with a feeling of desire.

But don't you understand, Massigher? Don't you feel sufficiently safe in this great old house? How can you feel doubt? Isn't it enough for you to be surrounded by these solid old walls, this nicely balanced peace, these impassive faces? How do you dare offend such dignity with your silly childish fears?

'You look like a soul possessed,' remarked his friend Fedri affectionately, 'like a painter . . . what prevented you from combing your hair? Please, next time . . . you know Mother's views on this,' and he burst out laughing.

He was interrupted by a peevish enquiry from his father: 'Well, shall we begin this bridge? We've still got time, you know. One game and then bed. Giorgina, would you be good enough to get the cards?'

At this point the butler appeared; he looked thoroughly dumbfounded by the turn events were taking. 'What is it now?' asked Signora Gron, with ill-concealed irritation, 'Has someone else arrived?'

'It's Antonio, the bailiff . . . he wants to speak to one of you, he says it's important.'

'I'll go,' said Stefano immediately, standing up quickly as though afraid of somehow being too late.

His wife did indeed hold him back. 'No no, you stay here. It's far too damp outside . . . you know quite well . . . your rheumatism . . . you stay here, dear. Fedri will go.'

'It'll only be the usual business,' said the boy, walking towards the curtain. From the distance there came a confused sound of voices.

'Are you going to play here?' asked the signora in the interim. 'Giorgina, take that vase away, please . . . then do go to bed, dear, it's already late. And what are you going to do, Martora – go to sleep?'

The old man roused himself, embarrassed: 'Had I fallen asleep? Yes, I believe I had, for a few minutes.' He smiled. 'The fireside, old age . . .'

'Mother,' the girl called from another corner of the room. 'I can't find the box of cards, they were here in the drawer yesterday.'

'Open your eyes, my dear. What's that on the side table? You never find anything . . .'

Massigher arranged the four chairs and began to shuffle the pack. At this point Fedri reappeared. Wearily, his father asked, 'What did Antonio want?'

'Absolutely nothing,' answered the boy merrily. 'Just the usual peasant's panics. The river's very swollen, they say the house is in danger – think of that. They wanted me to go and see – in this weather! They're all praying there now, and ringing the bells – can you hear?'

'Fedri, let's go and see together,' suggested Massigher. 'Just for five minutes. Will you come?'

'And what about our game, Massigher?' enquired the signora. 'So you'd leave Dr Martora in the lurch? And get a soaking too.'

So the four men began their game, Giorgina went to bed and her mother sat in a corner with her embroidery.

As the game progressed, the thuds they had heard earlier became more frequent. It sounded as if some heavy object were falling into a deep mud-filled hole, a sound of doom coming from the bowels of the earth. After each thud there was a feeling of unease, the players hesitated to play their cards, caught their breath, fumbled, but the tension vanished as quickly as it had come.

No one, it seemed, wished to talk about it. Except Martora, who observed at one point: 'It must come from the sewer underneath here. There is one very old water pipe which runs into the river. Probably some sort of overflow . . .' No one said anything.

Now it is time to study the reactions of Signor Gron, that true nobleman. He is looking at the small fan of cards in his left hand, but occasionally his glance steals out beyond the cards to take in the head and shoulders of Martora, who is opposite him, and finally to include the far end of the room where the polished floor disappears under the fringes of curtain. And now he no longer looks at the cards or at the face of his old friend, but stares beyond him at the back of the room, at the bottom of the curtain; his eyes widen further, kindle with a strange light.

At last the old nobleman says simply – dully, but in a tone of great desolation – 'Look.' He is not addressing his son, nor the doctor, nor Massigher in particular. He simply says 'Look', but that one word is frightening.

He uttered this one word and the others looked up, even his wife, who was sitting in a corner with great dignity, absorbed in her embroidery. Slowly, from beneath the lower border of the dark curtain, something black and shapeless crept across the floor.

'Stefano, why on earth do you have to use that tone of voice?' exclaimed Signora Gron, who had already jumped to her feet and was walking towards the curtain. 'Can't you see that it's water?' None of the four players had stood up.

It was indeed water. It had finally crept into the villa through some crack or gap, sneaking like a snake along corridors before finally entering the drawing room, where it looked black because of the shadow. It would have been amusing had it not been such a blatant outrage. But behind that negligible tongue of water, that merest trickle, might there not be something else? Could one be quite certain that that was the full extent of the damage? Was there no water trickling down the walls, no pools between the tall shelves in the library, no slow dripping from the arched ceiling of the next room (the water falling on the great silver salver – a wedding present given by the prince many years ago)?

'Those idiots have left a window open,' exclaimed Fedri. 'Go and close it then,' said his father.

But the signora intervened. 'Out of the question – stay where you are; someone else will come and close it, I trust!' She pulled the bell-pull nervously and they heard the distant sound of the bell. At the same time the mysterious splashing sounds began to occur with ominous, ever-increasing frequency; now they could be heard throughout the whole house. Old Gron, frowning, was staring at the tongue of water on the floor; it seemed to swell at the edges, then spill over, spreading a few inches, swell again, spread and so on. Suspecting that something unusual was about to happen, Massigher shuffled the cards to hide his own emotion. And Martora shook his head slowly, as if to say: 'Such are the times we live in – one can no longer rely on one's staff'; or perhaps, resignedly: 'Nothing to be done about this now, my friends, you noticed it all too late.'

A few moments passed without any sign of life from the other rooms. Massigher plucked up his courage: 'Signora,' he said, 'I did tell you that –'

'Good God! You again, Massigher!' snapped Maria Gron, without letting him finish the sentence. 'All because of a bit of water on the floor! Ettore will wipe it up in a minute. These wretched windows let in water all the time, we must have the fastenings seen to!'

But Ettore did not appear, nor did any other of the numerous staff of servants. There was a sudden feeling of oppression and hostility abroad in the night. Meanwhile the mysterious splashes had developed into an almost continuous roar, as if barrels were being rolled around in the foundations, so that even the sound of the pouring rain outside was barely audible.

'Signora!' shouted Massigher suddenly, jumping to his feet determinedly. 'Signora, where has Giorgina gone? Let me go and call her!'

'What now, Massigher?' Maria Gron's face still expressed coldly polite amazement. 'You are all terribly nervous this evening. What do you want Giorgina for? You don't actually wish to wake her up, I trust?'

'Wake her up!' the young man retorted, almost mocking. 'Wake her up! There you go again!'

From the passage hidden behind the curtain, as from an icy cave, there came a sudden violent gust of wind. The curtain billowed like a sail and twisted around itself to allow the lights of the room to shine beyond it and reflect in the pool of water on the floor.

'Fedri, run and close it quickly,' cursed his father. 'Good Lord, call the servants!'

But the boy seemed almost amused by this unusual turn of events. He ran across the dark hall shouting: 'Ettore! Ettore! Berto! Sofia!' but his shouts were lost unanswered in the empty corridors.

'Papà!' he called suddenly. 'There's no light out here. I can't see a thing . . . Oh God, what's happened?'

Back in the room all had risen to their feet, alarmed by his sudden call. Suddenly, inexplicably, water seemed to be pouring through the whole house. The wind blew fiercely through it as though there were holes in the walls, shaking the lamps, scattering cards and papers, upsetting flowers.

Fedri reappeared, looking as white as a sheet and trembling slightly. 'Good God,' he kept saying mechanically. 'Good God, how awful.'

Did he still need to explain that the river had burst its banks and was right here, below the house and was pouring past, implacable and uncaring? That the walls on that side of the house were about to collapse? That the servants had all vanished into the night and that soon no doubt there would be no light at all? His white face, his panicked shouts (he who was usually so elegant and self-confident), the frightful roar welling up from the bottomless abyss beneath them – was not all this sufficient explanation?

'We must leave immediately, my car's out there, it would be mad not to . . .' Martora was saying, he being the only one who had retained any semblance of calm. At this point Giorgina reappeared, wrapped in a thick coat, accompanied by Massigher; she was sobbing a little, though quite decorously, almost without making a sound. Her father began searching around in the drawer containing his important papers.

'Oh no, no!' Signora Maria burst out in sudden despair. 'I don't want to go! My flowers, all my beautiful things – I don't want to go, I don't!' Her mouth trembled, her face contracted as though it were about to fall apart, she was on the verge of consent. Then, with a marvellous effort, she smiled. Her mask of wordliness was intact, her highly sophisticated charms unimpaired.

'I'll always remember it,' said Massigher, suddenly cruel, hating her with all his heart. 'I'll always remember your villa. It was so lovely on moonlit nights.'

'Get a coat quickly, Signora,' said Martora firmly, turning to her. 'You get something warm too, Stefano. Let's go before the lights fail.'

Signor Gron was quite genuinely unafraid. He seemed devoid of all emotion and was clutching the leather wallet containing the papers. Fedri was pacing round the room, paddling in the water – he had completely let himself go. 'It's all over, then, all over,' he kept saying. The electric light became weaker.

Then there came a long, resounding thud, more awful and much nearer than anything that had preceded it, a sound of catastrophe. Fear held the family in its icy grip.

'Oh no, no!' the mother shrieked again suddenly. 'I won't, I won't!' Very pale, her face fiercely set, she began to walk anxiously towards the billowing curtain. But she was shaking her head, as though to say that she didn't allow it, that she was coming in person and that the water could not dare to come any closer.

They saw her pushing aside the flapping edges of the curtain with an angry movement and disappearing into the darkness, as though she were going to disperse an irritating band of beggars the servants had been unable to drive away. Did she hope that her aristocratic disdain could keep tragedy at bay, could intimidate the yawning abyss?

She disappeared behind the curtain and, although the frightful rumbling sound seemed to swell, there was a feeling of silence.

At last Massigher said: 'There's someone knocking at the door.'

'Now really,' said Martora, 'whom do you imagine that could be?'

'No one,' replied Massigher. 'Naturally, no one, at this stage. Yet there definitely is someone knocking. Probably a messenger, a spirit, a warning soul. This is a noble house. I think the powers that be sometimes take this into account.'

'*Eppure battono alla porta*'
First published in the literary supplement *La lettura*, XL, no. 9, September 1940. It was later included in *I sette messaggeri* (Mondadori, 1942) and *Sessanta racconti* (Mondadori, 1958).

MASSIMO BONTEMPELLI
1878–1960

'*Funambolismo*' is a word often used to describe Bontempelli's art – that of a tightrope walker. Among the most audacious of writers in this volume, he is also the most graceful. Everything Bontempelli wrote was brief, taut, exquisitely controlled. A precursor to Calvino, he was a key figure of the Italian avant-garde, formally anomalous even today. He began working as a school teacher and his first important book, a collection of stories called *Sette savi* (Seven Sages), was published in 1912. At around forty years of age, after covering the First World War as a correspondent on the front-lines, he went through a form of literary conversion, renouncing much of his preceding work. His new phase began with *La vita intensa* (The Intense Life), an emphatically experimental and ironic volume which contains ten micro-novels, all set in Milan and published in 1920. In his own preface to the book he declared his intention to 'renew the European novel'. Much has been said about Bontempelli's nationalist agenda and early role as Secretary of the Fascist Writers' Union, his collaboration with Curzio Malaparte,[1] his close friendship with Luigi Pirandello. And yet he refused to accept a university post denied to a Jewish professor in 1938, was forbidden, for the following year, to publish his work, and was forced into hiding in Rome for nine months during the Resistance. In 1937, when he was nearly sixty, he became a companion to the writer Paola Masino, thirty years his junior, who gave up writing to curate all of his work after his death. This story, exuberant, spare and post-apocalyptic, was written after his break with his former style. Describing a virtual reality before the term was invented, its themes are various: the transformation of space, the dividing line between nature and built environments, the contrasting ways that men and women sustain each other and survive. Bontempelli loved music, wrote about it, and composed it. He was also the first to apply 'magic realism' – an aesthetic term borrowed from German – to literature.

The Miraculous Beach, or, Prize for Modesty
(Aminta)

Translated by Jenny McPhee

At the first threat, people began to stay off the streets of Rome, then, after a few days, a generalized fear took over and the city itself began to empty out. Seized with fear, hour after hour, the citizens of Rome stormed the train stations, and, shoving their way on to train carriages, had fled far away. The richest people glutted their cars with oil and gas before bolting out of the thirteen city gates and, kicking up dust, headed to the most distant cardinal points.

And so it was for ten days. Then suddenly the train stations were deserted and throughout Rome it was only the peddlers' carts that raised any dust, the peddlers being afraid of nothing. At that point, no one was left in the metropolis.

Only a few heroes and heroines stayed to watch over the city. At midday, the heroes roamed imperiously through the streets. Jacketless, they allowed the sun to whip their silk shirts to shreds while vainly regarding their reflections in their belt buckles. When seeing each other on opposite pavements, even without knowing one another, they smiled proudly, confident that from Laterano to Monte Mario, from Valle Giulia to Saint Paul's, their supremacy would last undisturbed and uncontested for at least two months.

The heroines didn't go out in the sun. They each waited inside for their heroes to return home when they would dry their sweat and iron their silk shirts. The women went out only at night and, exercising their wily ways, they would flick flirtatious glances with their stray-cat eyes behind their companions' backs.

*

Since I adhere to the laws of nature, and love the heat of the sun in summer, the heat of the stove in winter, I was among those heroes who hadn't fled the city during the summer onslaught. The heroine chosen to dry my sweat was called Aminta.[1] This was once a male name, but my girlfriend's father did not know literary history, and eighteen years earlier, trusting his own ear, he had imposed that name on his newborn daughter. The priest who baptized her didn't dare inform the father of his innocent error.

Aminta, at the first heat of summer, conceded immediately to the excellent reasons I had used to convince her that we should stay in Rome instead of departing for the mountains or seaside.

And so the first eight days of the heatwave passed easily.

On Aminta's pale face, I never once detected the slightest indication of regret, repentance, disrespect or desire.

I was therefore astonished when, on the afternoon of the ninth day, having returned from my rounds on the blazing streets, Aminta, after a jubilant greeting, approached me where I had sunk down upon a couch in my study and, placing a hand on my shoulder, said suddenly:

'Darling, you must give me a small present, you must have a beautiful bathing suit made for me.'

I felt my brow furrow.

My disparaging masculine soul became muddy with suspicion.

I stared at her grimly:

'What for, Aminta? What has come over you? Aren't we divinely happy in Rome? Are you thinking of leaving? Of perhaps going to the beach? Oh, I have explained to you again and again that –'

'No, no,' she interrupted, her eyes, her brow, her mouth, her whole body laughing, 'I didn't mean that at all. Yes, we're very happy here in Rome. Who would dream of leaving? I simply want a beautiful bathing suit in order to have a beautiful bathing suit.'

'And once you have it?'

'I will put it on.'

'When?'

'Every so often. For a little while every day.'

'And then?'

'And then after a while I will take it off.'

'That's it?'

'That's it. I swear.'

She was so transparent, all suspicion vanished from my soul.

I kept quiet for a minute in order to give greater weight to the words I was about to utter, then declared:

'Very well, all is fine. Yes, darling, go ahead and have a beautiful bathing suit made for yourself.'

She clapped her hands and jumped for joy, then tenderly kissed all of the sweat off my face in gratitude.

Over the next few days she was very busy. As for her research, studies, attempts, doubts and resolutions regarding the construction of her bathing suit, I wasn't privy to her secrets. She went out a few times during the day and stayed in her room for long hours with a seamstress. She wouldn't allow me to know a thing. She wanted to surprise me with an unexpected masterpiece. Her face was full of happiness, day and night.

Preoccupied with my virile thoughts, after a few days I had almost forgotten about her feminine pastime. But on Wednesday morning, when I took off my jacket before heading out, Aminta said goodbye, then added:

'When you return in an hour it will be ready.'

'What will be ready?'

'Oh, the bathing suit.'

'Really?'

'Yes, hurry back and you'll see. It's absolutely marvellous.'

When I returned home less than an hour later, a sliver of suspicion was still trying to insidiously act upon me. Was it possible that this little story concerning the bathing suit marked the start of a campaign to get me to take her to the seaside?

I went into my study where I heard her voice coming from the other side of the door to her room.

'Don't come in. I'm ready. Sit down on the couch.'

'OK, I won't come in. OK, I'm sitting on the couch.'

I stared at the door to her room.

When it opened a great light entered the study, and at the centre of that light Aminta stood wearing her bathing suit. My heart skipped a beat.

Aminta came towards me. She seemed to be lit up, propelled by all the light in the sky. Trembling in ecstasy, I didn't move from where I was. Aminta stopped in the middle of the room.

It was truly marvellous. Pale-rose silk draped down from her throat accentuating her breasts, then gathered around her hips in a band of tiny pleats flaring into a short skirt that didn't dare graze her flesh, the undulating hem quivering suggestively. Layered on top of the minuscule skirt's pink material was a flounce of acute triangles, their colour emerald green. Aminta stood in the middle of the room; in the light cascading from her eyes, the pale rose of the silk bathing suit changed from minute to minute into a thousand mother-of-pearl reflections. The green of the flounce suggested a swarm of shiny scarab beetles flying across a sunset.

Amidst that effusion of tender colours, the white of her arms and legs became even paler. On her feet she wore two small green satin slippers. Aminta was laughing with all of her soft flesh, with her entire green-and-pale-rose bathing suit; she laughed and shook like a plant in a garden; and the room was filled with the scent of paradise.

I didn't have the courage to move. Aminta was happy to be alive. Her laugh sounding like silver bells flying out the window and rushing up to heaven, Aminta sat herself down on the carpet in the middle of the room, her arms behind her and her white legs crossed, her torso reclining backwards and stretched out as if she were offering herself up to God.

Her gaze landed on me. I still hadn't moved and I held my heart in my hands. At the sight of my emotion, she was touched with affection and gratitude.

Still trembling, I approached her. I sat beside her on the carpet and gently took her hand. I caressed her whole body with my eyes, then I timidly touched the pale-rose silk of her bathing suit with my forehead. Aminta's eyes, full of smiles, were swelling with tears of affection. They contained a message for me. In a trembling voice, she said:

'You see how beautiful it is, with no need to go to the seaside?'

I felt the entirety of her innocent soul pressing against me. I was overcome by love. And I, too, now searched for something simple to say to her. With my cheek resting on her cool arm, I whispered:

'Your modest desires deserve a prize.'

She softened and once again laughed joyfully. But when I didn't join in she stopped laughing and looked at me expectantly. Something fluttered in the air and touched me. I saw that she also had felt something. Her shoulders instantly trembled and she said:

'What is it? How beautiful!'

The whole room filled with a kind of light breath which then immediately disappeared. All around me I saw a flickering light; this too passed before my and Aminta's eyes, then fled away.

'Oh, how fabulous this is!' Aminta murmured.

She was sitting at the edge of the carpet and I was further back, almost behind her. A sweet, strange murmuring sound reached us, fading at her feet. I saw that she was listening intently.

The ground murmured again, while before our eyes everything in the room vanished into a light mist infiltrated by blue shadows and silver flashes.

By now the murmuring coming from the ground had become regular and frequent. It originated far away, swished nearby and died down at her feet. The murmuring then became prolonged: one, coming close, seemed to expand. Suddenly, she let out a cry and drew back her feet.

'Look, look,' she cried.

I looked. Her green slipper was wet, as was her foot up to her ankle.

And again, again . . .

The gushing increased. The sound of tiny waves arriving at the edge of the carpet continued, pushing at her feet and alongside her legs. Fearlessly, she leaned forward, plunged her hands into those waves, then lifted them out dripping with water.

'The sea, the sea.'

The silver and blue mist around us filled with light and the carpet burned like sand. Aminta dived in, outstretched, her breasts extending over the edge, then she came back up, the wet silk clinging to her chest, her nipples erect. I stared at her, ecstatic, and listened to the sea, which had come to visit us.

Suddenly, a bigger wave reached me and I felt the water rising as far as my calves.

I jumped to my feet, alarmed: 'Aminta, I'd better go and put on my bathing suit too.'

'Yes,' she cried. 'There's one in the bottom drawer of your bureau, but hurry.'

And both of us were very happy.

'*La spiaggia miracolosa ovvero Premio della modestia (Aminta)*'
Written between 1925 and 1927 and published in a national newspaper, then included in *Donna nel sole e altri idilli* (Mondadori, 1928) and in *Miracoli* (Mondadori, 1938).

ROMANO BILENCHI
1909–89

Bilenchi, from Florence, is an elusive figure, and an interesting study in extremes. He was known for obsessive revising and rewriting, admired for his unconventional and abstract coming-of-age tales. And yet he has slipped, somehow, through the literary cracks, still without a volume in Mondadori's *Meridiani* series to his name. Fascist as a youth, he broke with the regime, disillusioned, and became a Communist, but given that he did not fully support Soviet policy, eventually left the party. He started publishing in his early twenties and wrote several collections of short stories and novels, including the celebrated long story '*La siccità*' ('The Drought') set in a deliberately unidentified place. Composed in 1940, it became part of a volume of three limpid, chiselled stories called *Gli anni impossibili* (The Impossible Years). He funnelled his energy into journalism after the Second World War, helping to found the magazine *Il contemporaneo* and serving as editor of the *Nuovo Corriere* of Florence, an influential left-wing newspaper of the 1940s and 1950s. In 1958, about midway through his so-called 'silent' phase, Bilenchi decided to publish a rigorously revised volume of his short stories. His objective was to prune his language to its essentials; his labours were rewarded by the Premio Bagutta '*vent'anni dopo*' (a prize to recognize work in retrospect; in this case, twenty years later), proof that his silence had been in fact an exceptionally productive one. In 1972 after the release of a novel called *Il bottone di Stalingrado* (The Button of Stalingrad), he won the Viareggio Prize. This story, from the collection *Anna e Bruno*, concerns a young boy's growing frustration with being misnamed, misconstrued and misunderstood. But its central theme – the inexorable specificity of place, and its correlation with identity – illuminates the intensely regional nature of Italy, even today.

A Geographical Error

Translated by Lawrence Venuti

The inhabitants of the city of F. don't know the geography of their country, of their own home. When I left G. to study at F., I immediately noticed that these people had a mistaken idea of the location of my native town. As soon as I mentioned G., they told me, 'Oh, you're from the Maremma.'

One day, then, while the professor of Italian was explaining the work of some ancient Italian writer I no longer recall, he began to speak of certain shepherds who in the windows of their huts hung sheepskin tanned very finely instead of glass. For some reason I stood up from the last desk, where I was sitting, and said, 'Yes, it's true: among us as well farm workers attach the skins of rabbits or sheep to their cabin windows in place of glass, so great is their poverty.' For some reason I stood up and said this. Perhaps I wanted to make myself seem clever to the professor; perhaps I was driven by a humanitarian impulse on behalf of poor people and I wanted to testify to my classmates, all of them city dwellers, that the professor had said something right, that such poverty really existed in the world. Apart from the poverty, however, the affirmation was a product of my imagination. In my life – God knows whether I had ever wandered around the countryside – only once did I happen to see a windowpane patched with a piece of paper; and the farmer's wife, moreover, had practically apologized, saying that as soon as someone from the family could go to the city, they would buy a brand-new windowpane. No sooner was I standing before the class than I felt every impulse checked, and I realized that I had said something very stupid. I hoped that the professor might not be familiar with the customs of my region, but at my outburst, he raised his head from his book and said, 'Don't talk nonsense.' After a moment, he laughed and everybody followed suit, if only to please him. 'But wait a minute,' he then said.

'Perhaps you're right. Your town, G., isn't it in the Maremma? In the Maremma they probably still dress in sheepskin.'

Everybody burst into laughter again. Someone, perhaps to point out that the professor and I were on the same level of stupidity, guffawed ambiguously. I turned to grasp that uncertain yet unique solidarity with my position, but the first classmate I encountered, to avoid compromising himself, called me 'Bagpiper' and imitated playing the bagpipes characteristic of rural areas. Another said, 'Did you ever see sheep dung?' and in a chorus the others chanted, 'Baa, baa!'

I began – this was my error – to respond to each of them as they opened their mouths. I was one of the smallest and most ingenuous students in the class, and very soon the whole gang preyed upon me. Although they belonged to distinguished families, the class included the son of a nouveau riche shopkeeper, as I gathered from the mammas and daddies who would come to the school every month: they spoke their minds to me. Finally, with tears in my eyes, taking advantage of a moment of silence, I shouted, 'Professor, G. is not in the Maremma.'

'It is in the Maremma.'

'No, it is not in the Maremma.'

'It *is* in the Maremma,' said the professor resolutely. 'I have friends all across your region and often I go to hunt larks with them. I know the town well. It is in the Maremma.'

'We natives of G. also go to hunt larks in the Maremma. But the Maremma is at least eighty kilometres from my town. We see it as a very different place. Besides, G. is a city,' I said.

'But I've seen herdsmen precisely at the market in G.,' he responded.

'That's impossible. I've always lived there and I've never seen any herdsmen.'

'Don't insist. You wouldn't be trying to suggest that I'm an idiot, would you?'

'I'm not trying to do anything,' I said. 'But G. is not in the Maremma. Travelling peddlers come to the market dressed as redskins. Because of this you could assert that G. is in America.'

'You're also witty,' he said. 'But before calling you stupid and throwing you out of the class, I shall demonstrate to your classmates that G. is located in the Maremma.' He sent a boy to fetch the map of the region from the science classroom, so that there too they knew about my dispute and were amusing themselves at my expense. On the map, despite the fact that I didn't allow a single one of his assertions to go unchallenged, the professor abolished the actual boundaries of the province, created new imaginary ones, and managed to convince my classmates, relying on the scale of 1:1,000,000, along with various other fabrications, that G. is really in the Maremma.

'It isn't true that G. is in the Maremma,' I finally struck back, 'since we take 'Maremmano' to be synonymous with an uncouth, ignorant man.'

'In you, then,' he concluded, 'we have the proof that the people of G. are authentic Maremmani. I have known few boys as uncouth and ignorant as you. You're still wearing those shaggy knee socks.' At that point, he looked me up and down. The others did the same. I felt I wasn't as elegant as my classmates. I fell silent, humiliated. From that day onward I was the 'Maremmano'. But what irritated me most, in the end, was the geographical ignorance of the professor and my classmates.

I could not bear the Maremma. I had been seized by an intense aversion at the first document that happened to come before my eyes concerning the territory and its inhabitants. I had previously read many books about the horsemen of the American prairies, and I had seen innumerable films about their astounding adventures – books and films that had excited me. A couple of years of my life had been dedicated to the horses, lassoes, huge hats and pistols of those extraordinary men. In my heart there was no room for anybody else. When they arrived to free sidekicks captured by the Indians, I felt that their fluttering little flag represented freedom; and I would have hurled myself at the throat of whoever declared himself on the side of White Deer and Son of Eagle. When the wagon train, forced to form a circle to brave the attack of the murderous Indians, would return joyful and ready to set forth over the immense deserted prairies and the deep mountain gorges, I felt as if men had again won the right to traverse the world. The names of those horsemen – I used to know the names of every hero of every serialized novel and every film – were always on my lips. I judged every person by comparing him to them, and very few withstood the comparison. When I read that a stone's throw from my house – one might say – there lived men who lassoed wild animals, tamed bulls, dressed in Far West gear (more or less) and camped at night beneath the starry sky wrapped in blankets around blazing fires with their rifles and faithful dogs close by, I burst into a fit of laughter. I couldn't even take seriously the stories about the faithful dogs, which are common and accepted throughout the world. I pored over many maps and increasingly convinced myself that in an area so close to me there couldn't possibly be wild animals, brave men or any likelihood of adventures. Nor could there be the sweetest dark-haired women who sang on canvas-covered wagons and, if need be, loaded their partners' weapons. No, the horsemen of the Maremma were poor copies of the heroes of my acquaintance. Those in the books and films constantly fought against Indians and robbers; but there, a stone's throw away, what robbers could there be? The era of the famous old bandits seemed to be distant, if they had ever existed; I had my doubts about them as well.

When I went to study at F., this is precisely the way I thought. I could not therefore stand the nickname 'Maremmano'.

I used to play football with skill, but also with a certain roughness, notwithstanding that I was small and thin. I immediately distinguished myself the first time I went on the field with my classmates, and they put me at inside left forward on the squad that represented the high school in the student championship. I played several games, earning much applause.

'The Maremmano is good,' they would say. 'He must've been trained with the wild colts. The herdsmen taught him a bunch of sly tricks.'

The gibes and taunts, since I was certain that they contained some sincere praise, did not in fact irritate me. I would smile and the others quickly fell silent. We were now close to the end of the championship with a good chance of coming in first, and I promised myself that, because of services rendered in the school's honour – imagine a game won by a single point that I had scored – I would not be called 'Maremmano' in future. In the last match, however, an ugly incident occurred. On the way downfield I happened to turn my back to the opposing goal. They passed me the ball from the right. I turned to shoot on the volley. The goalie had guessed the move and dived forward to block both leg and ball, but my kick caught him squarely in the mouth. He passed out. I had broken three of his teeth. His mates heaped threats on me. I said that I hadn't done it on purpose, it was an accident, I was a close friend of the goalie, who was staying in the very same *pensione* as me, but the students supporting the other squad, who were very numerous in the audience, began to shout, 'Maremmano, Maremmano, Maremmano.'

I saw red, and turning towards the spectators who were shouting more loudly, I made an obscene gesture. The referee sent me off the field. As I was leaving, the shouts and insults intensified. I saw that even the girls were shouting.

'Maremmano, Maremmano, Maremmano – he comes from G.'

My team-mates must have been among those who were shouting. How else could everyone know that I was born in G.? I felt deprived of any solidarity and, head lowered, I walked towards the dressing room.

'Maremmano, Maremmano, Maremmano, you're still wearing those shaggy knee socks.'

The fact that the others didn't like my knee socks was unimportant to me. It was a question of taste. I have always liked woollen things, hand-made and rather heavy. To me the socks were very handsome, and I didn't blame them for my troubles, even though they were constantly the object of critical remarks and satire. On that occasion too, I was angered above all by the injustice my tormentors were committing against G. by continuing to believe that it was located in the Maremma. I went back to the spectators and sought to explain the error that those ignorant people were making, but by dint of the laughter, shouts, pushes and even kicks in the trousers, I was chased to the dressing room.

The next day the headmaster summoned me and suspended me for a week because of the gesture I had made to the spectators, a gesture that dishonoured the school. I opened my heart to the headmaster, hoping that at least he might understand that G. was not in the Maremma. He listened to me at length, but his face wore the same derisive expression as my classmates', and at the end of my speech, he confirmed the punishment. Perhaps he believed that I was something of an idiot.

My first impulse was to write home and beg my father and mother to send me to study in another city. But how could I explain my punishment? I would not have been understood; in fact, they would have scolded me. They were making sacrifices to support me at school. I decided to put up with everything. On my return to school after the suspension, the offences against G. and me multiplied. Summer was approaching, however, and with summer, vacation would come. At home I would think about what to do the following year; perhaps I would abandon my studies and find a job. But just then the worst trouble befell me.

One Sunday morning, having left my *pensione* early to enjoy the bright colours of late spring, I saw the walls plastered with vivid posters and groups of people lingering to admire them. The three figures that stood out in the posters immediately made me turn up my nose: a bull, his head lowered as if in the act of hurling himself into the street; a slender colt pawing the ground; and a herdsman who was looking at the two animals with contemptuous self-confidence. I drew closer. The posters announced that next Sunday, in a field near the hippodrome, for the first time in a city, the horsemen of the Maremma would perform in thrilling feats of derring-do.

I had never been in the Maremma, nor had I ever seen the herdsmen except in photographs. A better occasion to laugh at them could not have been offered to me. Besides, I liked immensely the place where the event would take place. As the river leaves the city, it withdraws into the countryside through bizarre bends, finally free of the houses and bridges. Between the right riverbank and a row of hills lie some very beautiful parks with wooden cafés and enormous trees; there are also pretty green meadows surrounded by well-kept boxwood hedges, which suddenly open up amid the trees. I liked the green meadows and hedges even more than the riverbank, and on the afternoons when I did not have class, I would never miss going to visit them. I would sit at the borders, next to the hedges, and from there observe the low, tender grass, which filled my soul with joy.

'I shall go there Sunday,' I decided, and at noon, on my return to the *pensione*, I invited my mess-mates, the goalie I had injured in the football match and two students in my high school to go to the performance with me.

'We've already seen the posters,' said the goalie. 'We'll come to admire your teachers.' The others also accepted and on the appointed day we walked to the site of the performance. I was not expecting the huge crowd, drawn there, I thought, more by the splendid day than by the herdsmen and their animals. There were beautiful ladies and girls, just like at the races. I had already begun looking at the women who went strolling near the hippodrome on Sundays. Following the crowd we entered a field, where on one side several stands had been constructed. I suddenly realized that I was no longer with my mates; perhaps the throng had separated us. I found a place to sit.

A wild colt entered the arena, along with a few herdsmen dressed in the style of cowboys from overseas. I was immediately annoyed by their clothing. The colt started to wander confusedly through the field. A herdsman rushed up behind it. His task was to mount the horse from behind on the run and to remain mounted despite the animal's fits of rage. But the colt, having noticed the man, stopped and allowed him to approach. Then the herdsman, perhaps unsettled by the presence of so many people, made a leap and wound up nearly astride the colt's neck. It was the way to mount a wooden horse, and yet horse and rider fell to the earth. The other herdsmen ran to help. The colt didn't want to stand up; it held the man prisoner, pressing its belly on his legs. The audience began to shout. The colt eventually decided to get on its feet again and, very calmly, allowed itself to be led out of the field.

'He won't be tamed,' shouted a spectator. 'He's a lamb.'

The crowd erupted into noisy laughter. I too laughed with relish.

A bull entered the green clearing. A herdsman confronted it at once, trying to grasp it by the horns and bring it down. The audience was hushed. The bull seemed more alert than the colt. In fact, the roles were quickly reversed – it seemed as if the bull had been assigned the task of knocking down the man. The animal began to behave with a kind of strange craftiness: it enacted a long series of feints like a football player who wants to pass an opponent. It finally charged the man, driving him to take to his heels. Yet it was a charge full of caution, without hostility, as if the bull had wanted to mock the enemy's gruff attitude, and the spectators immediately realized that the herdsman had not suffered any harm. Once again the other herdsmen ran to help their mate. Then the bull began running merrily after those poor devils. It headed for the hedges and, after completing two laps around the field, dashed in the direction of the river. The herdsmen, now in despair, also vanished beyond the hedge amid the uproar of the audience.

The crowd was yelling and cursing. In the end, aware that there would be no other attractions, they began to disperse.

'Swindlers,' they shouted.

'It's a scandal.'

'What robbery!'

'Down with the Maremmani!'

'We want our money back.'

I shouted along with the others. Someone landed several blows on the booth where the tickets for the stands had been sold. I threw a stone at the wooden tables: I wanted to see everything destroyed. At the exit my mates surrounded me.

'We were looking for you,' said one.

'You were hiding, weren't you?'

'Your paisans were just great. All of you should reimburse the spectators for the price of the ticket.'

'He too is a Maremmano,' said the goalie, pointing me out to people nearby.

'He's a Maremmano, just like these swindlers who jerked us around.'

A crowd of boys gathered and started to ridicule me as if they had always known me.

'Don't you think he's a Maremmano?' said the goalie again. 'Look at his knee socks. That's the kind of stuff they wear in Maremma.'

'Tomorrow I'll wear cotton socks,' I said. 'I wear them every year when it gets warm.' Then I added, 'G. is not in the Maremma.'

At the mention of G. several adults made common cause with the boys.

'Tell your countrymen they're thieves,' said a young man. The others laughed. With tears in my eyes I then tried to explain the grave error they committed by thinking that G. was located in the Maremma.

'Is he a bit touched?' someone asked one of my mates.

'More than a bit,' he replied.

The boys were shouting more loudly than before. They started pushing me, the adults no less than the boys.

A young man ran up; he was laughing and said that he had been to the river. The bull had thrown himself into the water, and the herdsmen were weeping, cursing and begging the saints and the bull, but they were unable to drag him out. At this news the attacks on me intensified.

'He must be the son of the herdsmen's boss if he defends them so much,' said a girl.

'No,' I hollered. 'I'm not defending them. I hate them. I have nothing to do with them. My grandfather owned farms. My mother is a lady. It was she who made these socks.'

'They're made of goat hair,' said an old gentleman. One boy emitted a 'Baa', another a 'Moo', and a third gave me a punch.

I turned around. I was standing in the middle of a street that leads to the city. People were gathering behind me in a semicircle. I was crying. It must have been a long time since I had cried. I broke away from the group and leaned against a tree. Far away, on the shore of the river, I glimpsed my mates running in the opposite direction. Perhaps they were going to see the bull who had thrown himself in the river.

'*Un errore geografico*'
Written in 1937 and first published in the collection *Mio cugino Andrea* (Vallecchi, 1943). It was then included in the collection *Racconti* (Vallecchi, 1958) and in the 1989 edition of *Anna e Bruno e altri racconti* (Rizzoli).

LUCIANO BIANCIARDI

1922–71

In 1949, Bianciardi, a recent graduate from the Scuola Normale Superiore of Pisa who had written a thesis on John Dewey and was teaching in a high school, launched something called a 'Bibliobus': a library on wheels. It was an act of cultural reconstruction and unification that promoted literature as a vehicle for social change, at a time when illiteracy rates in Italy were still remarkably high. Bianciardi didn't have a licence, so the bus was driven by his friend Cassola who, like Bianciardi, was raised in the Maremma. Among the circulating volumes were works by Shakespeare, Conrad, Steinbeck, Dostoevsky, Moravia and Hemingway (the latter two were the bestselling authors at that time). The Bible, the Koran and various agricultural manuals were also available. Bianciardi, a translator of Henry Miller and Jack Kerouac, remained an activist-intellectual throughout his life. He was wary of cities, opposed to industrialization and consumer culture. In 1954 he moved to Milan to work as an editor at Feltrinelli. The experience alienated him utterly but inspired his most successful work, a novel called *La vita agra* (published in English as *It's a Hard Life*). It is a bilious portrait of that city's bohemian intelligentsia. The original title of 'The Streetwalker', also set in Milan, is '*Il Peripatetico*', the title story of a posthumous 1976 collection that gathered together, for the first time, various short stories previously published in newspapers, magazines and assorted anthologies. The title alludes to the Ancient Greek school of philosophy, but the title in Italian has a double meaning: a '*peripatetica*' is also a term for a prostitute. One key to appreciating the story is knowing about the Merlin Law of 1958, which made brothels illegal in Italy. Bianciardi died of complications from alcohol. His final novel, *Garibaldi* – a fictional portrait intended to render Italy's legendary general more 'human' – was published a year after his death.

The Streetwalker

Translated by Ann Goldstein

When I can, I make a small financial contribution to the friends of family planning. It's unsung, deserving work, which should be encouraged. Dr Trabattoni and the others have nothing to gain, in a country like ours, and everything to lose. And yet there they are, and for a laughable fee one can always simply walk into their clinics, where they give advice and medical assistance. Of course, you'd need very different means, and very different advertising, to properly solve the problem of birth control.

In Italy today – or, rather, in that tiny fraction of Italy that knows about and practises birth control – there are basically three methods of contraception. The physiological method, also called the rhythm method, or, popularly, the Ogino-Knaus rule (from the names of the two scientists, a Japanese and a German, who discovered it). Once you've established that the woman has phases of fertility and phases of sterility every month, you try to distinguish the cyclical start of the former and abstain from sexual relations until it's over.

It's a method that even the ecclesiastical authorities tolerate (without, naturally, wanting excessive publicity about it), and it's also, in theory, the healthiest. In theory: in practice, ovulation (as in fact the 'fertile period' is called) varies greatly from person to person and is influenced by both external and internal factors – for example, by the change of seasons, body temperature, even mood – and nothing prohibits it from occurring not once, but twice in the same month.

Certain clever gynaecologists, I no longer remember whether American or Swedish, would even like to name the maternity ward of their clinic after Ogino and Knaus, to indicate how many new births owe their good fortune (?) to those famous scientists. My son Augusto, born in 1948, is

415

of that batch. We married young, Viola and I, and at the time knew very little about such things.

The chemical method seems to be more secure: as everyone knows, sperm prosper in an alkaline habitat and, on the contrary, react negatively when they find themselves in the presence of acids. So one has only to create an acidic internal environment (through special foam-generating suppositories) to kill or at least neutralize the sperm. The inconveniences are obvious: you feel the acidity, and not pleasantly, on the mucosa of the glans and especially in the balanopreputial sulcus.

Finally, there is the mechanical method: placing a pure and simple barrier between the sperm and the fertilizable egg. The barrier can be positioned either directly at the opening of the urethra (that is, using the common rubber *condom*) or in front of the cervix, using the diaphragm: it's a disc, also made of rubber, with a diameter of eight centimetres and a reinforced edge, which, with an adroit manoeuvre, is suspended between the pelvic bone and the muscles of the anal sphincter, in such a way as to entirely block the mouth of the uterus. Best to dampen the diaphragm with a spermicidal substance when it's inserted, as a guarantee against the possible porousness of the rubber. At first, to position it, the woman will likely resort to a special little plastic rod, jointed and serrated; then she'll be able to do it using just her fingers.

In everyone's opinion, the diaphragm (hardly noticeable after a short period of adjustment) is by far preferable to the *condom*, which is annoying and, let's face it, humiliating. But a doctor has to measure the position and angle of the woman's cervix, the contractibility of the striated muscles, the relative angle of the vaginal duct. Otherwise the diaphragm may not form a perfect seal, as, for example, in the case of my second-born, Cesare. My son was born in 1950, and my wife, Viola, accepted the new pregnancy with the tacit submissiveness that is her most admirable gift.

Her eyes turn soft and moist, her body is fuller, her skin clear: I have to say that she becomes beautiful. The trouble begins later, around the seventh month, when she loses her shape, along with her serenity: she's no longer a woman but an animal, a plant that Mother Nature destined for procreation, and then she stays in bed, with the meek, vacant gaze of a sheep, and waits, waits to expel the infant, nurse it, clean it, cradle it in her arms.

Tiberius, the third-born, came into the world by mistake. It was in 1954, a Saturday evening when Cesare and Augusto were spending the night at their grandparents', and we decided, on the spur of the moment, to spend the weekend out of town, stopping in the first motel we found on the road to the lakes. Viola had left her faithful diaphragm in the medicine chest, but the evening was beautiful, the wine light, pale and sparkling, and I didn't manage to pull out. The pregnancy was smooth, as always: in the seventh month Viola fell into lethargy – lethargy, so to speak, of course: she ate, slept, took walks – and sent me to sleep in the guest room, so she wouldn't bother me in the night, she said. Indeed, when she's expecting a child, she's always hot at night and wants the window open and scarcely a blanket on the bed.

Now, I love my wife, who is a wonderful, calm woman, who never asks where I'm going or why, even if I come home after ten at night. I know wives of others, meddling, capricious, tiresome, always ready to criticize, ask questions and so on. Not Viola: especially when she's pregnant, she thinks about the children, about what's to come, about the house and that's it. That's precisely the situation now she's expecting the fourth, and I have a vague suspicion that this time she did it on purpose – she took out the diaphragm.

On the other hand, what am I to do? Honestly, I think I'm a worker. The antiquarian bookshop is my father's and, no doubt about it, he's the one who built it up. From his father, my grandfather, he inherited little more than a stall in Piazzale Nord. My grandfather – it's not a figure of speech – arrived from Pontremoli with a basket of used books. For years he lived on chick-pea pancakes and drank water from the fountain, and he gradually put down roots in the metropolis, which was just then start-ing to expand. He and my father deserve credit, agreed, but you have to acknowledge that without what I contributed to the business myself we wouldn't be the best-known antiquarian bookshop in Lombardy today.

All the Milanese collectors seek us out, who are more numerous than you might think, and people write from all over Italy. Modesty aside, I was the one who taught my father that a nose for the business isn't enough, that it takes a minimal cultural framework as well: ranging from the plain old Piedmontese editions of Bona, and the versatile little volumes of Le Monnier, with their pink covers, all the way up to truly rare pieces. I have about a dozen books from the sixteenth century, sixty Aldine books, a good thirty-seven of which have the original dolphin-and-anchor printer's mark. I have Abramo Hortel's *Imago Mundi*, a marvellous atlas from the late sixteenth century. My father wanted to take it apart and sell the maps individually. In fact, five or six years ago it was very fashionable to have, as decor, old maps put into frames. I was against it, and I was right. Today I've been offered upward of four hundred thousand lire for that *Imago mundi*, but even now I can't make up my mind to sell it, because every now and then I like to sit and look through it.

In the morning I always get up at seven, and an hour later I'm in the shop, before my four salespeople, before the woman who does the accounts. My father sometimes comes by and sometimes he doesn't, and I can't blame him: he's seventy, and deserves a break. But, for his part, he should also recognize that I keep the business going and, if nothing else, add an '& Son' to the business name. He has me on a salary – a good one, moreover – but he doesn't give me any share in the profits. I leave at six every night, except on Tuesdays and Fridays, when I know that the important customers come by, the ones you have to tend to personally. So it's not at all an easy life, even though I don't lack comforts that my grandfather certainly didn't have: a car, a nice house, two weeks of vacation a year, a seasonal outing to the Frankfurt Book Fair, for business but also pleasure.

I'm not a Catholic, even though my parents had me baptized (I could, in good conscience, declare that 'I don't remember the event'), and even though my three sons were baptized: to keep the peace, because it's what Viola and my parents and my in-laws want. My point is, I don't have the sense of sin that plagues Catholics. And I'm obviously a man of my time, by which I mean prey to the tensions and suggestions – contradictory, of course – of our age. Certainly I feel the influence of advertising, all the more pernicious the more subtle and clever it is. Now, the most widely advertised 'item' in Italy today is, precisely, sex. Literature, cinema, fashion and custom impose it on us continuously. My natural inclination to give in completes the picture.

So without regrets and without complexes, one fine day I made up my mind and telephoned the number a friend had given me. I had only to mention his name, and the female voice, at the other end, invited me to appear, that very evening at five, in an establishment in the neighbourhood of Via Archimede, in the name of a certain Armida Ceccarelli, renter of rooms by profession. She was a woman of around fifty, jovial and still attractive. She welcomed me politely and immediately led me into the living room, where the girl, who said she was called Milly, was watching television.

It was a Thursday afternoon, and so *Passport*, an English lesson with Jole Giannini, was on. I remember that the screen showed a mock-up of a green-grocer, and the professor was reeling off the various names. 'Beans,' she said in perfect English. 'Peas, cucumbers, onions, garlic, avocado, artichoke.' It occurred to me that *articiocco* is a term for *carciofo*, artichoke, widespread in various northern dialects, in an area, perhaps, of Lombard contamination. But I wasn't sure and resolved to ask confirmation from a friend and customer, a philologist.

The girl, Milly, was watching, interested, then Signora Armida returned with two small Turkish towels, handed them to us, and asked if we wanted to make ourselves at home, pointing to the door of her bedroom. The cost was ten thousand lire. Not bad. I realized later that half the amount went to the girl, half to the landlady. Before she left, Armida urged me to come again soon.

After that I returned several times to the Via Archimede neighbourhood, always after calling to make an appointment. I ended up becoming friendly with the signora, who recounted her troubles – her widowhood, her rheumatic pains, her gossiping and nosy neighbours, the demands and hang-ups of certain girls. For my part, I managed to tell her my tastes, because I like women who are a bit short and plump, with curves in the right places, in other words. And I have to say that the signora always tried to please me and that we always got along until the day I read in the newspapers of a police raid at that address in the Via Archimede neighbourhood: they had jailed Armida Ceccarelli and also a Gennaro Lo Cicero, twenty-eight, her lover and business partner in the exploitation of the prostitution of others: under the Merlin Law it's up to seven years flat. After that, I never heard about Signora Armida again.

But in Milan it's not hard to find another solution, so already, after a few weeks, I had another address, in the Viale Bianca di Savoia neighbourhood (an area I know because I went there once to put in some ads in the popular magazine *Epoca*), and a meeting with Signora Andreina. I never learned her surname and the number doesn't appear in the telephone book. Anyway, there, too, it was ten thousand lire each time, half, as always, to the girl, and half to the landlady.

Now, I usually go once a week, and that adds up to forty thousand lire a month. I don't deny that the madam has the right to take care of her own affairs, but I think that the right to look after my interests is up to me. So, I thought, if I could cut the expense of the five thousand lire I give Signora Andreina and spend only five thousand on the girl, I would save twenty thousand lire every month, which I could use to rent a pied-à-terre somewhere. In fact I found one, with two rooms, for fifteen thousand a month, which I shared with a friend: even including the expenses for the cleaning woman, electricity and heat, it came to no more than ten thousand a month, and, once the minor expenses of setting things up were paid off, there was still money left over.

So when at Signora Andreina's I met a certain Linda, a girl of about twenty-five who worked as an operator at Stipel, the telephone company, whom I liked, and who also seemed to me intelligent, I asked for her number, and we agreed to meet outside. With her I inaugurated the pied-à-terre in the Bianca di Savoia neighbourhood: I had a record player there and a small bar, so that we could get in the mood first with a drink and a slow foxtrot.

I like to start by taking the woman standing up, which is uncomfortable but exciting. We dance a little, then when I feel ready I break away and untie my shoes, while she takes off her dress. But I want to take off the slip or the girdle myself. I tell her: 'Hold on, little girl. Let me do it,' and I unhook her bra. Then I start to take her like that, standing up. Then I break away again and finish undressing, lie on the bed, invite her discreetly to take over, but not for long, because I like intercourse best. I tuck the five thousand lire in her purse while she's washing up in the other room.

With Linda, the telephone operator from Stipel, there was the beginning of an affair. One Thursday she was free, and since I had called her for the usual appointment she asked me to take her in the car to buy a few things and do some errands. It was June, and she was already planning her next vacation, and wanted to buy a bikini, a straw bag, sandals and other things I no longer remember. I drove, and we looked in several boutiques, and she even asked my opinion, before choosing the suit. We agreed that the one with white and green polka dots would look good. But there was no way to try it on, because the fitting room was occupied by a fat lady, so the salesgirl agreed to let us take the bathing suit home. If it fits when she tries it, she said, you can pay tomorrow, no trouble.

We went back to the neighbourhood of Bianca di Savoia so that she could try it on. It was very entertaining: I began listening to Rachmaninov in the other room, while Linda changed, and suddenly she appeared before me in bathing suit and sandals, hips swaying; she took off Rachmaninov, put on a cha-cha she liked, and started dancing, just as she was. Then she had a drink, got excited, and I had the sensation that this time she had a real orgasm. I told a friend, but he's a sceptical type, and he responded that maybe the wetness I'd felt was only the acid-foam-producing suppository, inserted for contraceptive purposes before the sex act. Actually I had an inflammation in the glans afterward, which would confirm my friend's hypothesis, but it was still a satisfying experience.

We decided to go away for a weekend together, as I'd once done with my wife, Viola, and we spent Saturday night in the same motel on the road to the lakes. Thus I was able to talk to Linda and get to know her a little better. She wasn't happy with her job at Stipel, she said, especially because of a female supervisor who was old and sour, who made fun of her, blamed her for the delays in service and the malfunctions and the customers' complaints. But, she added, now she was becoming friendly with a big shot there at Stipel, a certain Manera, fifty and married, and thanks to him she would find a way of getting even with that nasty old maid.

She had talked to me about Manera at other times, partly admiring, partly mocking. Because he had strange tastes: for example, he would invite two girls to his house, besides Linda, have them strip and line up, crouching, under the window, between the wall and the curtain, so that only their rear ends were visible, sticking out. Then he'd enter, in tailcoat and striped trousers, a bowler on his head, parade past the bottoms with short steps, and, taking off his hat, say: 'Hello, little asses!'

Apart from that he was a gentleman, polite and lavish in his spending. He had even taken her with him to Campione, where they gambled until three in the morning. 'Why don't we go, too?' Linda asked me one night. 'Why don't we spend a *westend* in Campione?' I didn't even correct her, and after that I stopped calling her, because I am certainly not the type to throw money away on the green baize, which seems to me in fact shameful and stupid.

Because he isn't wrong, that friend of mine, when he says that I'm still basically a man from Pontremoli, that I haven't forgotten how my grandfather and my father built up this little fortune, book by book, lira by lira, living on chick-pea pancakes and water from the fountain. In fact, every so often I get in the car and make the trip: it's a lovely drive, below Monte Cisa and through the narrow valley, up to the old houses of Pontremoli, along the river. Above all, there's always a chance you might find something, rummaging through the shops of the secondhand-book sellers. Or when they give the prize, and then publishers, writers and cultural figures come to Pontremoli, most of them from Milan. I spent a couple of holidays right nearby, at the quiet little beach of Bocca di Magra, which Elio Vittorini and the critic Giansiro Ferrata[1] discovered after the other war.

Now I have to tell about one evening when, passing near Largo Cairoli, I was stopped by a flashy hooker, and I went up to her room with her. After the sex act we chatted a little – she was a mature but talkative woman – and so I learned that she had actually moved from Pontremoli, after this war, and had settled with her husband in Milan. Thanks to her work, and saving, she had managed to set up a small apartment in the Porta Ticinese neighbourhood, and now she continued to work, just to finish making the payments on the furniture and the sewing machine. She explained what the bedroom was like, the armoire with three mirrors and the marble-topped night table. She invited me to come and visit her, promising that for the occasion she would organize some 'numbers'.

That was the word she used, and, curious, I telephoned her one day and made an appointment for seven. It was a nice bourgeois apartment, well kept, clean, with the bathroom tidy and a small poodle and the coffee-pot always ready in the kitchen.

'Oh, here we drink coffee from morning to night,' said this woman from Pontremoli, whose name was Signora Anna. The room was as she had described it: she showed me a book of French pornographic photographs, and left me there while she phoned the neighbour upstairs, who was to take part in the famous 'number'. After that I returned several times to Signora Anna, who arranged the number, always calling on a different friend. Between the two of them they wanted ten thousand lire, and that was fine with me. Usually Anna participated only in the foreplay, then when she saw that we were getting into it she got dressed, leaving to the other the responsibility of finishing the job, and she returned near the end to change the sheets. I was very happy with this arrangement, and I even gave her the phone number of the bookshop, so that she could notify me. One evening around seven she called.

'Pierclaudio,' she said (in fact, my name is Pierclaudio), 'there's a brand-new model.'

'What sort of model?' I said, not having understood right away.

'A niece of mine. Seventeen years old. A real jewel.'

'Really?'

'So we'll see you?'

And we made an appointment for the next day. The niece, named Rita, was really sweet, slender, blonde, modest in her printed calico house dress. We went to the room together. Anna helped the niece undress, showed her off front and back, praising her features, then left us. Meanwhile I, too, had undressed and was lying on the bed. I nodded to her to join me. When she was at the foot of the bed, and had already put one knee up (because women get in bed knees first – I don't know if you've ever noticed), she stopped and said:

'Would you like to have some fun or should we move on to the material act right away?'

I was a little puzzled, and I wondered if Rita had said 'material act' or 'material fact'.

I said: 'What?'

'No, I meant, do you want us to do something material right away or should I entertain you?'

After a while I was about to enter her, but she interrupted me again. 'Excuse me,' she said and naked as she was went to the door, opened it and called out:

'Mammaaa!' and then again: 'Mammiiina! Mammina, the rubber!'

Anna arrived, smiling, holding the envelope with the rubber, put the head into it, asked me if everything was all right, explained to me that Rita, her niece, was afraid, so young, of getting pregnant and losing her figure. I must admit that I was disappointed, partly because, given Rita's youth and freshness, Anna, with the rubber, wanted fifteen thousand lire instead

423

of the usual ten, and she had added nothing of her own. I didn't ask the girl if Anna was her aunt or, rather, her mother; anyway I never went back. Anna called me a few more times, but I always declined the appointment, making up an excuse, and now she, too, has stopped calling.

Finally she got it, that business is business, it's true, but I, too, have to think of my interests, and I can't spend fifteen thousand lire for a girl, as young as you like, but cold as a fish, and afraid of getting pregnant besides. No one understands that fear better than I do, but, on the other hand, if a woman wants ten or fifteen thousand lire for a single sex act, which lasts at most half an hour, all-inclusive, she ought to run some risk, no?

Call girls definitely have some advantages certainly. They are almost always cute and young, clean and probably healthy (we men, too, have to run a slight risk, I'll admit). But usually you have to take them sight unseen, trusting the taste of the madam. Certainly, after you've met one you liked, you can return to her; but the trouble is that these madams don't like to keep the same women around all the time. Partly because the client likes novelty, partly because after a while two women always end up quarrelling – always for some foolish reason, you know how women are – and then a girl who's offended is quick to blow the whistle, or get someone else to blow the whistle, to the police. Behind the girl there's always a man – a 'boyfriend', they say – and it's he who goads her to go to the police when the madam has done a real or apparent wrong. Anyway, it's well known that with the new Merlin Law the one who gets caught is the madam/pimp, never the girl.

Then, there are the neighbours, who are envious and gossipy, and the concierges, generally female, who are stuck in the Hapsburg era and act like spies. If they always see the same woman going up the stairs, they begin to talk, and the rumour sooner or later reaches the right person. So the madam also makes sure to move house periodically, but stays in the same neighbourhood, so that, for a tip, she can keep her old telephone number. Thus the clientele remains the same, on the whole, but the girls change often, and, since they never go more than two or three times with the same man, on the one hand, they have no way of gaining real professional experience; on the other, they're not concerned with satisfying their partner, and always try to hurry the session along.

Anyway, satisfied or not, the man won't turn up again tomorrow, and tomorrow his neighbour will fall for the same scam, let's call it that. It's a vicious cycle of professional decline: certain attentions, certain considerations, that you could count on in the old brothels have become a memory of the past. In fact, I was in favour of the Merlin Law, and during the debate in Venice that accompanied the showing of *Adua and Her Friends*[2] I stood up to speak in favour of that honourable lady, whose tenacity was highly commendable.

It's unjust and obscene that in a country with a republican and democratic constitution, founded on work and not on exploitation, it is the government that exploits prostitutes. Other countries, truly civilized ones, have long since abolished regulation, both of brothels and the other kind, which, disguised as a health inspection, registered streetwalkers and exposed them to the continual risk of a police round-up. Those round-ups were almost as offensive as the brothels.

Just arguments, all, and sacrosanct, and I am ready to defend them even now. And don't say to me: 'What will our soldiers do?' People who say that couldn't care less about how the soldier will eat, dress, live or about his pay and his rations. And don't tell me that regulated prostitution was a social service, either. Because if you truly want to talk about a social service, then, *per absurdum*, let's organize obligatory, forced prostitution, for all women older than twenty-one – all of them, indiscriminately, none excluded.

They'll say that not all women older than twenty-one, indiscriminately, feel like being prostitutes. And I will answer that not all men of that age feel like being soldiers, either, and yet they certainly do it, since the social need, in fact the national and patriotic need, for military service is acknowledged.

They'll also say that the prostitute's trade (giving oneself, for compensation, to the first comer) isn't noble. And I'd respond that the soldier's trade (killing, without compensation, the first comer) doesn't seem noble, either. In other words, I supported and I support the Merlin Law, even if I see its limitations and deficiencies. Which are basically two.

First: the higher prices. When brothels existed, two hundred and fifty lire was on average enough for a satisfying connection (at least for youthful clients, who ejaculate easily). Today the same thing, and complicated by the hassle of hotels etc., costs no less than three thousand lire. The unemployed man, the soldier (this time, yes), and the humble factory worker have no way of getting off for less. And one could even go so far as to say this: that the rise in prices has caused an increase in pederasty, and the manifestations of this have spread *à ciel ouvert*, in public places.

Anyone who goes to the city park, or certain clearings on the outskirts, near the stadium or the reservoir, knows that decrepit prostitutes wander in those areas; they're older than sixty, almost horrendous to look at, and for five hundred lire they service the less prosperous client, behind a plane tree, in the shelter of a wall, against an escarpment. Now, the men who frequent these old hookers obviously seek nothing more than seminal evacuation. If that's their purpose, it's hard to see what real difference there is between achieving it with the prostitute and giving in to some pederast. (We could add, to the choices, getting off autonomously, by masturbating: but that isn't completely true, as I could explain if I had more space.)

In fact, rather than the old streetwalker, who still costs five hundred lire, the seminal evacuator might even prefer the rapid contact with the pederast, who is willing to pay him. Not much, because the pederast is usually a crafty, cheap man, but he does pay.

Second: the decline of the profession. We've seen how fleeting and precarious the human relation between client and call girl is. The girl has neither the time, nor the way, nor the will to refine the quality of her performances. As for high-class prostitutes, their main goal is to establish as good a price as possible: the man who is unprepared, or even just a little shy, will feel that he can't refuse five thousand lire. The woman will then equivocate about the price of the room. Once the act is over and he's gone down with the girl to the front desk, the client, who had understood that everything, room and service, was included, all together, in the five thousand lire, will hear her innocently ask him to pay for the room. He doesn't have the courage to argue in front of the desk clerk, who is looking at him with a single sarcastic eye. So he pays.

The act itself, which was supposed to be intercourse – and for this the client has agreed on a price – becomes an operation of emptying the epididymis as rapidly as possible. Sometimes it makes you think that if the prostitutes knew by what means the torturers of the SS extracted seminal liquid from the testicles of their victims, exhausted by malnutrition and ill-treatment, to be used for who knows what laboratory experiments – if prostitutes, I repeat, knew that, they wouldn't hesitate to do likewise.

Even the ones who are reputedly more skilled, and during the hurried act fake excitement and orgasm, and moan, and mumble, will open their mouth – note – only to demand and stimulate a rapid ejaculation. Thus young clients don't learn properly; in their turn they have neither the will nor the imagination necessary to ask for a larger and more complete sexual service, and the vicious circle drags on, who knows since when and who knows until when.

There is a remedy: not, certainly, a return to the old brothels, which I continue to disapprove of and condemn, but, instead, an effort to spread a healthier sexual morality in Italy. To preach clearer and more open relations between man and woman, from puberty, liberalize the mentality of both young men and young women, teach them that a sexual relationship is a mutual joy and that as such it should be practised and granted freely. All I ask is not to have to pay that ten thousand lire every time.

But these are debates, the goal is quite far off, and, given the way the wind blows, the worst is to be expected. I've tried to do what I could, in the current conditions and with current means. For example, establish a steady relation with a young call girl, setting a fixed price in advance, cultivating her, so to speak, getting her to understand my demands (which are, more or less, the demands of an average Italian client), educating her, in other words, in her trade. A vile trade, someone will say. But come on, read what Croce writes about it! The concept of a trade entails the beginning of an economy, and so is, in its sphere, a value. It produces a value, as a trade, and so, in the economic sphere, it's neither reputable nor disreputable, neither reprehensible nor commendable.

But this type of behaviour also includes some inevitable risks. Every human relationship requires participation, in effect, commitment, dedication, beyond giving and receiving. To put it simply, I should dedicate myself (member, feelings, thoughts) to the call girl. Absurd though it may seem, I sincerely tried that, too. With Pinuccia, for example: the madam called her Pinuccia, while she insisted on being called Giusi.

After sex this Pinuccia, or Giusi, went to the bidet and sang the song that goes:

From the cliff, gleaming and white,
I talk to the sea about you every night
And every night you entrust to the sea
Thoughts of love for me.

It's a song I like, so I followed with my voice, which is fairly well trained. She said:
'You like that song?'
She spoke with a northern Emilia accent, maybe from *Piatzenza*, as they say in her town: stashion of Piatzenza, don't crosh the tracks. And she continued, in her drawl, to explain to me that she liked the song, but not sung by Sergio Bruni – handsome profile, that Bruni, he hadn't booed Villa, in Naples, he had paid his thugs to boo Villa, but now he had to pay some nice millions, to Villa, who had sued him.[3]
And she had the courage to ask me, I who am of Tuscan-Ligurian lineage, transplanted to Milan, used to dealing with respectable, educated people, priding myself on speaking an unaccented Italian: 'But you, you're maybe a hick from the south?'
Now, I say, how can one create a satisfying human relationship with a dog-faced woman like that? I tried to get close again to my wife, Viola, but there, too . . . Above all, she demands that copulation take place in the pitch-dark, *more canonico et interposito lino*. That is, she doesn't take off her nightgown and she lies there, always lies there. And everything has to be resolved in a quarter of an hour at most, because she has to sleep afterward, and read before, and see to the house and the children for the rest of the day. All things considered, I really don't know which way to turn. The other night I was overcome by despair, my nerves were tense, my blood was pulsing, and I had to do something.
As twilight falls, Viale Maino is already crowded with streetwalkers, standing at their posts, waiting for cars. And I drove up and down the entire avenue three times. At first sight, only an embarrassment of riches. But in reality . . .
For example, the one who kept slightly to the shadows, away from the

street light, seemed pretty. But can one, honestly, venture to nod to a woman standing in the shadows? What if later, in the light, she reveals some outrageous physical defect? Others remained clearly visible: one, with her coat open, showed the swell of her breasts, which seemed promising. But can one trust what one sees of breasts with the shirt on? Who protects us from the tricks of bras, corsets, girdles, elastics and straps that, once released, often reveal devastation?

Another had a figure that seemed to me, all in all, acceptable, but her face was obtuse and hostile, so I preferred not to signal to her. I drove slowly, staying near the edge of the pavement, three times up and down. But, however slowly you go, there's no way of looking carefully, of reflecting on the pros and cons, of making a considered decision. These things are done better on foot. So I returned to Via Borgogna, parked the car, glanced at the photographs outside the Maschere, where they do stripteases, traversed the porticoes, crossed the temporary bridge that passes over the excavation for the metro in Piazza San Babila, and arrived at the porticoes of the Corso.

The traffic is on a detour there, too, because of the metro, and since at that hour the creak of the buckets and the breathing of the cement mixers ceases, I heard no more than the tapping heels of people walking. Women walk rapidly, alert and sullen, all alike, whether they're hookers or not. But I know how to distinguish them: that one, for example, maybe would have the face, but besides her purse she's carrying a package, so she isn't. The rule doesn't admit exceptions: package plus purse – to be excluded. Also a book, a magazine, a Sunday supplement. The hooker on the job has always and only the small purse.

Not only: while others keep their eyes fixed straight ahead and head high, when a prostitute meets up with you she turns her gaze slightly and gestures with her head. In this way I picked out three or four. One tall, shapely, with a shiny black leather coat; another smaller and round, plump, the way I like, with teased hair and a flared skirt; a third very thin and long, with a horsey face.

I followed the small one; she noticed and slipped off along Via Agnello. She stopped in front of a shop window and when I was close she said immediately, 'Will you give me ten thousand?' I kept going, and from Via San Paolo arrived again at the porticoes. There I immediately found a buxom brunette who advanced at a comfortable pace, with a nice smile.

She looked at me, and I immediately said 'Good evening, Miss.' She turned, faced me and tried to respond, but with gestures more than with her voice. From her throat issued a faint, dull sound, 'Uuuh, uuuuh,' and yet she didn't abandon her friendly smile. She held her hand open, as if to say five thousand. 'Eeeh, annn, eh!' she said again.

I was stunned, in disbelief that a deaf-mute could be a streetwalker in the centre of Milan. I turned on my heels and went back over the bridge, having decided to get in the car and go home. But the car wasn't there. I retraced all of Via Borgogna, went back, turned on to the side street, went as far as the Rivoli cinema, asked the parking attendant, but he didn't even answer, because I leave the car in authorized spaces only, and that wasn't one. In other words, it had been stolen.

I went into a bar, asked for a phone token, dialled the number of the police station in the area. A blonde at the counter was looking at me, but I had other things on my mind. A southern voice answered, asking for the number of the licence plate, and assuring me that they would investigate. But for now all I could do was go home.

There was no one left on the Corso at that dead hour between eight and nine, when people are having dinner and haven't yet emerged for the evening's entertainment. Only the streetwalkers are out, bolder now, hips swaying, majestic as galleons. That night they were even humming; a couple spoke to me but I kept going. The windows of Rinascente, the Galleria: in front of the cafés some painted women, sitting with their knees on display. La Scala, with the usual merry-go-round of trams, taxis, cars.

But I didn't feel like waiting for the tram on the narrow traffic island, in line with motionless, tense people. Trams went by, full of tired and drawn faces. I kept walking on Via Verdi, turned into Monte di Pietà, then along Via Cusani. Going off to the left was Via Rovello, with the Piccolo Teatro (to which I have a subscription) at the end and in the middle the regular prostitutes, the usual handful, the same for the past ten years, in position, like vultures. Since at that point the street is dark, they solicit you out loud, and if you don't answer they insult you. I passed by almost at a run.

Maybe in that bar in Largo Cairoli . . . But there was no one. I stood there a while, looking at the posters outside the Olimpia, the photos at Le Roi, then I headed towards the castle. Farther on, the gates of the park were locked, and around it, at regular intervals, other women loiter. There are some pretty ones, and I didn't fail to look at them, and let them know I was looking. But none answered: in that area there are no hotels nearby, so the streetwalkers accept only clients with cars.

I thought of my car, stolen, so without hesitation I cut across towards the bridge over the Ferrovie Nord tracks. There are always some young people in blue jeans and soldiers loitering there, talking and laughing. But as soon as they saw me they went silent and began to look at me. I seemed to hear a *psst–psst*. I went down the steps with my heart in my throat, and now I was in Via Venti Settembre. At one time certain hookers used to be stationed there, but I noticed that after the murder of Maria Maglia, who worked precisely in that area, they don't stick around after dark.

My feet began to hurt and a cold wind had risen. I was worried about my sinusitis, but still I kept walking. After the barracks on Via Mascheroni there is a dark avenue that borders the dirt road next to Leone XIII, a school for priests; it also has a large theatre that shows movie-club films (I've been a few times, because Father Nazzareno Taddei is an intelligent person, I'm the first to acknowledge it). And right there are thousand-lire women, who usually get in the car but will also agree to follow you on to the dirt road beyond the barbed-wire fence, which is broken in one spot.

I went with a fifty-four-year-old (so she told me) and we had a quickie against the wall of the Leone. Since shadows were passing, perhaps voyeurs, I preferred that she do everything, covering her head with an edge of my raincoat. My legs were shaking when I finally got home. That evening my mother-in-law and my mother had come to visit Viola, who is expecting the happy event any day now. They had already had dinner, and when I sat down in front of the bowl of cold soup, they continued their conversation. I thought it best not to say a word, for now, about the stolen car. They seemed happy and excited, all three of them.

They asked my opinion: whether it made sense to call the fourth-born Tito, and to combine the child's baptism with Cesarino's First Communion.

'Il peripatetico'
First published in the anthology *L'amore in Italia: antologia di racconti italiani* (Sugar, 1961) and later included in *Il peripatetico e altre storie* (Rizzoli, 1976).

ANNA BANTI
1895–1985

She was born in Florence with the name Lucia Maria Pergentina Lopresti. In 1916 she sent Roberto Longhi, an art historian who was her teacher in high school, a letter signed 'Anna Banti', the name of a relative who intrigued her. The following year she took part in an initiative to fabricate toys made in Italy, an alternative to German imports. These creations were also signed 'Anna Banti'. She gained a degree in art history and began teaching and publishing essays on art. In 1924 she married Longhi, who was to establish himself as a legendary connoisseur, critic and scholar of Italian painting. In 1930 she sent a short story by 'Anna Banti' to a magazine contest. She explained her decision: 'I was Roberto Longhi's wife and I didn't want to expose myself or him with that name. Nor did I want to use my childhood name . . . so I chose Anna Banti, which is my real name, given to me neither by my family nor my husband.' Thus was born Anna Banti, author of numerous novels, story collections and critical works whose official profession remained 'housewife'. Hers was a twinned passion for art and literature. She wrote biographies of Claude Monet, Fra Angelico and Matilde Serao, the first Italian woman to found and direct a major newspaper. *Artemisia*, her best-known novel, is about the Renaissance painter Artemisia Gentileschi, whose talent flourished when women had no place in the art world. An enthusiastic translator from both French and English, Banti brought works by Virginia Woolf, William Makepeace Thackeray, Jane Austen and Colette into Italian. In 1952 she won the Viareggio Prize for the collection *Le donne muoiono* (The Women Are Dying). This story, about a nameless woman, appeared in her last collection. Composed in the third person, but palpably autobiographical, it is essential to understanding Banti's attitude – divided and doubled – towards her creative formation, her words, herself.

Miss

Translated by Jenny McPhee

Twenty-three years old seemed ancient to her, as if the sun were already setting on her life. Other people, however, didn't see it that way. So for decorum's sake, and because she was well mannered, she acted as if she were still eighteen, her laughter disguising how terribly old she truly felt. She had already been quite alarmed when, as soon as she turned twenty, her name – the one she had been baptized with and used in childhood – was replaced, both at home and elsewhere, by 'Miss'. It was the *toga praetexta* worn by unmarried girls until . . . she shrugged off the alternative, but knew, at least in the eyes of others, that she would be unable to avoid her candidature for this 'promotion'. And it greatly disturbed her.

Her ally was a troubled passion: desired, consented to, abstractly imperious. One does not love in order to dominate and conquer life – life being just a silent sequence of woes, interrupted, but not mitigated, by ephemeral sparks of distressing exaltation. Miracles were rare, yet they did happen – the approaching step of her Beloved seemed to be one. In fact, here he is, deigning to exist. For an hour – or for a few minutes – they take a walk together, words flowing between them, but then perhaps he's a bit thoughtless and his words hit her straight in the heart, stab her even, but it doesn't matter, blood coagulates. Like a terrified soldier pretending to be brave, she grows rigid with reserve.

It could not, and did not, last. What are three years of a rapidly beating heart, of abandoned hopes, of constant disillusionment? A flash of lightning. Her bitterest ordeal, very nearly unbearable, was when convalescing she'd hoped that by appearing so delicately beautiful to him, with her feverish eyes and wan complexion, he would become tender towards her. Before going out, she had looked at herself in the mirror – a shepherdess, wearing an aquamarine dress that made her seem transparent, and a broad-brimmed straw hat blooming with violets. A fiasco. The Adored One was frowning and impatient. It's over, she said to herself, fighting back stinging tears; her voice – a violin, according to university friends – babbling away in an attempt to casually avoid the ever-present and catastrophic threat of a permanent goodbye. But apparently today he is in a hurry, so the the goodbye is quick but not definitive. Her parched lips refuse to open even to utter a timid 'See you tomorrow'; and then she is alone, the light silk of her dress weighing upon her like lead, her fever back.

A slow summer of separation, a rare letter now and again, then final exams, graduation ('Ah, yes, I had forgotten I graduated'). This display of indifference to academic affairs is *de rigueur.* He stops to light a cigarette, inhales: 'Congratulations.' Why bother taking another walk together? Ah, here it is: 'You must do me a favour. I have been given a Maltese puppy and promised him to my friends as a Christmas present. Would you look after him for a couple of months? You might even have fun. He's cute.'

In a drawer, she found an old postcard-sized photograph, a document of an almost majestic unhappiness, the heraldic undertaking of an accepted defeat. She remembered the empty hours during the autumn in which she was terribly free; it made no difference to her if she stayed home or went out, if she was alone or with a friend. An acquaintance passing through town, a public park, an amateur photographer (who was he?), the latter a necessity because the inevitable is concretized in an image. The acquaintance chattered on unheard; adoring and adored, the puppy, on a leash, followed his temporary mistress with tiny steps. The shadows under the trees favoured, as in a half-sleep, tenuous hopes; perhaps the deal won't stick, to deprive her of the animal would be too cruel. He had said: 'Give him back to me whenever you want, sometime during the week before Christmas.' She'd hoped he'd forget the whole thing; the wretched cling to anything. If he lets me keep Toby, we could meet again, if only to play with the puppy. She knew she was deluding herself, but didn't dare deny herself this little reprieve.

She had sewn Toby a ruff made out of Scottish silk, a kind of Spanish *golilla.* 'Adorable,' people would say, stopping to admire and stroke him. She would never have guessed that those compliments were really a pretext for erotic adventure. She was out of that game, she no longer existed. She had been surprised when the young photographer asked her to pose on that rustic bench ('Just you, please, something for me to remember you by, Miss'). And then she understood: the honour of becoming a stranger's souvenir was the sum of her fate. She'd picked up the puppy and consented meekly to the request. At least in the photograph, she reasoned bittersweetly, the little Maltese dog would be hers forever. She sat down, hugged him to her chest and stared at the trees – the golden leaves, the sun's rays at the very tops of the pines – with an almost religious devotion so as not to forget anything about this already memorable moment. The puppy was not all that mattered to her just then; she sensed that she had arrived at a unique moment of reckoning with herself, a reckoning with the 'Miss' who was about to sign away her future. She seemed to have inadvertently prepared for this ceremony: gone were the usual delicate colours, replaced by wisely appropriate dress, a dark suit trimmed with silk ribbon, almost a guarantee of professional seriousness. Her great mass of hair, however, was gathered beneath a cherry-red velvet turban, the one provocation she had permitted herself. Legs crossed and leaning slightly forward, she holds in her gloved hands the white Maltese, his mug hiding her neck. A disenchanted, slightly ironic smile, barely visible in the impending twilight, wanders across her face and says no to youth. Her lips thin, but do not part to reveal her teeth. From the depths of her wide eyes rises an ominous darkness that hides her emptiness, stills her sadness. 'A masterpiece,' exclaims the photographer. But she had stood up, saying one photo was enough.

Copies of the photograph, including the one she was looking at, were delivered to her just after the worst had happened, adding to her childish sorrow over parting with the puppy. Having dodged it so many times, the lightning bolt of extreme renunciation had finally struck and was now suffocating her. After that final elusive squeeze of her hand ('You're a clever girl, you'll get married'), he had turned his back on her, walked among the crowd, retreated into the distance. She felt she couldn't move, but somehow did, heading very slowly in the opposite direction. Finally, shattered to pieces, she sobbed openly in the streets, shamelessly, eventually entering a church gauchely lit with Christmas candles. In a merciful corner there, she realized to her horror that twenty-three years were few, that many still needed to pass for her to arrive at the end of an average human life – the life that she must live, alone, with dignity and courage, her only redemption. She didn't pray for death, but prayed, for pity's sake, that the time she had left would pass swiftly.

She gradually learned how to ride the waves of her days, as if she had a chronic, but not fatal, illness, her lack of confidence conditioning her thoughts, her studies, her work. Now and again, she would look at the photograph, and one day she made a discovery: indeed, that melancholic damsel really was a beautiful young woman. But this wasn't the issue; that image actually represented the quintessentially eternal 'Miss' – a substitute teacher, later a proper teacher, but always defined by that diminutive label that straddled pathetic and charming, and as she grew older, was even a little ridiculous. Even now, she stubbornly clung to this label – devoid of a first and last name – that society had branded her with. Her memories, secretly stored away (and woe to that sentimental colleague who mentioned them), kept her in a state of permanent adolescence.

Sometimes when she comes early to class and the room's still empty, she leans her forehead against the window. The street the high school is on leads to a piazza where He – she refuses to name him – once lived. Blushing, she remembers the one time she'd entered that rented room dressed in blue and white and he'd said nervously: 'You intimidate me.' In the tiny space of that messy room, and in half an hour of costly spontaneity, the future that awaited her had been born and died. 'Good day, Miss,' one of the eighteen-year-old numbskulls greets her, the first of thirty high-school students who will enter the classroom. Today Petrarch, tomorrow Tacitus, her duties. She, who for years had contented herself with any crumb he left her, and for which she paid dearly, would not die from a lack of love. But the deprivation leads to a terrible serenity. Proudly, making fun of herself, the 'Miss' attends a dance or two, proof that certain dangers don't exist for her. And, in fact, whenever she dances she never looks at her partner, never says a word, but she likes the rhythm, even if she would have preferred to dance alone, inventing steps and moves. As for her reputation for being arrogant, she explains that it's really only shyness, but knows that her timidity is actually an intolerance for banal conversation and clumsy compliments. She often dreams of being forced to marry someone – she had no idea whom – and they meet at the altar where she is unable to dislodge a 'no' that strangles her. When she then awakens with a jolt, she is delighted that her freedom is still secure. If anyone hints that she is in love, she responds disdainfully and denies it completely: how could anyone possibly dare to take the place of Him, the one who had rejected her? This is more or less the reason for her outrage. Her heart shut down, she becomes a little quarrelsome and admits, annoyed, that she is attractive and turns morose when, in spite of herself, she is undermined by a spark of vanity. She is not one to accept a bourgeois marriage proposal whenever asked – such a nice young man and so in love. The word 'Miss' sits like a crown atop her lightly bronzed hair, and woe to anyone who dares touch it. In the meantime, as she trains for a harsh maturity, enough already with anonymous floral homages and silly notes hidden in the pages of borrowed books. Very soon she will be a respectable, old-fashioned old maid. She travels alone, goes to the theatre alone, overcomes ignoble and wretched fears when, going home, she realizes she is being followed. She has no female friends.

How was anyone to know, however, that the thing everyone called 'life' had yet to even begin for her, that destiny would turn everything upsidedown and thrust her into the hands, the clenched hands, of that unforgettable Friend? Happiness is terrible, it leaves you naked, defenceless, anonymous. One Easter morning, the 'Miss' was walking among the columns of the Roman forum, dissolving in the morning air, disintegrating under the sun, amidst the sound of church bells; neither of them offered an explanation or recrimination, the naturalness of this new encounter assuring a perfect congruity that years of ambiguity – oh, how futile! – never succeeded in corroding. Younger at twenty-five than she had been at eighteen, the young woman, who had been so covetous of her own unhappiness, now reveals absolutely no trace or sign of her former self, her wide smile showing bright white teeth, all her pores exuding a steadily ecstatic amazement. Perhaps the Friend says, How beautiful you are, but she doesn't react. She has no interest in comparing herself to any former images of herself now that she is being offered – but she was a little afraid of it – a new name, a new situation, new tools that she didn't know how to use. On her horizon everything is too 'ready', too planned out in advance. It is not easy to get used to being a 'young wife'; it embarrasses her, makes her ashamed. She feels she no longer has any words or actions of her own, that her joyous triumph actually conceals a trap that every so often paralyses her, despite the enchantment of living in the Beloved's home, sitting at his table, certain that every evening, sooner or later, delightedly, she would hear the sound of his key turning in the lock, the sound of his approaching footsteps. A boundless sweetness suffocates her, clouds her eyes and ears, tatters her will. Passivity is dangerous: her life now like that of a sated and playful animal, she's aware of the hidden perils of swathes of free time, her susceptibility to caprice. The acts of love, once nettlesome and shocking, from one day to the next are not only validated, but virtually imposed by a new code. And it greatly disturbs her. Something, then, has changed: for better or for worse? For the better, for the better, she swiftly concludes, but instinctively she hesitates. In fact, the imposition of certain rights seems to her a vile hoax.

Unemployed, she throws herself into the subordinate work of secretarial duties. This is a misguided fallback plan since order, precision, patient study eludes her nature. Her husband – indeed yes! her husband – laughs good-naturedly, corrects the oversights, and she, recognizing her incompetence, hates herself, retreats, proposes that she do even more menial tasks such as typing, filling out forms. What does it matter? Even hidden in a corner she would be happy. It's nice that each day is the same as the next, and abandoning herself to their passing, it's no longer necessary to use her brain. Not that her brain can just stop working: but it wanders aimlessly or ruminates on frivolities, oddities, petty rebellions. Her will oscillates, swinging like a little monkey from tree to tree. Deciding whether or not to cut her long hair – one of her more attractive features – is a profound event. Leaping into the abyss, she returns to practising the piano; the generous Listener is surprised, tells her she's not bad, gives his approval. Suddenly a black cloud appears, the worst of all threats – eventually he's sure to get tired of a companion with no interests or problems. She's too docile, always happy, a silly kitten who romps about his feet.

No use deluding herself. Happiness has extinguished her intelligence and confines her to the role of scheming scrounger. The betrayed 'Miss' seeks revenge. It's impossible to return to her former solitude, reignite her initiative, her appetite for a challenge, her steadfast ambition to prove her overlooked worth. Who have I become? A wife who doesn't argue, attentive to every glance of fierce disapproval, to the shifting moods of a fickle largesse. Basking in the renunciation of decision-making, she no longer knows how to say 'I like that' or 'I don't like that'; she's even unlearned how to choose, her clothes falling on to her as if by magic. Unexpected trips transform her into a small suitcase convenient to the traveller. He knows what is worth seeing and, in his hands, the world opens up, there's nothing to do but listen and applaud. And thus France, England, Holland, the sombre Germany pass by. But suddenly, unexpectedly, something snaps: No, the young wife will not continue on to Berlin. 'I've had enough,' she declares in Munich, as she leaves the Alte Pinakothek and departs alone for Brenner. A troubled night of desolation and remorse. In Verona under a chilly sun, the 'Miss' reappears in front of the bronze door of the Basilica of San Zeno and before the Pisanello fresco in the church of Sant'Anastasia, pale, sad, ghostly, a shadow of herself.

It was an acrimonious trip. The sensation of having betrayed something precious plagued her, but the momentary solitude allowed her to recover some of the clarity that happiness had muddied. 'He who hesitates is lost,' some idiot once said, but actually this was now her situation. Going forward, she could live on her illusions – now that she knows that, from the start, the problems she faced had already been resolved. It was always a question of take it or leave it. So I fooled myself and took the wrong path. But what was my path? A deep dive into my childhood and adolescence and all would be revealed. But she didn't want to risk concluding that if love was by now indispensable, it was insufficient, indeed, unjustifiable. Banish the dreams depleted by doubt, excited by small successes and sometimes by the certainty her goal would be achieved – these ambitions were no longer for her. But at least some autonomous occupation, something she devised for herself, which would salvage her self-esteem, save her from laziness – she contemplated this as the train carried her home, vaguely irritated by, but also vulnerable to the stares she received; alas, the habitual experience of a 'pretty woman'. A job, a job. The most modest, the most humble, as long as it was outside the home and in no way reliant on the fact that she didn't need to earn a living because others 'kept' her; she was 'a kept woman'. Unfortunately, this banal, clichéd definition of who she was today fit her like a glove.

Resuming normal life, she had to hide her determination to get a job no matter what. This was no easy task, since her existence was filled with her obligations to love: the happy and sated animal reappeared. But every day, the clock struck zero. The abeyance painful, she reviewed her possibilities, acerbically and brutally rejecting all opportunities intellectual in nature. She wondered if she shouldn't humble herself and look for manual labour, as many women did in order to support themselves. It was useless to even consider sewing or needlework – she was entirely incapable – but as a young girl she had learned to knit. She wouldn't mind making little sweaters for newborns, booties, scarves, blankets, but there was still the problem of how she would sell these items. Idly wandering through the narrow streets in the centre of the city, she had noticed a small haberdasher's shop displaying exactly these sorts of garments. She passed by the shop repeatedly, and finally, with embarrassment, offered to bring the haberdasher a first sample of her work. She bought pink and blue yarn, then closed herself in her bedroom with the balls of wool and her knitting needles. She knit furiously, terrified that someone would surprise her and think . . . In fact, the maid, seeing her occupied by that unusual activity, had smiled and winked. Obviously, she thought her employer was expecting. Of course, it was a legitimate supposition and not at all out of line, and yet, even expressed by that simple girl, it made her seethe with resentment. She did not want to lie so, instead, firmly denied it with a harsh glare.

The little jacket was soon finished and she considered it a masterpiece, but as soon as she wrapped it up in tissue paper, her heart sank, feeling she had forfeited the last shred of herself: her past as a rigorous intellectual shamed her, condemned as she now was to this petty deception that was also badly paid. Passing her own work off as that of a poor young girl, she had tried to sell it to the haberdasher, a bitter woman who, after sizing her up, refused to do business with her, as if refusing to give alms to a beggar. Having left the awful shop, all she wanted was to get rid of the bundle, which she couldn't even look at, as if it were stolen goods. Her attempt to inadvertently drop the bundle failed; a boy picked it up and gave it back to her with a smile, the delicate pink wool visible through the now ripped tissue paper. A pew in an empty church finally offered a solution, but while in the act she was overcome by a profound longing, as if actually abandoning an infant. She had given no thought to maternity, and even as a little girl declared herself aunt, not mother, to her dolls. It had never occurred to her to discuss with her husband the legality of not procreating. She had intuited that paternity would have disrupted his work, and this was enough to silence her scruples, if she'd had any. But she didn't have any. She liked children, but her attitude towards them was one of a respectful lack of interest.

Having rid herself of her craving for manual labour, she headed towards what she believed would be the definitive loss of her personality, an irrelevant loss, after all, since every day the lightning-like brilliance of her Partner enriched her and simultaneously obliterated her. For her own amusement, and, in a certain sense, out of a pathetic celebratory pleasure, she started to visit museums and famous churches again, to go regularly to libraries where as a girl she had spent entire days drunk from reading obscure literature and delving into random research. The renewed pleasure of engaging in these activities soon included an active desire to pay secret homage to the great scholar whose name she shared. Scrutinizing old texts, and occasionally finding signs – pencil scribbles in the margins – of her own work as a student, she was stunned by some of her own interpretations. Raising her eyes from the page, she became lost in evoking quasi-optical images of mad warriors, wily monks, plundered cities, dense virgin forests. The historians, the medieval poets, the ugly mugs of Barbarians and Huns fascinated her, but she understood that regrettably none of this was of any use, all of it just a fairy tale she would recount to no one.

Although she was reluctant to engage in relationships of pure convenience, her husband eventually introduced her into the society of artists, writers and poets. Among them she was determined by all to be the beautiful and aloof Mrs X. Whenever in this illustrious company, she was careful not to mention her youthful achievements. But what, in fact, did she actually have to boast about? Certainly not her university studies, or her work as a substitute teacher in high schools, and even less about the few articles she'd published in academic journals. The wives she met were young and vivacious, with some knowledge of literature, art and above all music. None of them had ever worked, but they knew a lot of people and were able to converse with ease. These women did not like her much, but seemed so seductive and intrepid that, almost defensively, she tried her best to improve her appearance, applying light make-up in the hope of not entirely disappearing among all those beauties. The probability was high that her husband could fall for a woman more attractive, more 'interesting' than she. Should that happen, there was nothing to do but resign herself to it without thinking of the future. Jealousy is a luxury allowed only to a woman once adored. Her jealousy flashed like lightning, silent and quick. When she was a teenager, she had been obsessed by a classmate who seemed a prodigy of gracefulness. She was sure that the boy she idolized was also smitten with this girl, and he was right to be. In some sense, by proxy, she loved her too. She would never have dared to compare herself with that alabaster face, that smooth coal-black hair, that tall, thin person with an undulating gait. But I am more intelligent, she consoled herself, though she was shattered. The danger passed, and perhaps it had never existed, but now, anticipating that sooner or later something more serious would happen, she tried to reassure herself by studying the effects her own attractiveness had on men. She was incapable of flirting, flattering, acting childishly, but instead became irritated, ironic, caustic. And yet, sometimes she could imagine herself being 'served' by a melancholy, yet respectful, dutiful knight. Didn't her disconsolate early love give her the right to some sweetness? Wasn't it fair that having given so much without receiving, she should now receive without giving?

No, it wasn't fair. She felt guilty and deplored herself. In truth, Mrs X's actual betrayals were limited to a tear or two shed over lines from an old sonata (written by a man dead some two hundred years) or a shiver over the refrain of a Spanish song. Then, after the last note faded, she realized that her steadfast, anguished, everyday love was actually expanding, absorbing every manner of feeling – that of a daughter, mother, sister, an eternally beloved – its roots growing ever more intricate and deep. Her emotions were overflowing to the point that she dared to ask what she had never before dared: 'Do you love me?' And she clung to his adored chest, took possession of it, insensitive now to the fear of annoying him. Her conquest had become solid as a rock, all doubts, regrets slipped away, disappeared: 'We were born to be together,' she said, inflamed, her ear pressed against his heart, every heartbeat ecstatic, her palm resting on his delicate, almost childlike upper arm.

Ultimately, living day by day is easy if one isn't too demanding. The world is a small stage and everyone has a role in the drama, even those behind the scenes, and, at worst, one can always sleep, and sleeping, dream. Mrs

X dreams a lot of things – for example, when she has a migraine, she dreams of beautiful music. The sets change: singing lessons, tennis matches, incredibly boring games of bridge and canasta, with occasional friends whom she curiously observed. Terrible player that she was, she didn't keep track of the cards. And she, who was silent once upon a time, began to chat. Without realizing it, this new loquaciousness of hers took on the rhythm of a story-teller: she recounted her childhood memories, the city where she spent her youth, and how much she loved her enchanting aunt who died so young. Talking, talking, digressing, telling fantastic tales. Somewhat dazed, the players ended up neglecting their spades and diamonds, and listened to her, riveted. Yes, there was no doubt, Mrs X was a terrible card player, but she knew how to tell a good story. This observation was not devoid of malice, the implication being that she revealed too much.

Blunt arrows. A delightful spring swept away the green felt of the card table, the cards, the chips, the whisky and cigarettes. Midway through April, the garden behind the house was covered with violet and blue, the rose thorns as delicate as baby teeth. After having planted the seeds, watered them, played with the latest litter of kittens, she was able to sit outside, in the sun and under shade. Nothing was missing from that idyllic scene in which, like the protagonist of a George Sand novel, she decided to diligently play the role of the lonely noblewoman who had been wandering in a fog for thirteen years. Under a thicket of holly oaks and eucalyptus trees, a chaise longue was ready to welcome her, along with a book, its pages still uncut, a notebook and a fountain pen. She sat down but didn't feel like reading, her attention captured by the blossoming azalea.

It was at this point that fate intervened: the notebook fell from her lap to the ground and opened to a blank white page, almost as if waiting for a sign. While picking up the notebook, the fountain pen slipped from her hand and the top fell off; she didn't put it back on, holding the pen instead for an instant over the paper. The midday sun peeping through the leaves highlighted their sinuous profiles with such grace that her hand, almost moving by itself, traced the leaves' outlines weaving a lofty tapestry of pearly shadows. The page was entirely covered and all she could do was turn it over and give herself up to the game. A lively breeze had ruffled the foliage, but hadn't dried the ink still flowing from the sharp golden pen point. Temptation triumphed and her tenuous scribbles became words:

it was as if the pen were an invisible arrow aimed at the centre of the page, its purpose unclear, controlled by an external, benign force akin to the gentle deceptions that cause young children to obey. Words, words, words: now her agile hand was moving at the same rhythm as the stories she often told her 'friends' with whom she played bridge. She was living the story of her first encounter with death, the death of an amiable old woman who was courageous and Voltairian, and on to the piece of paper she crammed her spiky, hasty handwriting, the very same handwriting the 'Miss' had once used to take notes on venerable and difficult texts, an entirely different handwriting from the rounded letters used by Mrs X for the frivolous communications of a socialite.

It started to rain and a thick drop spread on the page, diluting a 'forever' to the point of vanishing. The word was crossed out and written again where the page was dry, and the notebook was closed.

Tucking the notebook and her book under her arm, she headed back inside, making her way slowly up the veranda steps, paying no attention to the rain as it drenched her hair and wrapped the silent stillness of the suddenly grey air in a silken rustle. Even once inside, the house was silent. Everyone had gone out. The study appeared abandoned, frozen in time. As on that singular day in the distant past, Mrs X rested her forehead against a windowpane and, her eyes closed, imagined a dusty classroom behind her. The present vanished. All that was left for her, or in her, was the act she had just carried out – tracing words she hadn't summoned, unnecessary words but still urgent, almost pleading with her to write them down, to give voice to images on the brink of disappearing.

Embarrassed, she realized that this was the secret of her anxieties – the dangerous conversation between the paper and the pen that promised a second life, and during her late years, if indeed they came, the only true peace. Her breath clouded the windowpanes streaming with rain. She blew on the ageing face of the neglected 'Miss'.

Her former self forgave her, but the price of redemption was high.

'La signorina'
Part of the collection *Da un paese vicino* (Mondadori, 1975).

GIOVANNI ARPINO

1927–87

In a 1981 interview, Arpino claimed that a real writer should write at least one hundred stories in his lifetime (he wrote nearly twice that number). He also compared the pressure felt by writers to fatten stories into novels to watering down a fine wine. Born in present-day Croatia, Arpino grew up in Liguria and spent summers in the Piedmontese city of Bra. He was a mediocre student, pressured by his father, a colonel in the military, to study law in Turin. He switched to literature and produced a slim book of poems. As he matured he wrote prose as well as verse. His first novel was published when he was twenty-five. He went on to write fifteen others, including *L'ombra delle colline* (The Shadow of the Hills), which won the Strega Prize in 1964. His most commercially successful work, the novel *Il buio e il miele* (1969), translated as *Scent of a Woman* in English, inspired a film starring Vittorio Gassman in the original 1974 adaptation, and Al Pacino in the 1992 remake. Arpino also was a prolific sports journalist (he covered the Olympic Games in Munich for *La Stampa* in 1972), published over a dozen books for children and wrote avidly about art and photography. While residing in Turin with his family, he rented a room without a telephone in Milan, nearly eighty miles away, commuting back and forth in order to write undisturbed. *Racconti di vent'anni* (Twenty Years of Stories) is an eclectic harvest of techniques, moods and styles: traditional, Surrealist, sarcastic, sincere, elegiac, farcical. This story, featuring an animal in a starring role, is a mixing of the absurd and the pathetic, of fable and verisimilitude. Call it a perverse, latter-day pygmalion, a mordant comment on chauvinism and possession; a paean, however oblique, to female desire.

The Baboon

Translated by Howard Curtis

Poor devil. It's really touching. She does all she can, whatever she knows, just to make me happy. There's no end to her good intentions. I hate scolding her, but that only ever happens when I'm tired, rattled by work, by constantly rushing around the city, by taxes, business deals, sales, down payments, not to mention my lawyer, my stockbroker, my insurance agent, those who claim I owe them money and those who refuse to pay what they owe me.

No sooner have I scolded her than I immediately regret it. She huddles in the corner of her armchair and weeps, she covers her eyes with her hand, then spreads her fingers and throws me a moist glance, and again she starts moaning in that shrill, desperate little voice of hers.

'Look, forget it, I'm sorry, let's make peace,' I stammer, and immediately she's a good girl again, she calms down, runs to me, empties and brings back the ashtray and stands there looking at me as I read the newspaper, sighing slightly. Then she remembers she hasn't yet made the coffee and rushes madly into the kitchen, giving vent to her obsession with doing things, doing them quickly, making herself useful.

I have to confess it: she's the best of the wives I've had. She's the fourth, I've been widowed three times, fortunately without the added burden of children. They all died on me when they were young: it seemed like a curse.

'What did you do to her?' my friends said after the funeral of the third. 'You have to tell us now.' They had become suspicious, unwilling to accept that it was a simple case of pneumonia.

But this Gilda, I admit to myself, is a treasure. A good girl, as I said, docile, helpful, all she needs is a cheap little necklace a couple of times a

449

year. She washes and irons her skirts for herself, and every day she combs and grooms herself with incredible care. The house gleams like a mirror. In the kitchen – well, there she doesn't manage so well. She's too predictable, she can't figure out more than the same three or four dishes. But I knew that right from the beginning, when I bought her from that circus that had gone bust after a tornado destroyed the tent and broke the tamer's leg.

'She can do everything,' the owner of the circus told me at the time. 'Better than a maid. I swear I wouldn't be selling her if it wasn't for that disaster . . . We gave her a good training . . . She doesn't eat much, you know? Nothing, really . . . You're getting a good deal.'

Gilda has been with me for three years now. She's robust and healthy, and takes care of herself from her ears to the tip of her tail. She smells of cologne, soap and talcum powder.

She loves me. Maybe even too much. Not that she expects me to be particularly effusive, sometimes all she needs is a caress, poor thing, but she moves around me with the huge weight of love that she feels, and I can smell its heat, its constant intensity.

'*Bee-ba*,' she says to me every now and again under her breath, closing her eyes and quivering, and then I know that I have to stroke her in a certain way, until her grunting gently fades into an almost imperceptible sigh.

Or maybe I give in, and then for the next three or four days she bustles about like a madwoman, polishing the furniture, beating the cushions, scouring the pans, lighting my cigarettes, humming in the bath, blowing me anxious little kisses with the tips of her fingers from the end of the corridor. Or else she summons her courage and grooms me, smoothly moving the brush back and forth between the top of my skull and the back of my neck. She loves grooming me, and it's a joy she knows she can obtain only in exceptional cases. As she moves the brush, I feel her warm breath blowing between my skin and my shirt collar, interspersed with the occasional very light, very shy kiss.

When she does that, I say 'Good girl' and continue to read my newspaper, while she resumes brushing my hair, placated and contented by the masterful tone of my voice.

*

Any comparison between this baboon, Gilda, and my first three wives might seem in bad taste. And yet when I think of them now, I remember them as three witches, always after money, things, words, diversions. Tired of staying in, but then immediately tired of being out for a walk, or at the cinema, or in a café, or by the sea. With sudden pains in their feet, or with headaches, snivelling for no reason. Lazy. And very stingy, when they weren't being spendthrift. Sometimes badly washed, and maybe churlish towards friends of mine who came to the house for a chat, a drink, a Sunday poker game.

Gilda doesn't have even one of these defects. She's limited, that much is true, but she's no burden, she doesn't make claims, she doesn't answer back, she doesn't argue, she couldn't concoct the smallest whim. Home and a little love are absolutely everything to her. And that's reassuring for a mature man like me, it makes him tougher, more solid, it doesn't disturb the equilibrium of his days, or his work.

Of course, there are a few bones of contention between Gilda and me, but they're more a matter of nature than of conflicts of character.

For example: Gilda is under the illusion, I don't know how or why, that she can grow, that she can become at least as tall as me. She's always thinking about it. Every now and again she takes me by the hand and drags me over to the mirror. She looks at our images standing side by side, me tall and strapping in my shirtsleeves, she in her little petticoat, barely coming up to my waist, and she shakes her head and her eyes grow dim with tears. Or else she takes the rolled-up tape measure from her workbasket and hands it to me, and I have to measure her against the wall as you do with children. But the mark on the wall is where it always was, it hasn't got any higher in three years, and Gilda stares at it, studies it, then wipes away a tear.

To console her at such times, but in a clearly playful tone, so that she won't get the wrong idea, I say, '*Bee-ba?*' And she shakes her head, I don't know if it's because of her despair at not having grown yet or because she has understood that in saying '*Bee-ba*' I am only playing a game.

For some time now, before going to bed at night, I've had to give her a mild sleeping pill. Since I suffer a little from insomnia, she gets nervous and worried, and would be quite capable of spending the night sitting watching me until I fall asleep. To avoid this needless complication, I give her the pill and take two of them myself, even though I know they have almost no effect on me these days, and then lie there for hours hearing her sleeping next to me.

She doesn't snore, although every now and again she lets out a long sigh. I have no idea if she dreams or not. They say dogs have the ability to dream, so why not creatures as evolved as baboons?

She was born in captivity, in that wretched failed circus, so she has no memory of Africa, the forests, the elephants. If she does dream, maybe it's about the circus, and the acts they made her perform, dressing her up as a grandmother knitting, a clown tumbling about, a sailor riding a bicycle, a waitress serving at a table . . . Or else, as is more likely, she dreams about her love, in other words, me. Because even at night her hand searches for me. She is content with a slight touch, I feel those fleshy, oh-so-delicate parts of her fingertips, and immediately I react, stiffening the muscles in my shoulder and in the arm she has touched, in order to calm her and lull her back into a deep sleep.

At night, I'm more aware of how small she is. If she were taller, everything would be much more convenient. I hear her breathing, and in the dark, with my eyes open, I'm a little scared of that bristly, frail little body of hers, wrapped in a summer blouse that's hardly any length at all. I bought a similar blouse in a large shop years ago, pretending it was for one of my daughters. Since then, Gilda has sewn herself another three, in different colours, and when she comes out of the bathroom in those few centimetres of cloth and gets ready for bed, I'm really touched.

My insomnia, though, poisons these thoughts. For some nights now, I've actually been wishing that Gilda were taller. I realize that the image of a Gilda who's at least one metre sixty tall is starting to upset me. You're being stupid, I try to rebut myself, your life is perfect, don't make it a matter of centimetres. And besides: how do you know what she thinks? How do you know that she doesn't dream of a male baboon of her own who's smaller and more efficient than you?

These are troublesome thoughts that I can't easily dismiss. And at such moments I am afraid to reach out my hand and feel that poor little heap of bones sleeping by my side.

Then the insomnia loses its grip and starts to recede, and as I fall asleep I somehow manage to free myself of these idiotic ravings.

I am cursed.

Why does a man always manage – never deliberately, but simply out of inertia and madness – to ruin what he has that's beautiful and good and useful?

Or does my curse depend on a conjunction of the stars, which, as soon as they see I'm at peace, immediately set about making me take the wrong step?

To be brief: I went to the zoo yesterday. It was Sunday, and the first sunny day after a very long winter. I didn't want to go alone, so Gilda went with me: she was a little reluctant, because she doesn't like leaving the house, she's scared of people and, especially, dogs. Seeing, though, that I insisted, and was laughing, and the sunlight in the kitchen was making me cheerful, she put on her best skirt and came with me, holding me by the hand.

There were lots of children at the zoo, but surrounded as they were by all those animals in cages or scattered around the enclosures, they were hardly surprised to see me with Gilda by my side. The air by the river, where the zoo had been built, was stimulating, with gusts of wind that seemed like razor cuts, though only very slightly biting and not pitiless.

Gilda seemed sulky, she let herself be carried here and there, and it was only when we came to the big monkey pit that she was reluctant to stop and her hand stiffened in mine. Obviously those dirty, mangy, quarrelsome apes embarrassed her.

It all happened when we lingered by the gorilla's cage. The gorilla was an extremely rare specimen. He sat there, huddled like an old carpet. Then he moved, and I saw that he wasn't a male, but a female, with a baby in her arms. She was at least one metre eighty tall, maybe more, a big, vigilant beast with glossy black fur and aggressive tar-black eyes, but with her fingers tenderly clasping the little one in her lap. I hoisted Gilda on my back so that she could see better. Immediately I felt her shaking as if she'd been stricken with a high fever. She bent her little arms and squeezed my neck, and her breath in my ear sounded fractured with emotion, or with terror.

'Good girl,' I whispered to her. 'Don't you see how beautiful she is? A giant. Would you let me make *'Bee-ba'* with her, eh?'

I felt the slight touch of her nails around my neck, and then a big shudder that shook her in every vertebra.

But when we got home, she shut herself in the bathroom and for a long time I heard her weeping desperately. I didn't say anything, didn't call her, because after three wives I know perfectly well how valuable silence is as a response to a female's tears.

She came out and served dinner, without the slightest sigh escaping her mouth. She obeyed each of my requests – the salt, the oil, a fruit knife – with her usual docility, but without the celebratory frenzy I know so well.

After dinner, she immediately went off to bed, while I sat up to watch television.

It's only now, in the bedroom, that I discover she's swallowed an entire tube of sleeping pills.

From her mouth the breath emerges thin, already wheezing. I've telephoned the Red Cross, someone will be here soon. Maybe they'll be able to save her for me.

My head feels empty, my hands alternately dry and moist. I stand here looking at her, waiting for the doorbell to ring. Yes, maybe they'll save her. But what then? Will she still be my Gilda, will she be what she was yesterday, what she's always been? Or will she start to grow suspicious and hate me, the way my other wives did? What little acts of revenge will she come up with in the labyrinth of her female mind?

But then, what do these women want of me, what do they expect, do they really not understand the efforts I make, just to keep going, to keep the peace? And yet . . . if I'm left alone, if Gilda dies, what will I be able to do with myself when I've become master of nothing?

'La babbuina'
Part of the collection *La babbuina e altre storie* (Mondadori, 1967).

CORRADO ALVARO

1895–1956

Alvaro is the only writer in this volume from Calabria, one of the poorest
regions of Italy, and though he moved away from it as a young man – sent
away to a Jesuit school outside Rome, serving in the army, studying and
working in Milan, and eventually settling in Rome – that arid, insular
landscape, the southern 'toe' of the Italian peninsula from which so
many migrated, inspired him all his life. A transitional figure who fused
Realism with Modernist and lyrical elements, he wrote poetry as well as
prose. He was keenly attuned to tensions between rural and urban society,
between the world of manners and the irrational realm. He started
publishing stories in *La Stampa* in 1929, and followed up, a year later,
with a powerful collection called *Gente in Aspromonte* (published in
English under the title *Revolt in Aspromonte*). His novel *Quasi una vita*
(Almost a Life) received the Strega Prize in 1951, but he remains finest in
his stories, which are ambiguous, ardent, psychologically driven and mor-
ally charged. He was known for labouring intensely over drafts; the year
before he died, he organized his short fiction in a definitive volume called
Settantacinque racconti (Seventy-five Stories). A fierce and open opponent
of Mussolini, he was among the intellectuals who signed Benedetto
Croce's Anti-Fascist Manifesto in 1925, and he hid under a false name in
Abruzzo in 1943 after the regime fell. Alvaro also worked as a journalist
throughout his life – he was an editor at the anti-Fascist newspaper *Il
Mondo* – and was at one point dispatched to the Soviet Union, where he
learned enough Russian to translate Tolstoy into Italian. In the last two
months of his life he befriended Campo, who was at his side when he
died. This story, a hybrid of conventional plot, intrigue and interior

rumination, moves rapidly and unpredictably, its slippery structure mirroring the rootless gypsy at its centre. A recurrent female figure in Alvaro's work, she symbolizes both desperation and freedom, and defies fixed notions of identity.

Barefoot

Translated by Jhumpa Lahiri

At times, as soon as I've closed the door to my house, I hear the phone ringing in my room. I go down a few steps, slowly, listening all the while to a sound that gradually sounds more like a voice that's calling. I climb back up the steps, open the door and go into my room. When I pick up the receiver, poof, the call vanishes, and in the Bakelite tube I hear that '*crac*', like a knot being tied that no one can undo.

I suppose it's strange to hear me use an expression like that: a sound that ties a knot. But it does. You have to realize that, since I live alone, everything that surrounds me strikes me in a singular way. Other times, instead of turning back, I stop at the first landing. I hear the phone ringing even more intently, almost desperately. It implores in the solitude of the empty rooms. I go down a few more steps, and now other calls from neighbouring apartments layer on top of that one, all of them blending into a single plea, almost as if they're asking to be freed from the device.

When the cleaning lady's here to tidy up my place in the mornings, she's the one to answer the calls. Coming back home I find, written on a pad, the name of whoever has asked for me. It's almost always people I don't know. Maybe because the cleaning lady mangles the names. I wouldn't know how else to interpret certain phenomena: certain people, a man or a woman, declare that they urgently need to talk to me, they say they'll call back; but no one ever does, or almost never. So, what's the hurry? I've noticed that this sort of thing tends to occur on specific days, on sunny days, for example.

It doesn't only happen with people who call me on the phone, but also with those who show up at my door. I'm often told that someone who absolutely must see me came by in a great hurry, and that he'll come back, as usual; and as usual, this person never turns up again. I must say that under other circumstances – were I to live in a small town, for example – such things wouldn't matter. But certain mechanical devices, like the telephone, have lent life a certain drama, and someone who calls you on that piece of equipment is nothing but the shroud of a man – his soul, his essence, all of him, reduced to that beseeching voice. As for why I care so much about who's been trying to get in touch with me, and even feel a bit anxious about it, that's another matter.

It stirs up memories of when I was younger, when people asked after you not to get something, but rather, to give. You might say I've gauged my life with this device. Once they were people who augured kindness, unknown women who proposed a walk, given that it was a pleasant day. It didn't matter that, later, they laughed at me. Not all of them, though. Others uttered scalding words into that tube, with brazen voices. Not to me, naturally, but to a stranger, to the unknown, to hope. Then, imperceptibly, the situation changed. Typically, the person who now calls asks for something. I've become a man. I expect nothing from others. I've got to give the little I can.

And yet the wishful thinking of those days remains. And every time someone calls and then doesn't show up, I remember that ancient longing. No, it doesn't only happen to me. In my salad days I saw old men who'd already gone grey, nearly falling over, anxiously waiting for someone who'd called once to call again; and they, too, would wait in vain. A man never tires of waiting.

Then lo and behold: after dropping by various times to no avail, someone turned up again. I opened the door – I was alone – and found a woman behind it, holding a child by the hand. I first took in the child. He was small, but possessed that adult air that the children of the poor have, also children in certain historic paintings: a tiny humanity, but the eyes, expression and experience of grown-ups, which is the case among animals, and in the truer world of men. The woman took a bold step, furtive and light. She was already in my study. Lowering my eyes, I saw that she wasn't wearing shoes; her feet were wrapped, instead, in some rags. I took a moment to consider those rags, and her silent step, and her sidelong gait, and only afterwards did I take in her thin, dark, resolute face, straight nose, whittled lips, small head at the top of her tall, straight body. I found myself behind my table; it was as if she'd cornered me against the wall. Her presence cut me off from the rest of the room; with her restless eyes she'd taken in everything around her, on the tables, on the furniture, on the shelves. I had a bad feeling and prepared, instinctively, to defend myself, when my eyes fell to her breasts, discreetly but confidently.

She began speaking with a voice that sought to be reassuring, but betrayed concern: she'd heard of me, and she cited the names of two or three people I knew; she spoke about my life, and here she reminded me of one or two incidents; in short, she wanted me to put in a good word to the director of an institute for the needy, so that he would welcome her among its residents, since she was poor, and willing to adapt to the jobs that impoverished women did to pay for their keep in that charitable institution. I lifted my eyes to look at her, and again I encountered that face, frozen in its secret, rough beauty. I couldn't help thinking of a man: I was convinced that some fellow had coached her preamble, and the things she'd said about me; the way she'd organized her speech, and that type of flattery, seemed to me of purely masculine inspiration. Moreover, while everything she'd said about my friends was true, she'd been wrong about one thing: I didn't know the director of the institute she was talking about, not in the least. I'm a man, with a man's thoughts. In fact, while looking at those strips on her feet, I was actually thinking that I'd never seen a woman so careless about her appearance. In other words, it struck me as a disguise. I must admit she spoke in polished sentences, and didn't lack a certain refinement. Whoever her Svengali was, he would have gone out of his way to procure a pair of shoes for such a beautiful creature. Beautiful, yes, but also harsh, almost in revolt against her femininity, with those eyes, quick and furtive, that took in, took stock, of everything. Including me.

She didn't want to sit down. She looked with disdain at the armchair I offered her, her eyes trained on me as if expecting the unexpected. I looked once more at the child. He was barefoot, and he stared at me, clinging to his mother's side, as if he, too, expected something inevitable to happen. Perhaps he was trembling, perhaps he was scared, but he controlled himself with the determination children are capable of.

'All right,' I said, 'I'll see to this director, I'll find someone among my friends who knows him. Why don't you leave me your address.' I motioned to offer her a pen; I wanted to see her writing. But the pen slipped from my hand, rolling on the table, and in the attempt to pick it up again, I gave it another nudge and it ended up falling on the floor. I heard a sudden cry, a shriek, and saw the child's mouth: it was red, a commoner's red, opened wide to reveal the few teeth among the gums. The fallen pen had ended up hurting the child's small bare foot.

I started to panic. The boy behaved as if he couldn't breathe, he seemed on the verge of choking. She took him roughly in her arms, without sitting down, and looked at me, stunned. I sensed a tremendous, powerful vitality, and a fear of evil that only simple people know how to convey. I rooted around for a small bottle of disinfectant and found a vial of iodine. I was about to pour a few drops on the wound, which was barely a scratch grazing that little foot, sensing that it was fruit from the maternal tree. The child caught his breath and asked, in a grown-up voice, using an incredibly reasonable tone: 'Will it sting?'

'A bit,' I replied.

Then he let out another cry, even louder, baring his mouth down to his tonsils. 'Calm down,' I said, 'I'll look for a medicine that doesn't sting,' and I started to look for a bottle of hydrogen peroxide that I remembered keeping in a drawer.

The boy quieted down at once and waited. When I came back, I saw a drop of blood creeping out of the wound: it was thick blood, bright vermilion, a perfect drop of it.

With impressive ease the boy started shrieking: 'Now it hurts, now it hurts.' He pulled at his hair and scratched his cheeks. Then suddenly he turned quiet again, while his mother looked at me and him the way animals watch strangers who approach their young, a look that deems their young the strongest, most precious things on earth.

I'd placed a cotton pad on the wound, and I watched it shrinking and staunching. While I did this I was seized by a violent feeling, due to some ancient memory, and I appraised that flesh dense with blood and strength, and those two pointlessly beautiful bodies, as if they were treasures that lay buried in residual gangue: a force of nature, hidden yet thriving at some unexplored depth. Looking around, at the things I'd accumulated in so many patient, lean years, everything seemed stupid and petty. These weren't thoughts of mine, but rather, vague impressions; I was thinking about that woman's silent steps through city streets, and the multiplicity of her life, unshackled from any law and norm, and about her mysterious affairs. At the same time, the woman's language – civilized, sly, cajoling – stood in contrast to those screams, the turning pale, the trembling for nothing, the sudden self-control, the fickle mutability of gypsies. That drop of blood, alive, dark-red, almost protean, multi-hued, had faintly repulsed me, like something too intense to bear. And yet it had enticed me, like a memory of lost vigour.

I'd barely managed to close the drawer with the bottle of disinfectant in it before something else happened, perhaps just what I'd been fearing and anticipating in the back of my mind. I heard the bustle of footsteps behind me, and the thud of that muffled stride: I saw the door open, and mother and son tumbling out, this time with the intelligence and accord that had already struck me when I'd observed the little boy next to his mother. They formed a single being. The little one must have been perfectly trained to make such an exit. I noticed, in a flash, that a silver vase that used to stand on a piece of furniture was missing. I'd thought about it all the while, mixed up with all my other thoughts. I moved towards the door and heard it close, violently. I stepped outside.

The two of them were already on the stairs. I caught up to them on the landing of the first floor; they were incredibly fast. I found them among the shadows. This time the boy was perfectly silent. I plunged my hands towards them and felt two lips graze me. Now I saw that feminine face – above me, since she was taller – with a new expression, smiling and frighteningly secure. During that temptation, I wavered, once again envisioning vast spaces that gave on to to the prison of urban life: dangerous streets, dark stairwells, secret rooms guarded by some old woman, hoary and slow, with the voice of a ready accomplice. But at the same time, under those alluring eyes that fixed me like an asp, I was unable to look away. And as I felt, under my grip, two arms that had surrendered but remained strong, the doors to the apartments on the landing opened. Still holding her (and later I was told that my position was somewhat strange), I said:

'She's a thief.'

The face above me clouded over. And then I saw another expression take possession of it, blooming once more like a distinct, stagnant shape on the surface of a suddenly agitated lake. Various voices were heard: 'Ah, you finally caught her!' 'Search her. She must have my purse, my lipstick, too. I can spot the lipstick right away, I bought it in Zurich.' 'Ah, it's her!' She was passed from one person to another. With her pilgrim's gait I saw her on the street, growing distant, in the grips of the porter and an officer.

I'd forgotten, in the hubbub, about my silver vase. When I was summoned by the judge, who gave the stolen item back to me, I told him I didn't want any harm to come to the woman. But I was told they'd been looking for her for a long time, and they thanked me for having brought her to justice. 'Anyway,' they added, 'you can't call a woman a thief without wanting to harm her.' She followed me, with her dangerous eyes, as I went out, watching me all the way up to the door. She understood men. She knew how vain we were. She didn't quit her act, even under those circumstances. As for me, I hope I never see her again. Men, as everyone knows, are tempted by mystery and deceit, riddles to solve and explain. But what mystery? Someone might say: we're talking about a thief. True, but why does such a beautiful woman become a thief? To stay honest?

'*Piedi scalzi*'

First published in *Incontri d'amore* (Bompiani, 1940). Later published as part of the collection *Settantacinque racconti* (Bompiani, 1955).

Notes

THE SIREN

1. William Shakespeare, *The Tempest*, act I, scene 2.
2. William Shakespeare, *The Sonnets*, 119.
3. The Opera Nazionale Dopolavoro (National Recreational Club) was the Italian Fascist leisure and recreational organization.

THE TOWER

1. *RAI3*: RAI stands for 'Radiotelevisione italiana', which, until 1954, was called 'Radio Audizioni Italiane'. It is Italy's public broadcasting company. RAI3, among the principal RAI channels, was controlled by the Italian Communist Party and dedicated largely to cultural programming. It retains a left-leaning audience.
2. San Francesco from the 1930s: San Francesco (Saint Francis), declared the patron saint of Italy by Pope Pius XII in 1939, was appropriated by Mussolini as a nationalist symbol. The Duce declared him 'the most Italian of saints and the most saintly of all Italians', and linked his evangelical missions in Palestine and Egypt to the Fascist regime's colonialist aggression.
3. *The festival for l'Unità*: The *l'Unità* Festival was launched by the Italian Communist Party in 1945 to foster Communist identity and raise funds for *l'Unità*, Italy's official Communist newspaper, founded by Antonio Gramsci in 1924. Italo Calvino, Cesare Pavese, Antonio Tabucchi and Elio Vittorini were among the writers in this anthology who wrote for *l'Unità*. Since the dissolution of the Italian Communist Party in 1991, the festival has continued under successor left-wing

parties and coalitions. As of 2017, *l'Unità* has ceased publication, but *l'Unità* festivals are still held in numerous cities in Italy.

4. *Emmanuelle*: *Emanuelle* was an erotic French film released in 1974, based on the novel of the same name by Emmanuelle Arsan. Its protagonist was a French diplomat's wife travelling to Thailand to meet her husband.

Goffredo Parise – Biographical note

1. From the *Avvertenza* (author's note) of the 1984 complete edition of the *Sillabari*. The original Italian reads: '*Ma all lettera S, nonostante i programmi, la poesia mi ha abbandonato.*'

Anna Maria Ortese – Biographical note

1. From Ortese's introduction to the 1994 edition of *Il mare non bagna Napoli*.

A MARTIAN IN ROME

1. The language used in this short story by Flaiano presents a variety of challenges, including a couple of expressions that cannot be precisely translated into English. The author's use of Italian is specific to the 1950s, and, in some cases, unique to the city of Rome and its inhabitants. The text is riddled with formal, journalistic language, which is in direct contrast with the fantastic, ironic and at times ridiculous nature of the plotline. One of the expressions that cannot be properly rendered in English is a play on words, not entirely dissimilar to the phrase 'Rome or bust'. When he describes a satirical drawing by Mino Maccari, Flaiano references the exclamation '*O Roma o Marte!*' ['Rome or Mars!'], an allusion to Garibaldi's historical battle cry '*O Roma o Morte!*' ['Rome or Death!'].

Another aspect of the Italian language that is difficult to translate is the degree of formality implied in conversation by addressing an interlocutor in the third person, without having to resort to words like 'sir' or 'ma'am'. Since it is customary to address strangers formally in Italy, the choice not to do so is inherently informal, familiar and possibly disrespectful. The decision to address someone in dialect or standard Italian also carries similar weight. Standard language would normally be used in school, in the professional world, and when dealing with figures of authority. It can denote a certain distance, but also respect and consideration for the listener, since he or she may not even completely understand the dialect in question. Hence, when photographers shout at the Martian to get him to move out of the way, they are being rude for more than one reason. The forceful request '*A Marzià, te scansi?*' is only truly clear to those who have at least a small understanding of the dialect known as Romanesco. To render the tone of derision and disdain in the original text, it was necessary to add an element of vulgarity, producing the following question: 'Hey, Mr Mars, will you move your ass?'

(Names of people and places have not been translated. The spelling of the Martian's name [Koont] has been graphically changed from the original form [Kunt] in order to avoid the vulgar connotation that this word implies in English, as it is non-existent in Italian.)

Massimo Bontempelli – Biographical note

1. *Curzio Malaparte*: Malaparte (1898–1957), born Kurt Erich Suckert to a Saxon father and Milanese mother, was one of Italy's most controversial and contradictory literary figures. Fascist and anarchist in turn, he marched on Rome with Mussolini but later collaborated with Moravia to oppose Mussolini's Racial Laws. And yet he was never forgiven by leftist artists and intellectuals for his Fascist links. Permission could not be obtained from the estate of Curzio Malaparte to include a selection by him in this volume

THE MIRACULOUS BEACH

1. *Aminta:* The title of a play written by Torquato Tasso in 1573 in which Aminta, a shepherd, falls in love with the nymph Silvia, who initially spurns him, but eventually the two are united.

THE STREETWALKER

1. *Giansiro Ferrata*: A critic and writer (1907–86).
2. *Adua and Her Friends*: A film made in 1960, starring Marcello Mastroianni and Simone Signoret, in which four prostitutes try to open a restaurant after the brothels are closed after the Merlin Law.
3. *she liked the song, but not sung by Sergio Bruni – handsome profile, that Bruni, he hadn't booed Villa, in Naples, he had paid his thugs to boo Villa, but now he had to pay some nice millions, to Villa, who had sued him*: Sergio Bruni and Claudio Villa were popular Neapolitan singers. Bruni dramatically (and famously) withdrew at the last minute from the Festival of Neapolitan Song in 1960, refusing to participate in the final evening because of an argument with Villa and the festival organizers about who was to sing last.

Chronology

Literary Events	Historical Events

1840: The historical novel, *I promessi sposi* (*The Betrothed*) by Alessandro Manzoni (1785–1873), originally published in 1827, is definitively revised by the author and republished to make his prose consistent with contemporary educated Tuscan, thus setting the standard for modern written Italian.

Giovanni Verga, the oldest author in this volume, is born in Catania, Sicily.

1861: The kingdom of Italy is founded with Vittorio Emanuele II as its king. At the time, the Italian language is spoken by fewer than 10 percent of the population.

1871: Rome, annexed to the kingdom of Italy the year before, is named its capital.

1883: Benito Mussolini, son of a Socialist blacksmith and a schoolteacher, is born in Predappio, Italy.

Chronology

Literary Events	Historical Events

1891: **Luigi Pirandello** submits his doctoral dissertation on Sicilian dialect, written in German, at the University of Bonn.

1901: Guglielmo Marconi transmits the first wireless signals across the Atlantic Ocean.

1905: James Joyce moves to Trieste, teaches English at the Berlitz School and befriends **Italo Svevo**, one of his students.

1907: Arnoldo Mondadori, a restaurant owner's son who has only five years' schooling, begins work that will lead to the founding of Mondadori, now Italy's largest publishing house.

1909: 'The Manifesto of Futurism' by Egyptian-born poet and theorist Filippo Tommaso Marinetti (1876–1944) is published, in French, in the pages of *Le Figaro*.

1912: Italy annexes parts of modern-day Libya.

1915: Italy enters the First World War, siding with Great Britain, France and Russia.

1916: **Corrado Alvaro**, a foot soldier in the First World War, is severely injured close to the Slovenian border.

1917: **Alberto Savinio** is sent to
Thessaloniki, Greece, as an
interpreter for the Italian army on
the Macedonian front.
Tens of thousands of Italian
soldiers are killed or wounded at the
Battle of Caporetto.

1918: General Armistice. An
estimated 600,000 Italians have died
in combat. The country is mired in
debt.

1921: The Communist Party of Italy,
which will become the largest
Communist party in Western
Europe, is founded in Livorno.

1922: On October 28, Mussolini's
Fascist supporters march on Rome.
Two days later he is charged with
forming a government.

1924: First radio transmission in
Italy. Early broadcasts provide a mix
of opera, weather and stock-market
news.

1926: **Massimo Bontempelli** and
Curzio Malaparte (1898–1957) found
the journal *900*, a forum for
Surrealist, Dadaist and other
experimental writing. The Premio
Bagutta, awarded to eight authors in
this collection, is inaugurated. The
prize will be suspended between 1937
and 1946 to resist pressure from
Fascist authorities on the jury.

1927: **Antonio Delfini** starts a literary journal called *L'ariete* with Ugo Guandalini (1905–71), who will go on to found the publishing house Guanda. Fascist censors shut down the publication after one issue.

    Grazia Deledda receives the Nobel Prize in Literature for the previous year.

1929: **Umberto Saba** begins psychoanalysis in Trieste with Edoardo Weiss (1889–1970), a student of Sigmund Freud. The Viareggio Prize, awarded to sixteen authors in this collection, is inaugurated. Bompiani, the publisher of the anthology *Americana*, is founded in Milan.

1933: The publishing house Einaudi, with close ties to the Communist Party of Italy, is founded in Turin. Leone Ginzburg and **Cesare Pavese** are among its first editors.

1934: **Luigi Pirandello** wins the Nobel Prize for Literature.

    Giuseppe Tomasi becomes the Prince of Lampedusa following his father's death.

1935: **Alba De Céspedes** publishes her first collection of short stories, *L'Anima degli altri* (The Soul of Others), at twenty-four.

1935: Italy invades Ethiopia and will occupy the country over the next six years.

Literary Events	*Historical Events*
1936: **Fabrizia Ramondino**, the youngest author in this volume, is born.	1936: Italy and Germany enter into an alliance later known as the Axis.
	1937: Philosopher and critic Antonio Gramsci (b. 1891), one of the founders of the Communist Party of Italy and imprisoned by Fascists since 1926, dies after being recently liberated, in a clinic in Rome.
	1938: Mussolini's Racial Laws take effect; Jews are excluded from public office and public education. Their works are banned.
1939: **Dino Buzzati** leaves for Addis Ababa, Ethiopia, to report for *Corriere della Sera*.	
1941: While convalescing from illness, **Romano Bilenchi** meets Ezra Pound in Rapallo.	
1942: **Silvio D'Arzo**'s novel *All'insegna del buon corsiero* (At the Good Steed Inn) is published, the only one of his works to appear in his lifetime.	
	1943: Germany occupies Italy; Mussolini is made the head of a puppet regime known as the Republic of Salò. In Cairo, **Fausta Cialente** founds *Fronte Unito*, a newspaper distributed to Italian civilians and Italian prisoners of war in Egypt, Libya and Eritrea.

1944: In February, Leone Ginzburg, husband of **Natalia Ginzburg**, is tortured to death by Nazis in a Roman prison.

1944: Rome is liberated by Allied troops on 4 June.

1945: **Lalla Romano** translates the diaries of Eugene Delacroix.

1945: Mussolini is captured and killed by the Partisans.

1946: **Carlo Emilio Gadda** writes a letter from Florence to the literary critic Gianfranco Contini (1912–90) about **Tommaso Landolfi**'s gambling winnings, mentioning that Landolfi spends the money on cashmere sweaters, opulent hats and a powerful motorcycle.

1946: Italian women vote for the first time. Italy becomes a republic.

1947: The first edition of the Strega Prize, Italy's most prestigious honour for fiction, is awarded to **Ennio Flaiano**. Though founded by a woman – writer Maria Bellonci – a woman has only won eleven times in seventy-one years.

1947: Enactment of the Constitution of the Italian Republic. The text, composed in strikingly simple language, with five women among the seventy-five commissioned authors, was defined by the linguist Tullio De Mauro (1932–2017) as *'parole di tutti e per tutti'* ('everybody's words, for everyone').

1948: The literary magazine *Botteghe Oscure* is founded in Rome by American-born Princess Marguerite Caetani (1880–1963). Each issue publishes work in American English, British English, French, Italian and, in alternation, Spanish and German.

1949: **Beppe Fenoglio** has his first short story published under the pseudonym Giovanni Federico Biamonti.

Chronology

Literary Events	*Historical Events*

1950: **Anna Banti** and her husband, the art historian Roberto Longhi (1890–1970), found the bi-monthly journal *Paragone*, dedicated to art and literature.

1951: **Elio Vittorini** is commissioned to edit the *Gettoni* series for Einaudi, an imprint of paperbacks designed to promote young Italian authors.

1953: The literary journal *Nuovi Argomenti* is founded in Rome. **Alberto Moravia** is its first editor-in-chief.

1954: Italian state TV commences broadcasts.

1956: Work begins on the 'Autostrada del Sole', a highway connecting Milan and Naples, and a symbol of the country's burgeoning economy.

1957: **Luciano Bianciardi** is fired from his position as editor at Feltrinelli, a publishing house founded by the son of one of the richest men in Italy.

1957: Italy produces the Fiat 500, an economical car for city drivers.

1960: Educator Alberto Manzi (1924–1997) starts hosting *Non è mai troppo tardi* (It's Never Too Late), an enormously popular television programme that teaches adult illiterates to read and write in Italian.

1962: The publishing house Adelphi is founded in Milan and is the first in the world to publish the complete works of Friedrich Nietzsche.

Literary Events	*Historical Events*
	1965: The manufacturer Olivetti, founded in 1908 and famous for its typewriters, launches the first 'desktop computer', nicknamed '*la Perottina*', at the World's Fair in New York City.
1966: **Goffredo Parise**, reporting for *Corriere della Sera*, visits China, Laos and Vietnam. In the following years, he will write reportage on several other South-east Asians countries.	1966: The Arno river floods in Florence, devastating the historic centre, destroying thousands of valuable works of art, millions of rare books and documents, and killing thirty-five people in urban and outlying areas. Immediately afterward, students from Italy and abroad arrive by the hundreds in a massive volunteer effort to salvage the city's cultural treasures.
1967: Publication of *Il Doge* (The Doge), **Aldo Palazzeschi**'s radically experimental novel, almost entirely lacking in dialogue.	
1968: **Italo Calvino** receives the Viareggio Prize for the short-story collection *Ti con zero* (*T Zero*, also published as *Time and the Hunter*). He refuses it, sending a telegram in which he declares that the age of literary prizes is over.	1968: Nearly four thousand students in Rome, including militant leftists and neo-Fascists, engage in a violent face-off with police. The incident, known as 'The Battle of Valle Giulia', inspires a provocative poem by Pier Paolo Pasolini in which the Communist writer defends the police.
1969: The poet Vittorio Sereni (1913–83) creates the *Meridiani* series for Mondadori, critical anthologies designed to honour classic Italian and international authors.	

Literary Events   *Historical Events*

1971: Einaudi publishes John Donne's poems, edited and translated by **Cristina Campo.**

1972: Close to eight thousand people attend the funeral of publisher and leftist activist Giangiacomo Feltrinelli, who dies setting out to destroy a power pylon. On his body were sticks of dynamite and a picture of his ten-year-old son.

1974: **Leonardo Sciascia**'s *Todo Modo* (*One way or Another*) is published, a novel critical of the Christian Democratic Party, the dominant political force at the time.

1975: Pier Paolo Pasolini (b. 1922) is murdered in Ostia. The exact circumstances of his death remain a mystery.

1975: **Giovanni Arpino**, in collaboration with Mario Maffiodo (1899–1976), launches *Racconto*, a journal dedicated to short fiction. The poet Eugenio Montale (1896–1981) wins the Nobel Prize for Literature.

1977: **Carlo Cassola** founds the League for the Unilateral Disarmament of Italy and campaigns for non-violence.

1978: The body of former prime minister Aldo Moro (1916–78) is found in the trunk of a car in Rome after being kidnapped and murdered by members of the *Brigate Rosse*, an extreme left-wing group dedicated to armed revolution.

1980: Publication of *Il nome della rosa* (*The Name of the Rose*), Italy's first international bestseller, by Umberto Eco (1932–2016), a professor of semiotics at the University of Bologna.

1980: The Bologna train station is bombed by right-wing terrorists, killing eighty-five people and injuring over two hundred.

Chronology

1982: **Elsa Morante**'s last novel, *Aracoeli*, about an Andalusian mother's relationship with her homosexual son, is published.

1983: The stories of Edgar Allen Poe, in three volumes, are published by Einaudi, translated by **Giorgio Manganelli**.

1983: Bettino Craxi becomes Italy's first Socialist prime minister.

1986: **Luce d'Eramo**, known for writing about Nazi Germany and the consequences of the Second World War, publishes an anomalous science-fiction novel called *Partiranno* (They Will Leave), about friendly aliens that land in Rome.

1986: In Palermo, the *Maxiprocesso* (Maxi Trial) begins, a criminal trial prosecuting 474 members of the Sicilian mafia.

1987: **Primo Levi** commits suicide in Turin.

1988: The ***Salone del libro***, Italy's most important book fair, is first held in Turin.

1991: The Communist Party of Italy dissolves.

1992: *Amore Molesto* (*Troubling Love*), the first novel by the pseudonymous author Elena Ferrante, is published.

1992: A series of judicial investigations into political corruption, known as *Mani Pulite* (Clean Hands), brings down the political career of Bettino Craxi, along with most of Italy's political establishment. Giovanni Falcone and Paolo Borsellino, prosecuting magistrates who presided over the Maxi Trial, are killed by the Mafia, their murders only months apart.

Chronology

Literary Events   *Historical Events*

1993: After years of financial hardship and neglect from the literary establishment, **Anna Maria Ortese**, seventy-nine, publishes the novel *Il cardillo addolorato* (*The Lament of the Linnet*) to critical acclaim.

1994: The *Scuola Holden*, Italy's first school for Creative Writing and named after the protagonist of J. D. Salinger's *The Catcher in the Rye*, is founded in Turin.

1994: Media tycoon Silvio Berlusconi becomes prime minister for the first time.

1997: Dario Fo (1926–2016), an actor, director, comedian, playwright, songwriter, illustrator and political activist, wins the Nobel Prize in Literature.

2002: The Euro replaces the Lira.

2009: President of the Senate, Renato Schifani accuses **Antonio Tabucchi** of defamation for an article published in the Communist newspaper *l'Unità*, suing him for over one million euros.

Further Reading

The following list contains a few short-story collections, in English, by Italian authors active during the twentieth century whose work is not included in this volume, as well as a selection of English-language anthologies.

Individual Authors

Bassani, Giorgio, *Within the Walls: Five Stories from Ferrara*, trans. Jamie McKendrick. London: Penguin Classics, 2016

D'Annunzio, Gabriele, *Nocturne and Five Tales of Love and Death*, trans. Raymond Rosenthal. London: Quartet, 1994

Pasolini, Pier Paolo, *Stories from the City of God: Sketches and Chronicles of Rome 1950–1966*, ed. Walter Siti, trans. Marina Harss. London: Penguin, 2019

Anthologies

Italian Literature in Translation, ed. James E. Miller Jr, Robert O'Neal and Helen M. McDonnell. With an introductory essay: 'Translation: The Art of Failure', John Ciardi. Glenview, IL: Scott, Foresman, 1970

Italian Short Stories, vol. 1, Penguin Parallel Texts Series, ed. Raleigh Trevelyan. London: Penguin, 1989

Italian Short Stories, vol. 2, Penguin Parallel Texts Series, ed. Dimitri Vittorini. London: Penguin, 1993

Italian Tales: An Anthology of Contemporary Italian Fiction, ed. Massimo Riva. New Haven, CT: Yale University Press, 2004

Italy: A Traveler's Literary Companion, ed. and trans. Lawrence Venuti. Berkeley, CA: Whereabouts Press, 2003

Modern Italian Short Stories, ed. Marc Slonim. New York: Simon and Schuster, 1954

Modern Italian Stories, ed. and trans. W. J. Strachan. London: Eyre & Spottiswoode, 1955

Name and Tears and Other Stories: Forty Years of Italian Fiction, ed. and trans. Katherine Jason. St Paul, MN: Greywolf Press, 1990

New Italian Women: A Collection of Short Fiction, ed. Martha King. New York: Italica Press, 2008

Open City: Seven Writers in Postwar Rome, ed. William Weaver. South Royalton, VT: Steerforth Italian, 1999

The Penguin Book of Italian Short Stories, ed. Guido Waldman. Harmondsworth: Penguin, 1969

Rome Tales: Stories, selected and trans. Hugh Shankland; ed. Helen Constantine. Oxford; New York: Oxford University Press, 2011

Short Stories in Italian, New Penguin Parallel Texts Series, ed. Nick Roberts. London: Penguin, 1999

Stories of Modern Italy, from Verga, Svevo and Pirandello to the Present, ed. Ben Johnson. New York: Modern Library, 1960

Twentieth-century Italian Literature in English Translation: An Annotated Bibliography 1929–1997, ed. Robin Healey. Toronto; Buffalo; London: University of Toronto Press, 1998

Unspeakable Women: Selected Short stories written by Italian Women during Fascism, trans., and with an introduction and afterword by Robin Pickering-Iazzi. New York: The Feminist Press at CUNY, 1993

Acknowledgements

Nearly every story I discovered, considered and eventually included in this volume arrived by word of mouth, by way of a friend or acquaintance who urged me to read a certain writer. I therefore begin by thanking the following people: Daniela Angelucci, Sara Antonelli, Maria Baiocchi, Andrea Bajani, Paola Basirico, Marco Belpoliti, Ginevra Bompiani, Caterina Bonvicini, Biagio Bossone, Patrizia Cavalli, Federica Cellini, Felice Cimatti, Leonardo Colombati, Fabrizio Corallo, Alessandro Cusimano, Angelo De Gennaro, Cristina Delogu, Maddalena Deodato, Tiziana de Rogatis, Paolo Di Paolo, Isabella Ferretti, Ilaria Freccia, Maria Ida Gaeta, Michela Gallio, Ornella Gargagliano, Francesca Virginia Geymonat, Ludovico Geymonat, Martino Gozzi, John Guare, Gioia Guerzoni, Francesca Marciano, Claudia Marques de Abreu, Melania Mazzucco, Chiara Mezzalama, Michela Murgia, Gabriele Pedullà, Anita Raja, Mario Raja, Antonio Ria, Marina Sagona, Italo Spinelli, Chiara Valerio, Pietro Valsecchi and Giorgio van Straten.

Of these, Dorina Olivo was particularly effusive in transmitting her passion for a series of Italian authors I had not heard of, and for giving me copies of their books.

Though I conceived of this anthology in Italy, I am indebted, above all, to two people I had the good fortune to meet in America, at Princeton University: Alessandro Giammei and Chiara Benetollo. Alessandro, in whose company Nassau Street nearly felt like Rome, was a font of knowledge like no other, filling in countless gaps in my knowledge and providing crucial insight, guidance and solidarity. And Chiara, my phenomenally capable (and extraordinarily generous) research assistant, meticulously compiled and collated the materials, verified an infinite number of details and ascertained the complex editorial history of many of these stories. Their unfailing attention to this project throughout each phase of its gestation was essential.

At Princeton, I wish also to thank: Pietro Frassica, who provided the

Acknowledgements

first set of photocopies that set me on my way; Michael Moore, Princeton's Translator-in-Residence in 2018, who not only contributed his own marvellous translations to this anthology, but patiently and sagely edited mine; David Bellos and Sandra Bermann, esteemed colleagues who have welcomed me to the world of translation at Princeton; Dorothea von Moltke, *libraia simpatica ed eccezionale*; Lavinia Liang, a student in the class which first motivated me to put together this anthology, who spent hours at the photocopying machine on my behalf; Noreen McAuliffe and Erin West, in the Program of Creative Writing, for their impeccable assistance.

I owe a great deal to Sara Teardo, with whom I co-taught the bilingual translation workshop 'To and from Italian' in the fall of 2017 at Princeton. That class, which we dreamt up together, was the laboratory for the Italo Calvino story in this volume, and I thank her for her collaboration, *consigli* and companionship. A special thanks to our five students for collectively producing the first translation of Calvino's text: Bes Arnaout, Owen Ayers, Charles East, Inés French, Jackson Springer. A pioneer class that did pioneering work, they did the heavy lifting, were undaunted, and went out of their way.

Enormous gratitude to all members of the excellent group of translators for their beautiful and invigorating work: Simon Carnell, Howard Curtis, Richard Dixon, Ann Goldstein, Jenny McPhee and Erica Segre, in addition to the aforementioned Michael Moore.

Thanks to the following intercontinental team of exacting readers, some in English, some in Italian, a few in both: Barringer Fifield, Stefano Jossa, Barry McCrea, Neel Mukherjee and Alberto Vourvoulias, my dear husband, who also happens to be an exceptional editor. My heartfelt gratitude goes to Tiziana Rinaldi Castro, a writer equally at home in English and Italian, who not only introduced me to Fabrizia Ramondino but has become my *paladina*, lending succour and support on the path of translation like no other.

Grazie di cuore to Marco Delogu for sustaining and championing the book when it was merely in progress; Domenico Starnone for friendship, encouragement and advice in making the final selection; Giovanna Calvino for leading me to an untranslated work by her father; Alessandra Ginzburg, for helping me to decide on the story by her mother.

Thanks to my Italian publisher at Guanda, Luigi Brioschi, for our many conversations about this project; Laura Bosio, my gifted editor, who kindly reviewed my work, this time in English; Cinzia Cappelli, for her helpful suggestions; Claudine Turla for her rigorous research. My agents: Eric Simonoff in New York; Fiona Baird, Raffaella De Angelis and Matilda Forbes Watson in London, Giulia Pietrosanti in Rome.

At Penguin Classics, I wish to thank Josephine Greywoode for inviting me to take on this project, for setting the parameters, and for steering the helm; Bianca Bexton and Ruth Pietroni for expeditiously overseeing the production; Louisa Watson for her heroic and painstaking copy-editing.

Thanks to the Centro Studi Americani in Rome and to Libreria Minimum Fax, my neighbourhood bookstore in Trastevere, for wonderful suggestions and for special-ordering innumerable titles and holding them for me, behind the cash register, sometimes for months at a time, always trusting that I would pass by to retrieve them.

I am also profoundly grateful to Firestone Library at Princeton, which houses nearly every Italian book I needed, and where I discovered a wealth of material that was out of print, including previously published anthologies, in both English and Italian, which paved the way for this one. If it is translation that allows the reader to cross linguistic borders, great libraries are what house those efforts, safeguard them in spite of neglect, collapse space and time for those who explore their depths and make a voyage like this one possible.

Finally, thanks to my son and daughter, Octavio and Noor Vourvoulias, for bravely crossing borders throughout their growing lives.

The following sources proved especially helpful:

Giulio Ferroni (ed.), *Storia della letteratura italiana*, vol. 4: *Il novecento*. Torino: Einaudi, 1991.

Enzo Ronconi (ed.), *Dizionario della letteratura italiana contemporanea*, vol. 1: *Movimenti letterari-Scrittori*. Firenze: Vallecchi, 1973.

Enzo Siciliano (ed.), *Racconti italiani del novecento*, with an introductory essay by Enzo Siciliano and bibliographic notes on the authors by Luca Baranelli. 3 volumes. Milano: Mondadori, i Meridiani 2001.

Copyright Information

About the Translators

Many of the stories in this publication have been newly translated by Jhumpa Lahiri and the following contributors

Howard Curtis has translated more than a hundred books, mostly fiction, from Italian, French and Spanish. Among the Italian writers he has translated are Luigi Pirandello, Beppe Fenoglio, Leonardo Sciascia, Giorgio Scerbanenco, Gianrico Carofiglio, Pietro Grossi, Filippo Bologna, Fabio Geda, Andrej Longo, Paolo Sorrentino and Marco Malvaldi.

Richard Dixon lives and works in Italy. His new translation of *La congnizione del dolore* by Carlo Emilio Gadda is published by Penguin Books under the title *The Experience of Pain*. Other recent translations include works by Roberto Calasso, Umberto Eco, Antonio Moresco and Paolo Volponi.

Ann Goldstein is a former editor at *The New Yorker*. She has translated works by, among others, Primo Levi, Pier Paolo Pasolini, Elena Ferrante, Italo Calvino and Alessandro Baricco, and is the editor of the *Complete Works* of Primo Levi in English. She has received a Guggenheim Fellowship and awards from the Italian Ministry of Foreign Affairs and the American Academy of Arts and Letters.

Jenny McPhee is the author of the novels *The Centre of Things*, *No Ordinary Matter* and *A Man of No Moon*. Her translations include books by Primo Levi, Natalia Ginzburg, Giacomo Leopardi, Curzio Malaparte, Paolo Maurensig and Pope John Paul II. She teaches in the MS in Translation program at New York University.

Michael F. Moore has translated, most recently, *The Drowned and the Saved*, by Primo Levi, *Agostino*, by Alberto Moravia and *The Animal Gazer*, by Edgardo Franzosini. He has just completed a new translation of the nineteenth-century classic, *The Betrothed*, by Alessandro Manzoni. A translator and interpreter at the Italian Mission to the UN, he also teaches literary translation at Columbia University.

Erica Segre and Simon Carnell are co-translators of three books by the theoretical physicist Carlo Rovelli, as well as of books by Leonardo Sciascia, Giorgio van Straten, Antonio Erediatato and Paolo Cognetti. Their translations of Italian poetry have appeared in numerous magazines and in *The Faber Book of 20th-Century Italian Poems*. Erica Segre is a Fellow of Trinity College, Cambridge, where she teaches Latin American Literature and Visual Art. Simon Carnell is the author of *Hare*.

Sara Teardo is a lecturer at the Department of French and Italian at Princeton University and holds a PhD from Rutgers University. She has published on Italian women writers and translation. In 2013, in collaboration with Princeton colleague Susan Stewart, she edited and translated Laudomia Bonanni's posthumous novel *The Reprisal* (Chicago University Press).